CREATED BY
JEREMY HAUN & SETH M. PECK

COLORS
NICK FILARDI

LETTERING & DESIGN
THOMAS MAUER

EDITOR
JOEL ENOS

COVER
JEREMY HAUN
NICK FILARDI

IMAGE COMICS, INC.

ROBERT KIRKMAN — CHIEF OPERATING OFFICER
ERIK LARSEN — CHIEF FINANCIAL OFFICER
TODD MCFARLANE — PRESIDENT
MARC SILVESTRI — CHIEF EXECUTIVE OFFICER
JIM VALENTINO — VICE PRESIDENT

ERIC STEPHENSON — PUBLISHER
COREY HART — DIRECTOR OF SALES
JEFF BOISON — DIRECTOR OF PUBLISHING PLANNING
& BOOK TRADE SALES
CHRIS ROSS — DIRECTOR OF DIGITAL SALES
JEFF STANG — DIRECTOR OF SPECIALTY SALES
KAT SALAZAR — DIRECTOR OF PR & MARKETING
DREW GILL — ART DIRECTOR
HEATHER DOORNINK — PRODUCTION DIRECTOR
NICOLE LAPALME — CONTROLLER

IMAGECOMICS.COM

THE REALM, VOL. 1
Standard Cover ISBN: 978-1-5343-0501-4
Bedrock City Comics Exclusive ISBN: 978-1-5343-0891-6
Forbidden Planet/Big Bang Comics Exclusive ISBN: 978-1-5343-0892-3
Special Edition Hardcover ISBN: 978-1-5343-0893-0
First Printing. March 2018.

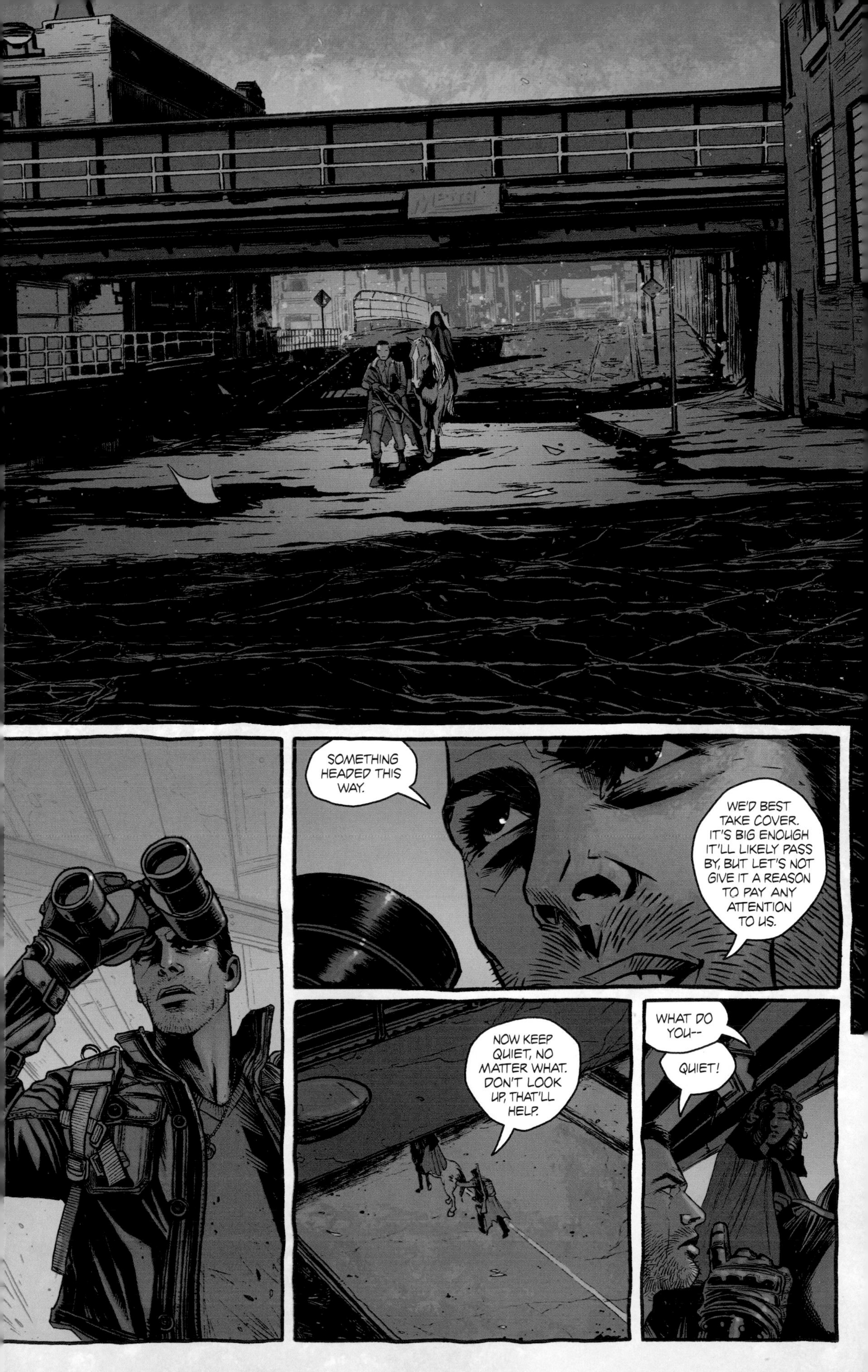

SOMETHING HEADED THIS WAY.
WE'D BEST TAKE COVER. IT'S BIG ENOUGH IT'LL LIKELY PASS BY, BUT LET'S NOT GIVE IT A REASON TO PAY ANY ATTENTION TO US.
NOW KEEP QUIET, NO MATTER WHAT. DON'T LOOK UP, THAT'LL HELP.
WHAT DO YOU--
QUIET!

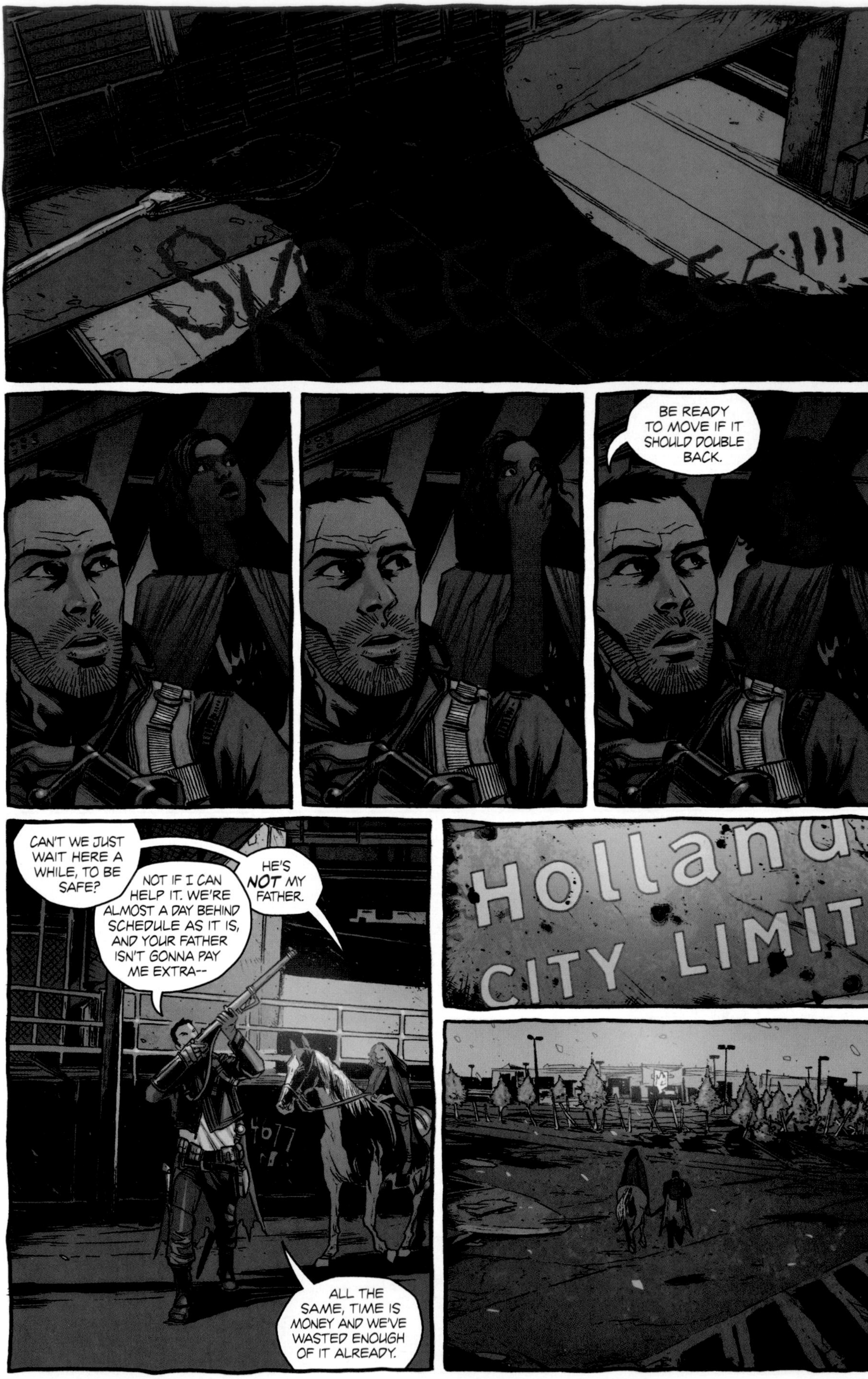
BE READY TO MOVE IF IT SHOULD DOUBLE BACK.
CAN'T WE JUST WAIT HERE A WHILE, TO BE SAFE?
NOT IF I CAN HELP IT. WE'RE ALMOST A DAY BEHIND SCHEDULE AS IT IS, AND YOUR FATHER ISN'T GONNA PAY ME EXTRA--
HE'S **NOT** MY FATHER.
ALL THE SAME, TIME IS MONEY AND WE'VE WASTED ENOUGH OF IT ALREADY.
Holland
CITY LIMIT

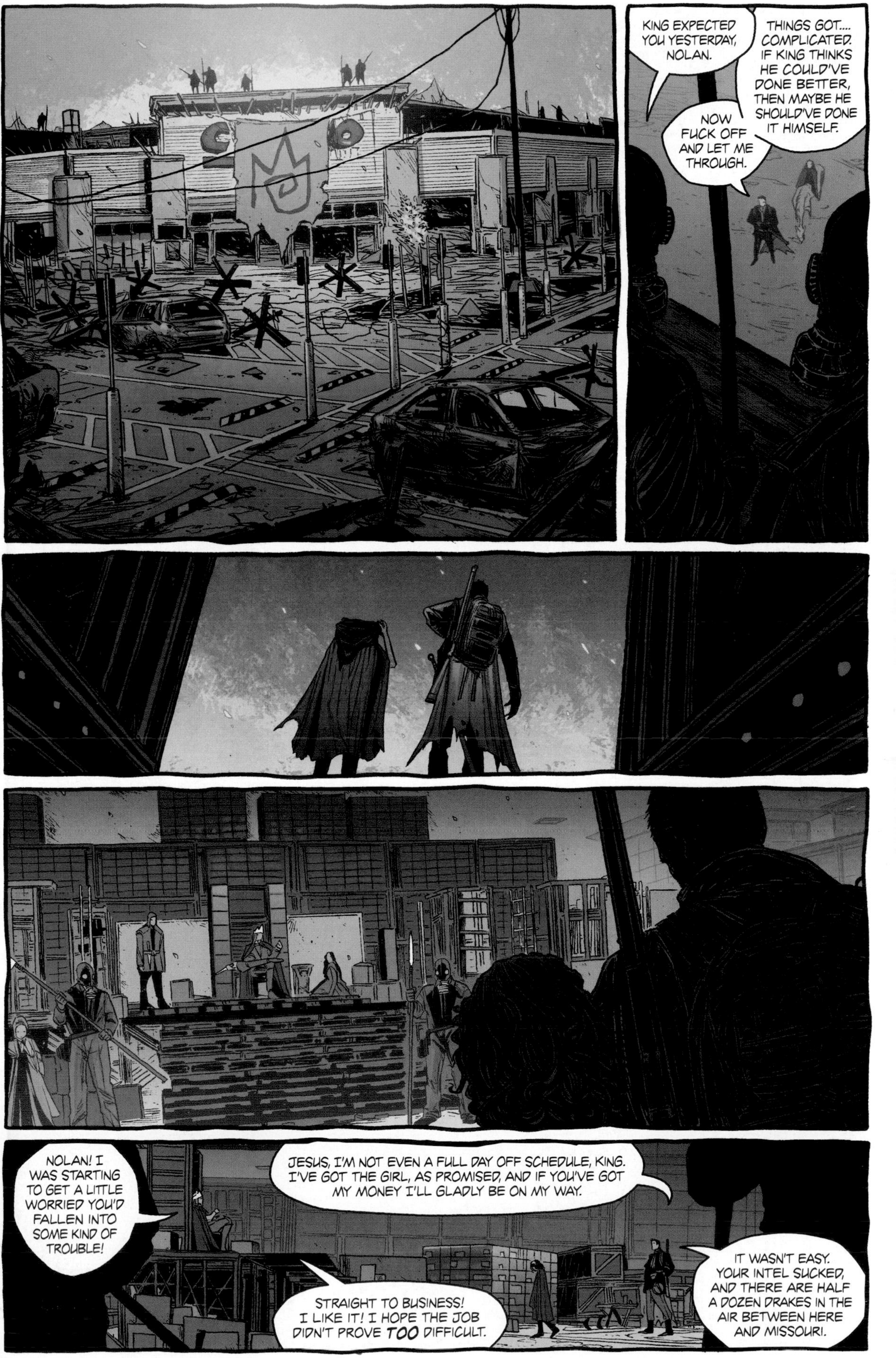
KING EXPECTED YOU YESTERDAY, NOLAN.
THINGS GOT.... COMPLICATED. IF KING THINKS HE COULD'VE DONE BETTER, THEN MAYBE HE SHOULD'VE DONE IT HIMSELF.
NOW FUCK OFF AND LET ME THROUGH.
NOLAN! I WAS STARTING TO GET A LITTLE WORRIED YOU'D FALLEN INTO SOME KIND OF TROUBLE!
JESUS, I'M NOT EVEN A FULL DAY OFF SCHEDULE, KING. I'VE GOT THE GIRL, AS PROMISED, AND IF YOU'VE GOT MY MONEY I'LL GLADLY BE ON MY WAY.
STRAIGHT TO BUSINESS! I LIKE IT! I HOPE THE JOB DIDN'T PROVE TOO DIFFICULT.
IT WASN'T EASY. YOUR INTEL SUCKED, AND THERE ARE HALF A DOZEN DRAKES IN THE AIR BETWEEN HERE AND MISSOURI.

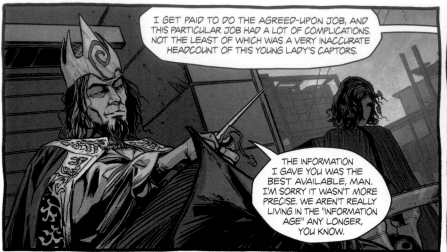

I GET PAID TO DO THE AGREED-UPON JOB, AND THIS PARTICULAR JOB HAD A LOT OF COMPLICATIONS. NOT THE LEAST OF WHICH WAS A VERY INACCURATE HEADCOUNT OF THIS YOUNG LADY'S CAPTORS.

YEAH, WELL, I THINK THE FAIR THING TO DO IS TO COMPENSATE ME FOR MY EXTRA TIME AND EFFORT.

THE INFORMATION I GAVE YOU WAS THE BEST AVAILABLE, MAN. I'M SORRY IT WASN'T MORE PRECISE. WE AREN'T REALLY LIVING IN THE "INFORMATION AGE" ANY LONGER, YOU KNOW.

AND IF I REFUSE? I COULD JUST AS EASILY HAVE YOU KILLED AND DUMPED IN A HOLE, YOU KNOW.

I DON'T THINK THAT'D PROVE AS EASY AS YOU MIGHT EXPECT.

I'D PREFER TO DO THIS WITHOUT BLOODSHED, BUT WE CAN DO IT THE HARD WAY IF YOU'D LIKE.

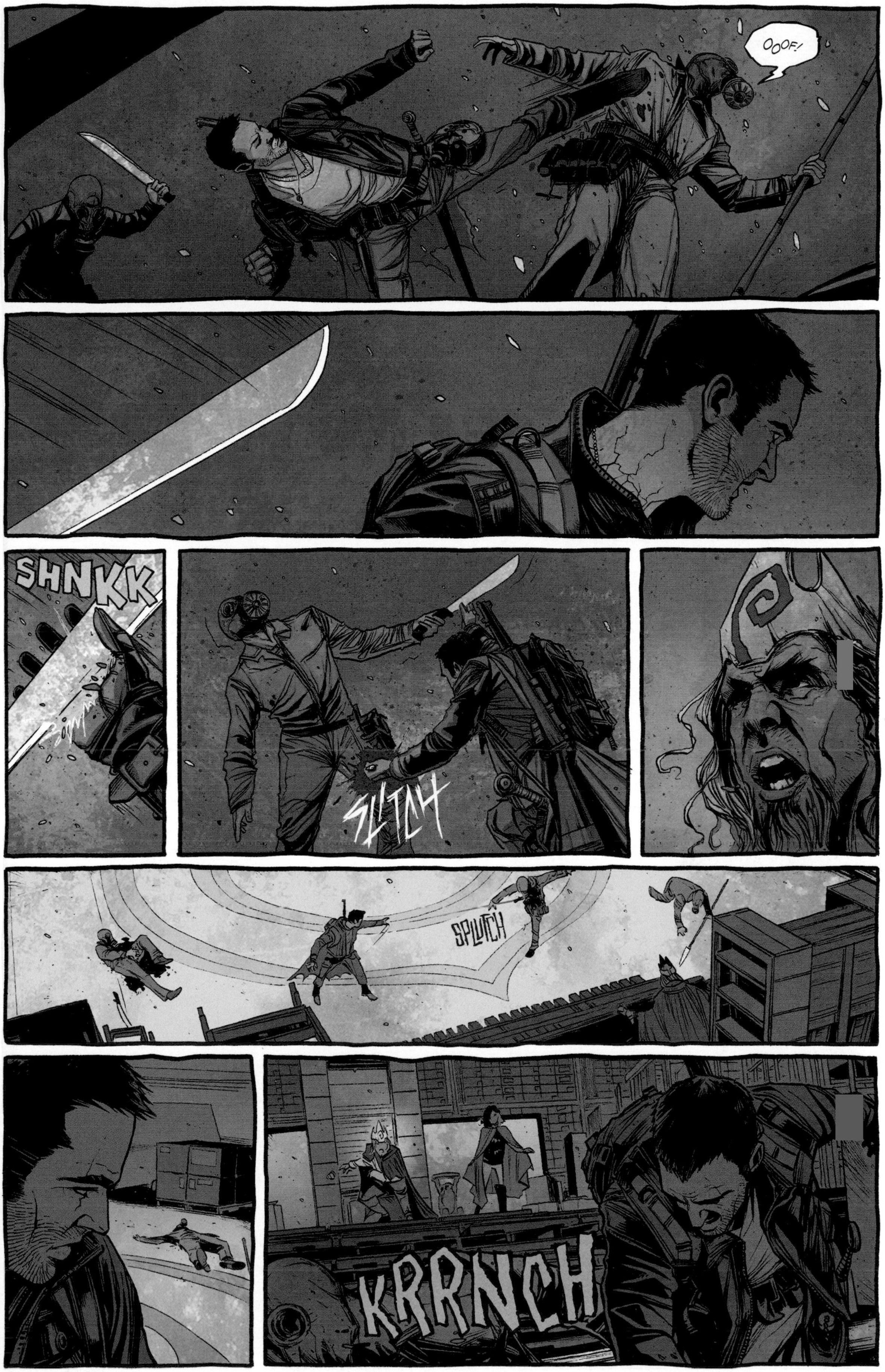
OOOF!
SHNKK
SLITCH
SPLUTCH
KRRNCH

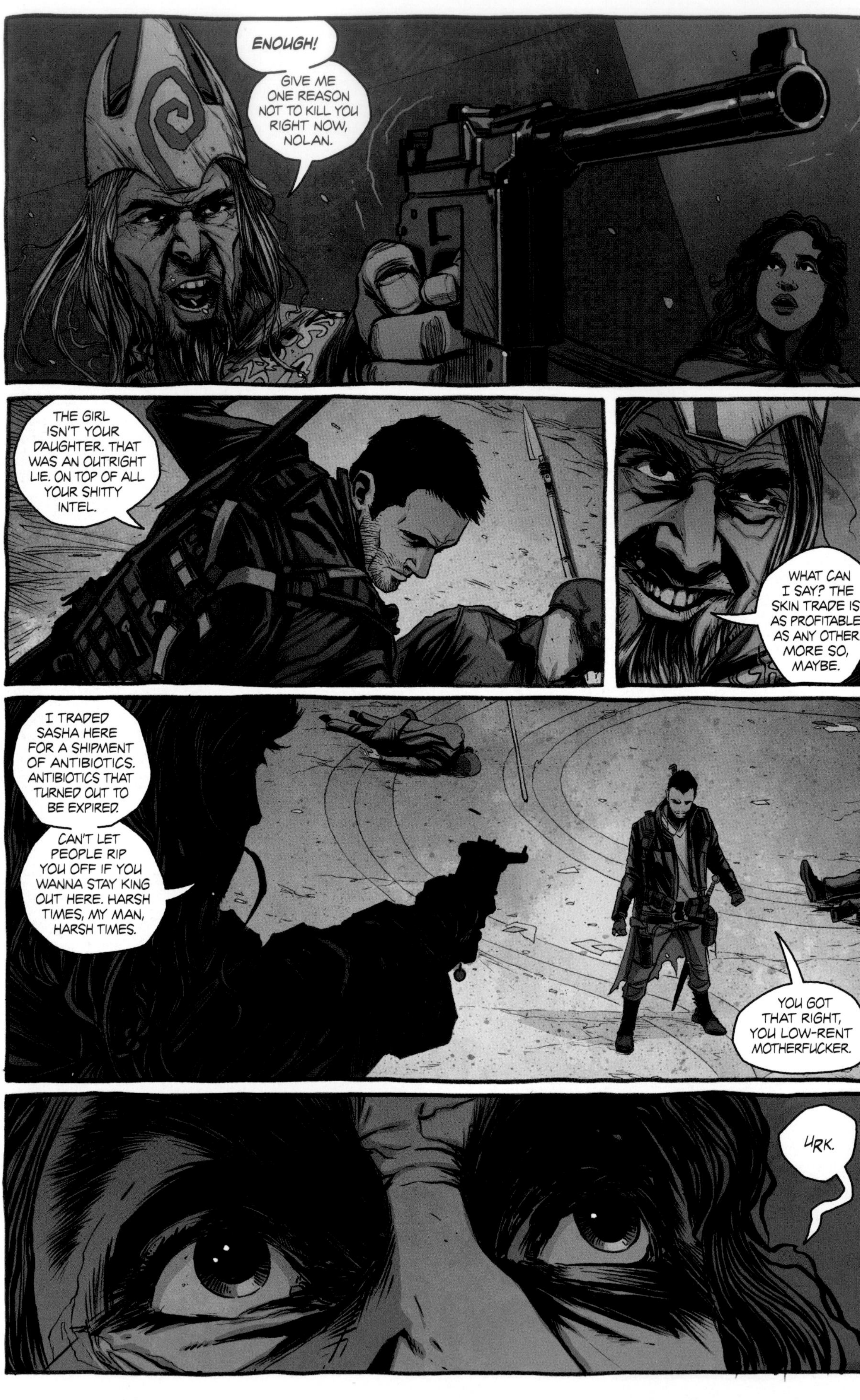
ENOUGH!
GIVE ME ONE REASON NOT TO KILL YOU RIGHT NOW, NOLAN.
THE GIRL ISN'T YOUR DAUGHTER. THAT WAS AN OUTRIGHT LIE. ON TOP OF ALL YOUR SHITTY INTEL.
WHAT CAN I SAY? THE SKIN TRADE IS AS PROFITABLE AS ANY OTHER. MORE SO, MAYBE.
I TRADED SASHA HERE FOR A SHIPMENT OF ANTIBIOTICS. ANTIBIOTICS THAT TURNED OUT TO BE EXPIRED.
CAN'T LET PEOPLE RIP YOU OFF IF YOU WANNA STAY KING OUT HERE. HARSH TIMES, MY MAN, HARSH TIMES.
YOU GOT THAT RIGHT, YOU LOW-RENT MOTHERFUCKER.
URK.

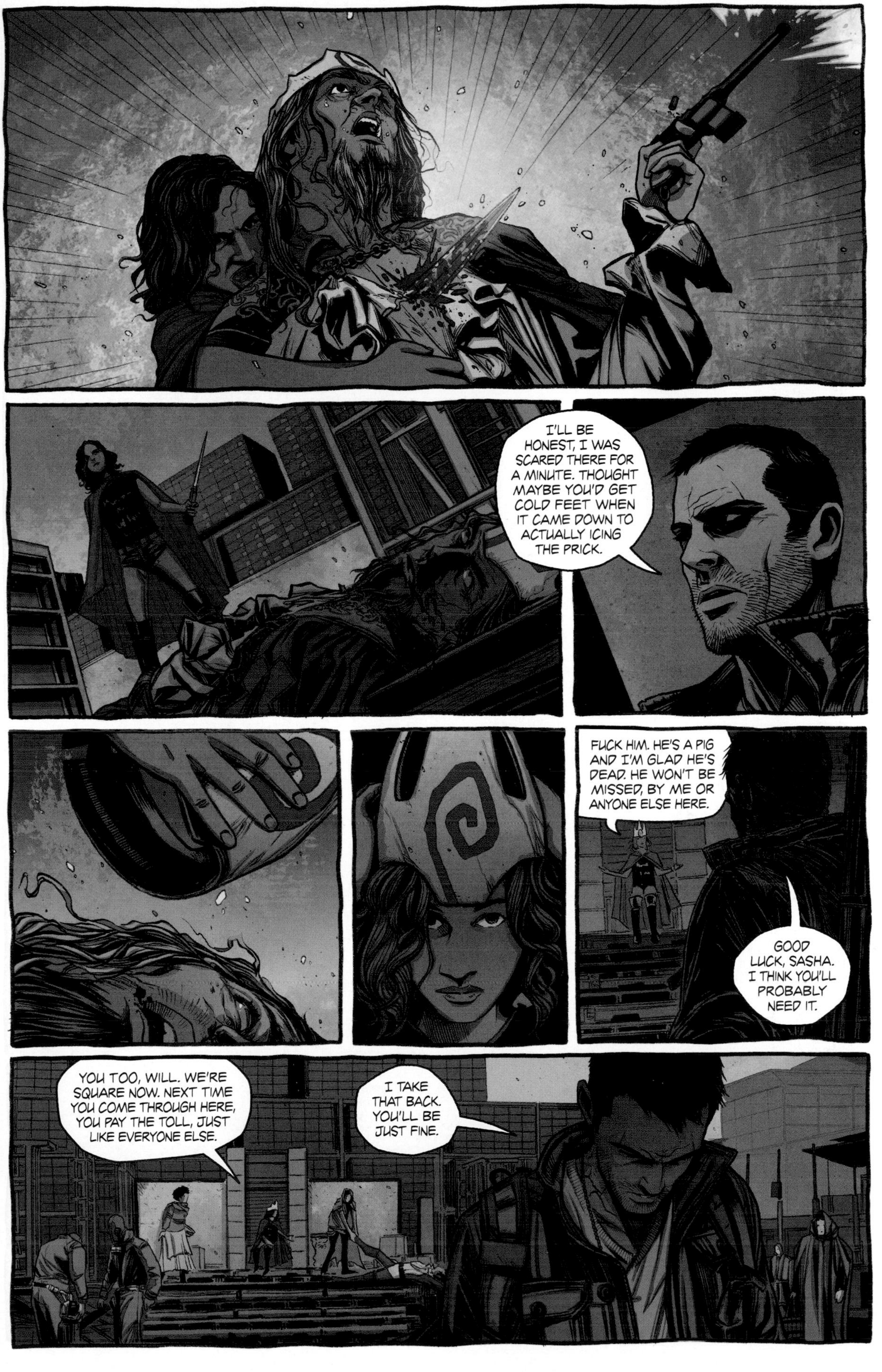
I'LL BE HONEST, I WAS SCARED THERE FOR A MINUTE. THOUGHT MAYBE YOU'D GET COLD FEET WHEN IT CAME DOWN TO ACTUALLY ICING THE PRICK.
FUCK HIM. HE'S A PIG AND I'M GLAD HE'S DEAD. HE WON'T BE MISSED, BY ME OR ANYONE ELSE HERE.
GOOD LUCK, SASHA. I THINK YOU'LL PROBABLY NEED IT.
YOU TOO, WILL. WE'RE SQUARE NOW. NEXT TIME YOU COME THROUGH HERE, YOU PAY THE TOLL, JUST LIKE EVERYONE ELSE.
I TAKE THAT BACK. YOU'LL BE JUST FINE.

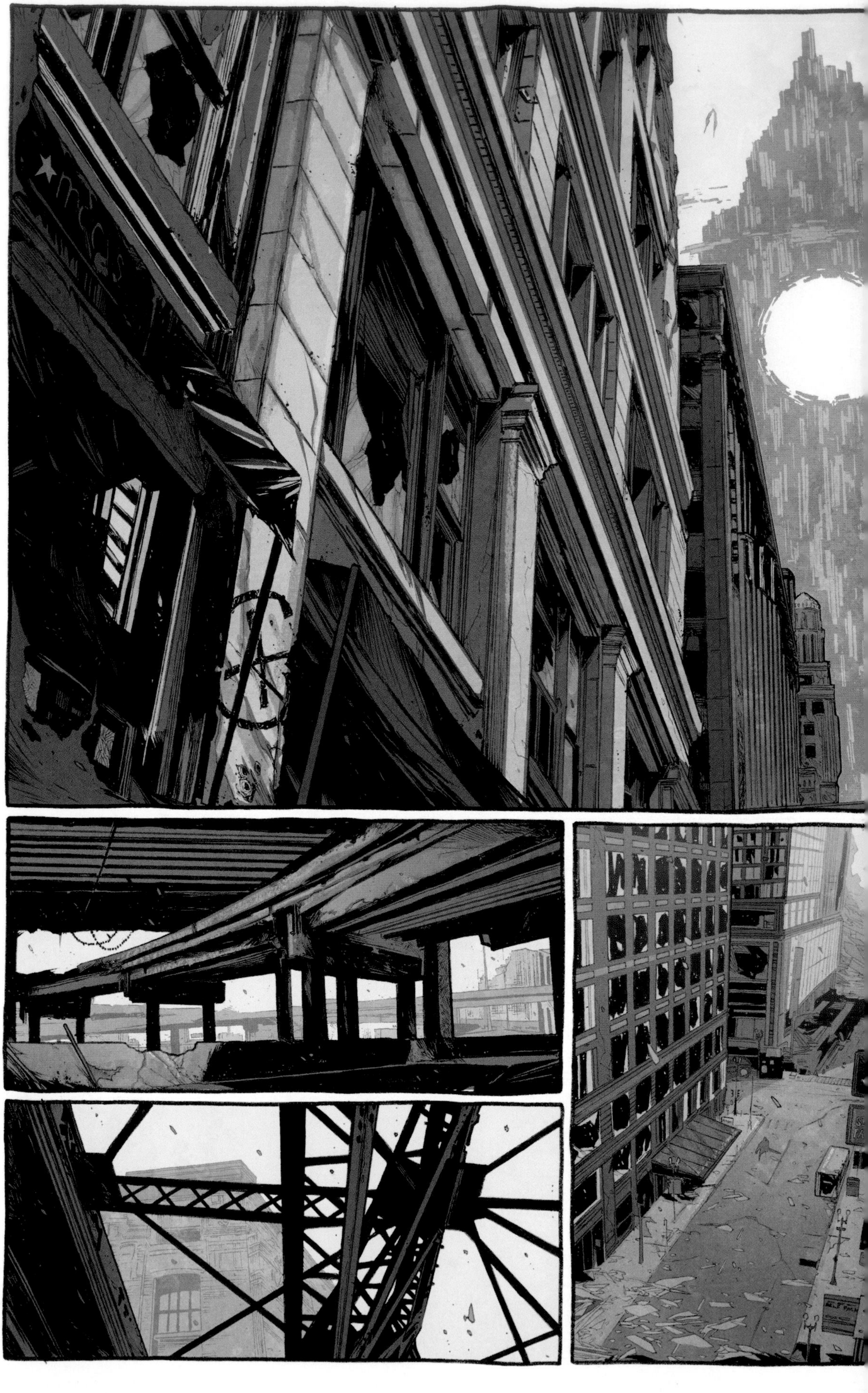

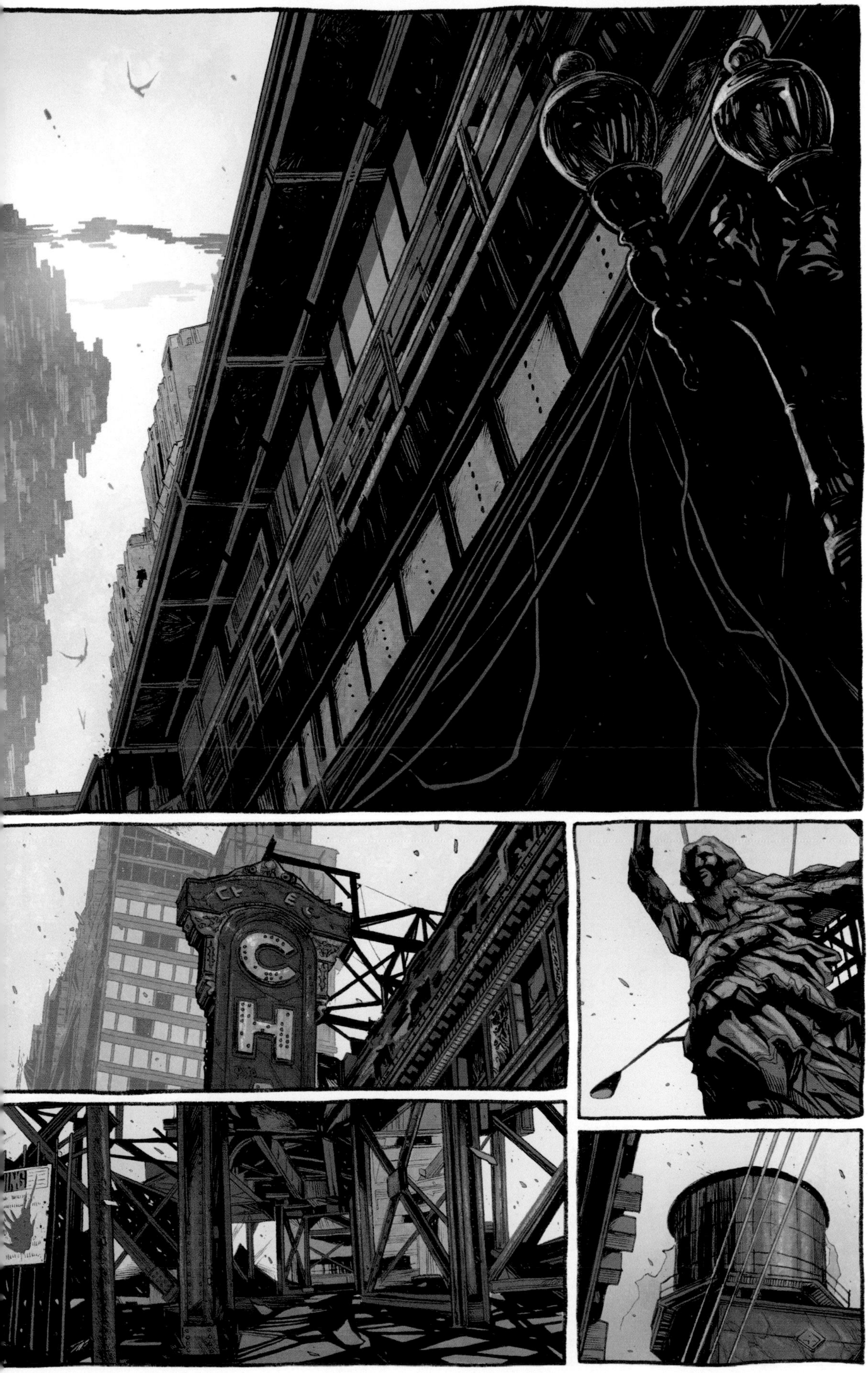

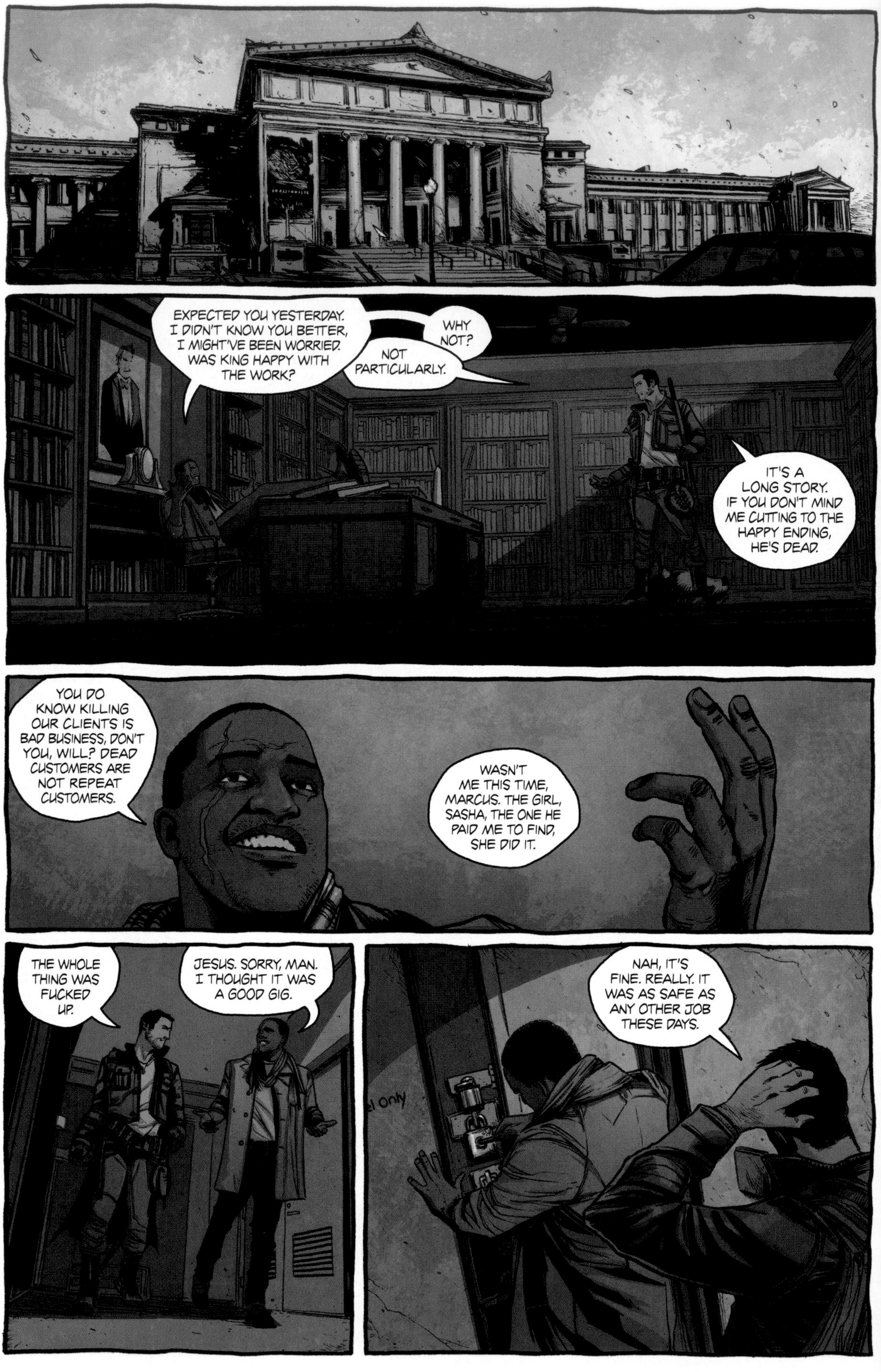
EXPECTED YOU YESTERDAY. I DIDN'T KNOW YOU BETTER, I MIGHT'VE BEEN WORRIED. WAS KING HAPPY WITH THE WORK?
NOT PARTICULARLY.
WHY NOT?
IT'S A LONG STORY. IF YOU DON'T MIND ME CUTTING TO THE HAPPY ENDING, HE'S DEAD.
YOU DO KNOW KILLING OUR CLIENTS IS BAD BUSINESS, DON'T YOU, WILL? DEAD CUSTOMERS ARE NOT REPEAT CUSTOMERS.
WASN'T ME THIS TIME, MARCUS. THE GIRL, SASHA, THE ONE HE PAID ME TO FIND, SHE DID IT.
THE WHOLE THING WAS FUCKED UP.
JESUS. SORRY, MAN. I THOUGHT IT WAS A GOOD GIG.
NAH, IT'S FINE. REALLY. IT WAS AS SAFE AS ANY OTHER JOB THESE DAYS.

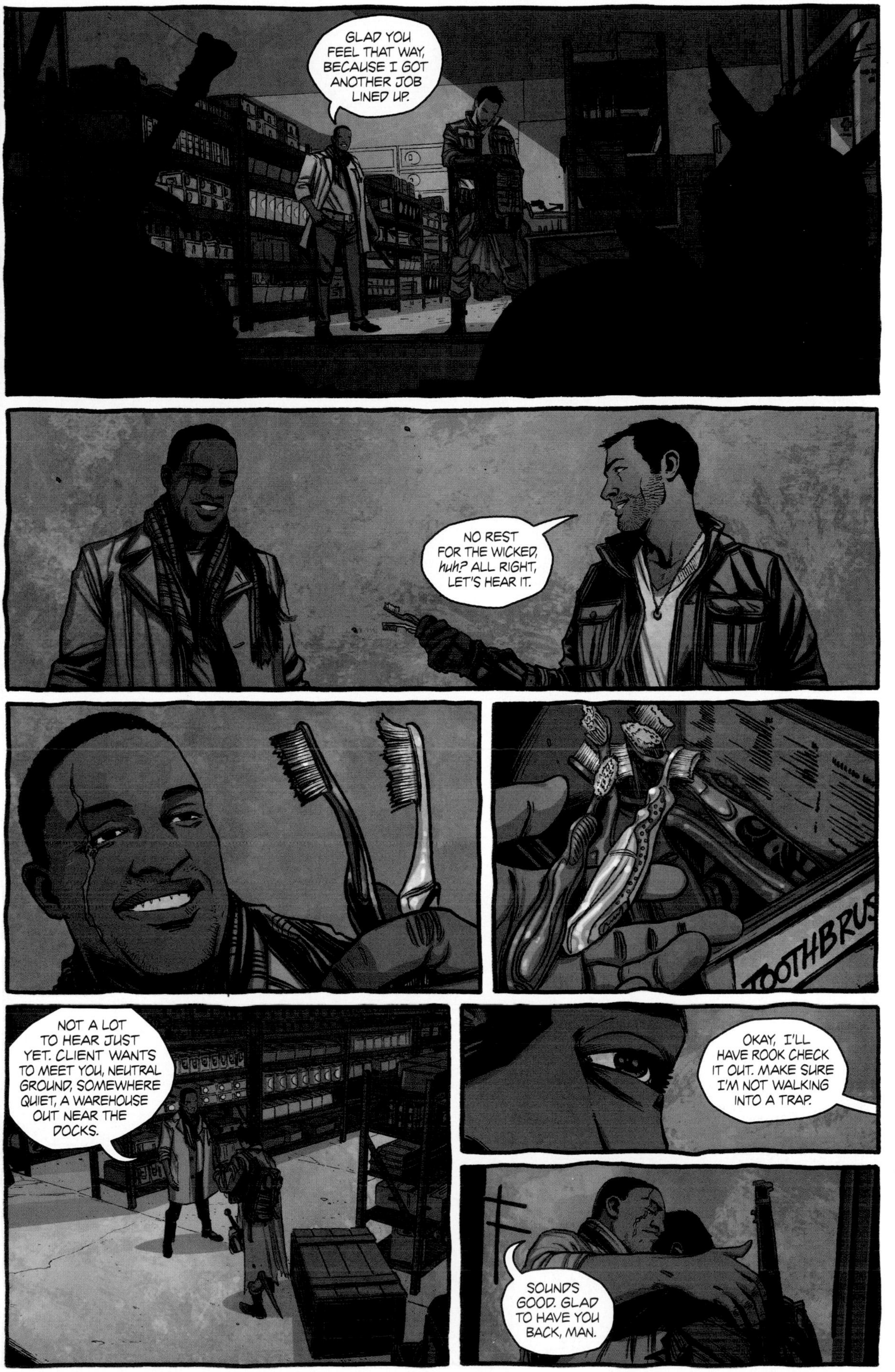
GLAD YOU FEEL THAT WAY, BECAUSE I GOT ANOTHER JOB LINED UP.
NO REST FOR THE WICKED, *huh?* ALL RIGHT, LET'S HEAR IT.
TOOTHBRUS
NOT A LOT TO HEAR JUST YET. CLIENT WANTS TO MEET YOU, NEUTRAL GROUND, SOMEWHERE QUIET, A WAREHOUSE OUT NEAR THE DOCKS.
OKAY, I'LL HAVE ROOK CHECK IT OUT. MAKE SURE I'M NOT WALKING INTO A TRAP.
SOUNDS GOOD. GLAD TO HAVE YOU BACK, MAN.

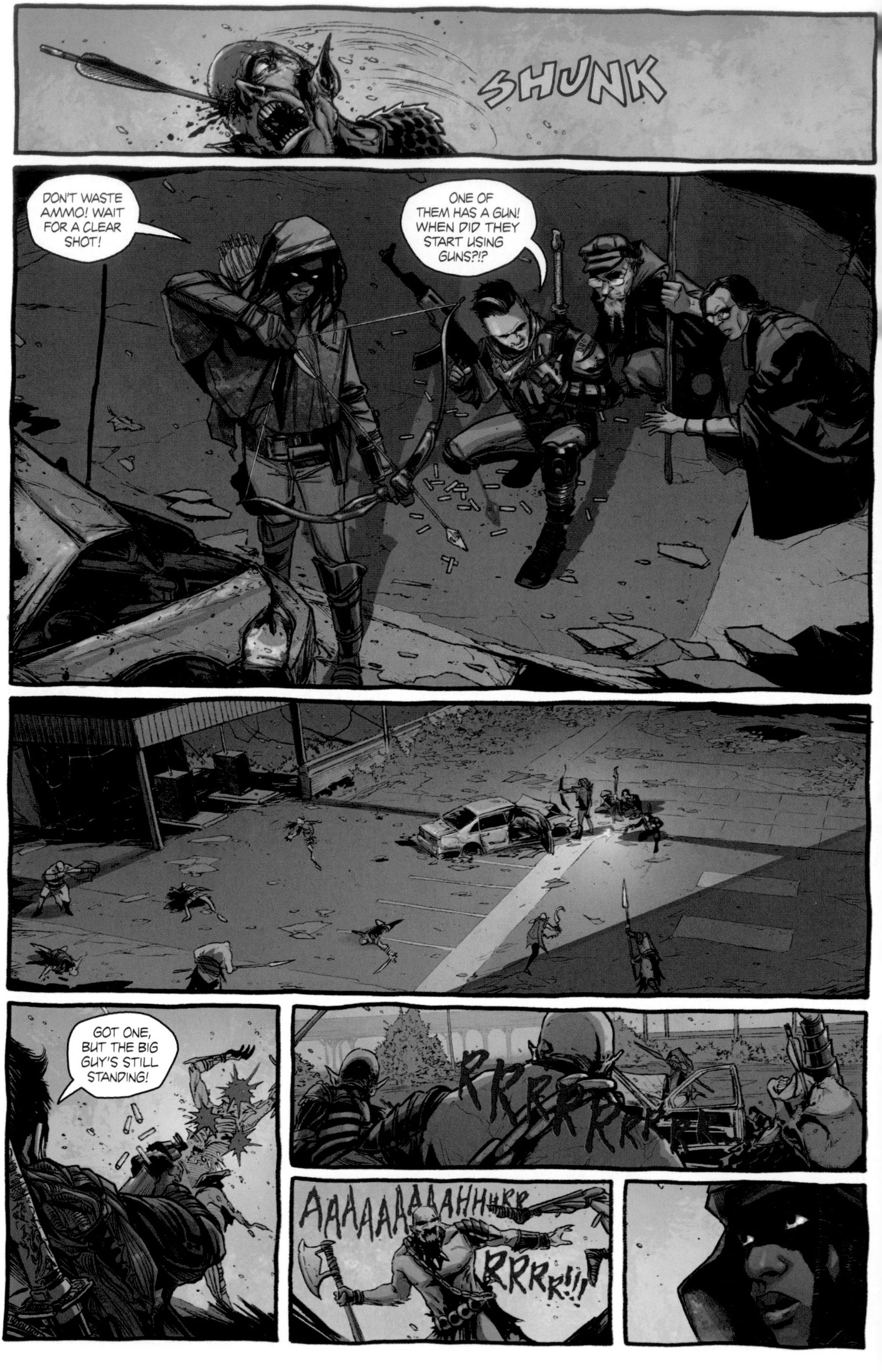
SHUNK
DON'T WASTE AMMO! WAIT FOR A CLEAR SHOT!
ONE OF THEM HAS A GUN! WHEN DID THEY START USING GUNS?!?
GOT ONE, BUT THE BIG GUY'S STILL STANDING!
RRRRRRRRRRRR
AAAAAAAAAHHHRRR
RRRR!!!

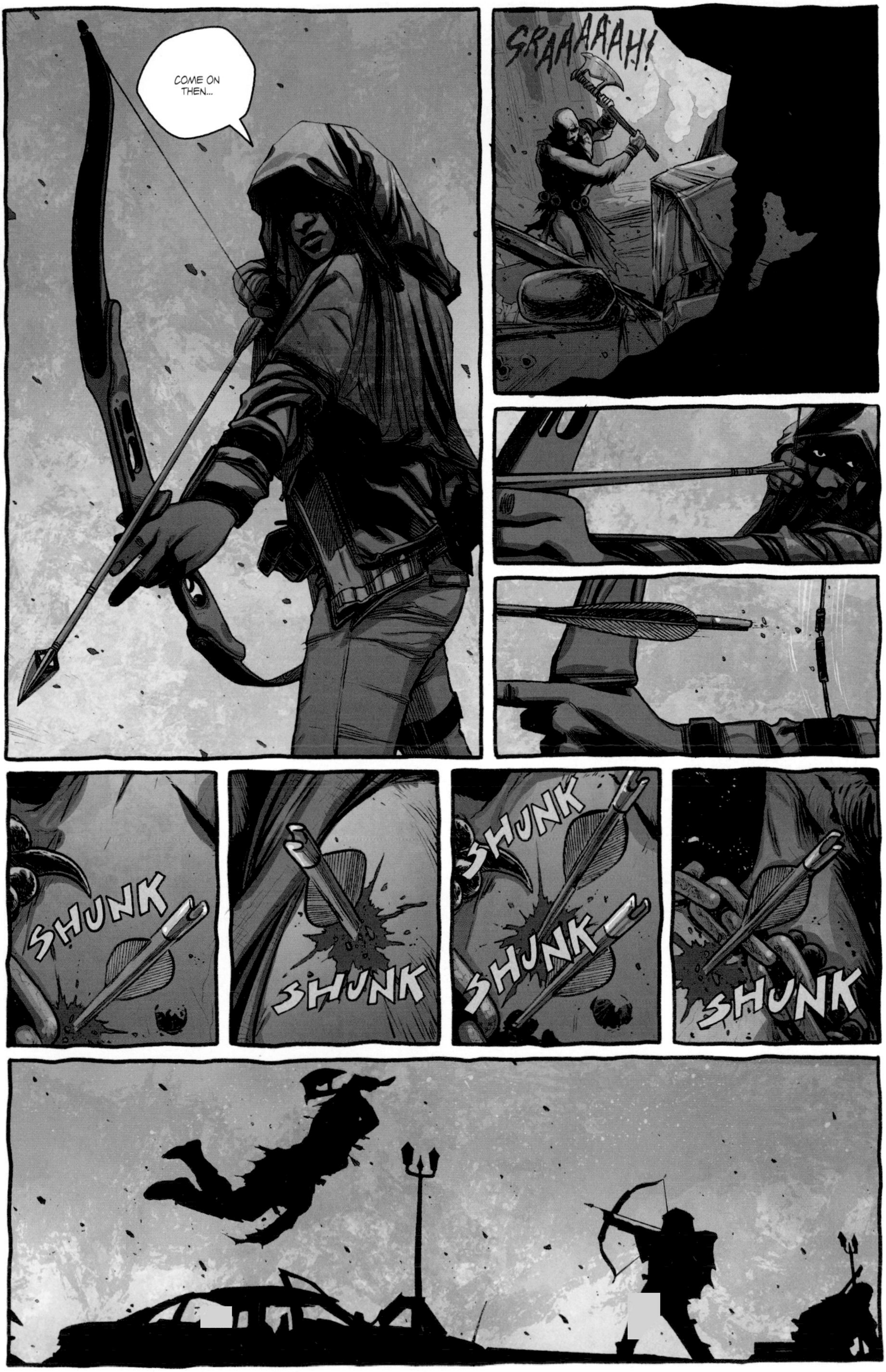
COME ON THEN...
SRAAAAAH!
SHUNK
SHUNK
SHUNK
SHUNK
SHUNK

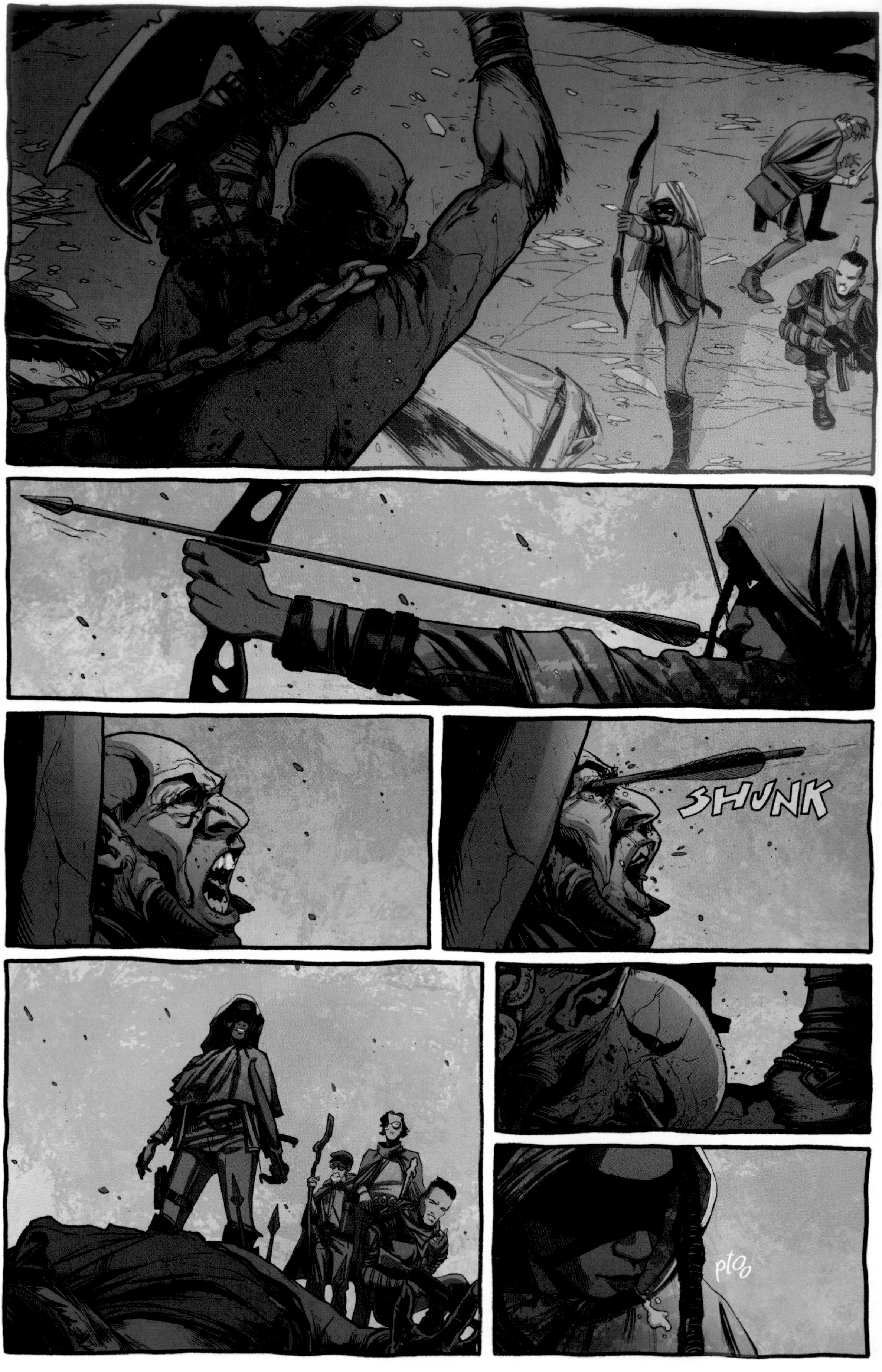
SHUNK
ptoo

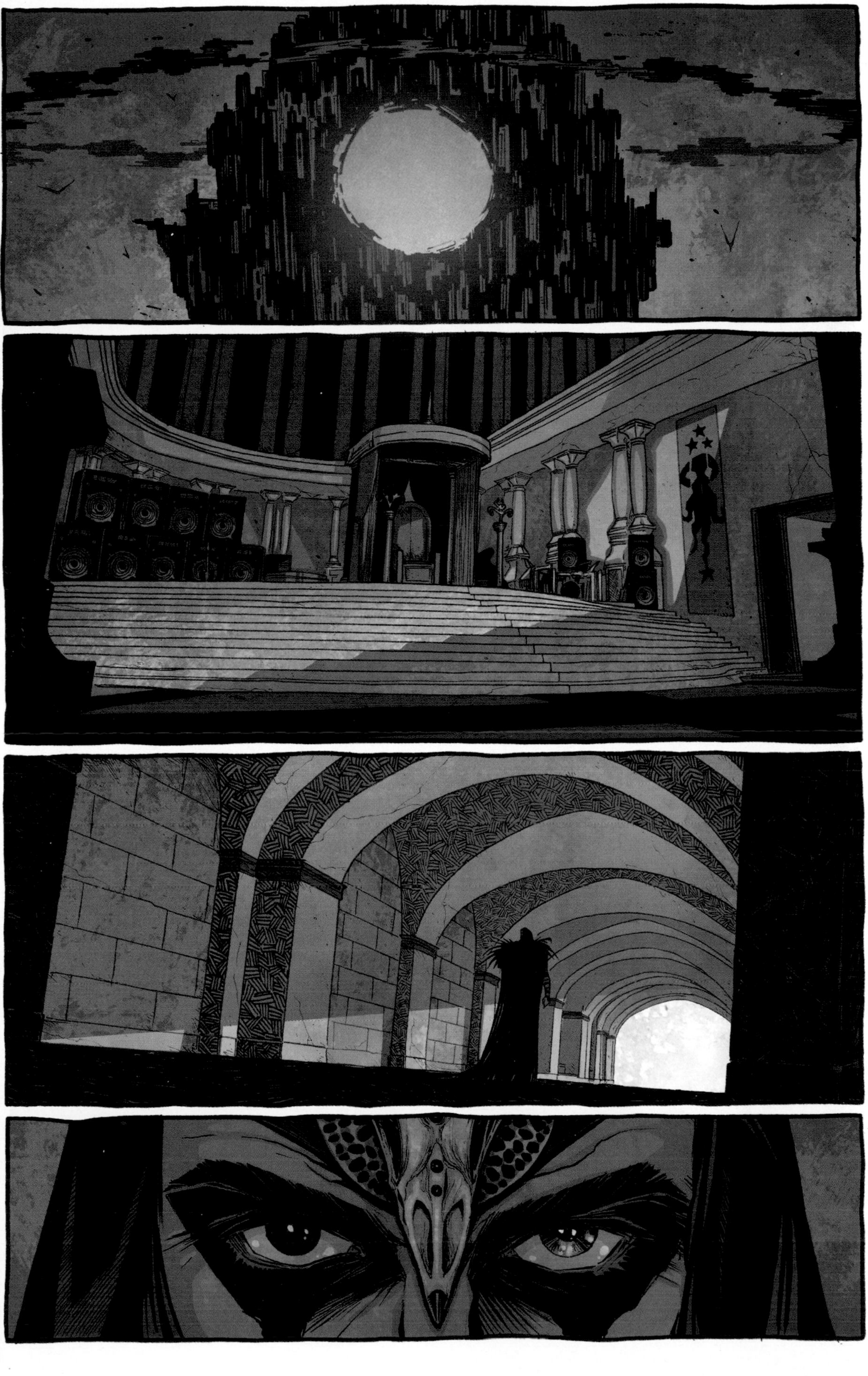

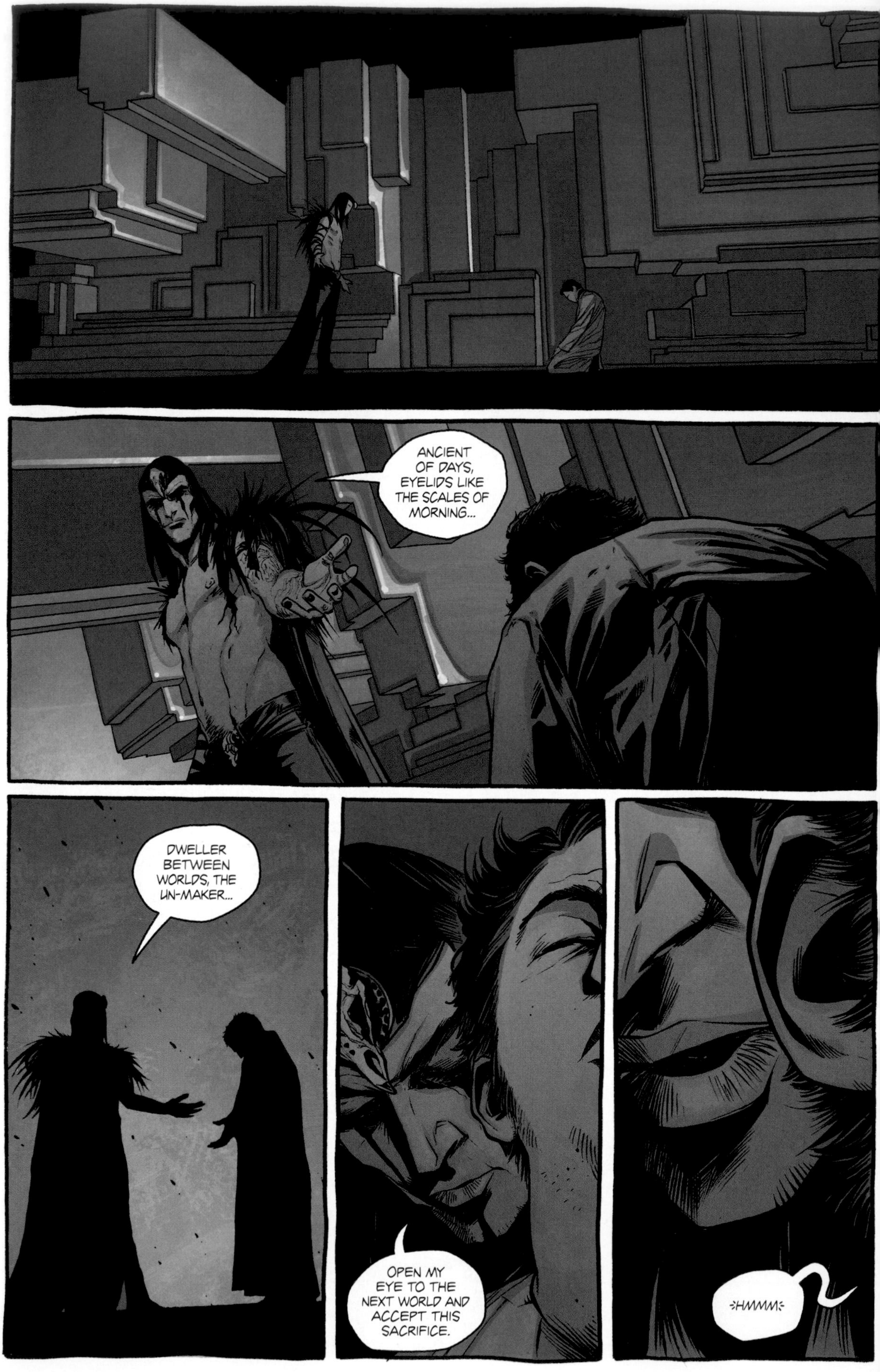
ANCIENT OF DAYS, EYELIDS LIKE THE SCALES OF MORNING...
DWELLER BETWEEN WORLDS, THE UN-MAKER...
OPEN MY EYE TO THE NEXT WORLD AND ACCEPT THIS SACRIFICE.
HMMM

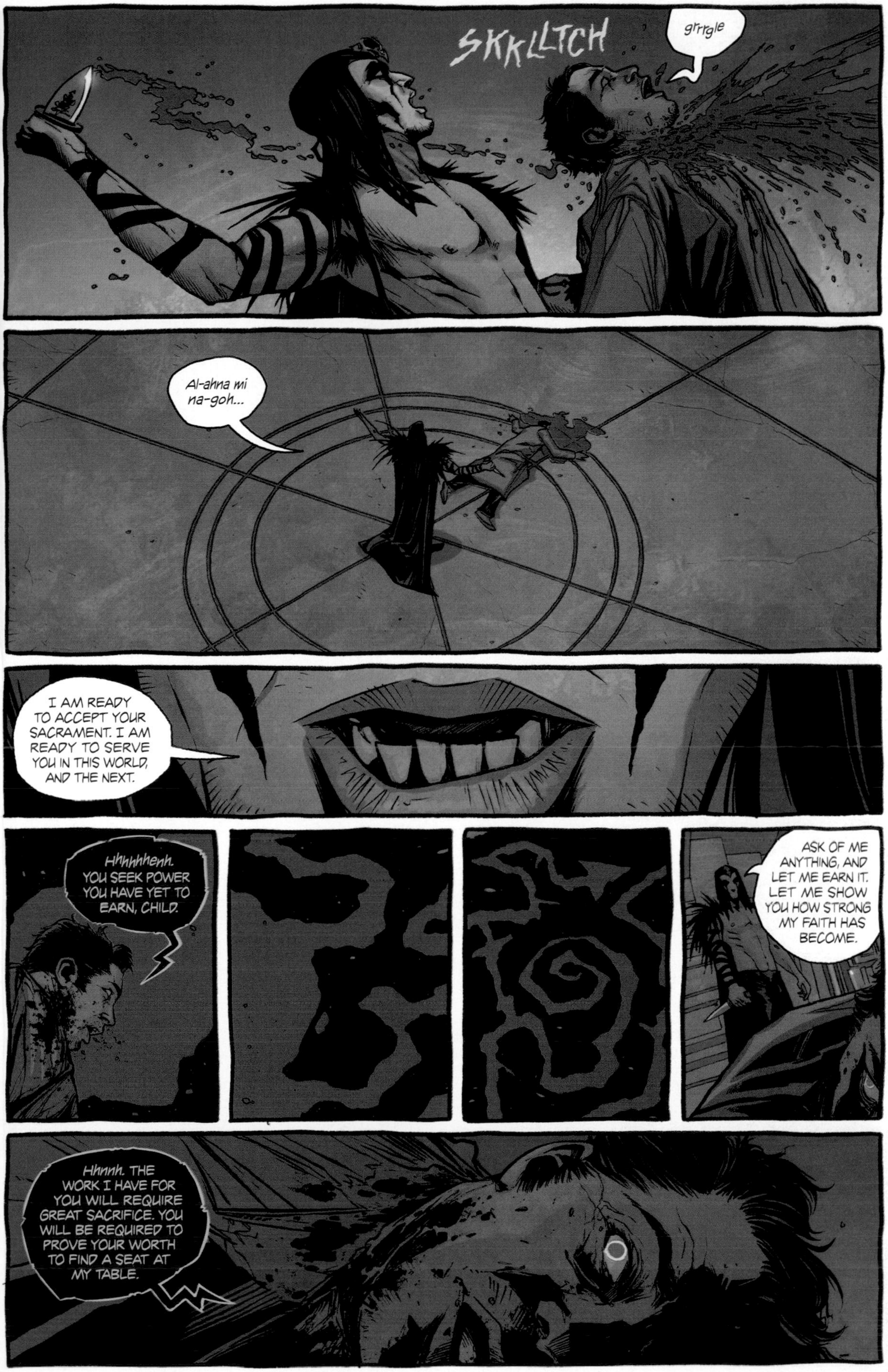
SKKLLTCH
grrrgle
Al-ahna mi na-goh...
I AM READY TO ACCEPT YOUR SACRAMENT. I AM READY TO SERVE YOU IN THIS WORLD, AND THE NEXT.
Hhhhhhenh. YOU SEEK POWER YOU HAVE YET TO EARN, CHILD.
ASK OF ME ANYTHING, AND LET ME EARN IT. LET ME SHOW YOU HOW STRONG MY FAITH HAS BECOME.
Hhnnh. THE WORK I HAVE FOR YOU WILL REQUIRE GREAT SACRIFICE. YOU WILL BE REQUIRED TO PROVE YOUR WORTH TO FIND A SEAT AT MY TABLE.

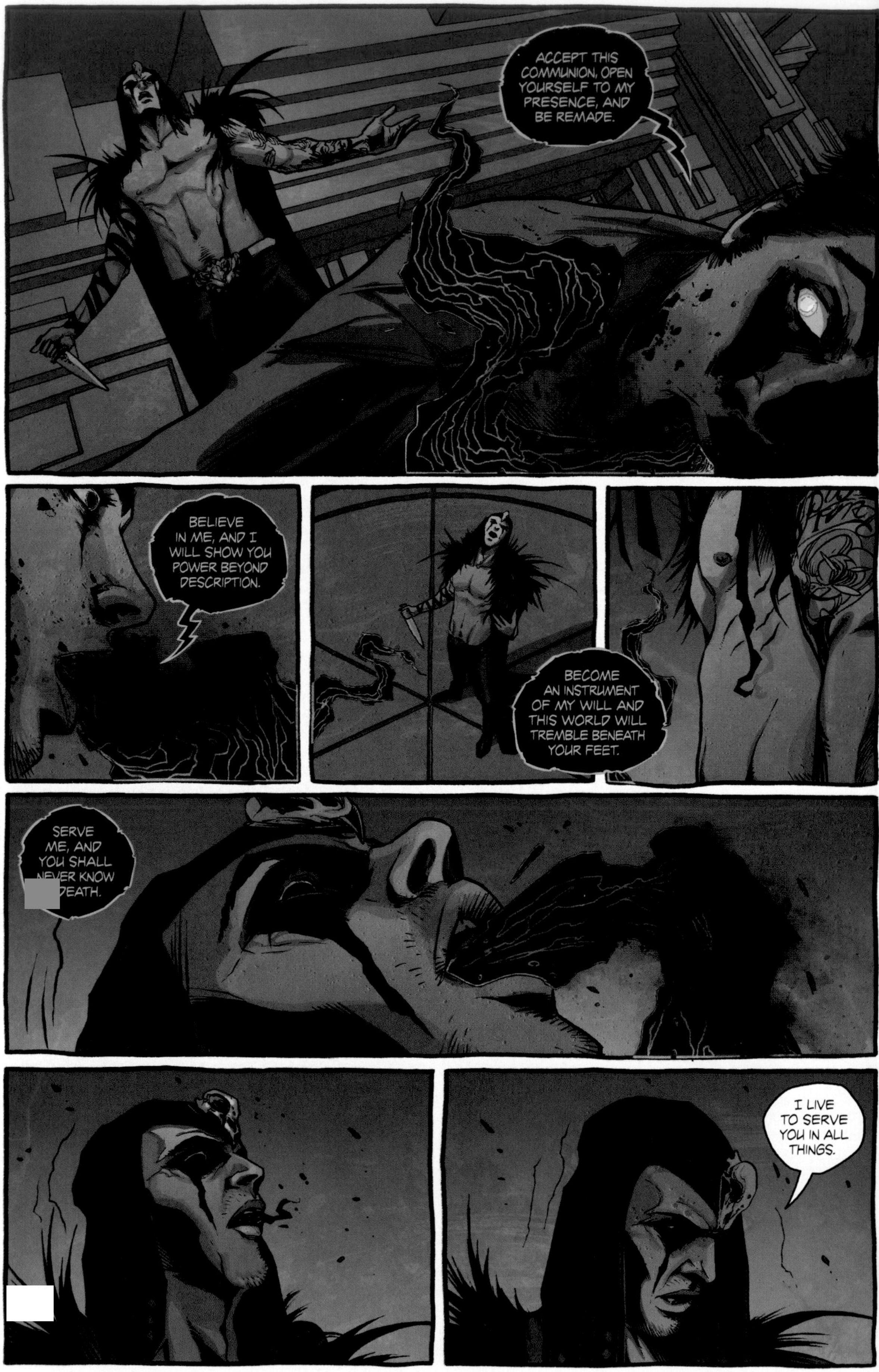
ACCEPT THIS COMMUNION, OPEN YOURSELF TO MY PRESENCE, AND BE REMADE.
BELIEVE IN ME, AND I WILL SHOW YOU POWER BEYOND DESCRIPTION.
BECOME AN INSTRUMENT OF MY WILL AND THIS WORLD WILL TREMBLE BENEATH YOUR FEET.
SERVE ME, AND YOU SHALL NEVER KNOW DEATH.
I LIVE TO SERVE YOU IN ALL THINGS.

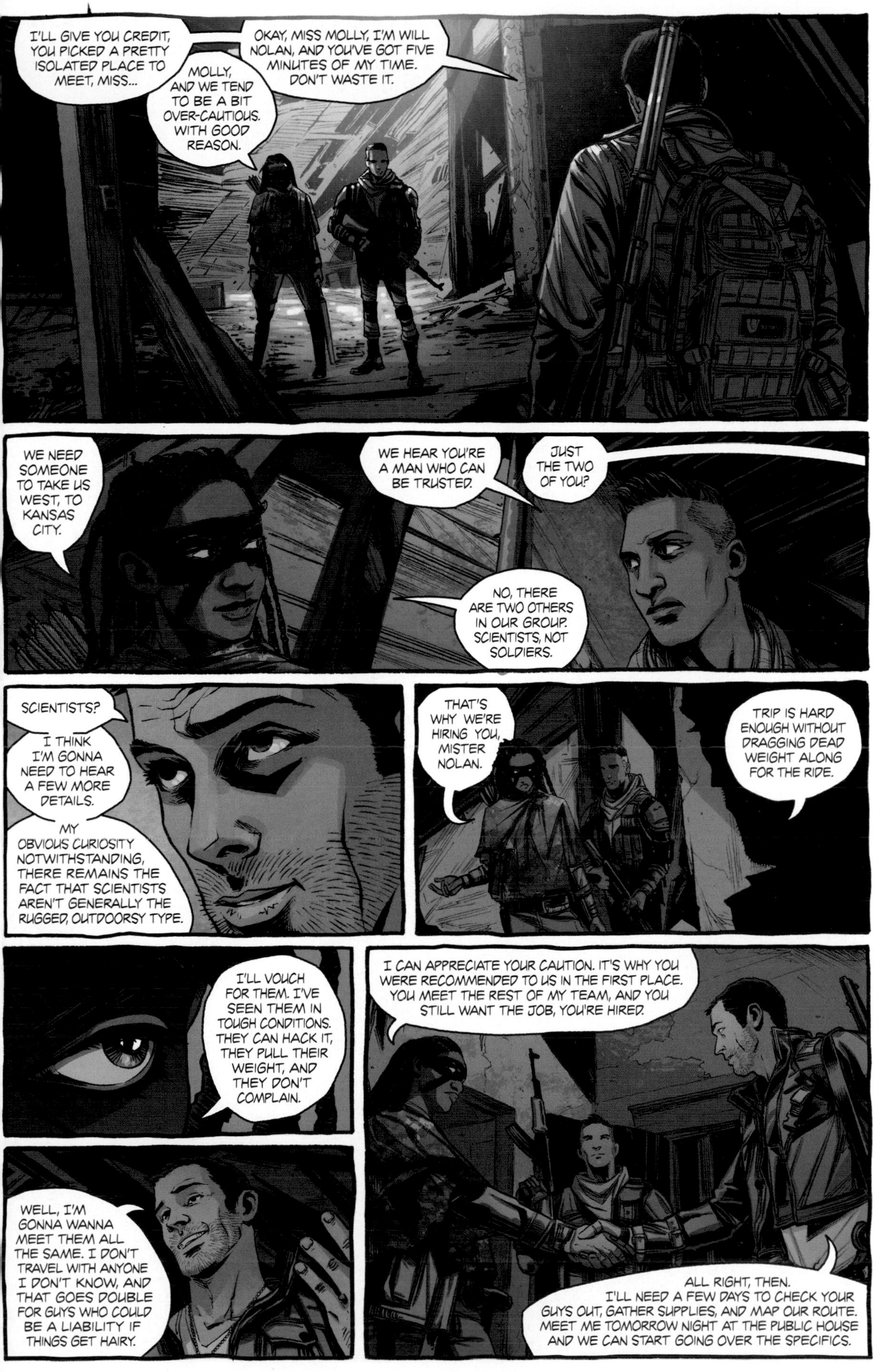

I'LL GIVE YOU CREDIT, YOU PICKED A PRETTY ISOLATED PLACE TO MEET, MISS...
MOLLY, AND WE TEND TO BE A BIT OVER-CAUTIOUS. WITH GOOD REASON.
OKAY, MISS MOLLY, I'M WILL NOLAN, AND YOU'VE GOT FIVE MINUTES OF MY TIME. DON'T WASTE IT.
WE NEED SOMEONE TO TAKE US WEST, TO KANSAS CITY.
WE HEAR YOU'RE A MAN WHO CAN BE TRUSTED.
JUST THE TWO OF YOU?
NO, THERE ARE TWO OTHERS IN OUR GROUP. SCIENTISTS, NOT SOLDIERS.
SCIENTISTS?
I THINK I'M GONNA NEED TO HEAR A FEW MORE DETAILS.
MY OBVIOUS CURIOSITY NOTWITHSTANDING, THERE REMAINS THE FACT THAT SCIENTISTS AREN'T GENERALLY THE RUGGED, OUTDOORSY TYPE.
THAT'S WHY WE'RE HIRING YOU, MISTER NOLAN.
TRIP IS HARD ENOUGH WITHOUT DRAGGING DEAD WEIGHT ALONG FOR THE RIDE.
I'LL VOUCH FOR THEM. I'VE SEEN THEM IN TOUGH CONDITIONS. THEY CAN HACK IT, THEY PULL THEIR WEIGHT, AND THEY DON'T COMPLAIN.
WELL, I'M GONNA WANNA MEET THEM ALL THE SAME. I DON'T TRAVEL WITH ANYONE I DON'T KNOW, AND THAT GOES DOUBLE FOR GUYS WHO COULD BE A LIABILITY IF THINGS GET HAIRY.
I CAN APPRECIATE YOUR CAUTION. IT'S WHY YOU WERE RECOMMENDED TO US IN THE FIRST PLACE. YOU MEET THE REST OF MY TEAM, AND YOU STILL WANT THE JOB, YOU'RE HIRED.
ALL RIGHT, THEN. I'LL NEED A FEW DAYS TO CHECK YOUR GUYS OUT, GATHER SUPPLIES, AND MAP OUR ROUTE. MEET ME TOMORROW NIGHT AT THE PUBLIC HOUSE AND WE CAN START GOING OVER THE SPECIFICS.

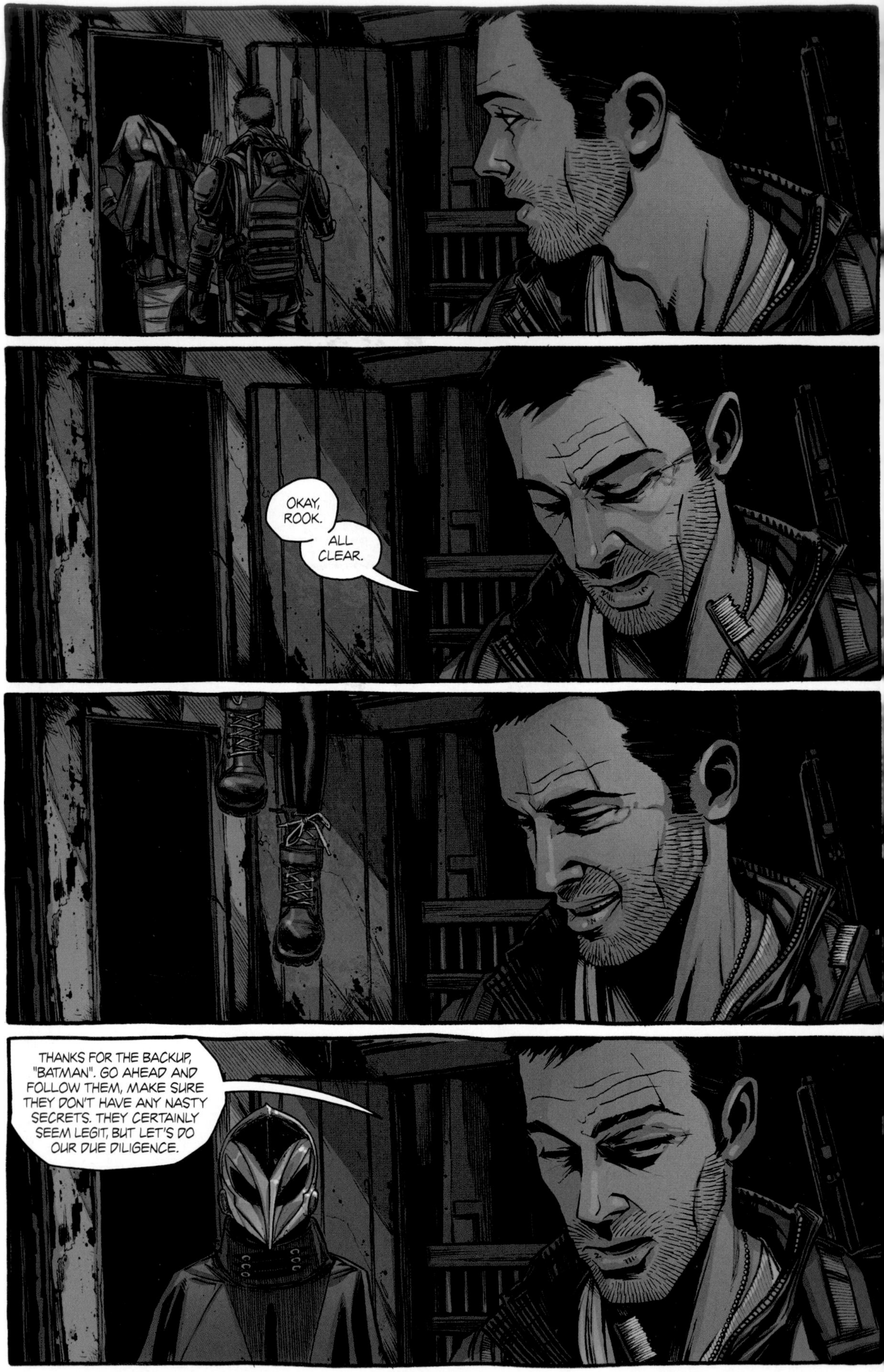
OKAY, ROOK.
ALL CLEAR.
THANKS FOR THE BACKUP, "BATMAN". GO AHEAD AND FOLLOW THEM, MAKE SURE THEY DON'T HAVE ANY NASTY SECRETS. THEY CERTAINLY SEEM LEGIT, BUT LET'S DO OUR DUE DILIGENCE.

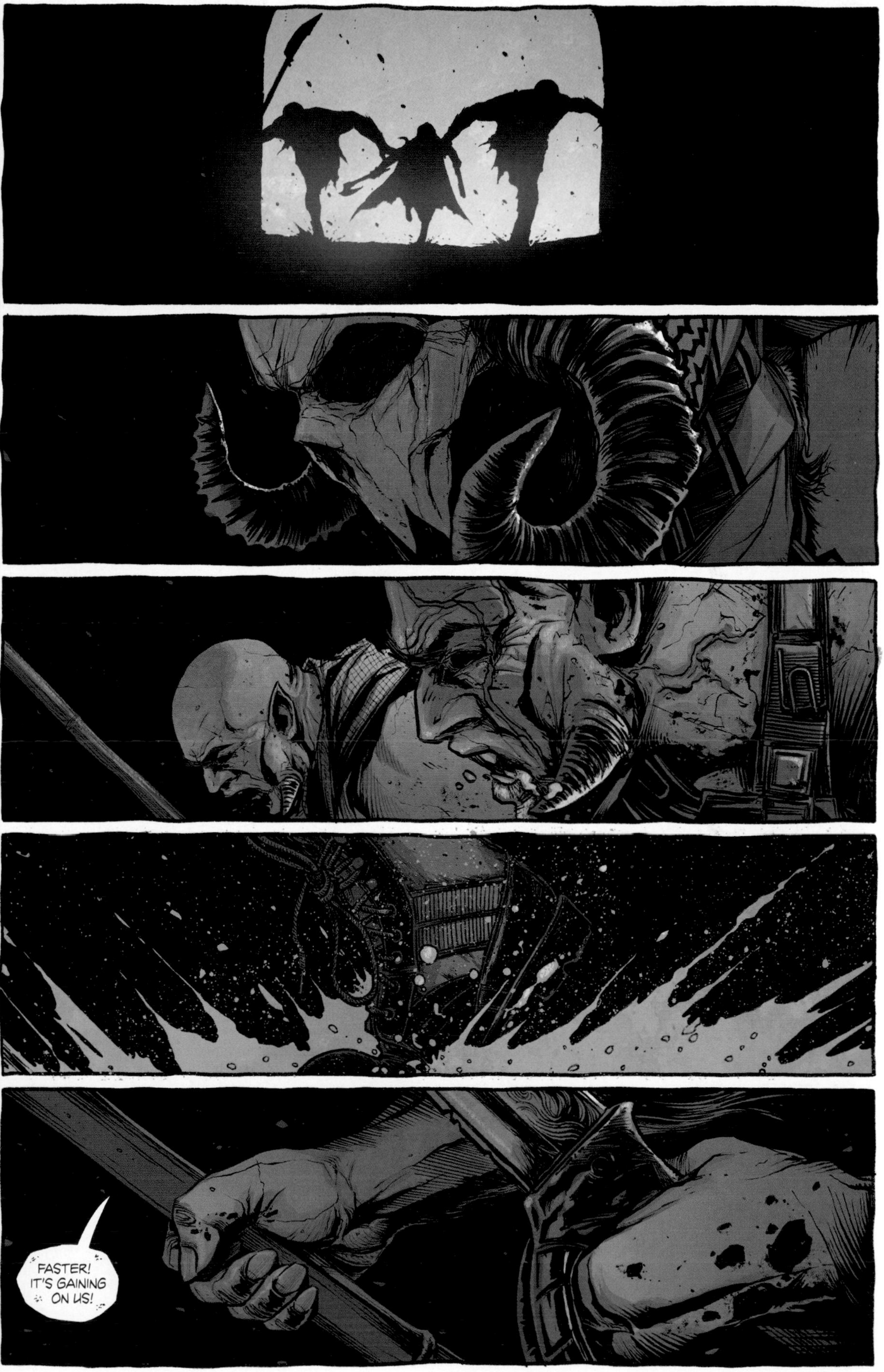
FASTER! IT'S GAINING ON US!

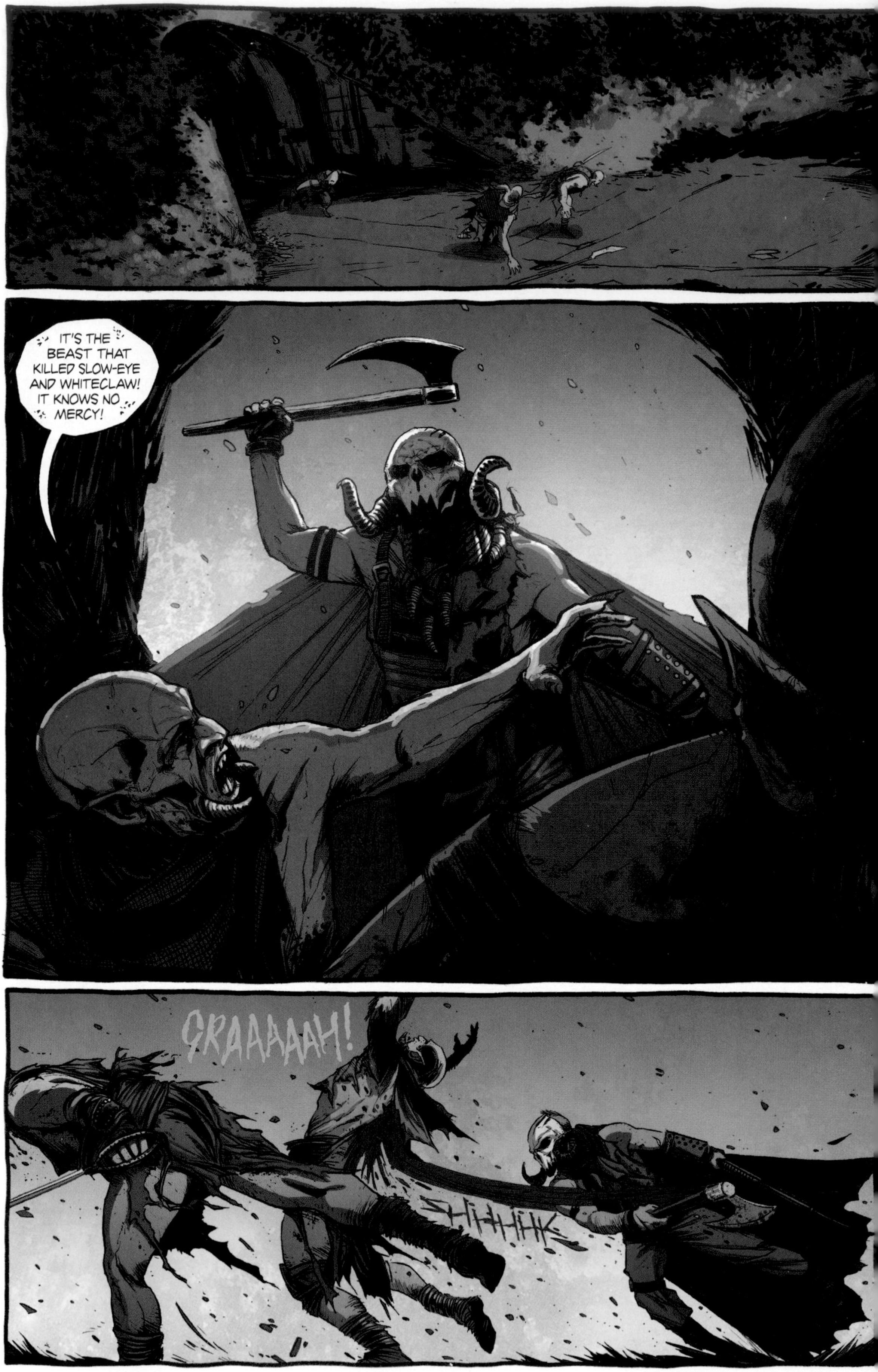
IT'S THE BEAST THAT KILLED SLOW-EYE AND WHITECLAW! IT KNOWS NO MERCY!
GRAAAAAH!

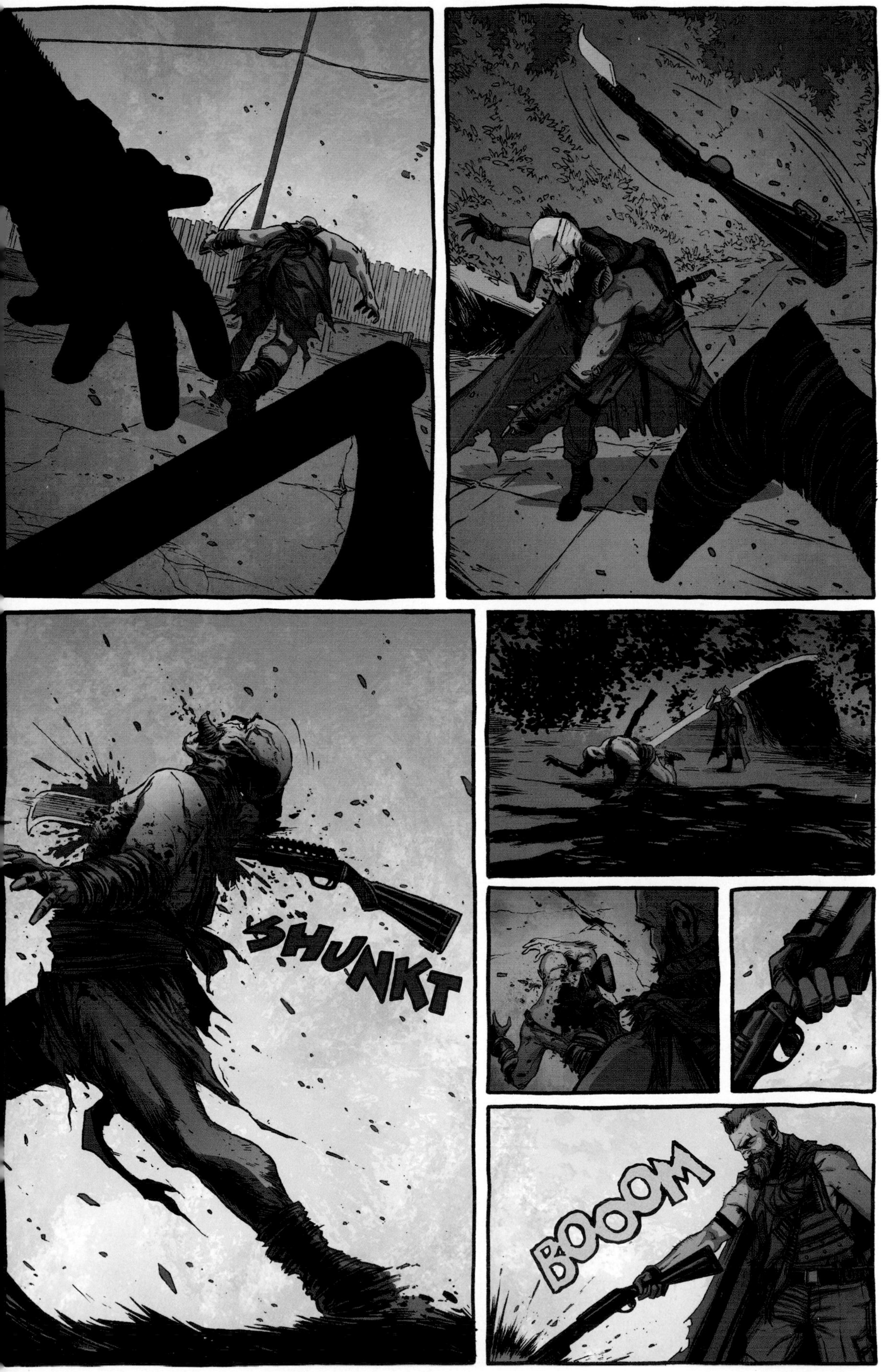
SHUNKT
BOOOM

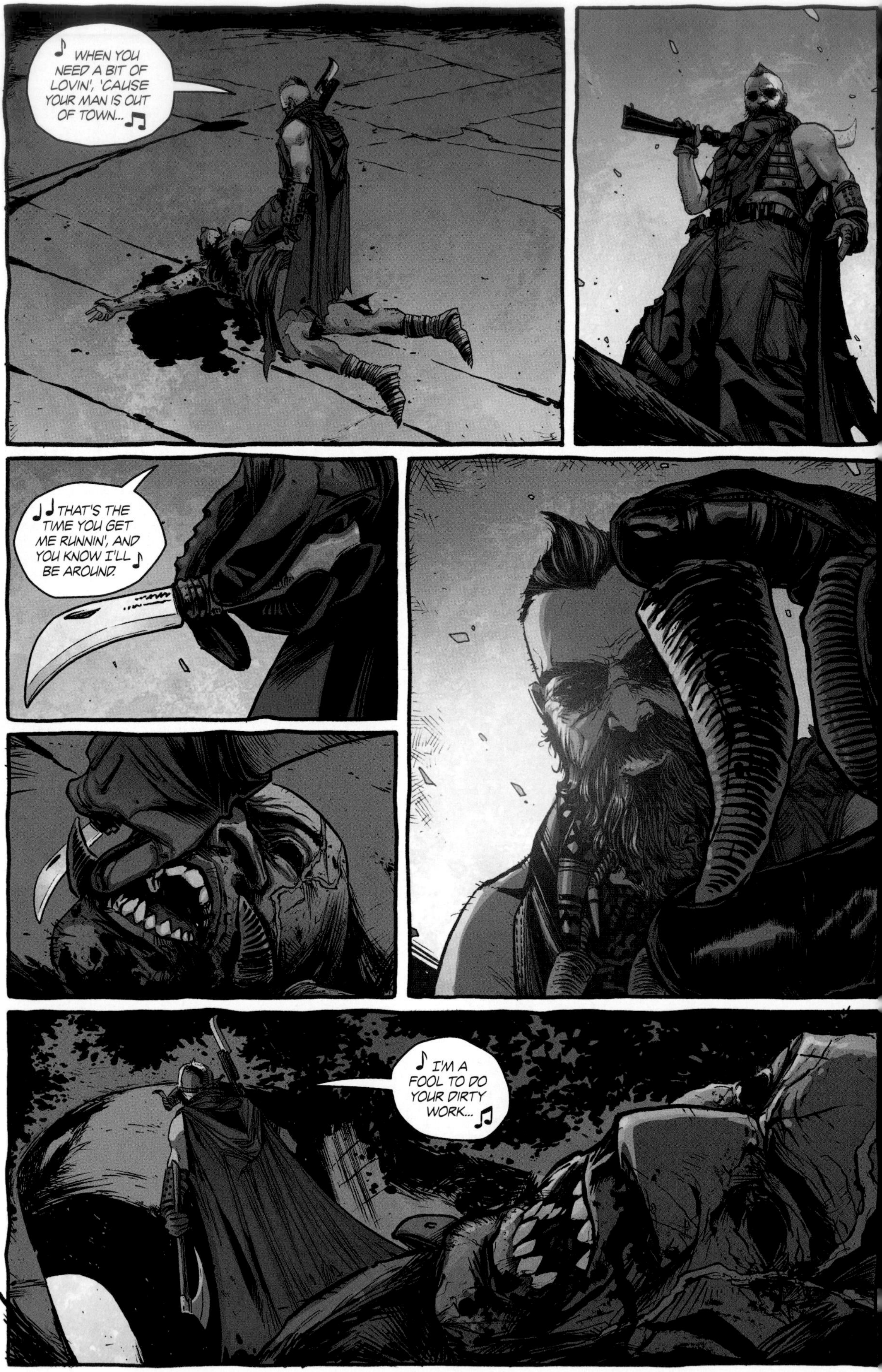
WHEN YOU NEED A BIT OF LOVIN', 'CAUSE YOUR MAN IS OUT OF TOWN...
THAT'S THE TIME YOU GET ME RUNNIN', AND YOU KNOW I'LL BE AROUND.
I'M A FOOL TO DO YOUR DIRTY WORK...

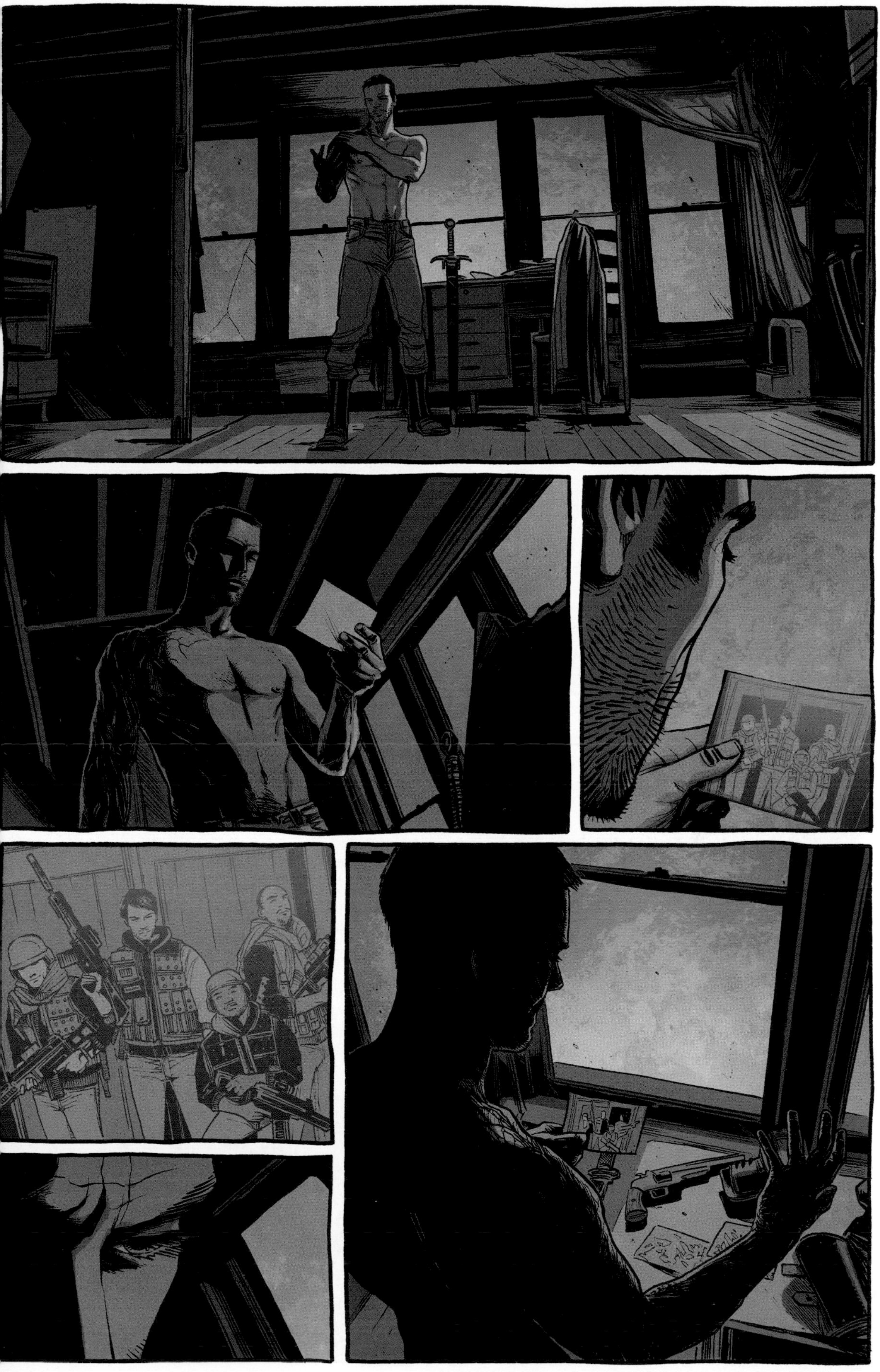

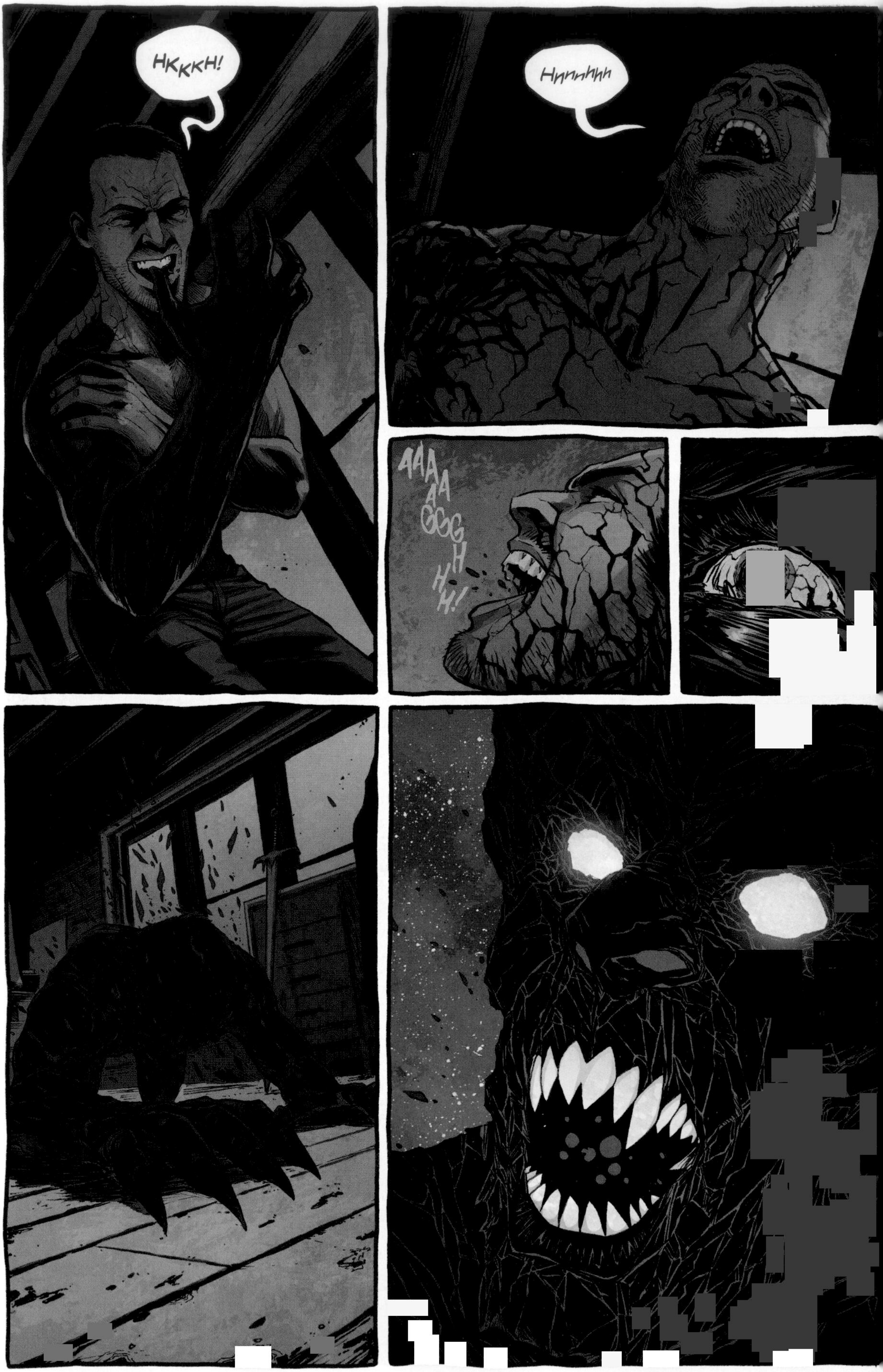
HKKKH!
Hnnnhhh
AAAAAGGGHHH!

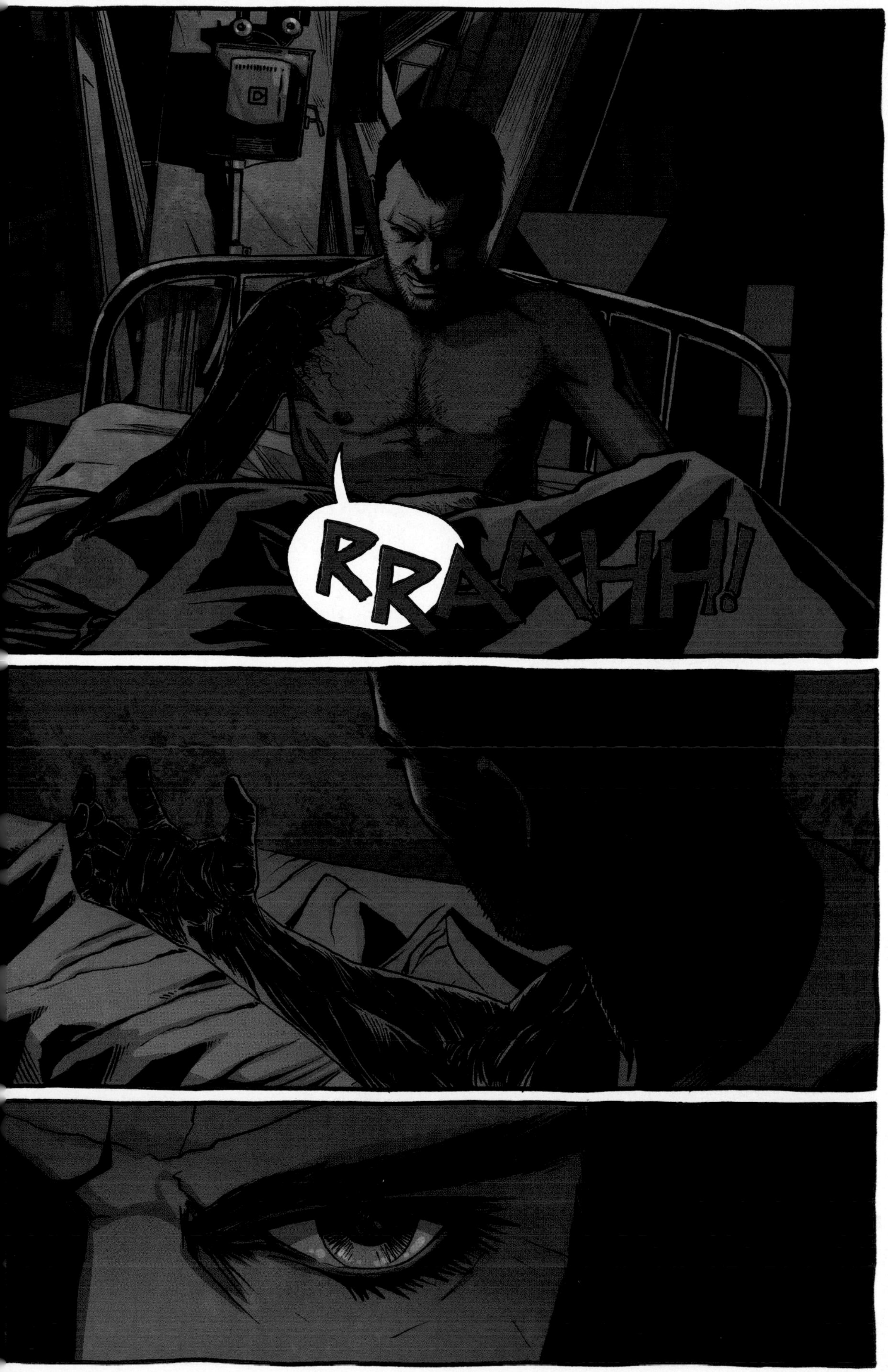
RRAAHH!

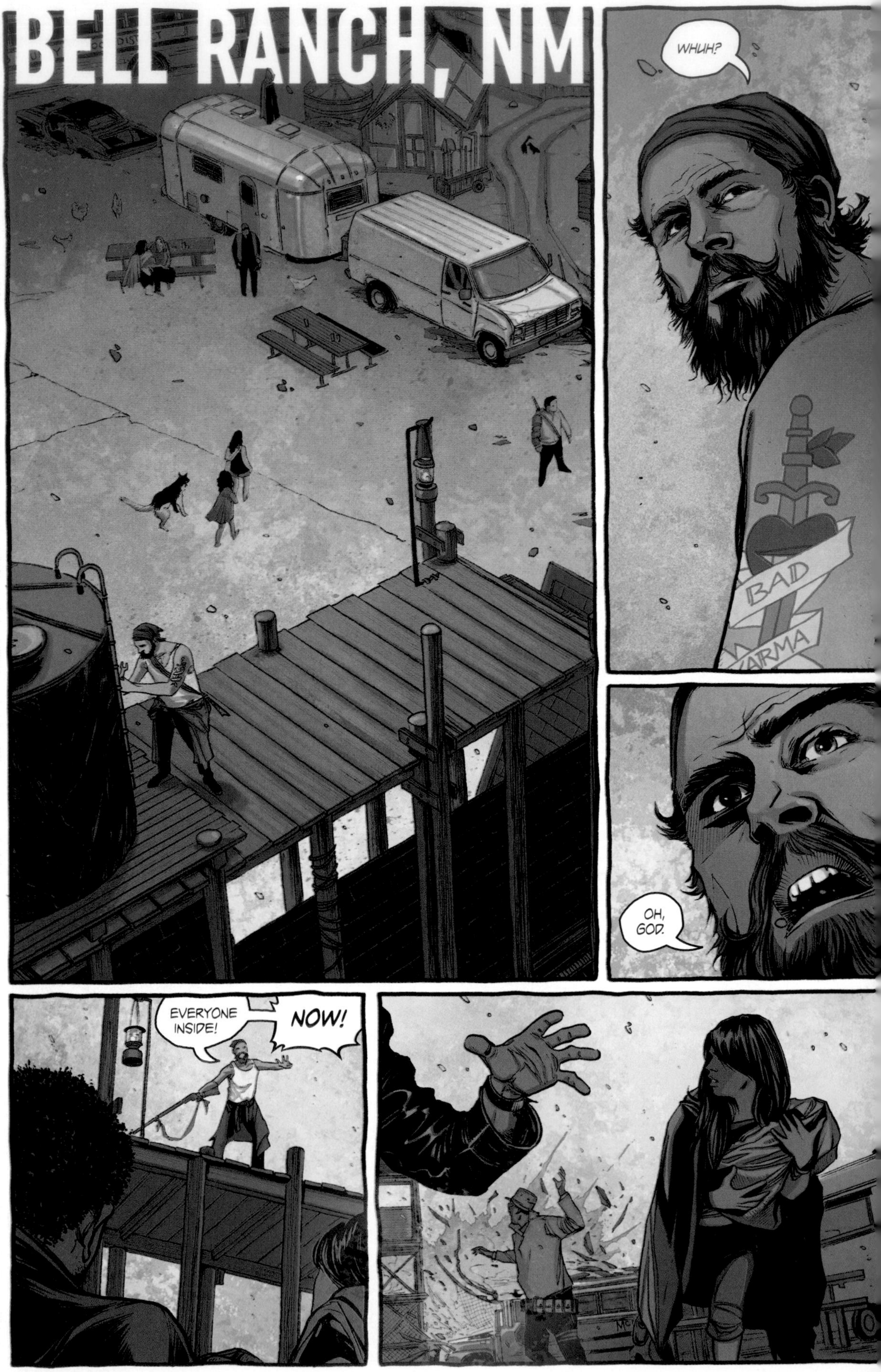

BELL RANCH, NM
WHUH?
BAD
KARMA
OH, GOD.
EVERYONE INSIDE!
NOW!

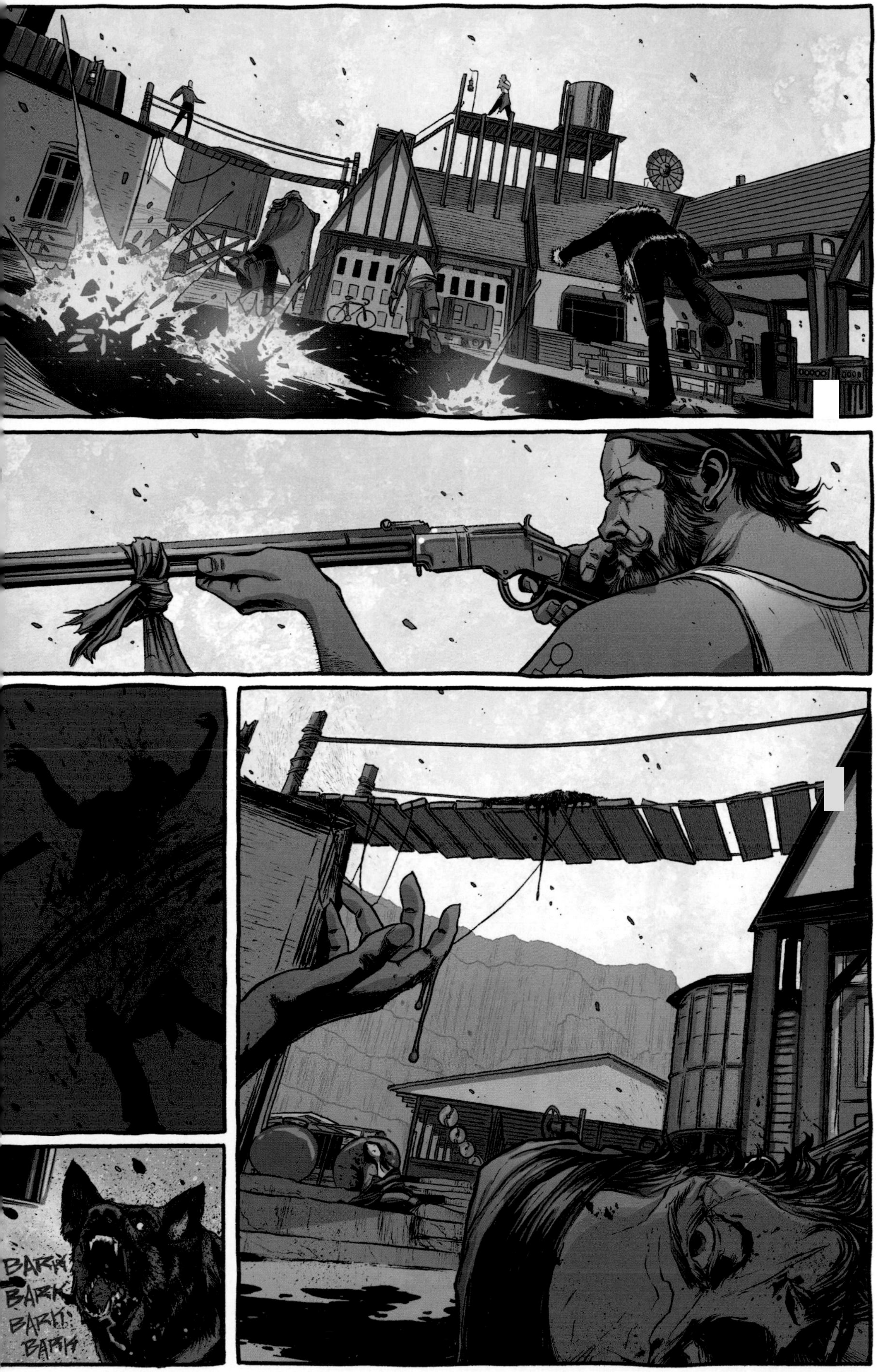
BARK
BARK
BARK
BARK

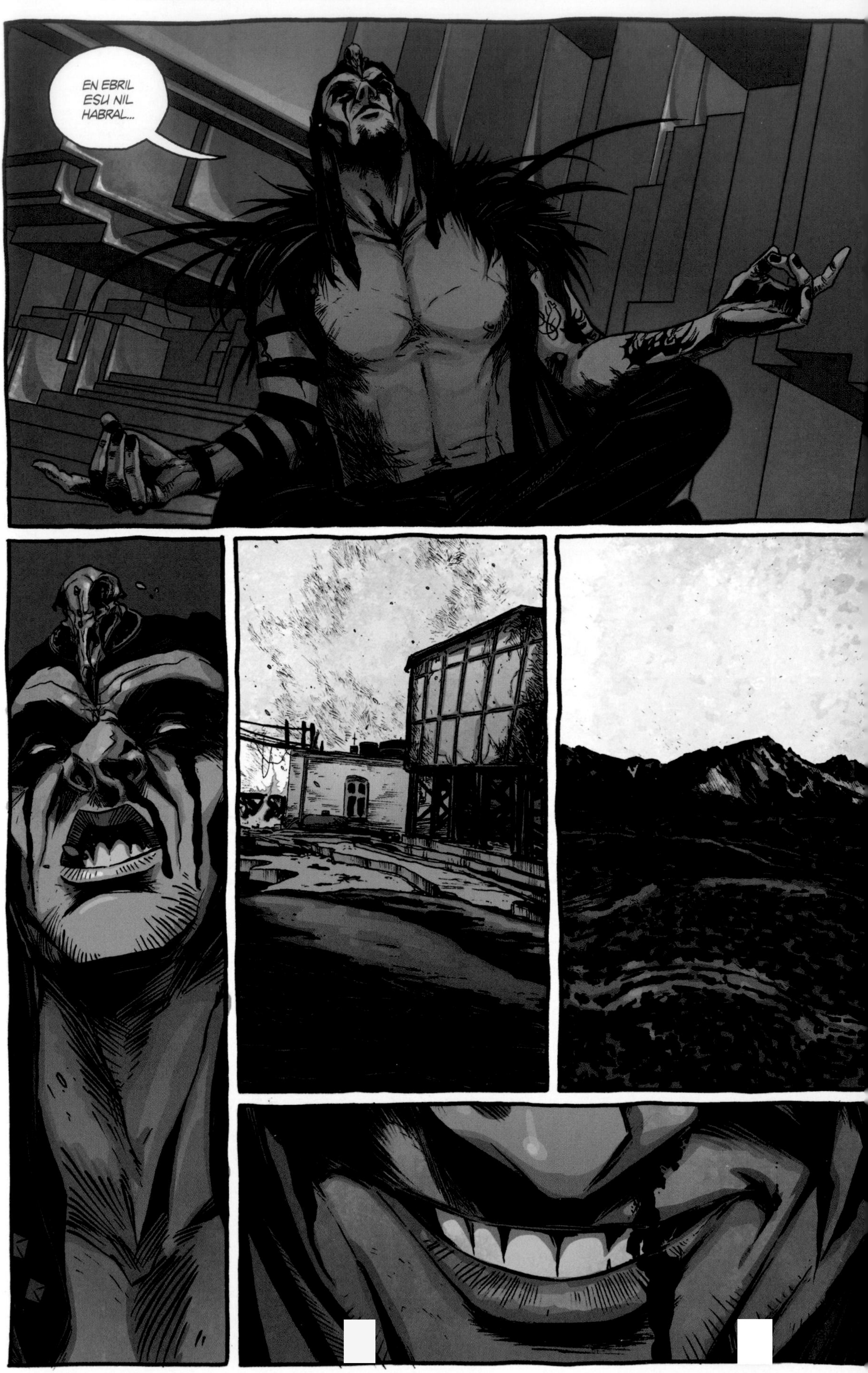
EN EBRIL
ESU NIL
HABRAL...

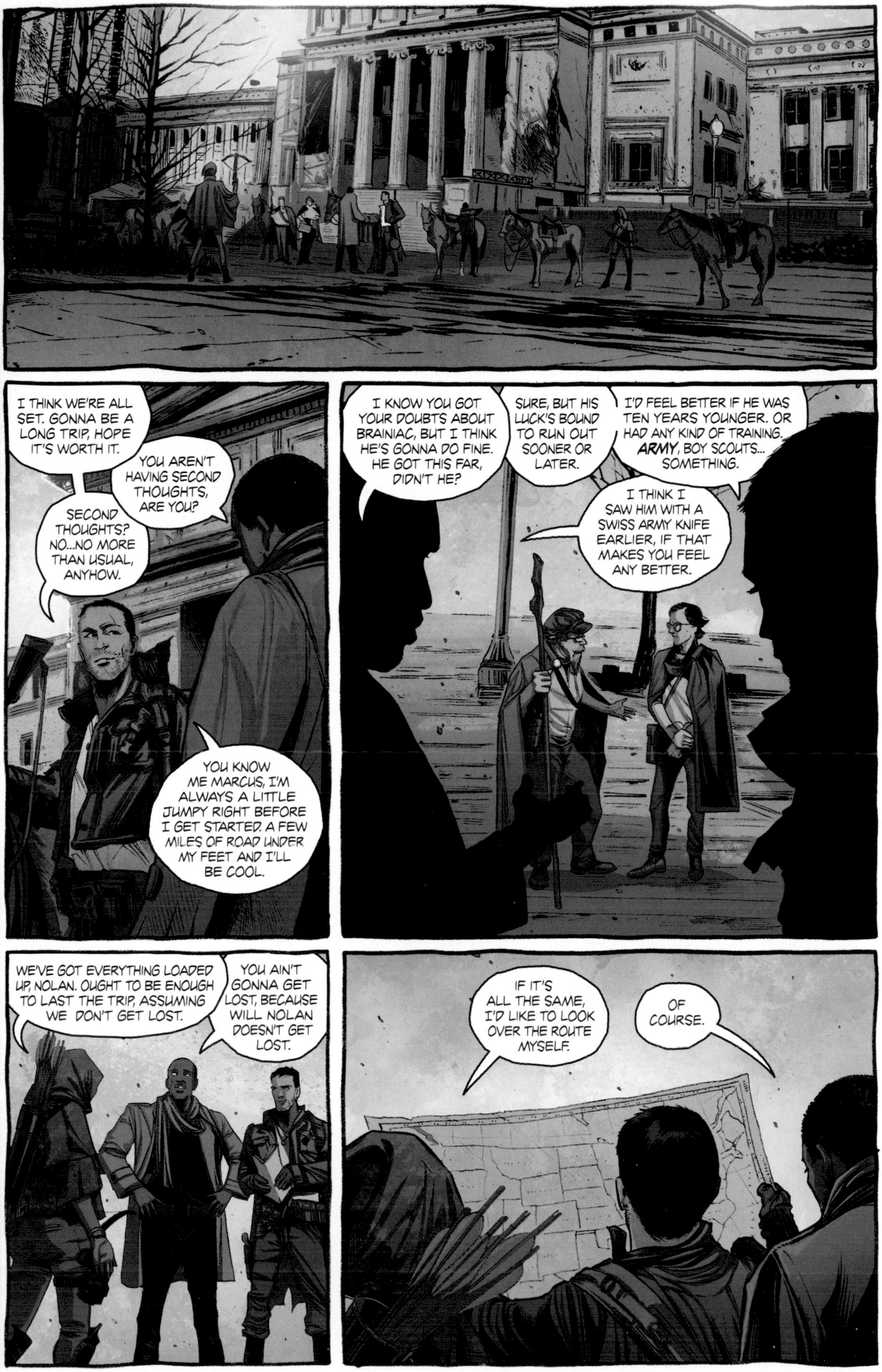
I THINK WE'RE ALL SET. GONNA BE A LONG TRIP, HOPE IT'S WORTH IT.
YOU AREN'T HAVING SECOND THOUGHTS, ARE YOU?
SECOND THOUGHTS? NO...NO MORE THAN USUAL, ANYHOW.
YOU KNOW ME MARCUS, I'M ALWAYS A LITTLE JUMPY RIGHT BEFORE I GET STARTED. A FEW MILES OF ROAD UNDER MY FEET AND I'LL BE COOL.
I KNOW YOU GOT YOUR DOUBTS ABOUT BRAINIAC, BUT I THINK HE'S GONNA DO FINE. HE GOT THIS FAR, DIDN'T HE?
SURE, BUT HIS LUCK'S BOUND TO RUN OUT SOONER OR LATER.
I'D FEEL BETTER IF HE WAS TEN YEARS YOUNGER. OR HAD ANY KIND OF TRAINING. ARMY, BOY SCOUTS... SOMETHING.
I THINK I SAW HIM WITH A SWISS ARMY KNIFE EARLIER, IF THAT MAKES YOU FEEL ANY BETTER.
WE'VE GOT EVERYTHING LOADED UP, NOLAN. OUGHT TO BE ENOUGH TO LAST THE TRIP, ASSUMING WE DON'T GET LOST.
YOU AIN'T GONNA GET LOST, BECAUSE WILL NOLAN DOESN'T GET LOST.
IF IT'S ALL THE SAME, I'D LIKE TO LOOK OVER THE ROUTE MYSELF.
OF COURSE.

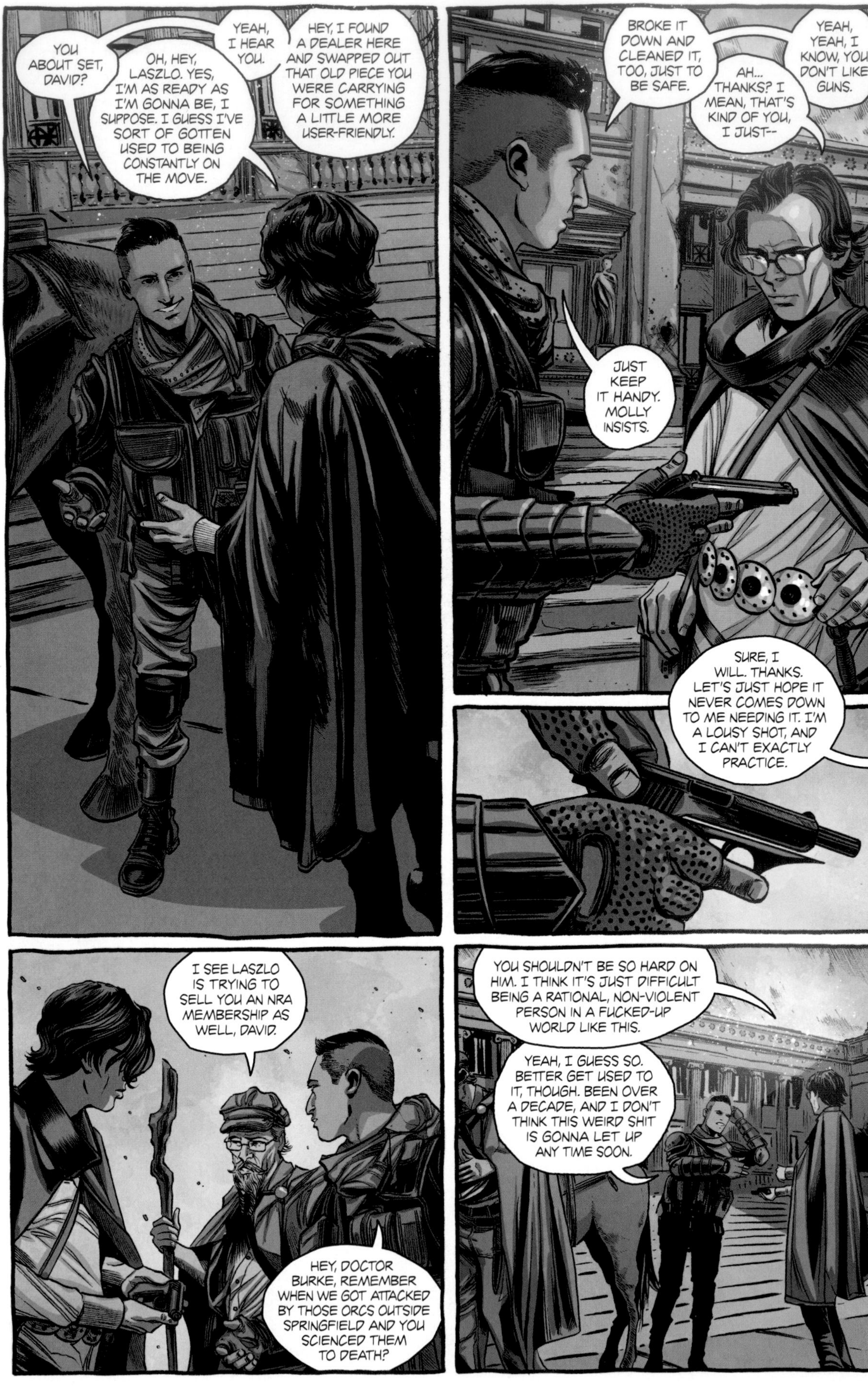
YOU ABOUT SET, DAVID?
OH, HEY, LASZLO. YES, I'M AS READY AS I'M GONNA BE, I SUPPOSE. I GUESS I'VE SORT OF GOTTEN USED TO BEING CONSTANTLY ON THE MOVE.
YEAH, I HEAR YOU.
HEY, I FOUND A DEALER HERE AND SWAPPED OUT THAT OLD PIECE YOU WERE CARRYING FOR SOMETHING A LITTLE MORE USER-FRIENDLY.
BROKE IT DOWN AND CLEANED IT, TOO, JUST TO BE SAFE.
AH... THANKS? I MEAN, THAT'S KIND OF YOU, I JUST--
YEAH, YEAH, I KNOW, YOU DON'T LIKE GUNS.
JUST KEEP IT HANDY. MOLLY INSISTS.
SURE, I WILL. THANKS. LET'S JUST HOPE IT NEVER COMES DOWN TO ME NEEDING IT. I'M A LOUSY SHOT, AND I CAN'T EXACTLY PRACTICE.
I SEE LASZLO IS TRYING TO SELL YOU AN NRA MEMBERSHIP AS WELL, DAVID.
HEY, DOCTOR BURKE, REMEMBER WHEN WE GOT ATTACKED BY THOSE ORCS OUTSIDE SPRINGFIELD AND YOU SCIENCED THEM TO DEATH?
YOU SHOULDN'T BE SO HARD ON HIM. I THINK IT'S JUST DIFFICULT BEING A RATIONAL, NON-VIOLENT PERSON IN A FUCKED-UP WORLD LIKE THIS.
YEAH, I GUESS SO. BETTER GET USED TO IT, THOUGH. BEEN OVER A DECADE, AND I DON'T THINK THIS WEIRD SHIT IS GONNA LET UP ANY TIME SOON.

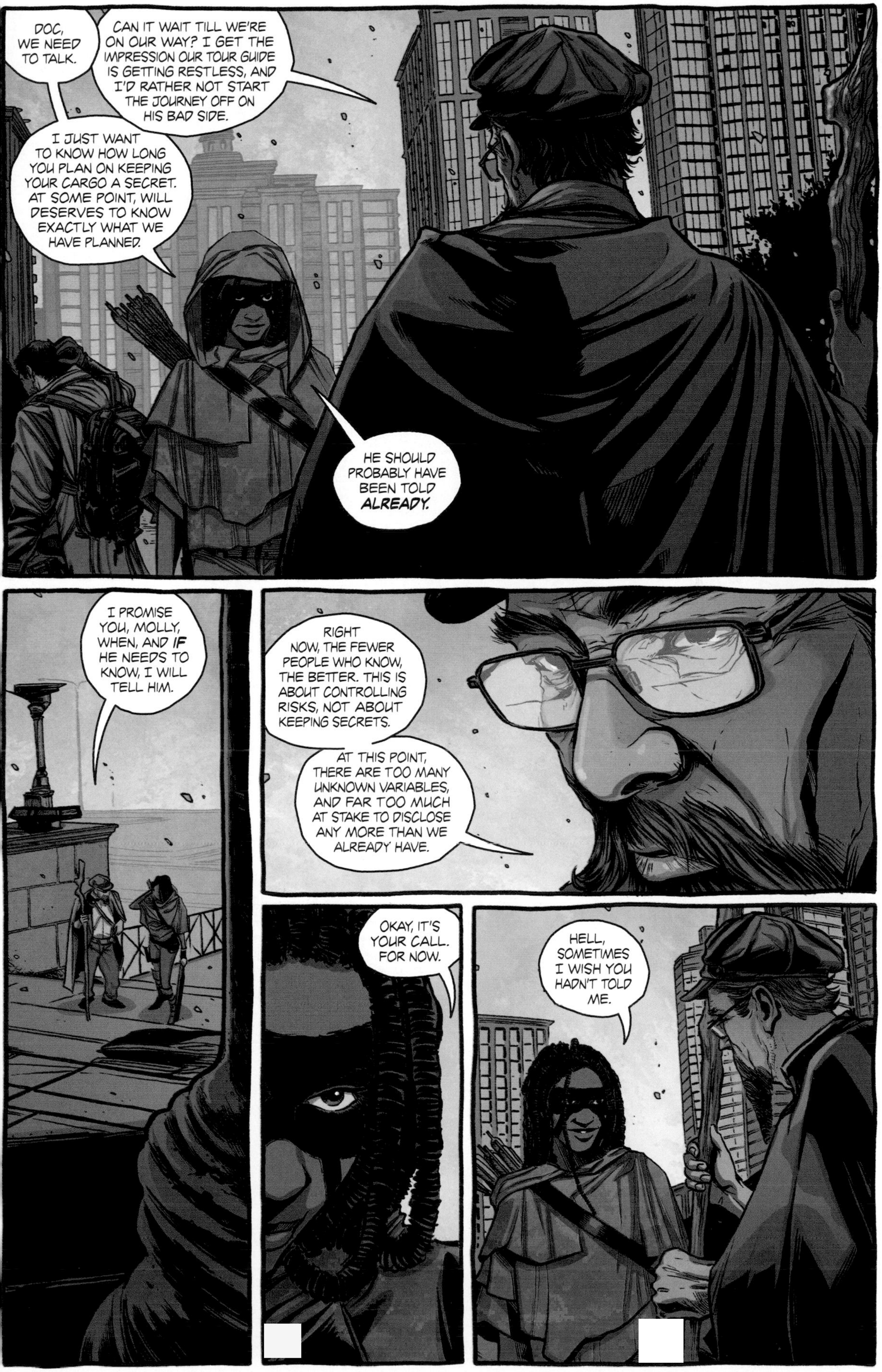

DOC, WE NEED TO TALK.
CAN IT WAIT TILL WE'RE ON OUR WAY? I GET THE IMPRESSION OUR TOUR GUIDE IS GETTING RESTLESS, AND I'D RATHER NOT START THE JOURNEY OFF ON HIS BAD SIDE.
I JUST WANT TO KNOW HOW LONG YOU PLAN ON KEEPING YOUR CARGO A SECRET. AT SOME POINT, WILL DESERVES TO KNOW EXACTLY WHAT WE HAVE PLANNED.
HE SHOULD PROBABLY HAVE BEEN TOLD ALREADY.
I PROMISE YOU, MOLLY, WHEN, AND IF HE NEEDS TO KNOW, I WILL TELL HIM.
RIGHT NOW, THE FEWER PEOPLE WHO KNOW, THE BETTER. THIS IS ABOUT CONTROLLING RISKS, NOT ABOUT KEEPING SECRETS.
AT THIS POINT, THERE ARE TOO MANY UNKNOWN VARIABLES, AND FAR TOO MUCH AT STAKE TO DISCLOSE ANY MORE THAN WE ALREADY HAVE.
OKAY, IT'S YOUR CALL. FOR NOW.
HELL, SOMETIMES I WISH YOU HADN'T TOLD ME.

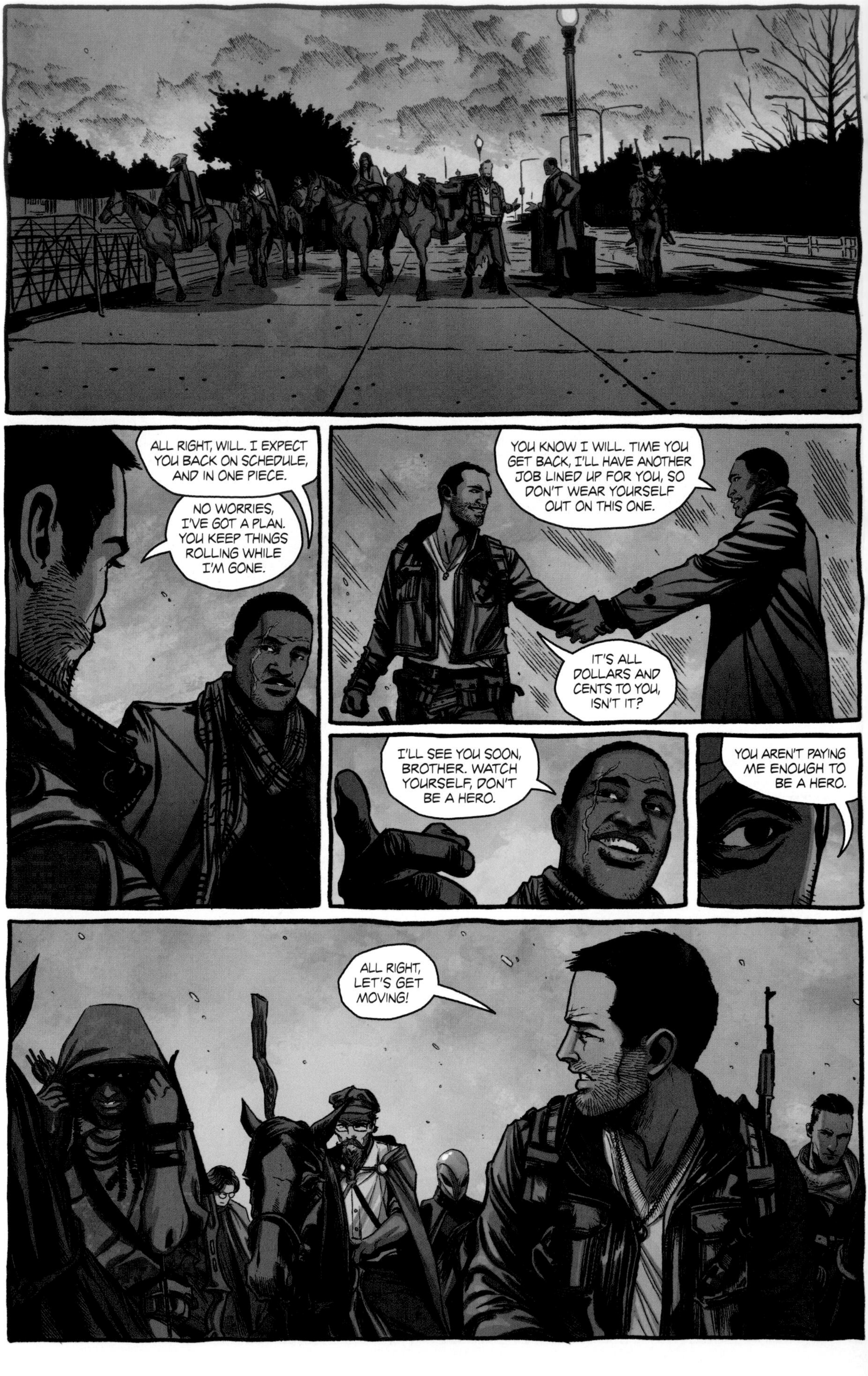
ALL RIGHT, WILL. I EXPECT YOU BACK ON SCHEDULE, AND IN ONE PIECE.
NO WORRIES, I'VE GOT A PLAN. YOU KEEP THINGS ROLLING WHILE I'M GONE.
YOU KNOW I WILL. TIME YOU GET BACK, I'LL HAVE ANOTHER JOB LINED UP FOR YOU, SO DON'T WEAR YOURSELF OUT ON THIS ONE.
IT'S ALL DOLLARS AND CENTS TO YOU, ISN'T IT?
I'LL SEE YOU SOON, BROTHER. WATCH YOURSELF, DON'T BE A HERO.
YOU AREN'T PAYING ME ENOUGH TO BE A HERO.
ALL RIGHT, LET'S GET MOVING!

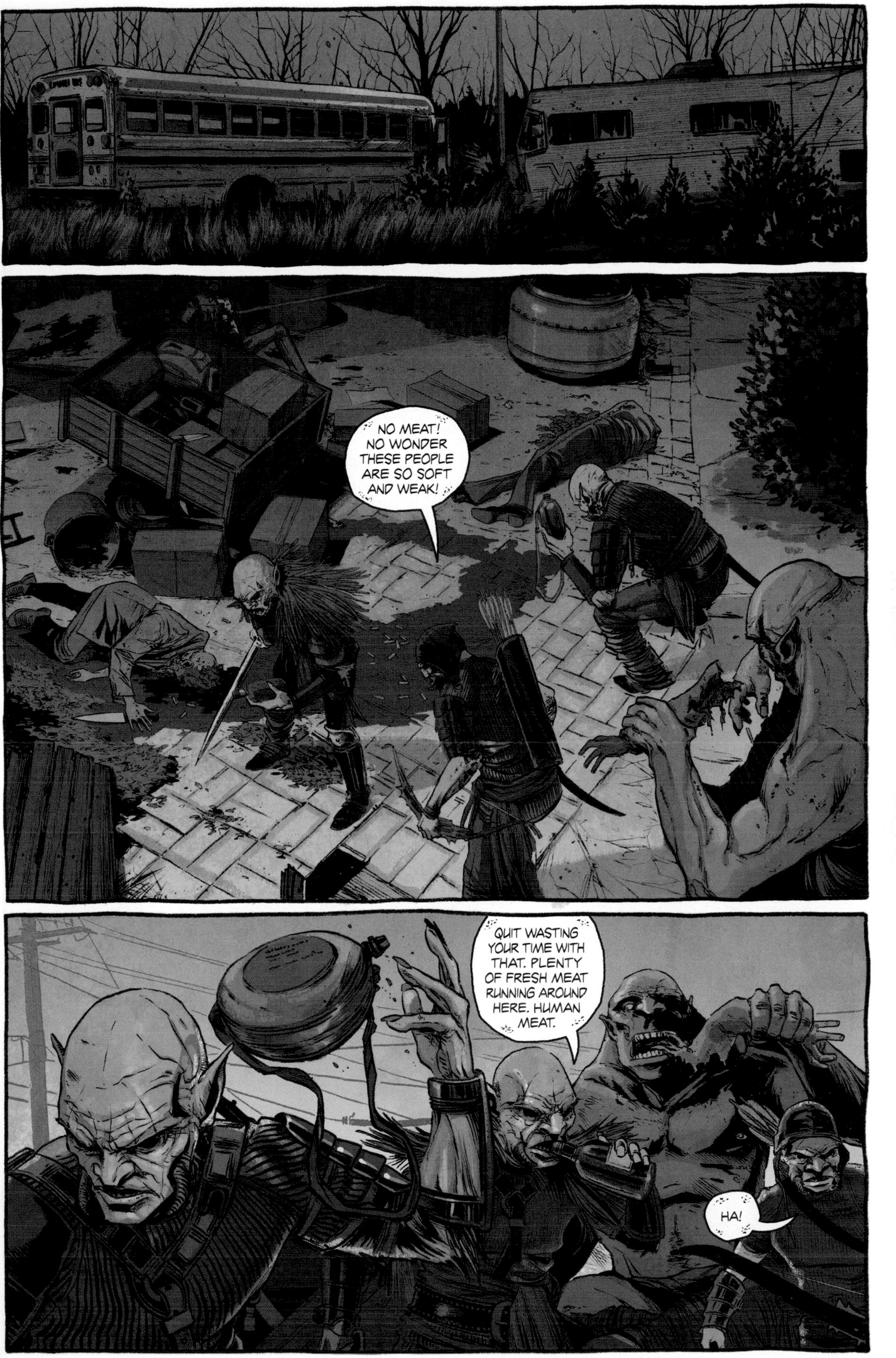
NO MEAT! NO WONDER THESE PEOPLE ARE SO SOFT AND WEAK!
QUIT WASTING YOUR TIME WITH THAT. PLENTY OF FRESH MEAT RUNNING AROUND HERE. HUMAN MEAT.
HA!

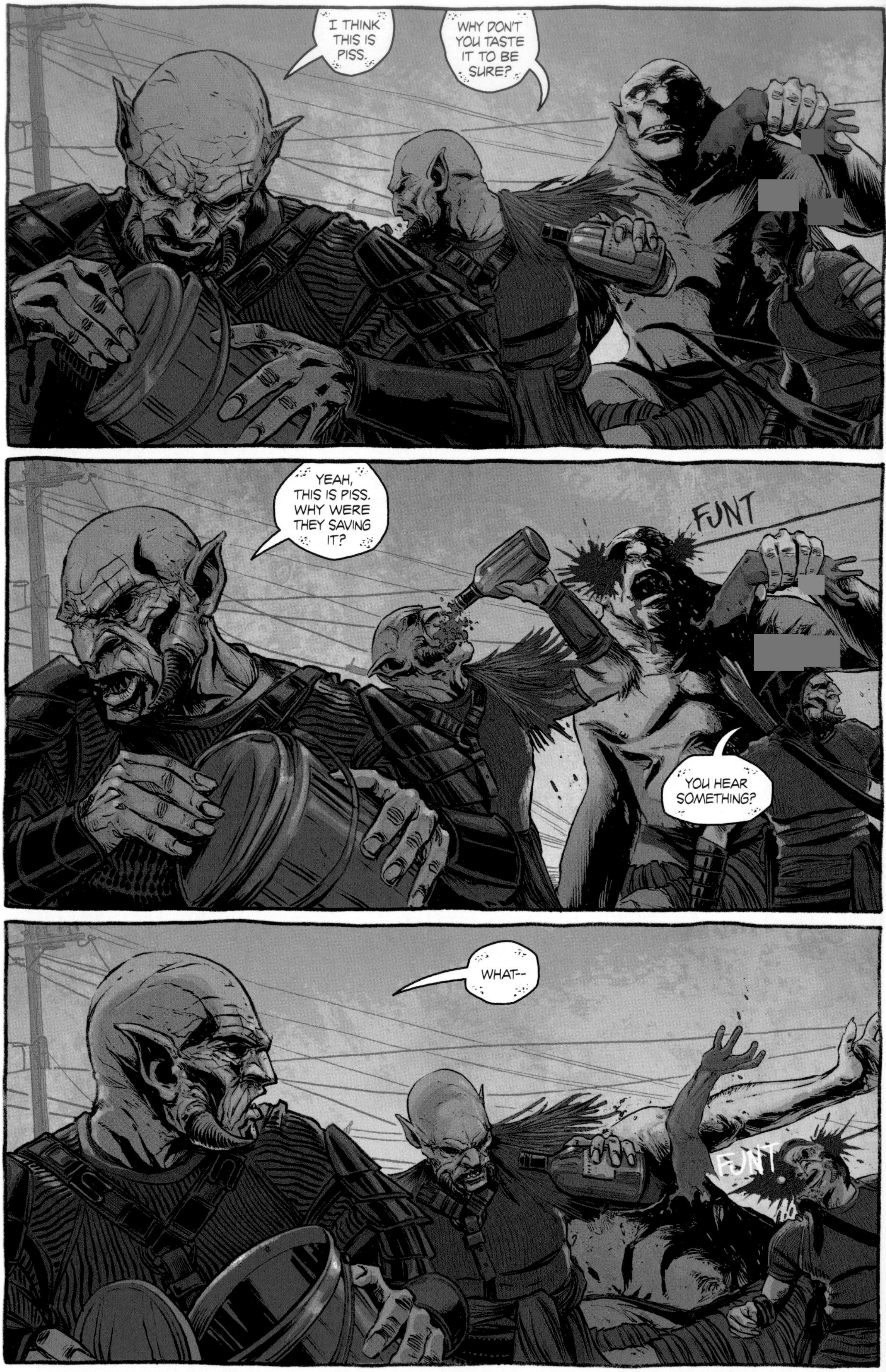
I THINK THIS IS PISS.
WHY DON'T YOU TASTE IT TO BE SURE?
YEAH, THIS IS PISS. WHY WERE THEY SAVING IT?
FUNT
YOU HEAR SOMETHING?
WHAT--
FUNT

--THE FUCK?

IT'S COMING FROM--

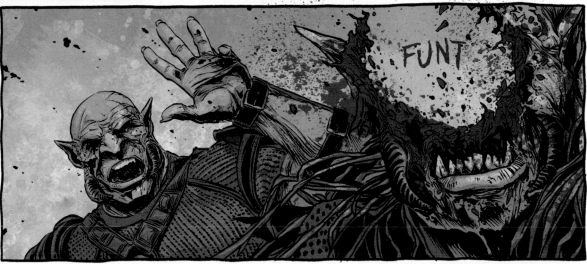

FUNT

MIGHT AS WELL MAKE THIS INTERESTING.

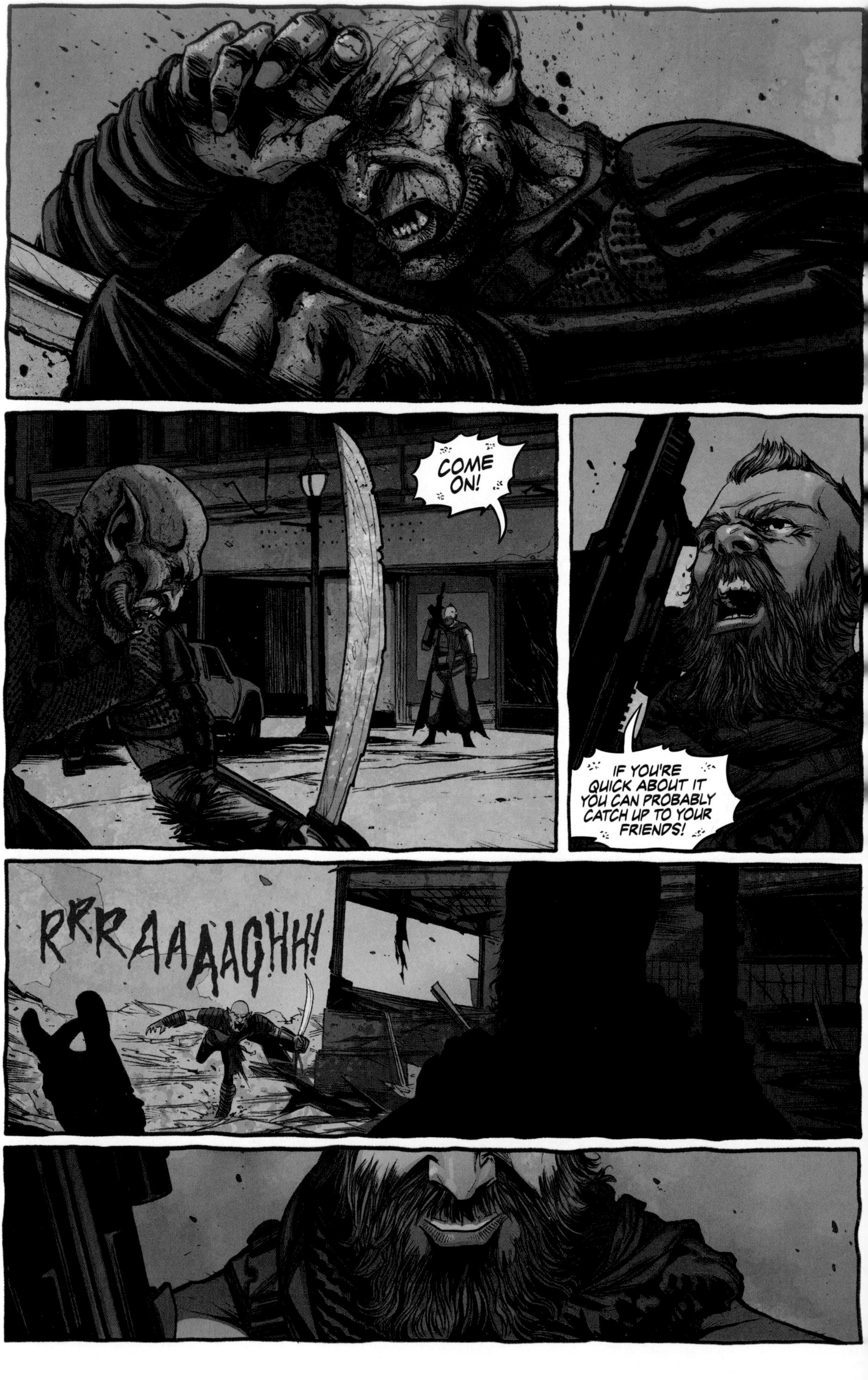
COME ON!
IF YOU'RE QUICK ABOUT IT YOU CAN PROBABLY CATCH UP TO YOUR FRIENDS!
RRRAAAAGHH!

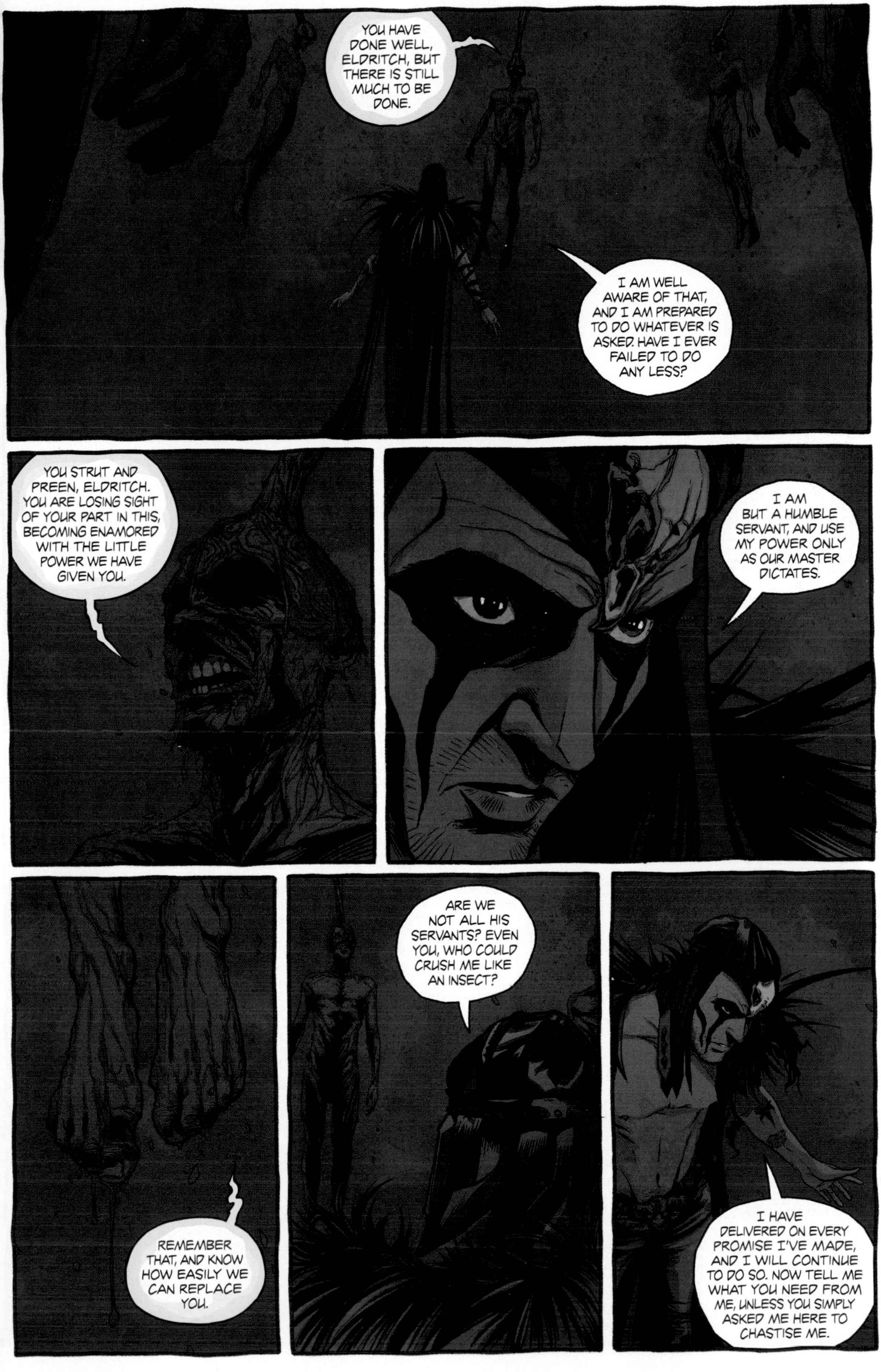
YOU HAVE DONE WELL, ELDRITCH, BUT THERE IS STILL MUCH TO BE DONE.
I AM WELL AWARE OF THAT, AND I AM PREPARED TO DO WHATEVER IS ASKED. HAVE I EVER FAILED TO DO ANY LESS?
YOU STRUT AND PREEN, ELDRITCH. YOU ARE LOSING SIGHT OF YOUR PART IN THIS, BECOMING ENAMORED WITH THE LITTLE POWER WE HAVE GIVEN YOU.
I AM BUT A HUMBLE SERVANT, AND USE MY POWER ONLY AS OUR MASTER DICTATES.
REMEMBER THAT, AND KNOW HOW EASILY WE CAN REPLACE YOU.
ARE WE NOT ALL HIS SERVANTS? EVEN YOU, WHO COULD CRUSH ME LIKE AN INSECT?
I HAVE DELIVERED ON EVERY PROMISE I'VE MADE, AND I WILL CONTINUE TO DO SO. NOW TELL ME WHAT YOU NEED FROM ME, UNLESS YOU SIMPLY ASKED ME HERE TO CHASTISE ME.

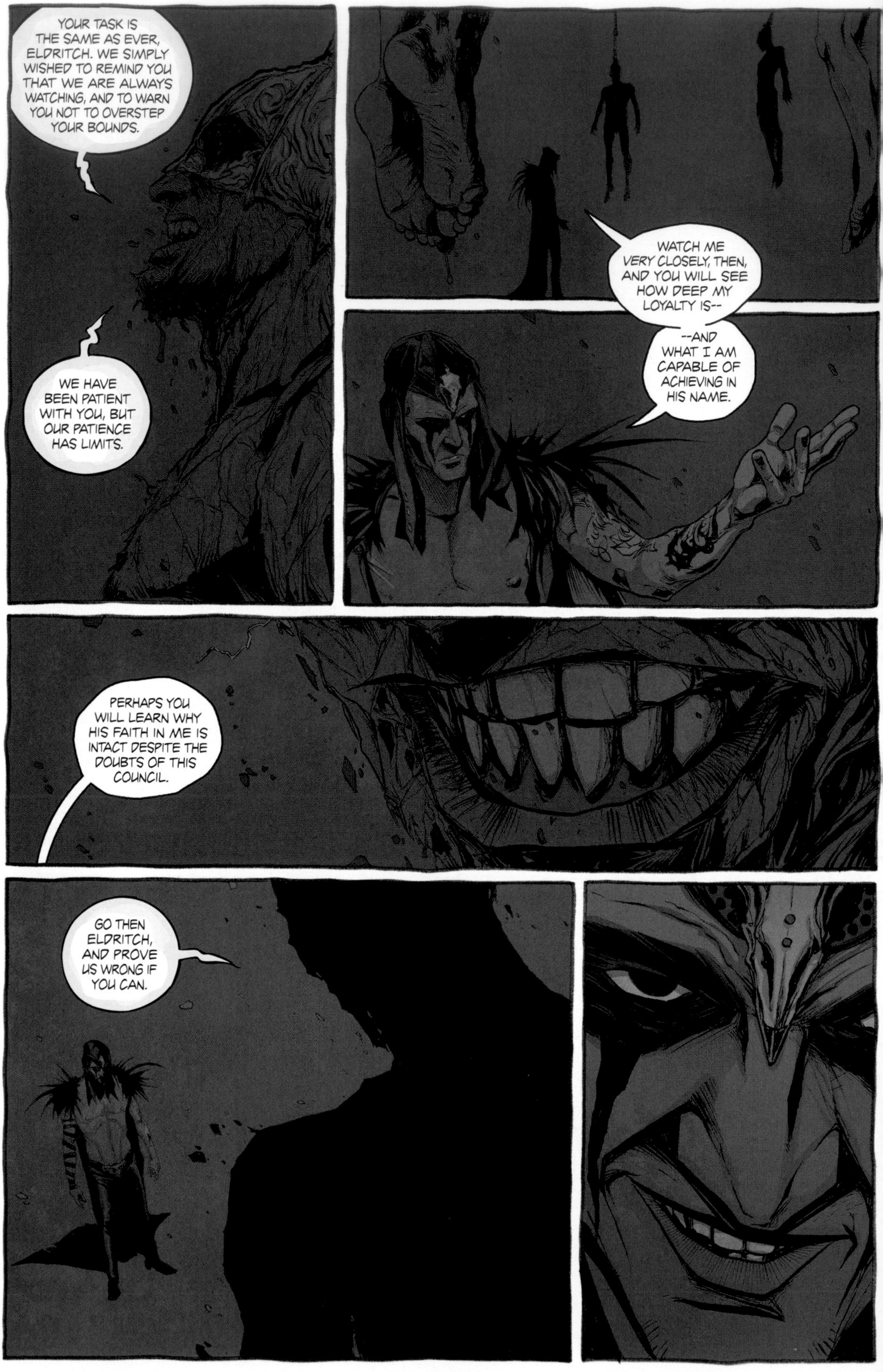
YOUR TASK IS THE SAME AS EVER, ELDRITCH. WE SIMPLY WISHED TO REMIND YOU THAT WE ARE ALWAYS WATCHING, AND TO WARN YOU NOT TO OVERSTEP YOUR BOUNDS.
WE HAVE BEEN PATIENT WITH YOU, BUT OUR PATIENCE HAS LIMITS.
WATCH ME VERY CLOSELY, THEN, AND YOU WILL SEE HOW DEEP MY LOYALTY IS--
--AND WHAT I AM CAPABLE OF ACHIEVING IN HIS NAME.
PERHAPS YOU WILL LEARN WHY HIS FAITH IN ME IS INTACT DESPITE THE DOUBTS OF THIS COUNCIL.
GO THEN ELDRITCH, AND PROVE US WRONG IF YOU CAN.

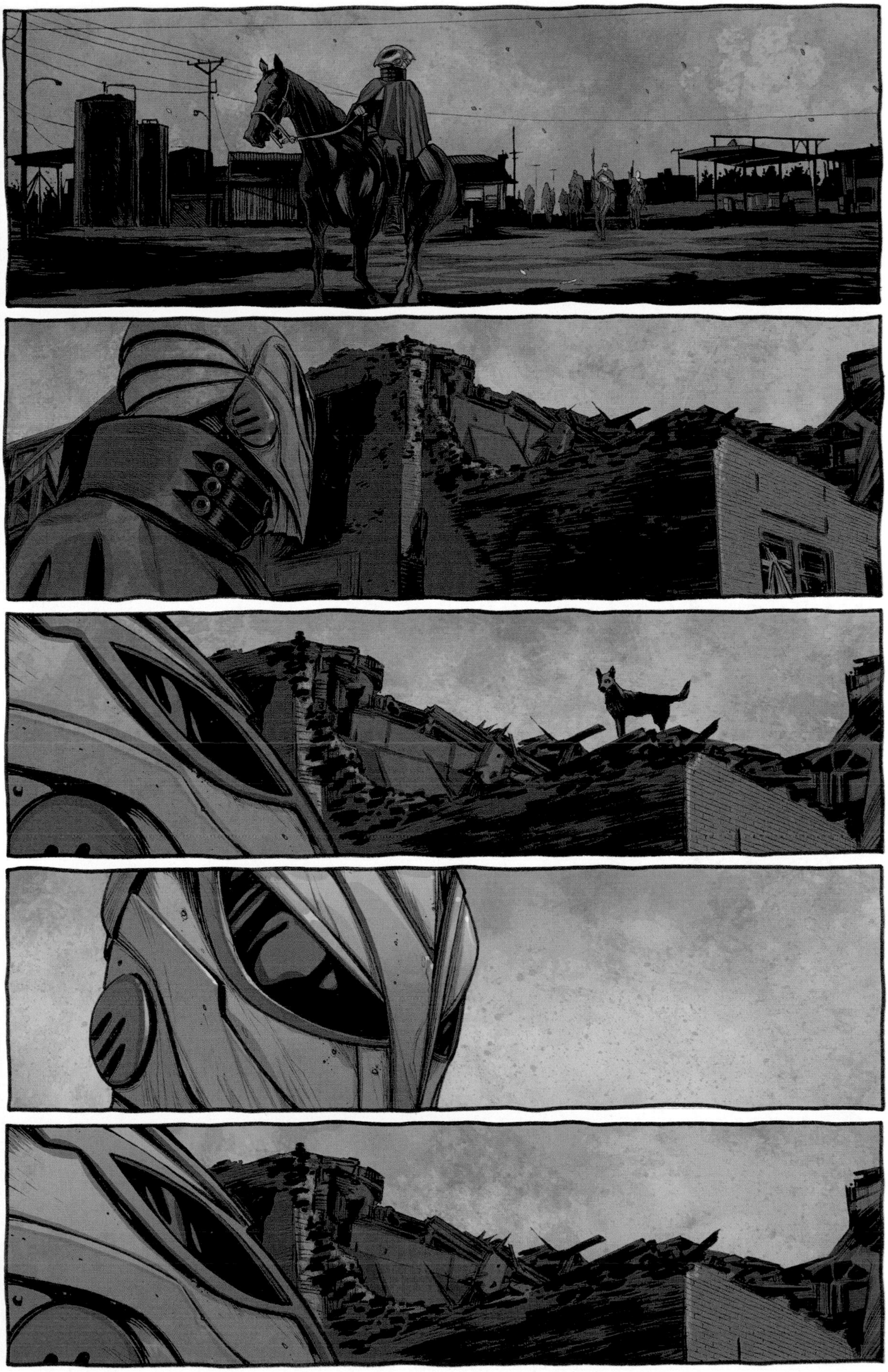

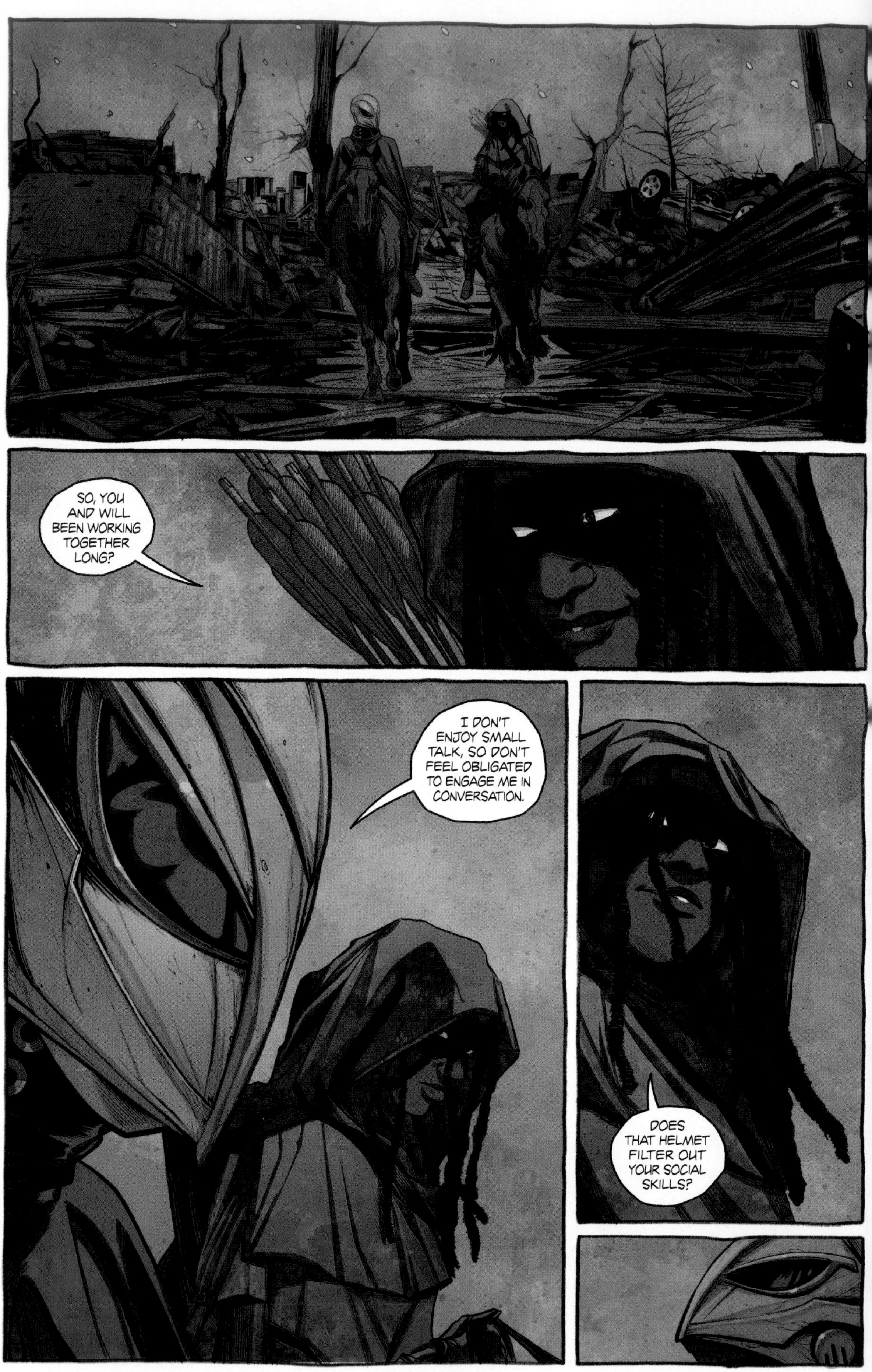
SO, YOU AND WILL BEEN WORKING TOGETHER LONG?
I DON'T ENJOY SMALL TALK, SO DON'T FEEL OBLIGATED TO ENGAGE ME IN CONVERSATION.
DOES THAT HELMET FILTER OUT YOUR SOCIAL SKILLS?

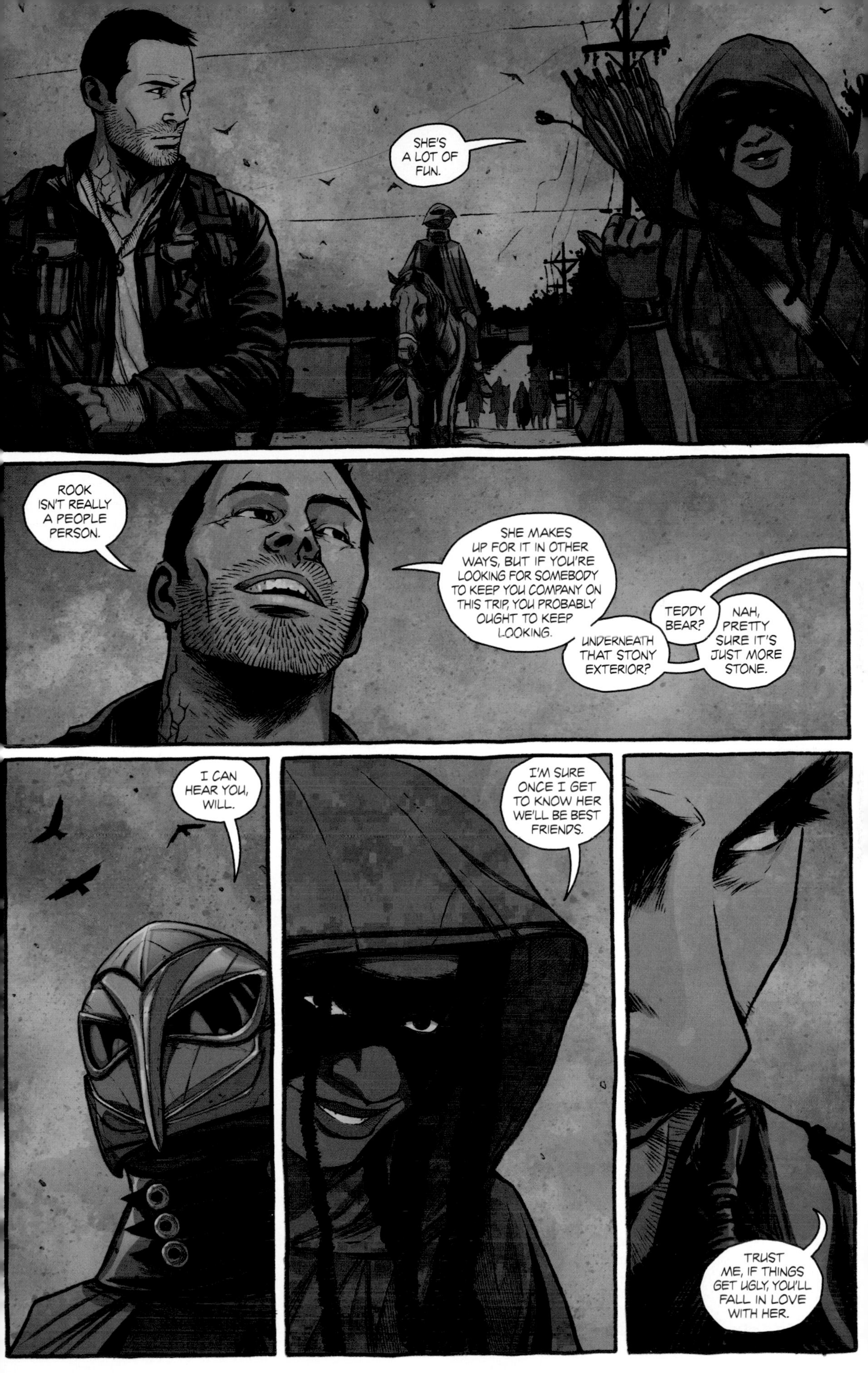
SHE'S A LOT OF FUN.
ROOK ISN'T REALLY A PEOPLE PERSON.
SHE MAKES UP FOR IT IN OTHER WAYS, BUT IF YOU'RE LOOKING FOR SOMEBODY TO KEEP YOU COMPANY ON THIS TRIP, YOU PROBABLY OUGHT TO KEEP LOOKING.
TEDDY BEAR?
UNDERNEATH THAT STONY EXTERIOR?
NAH, PRETTY SURE IT'S JUST MORE STONE.
I CAN HEAR YOU, WILL.
I'M SURE ONCE I GET TO KNOW HER WE'LL BE BEST FRIENDS.
TRUST ME, IF THINGS GET UGLY, YOU'LL FALL IN LOVE WITH HER.

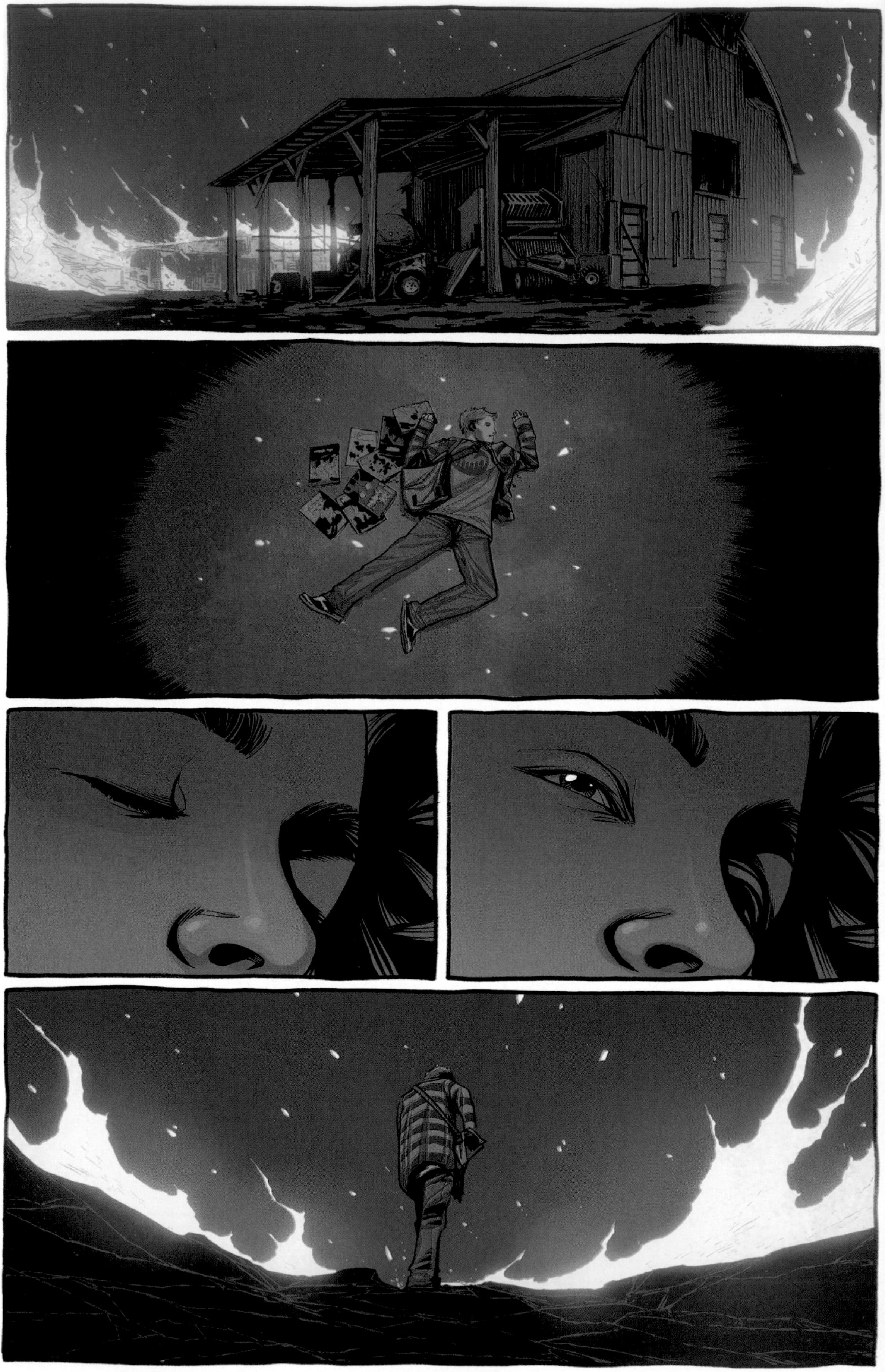

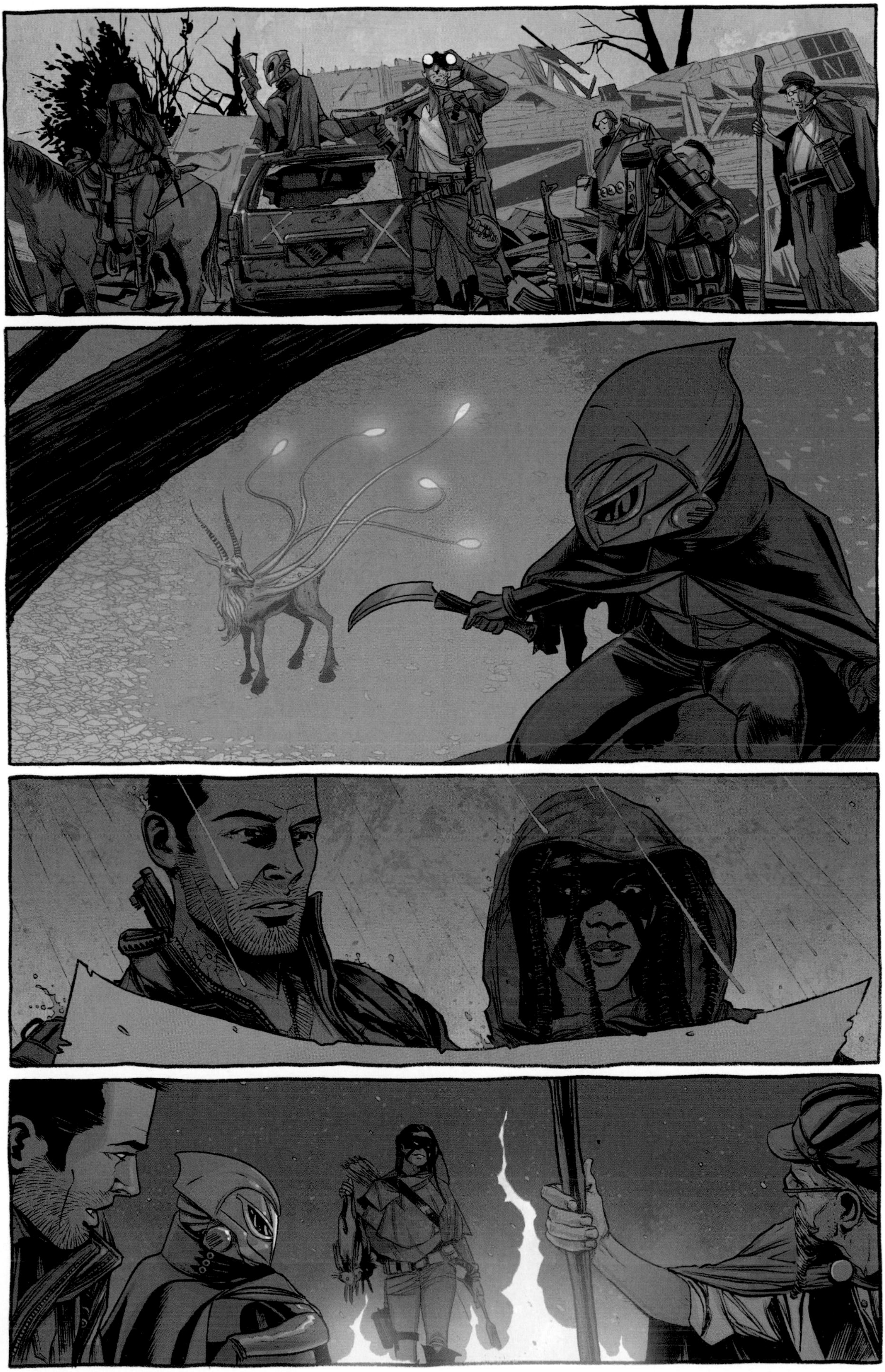

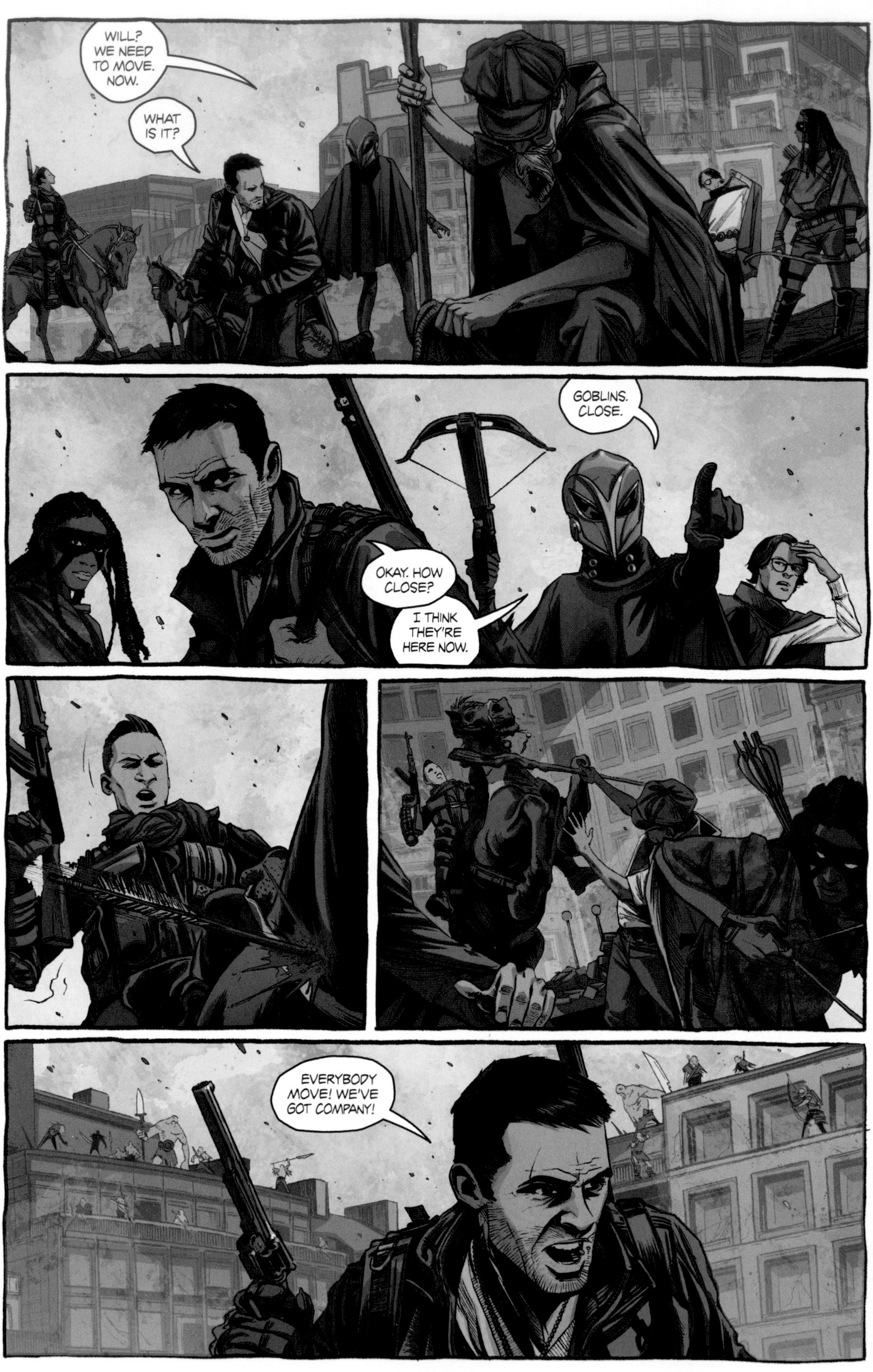
WILL? WE NEED TO MOVE. NOW.
WHAT IS IT?
GOBLINS. CLOSE.
OKAY. HOW CLOSE?
I THINK THEY'RE HERE NOW.
EVERYBODY MOVE! WE'VE GOT COMPANY!

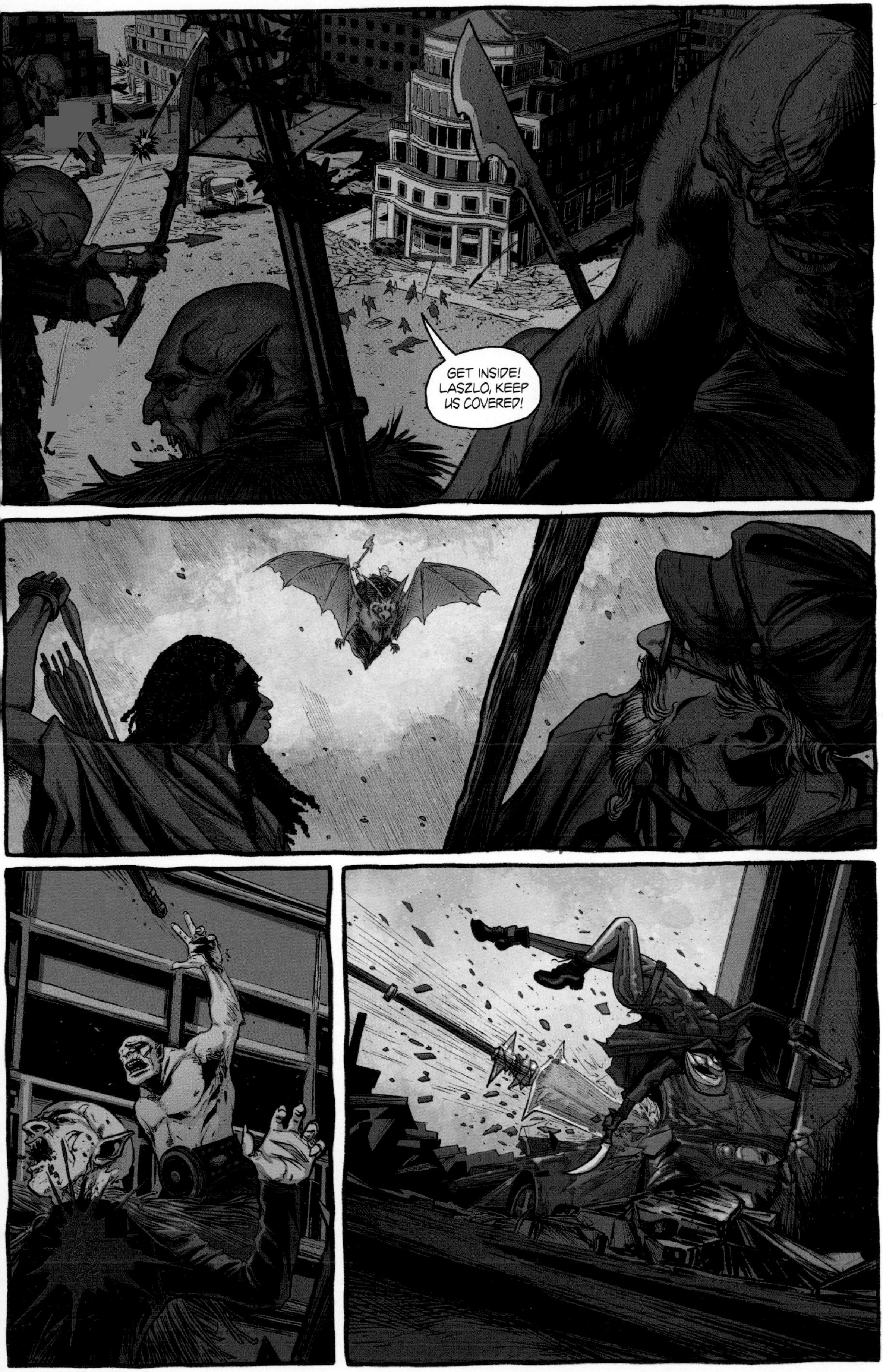
GET INSIDE! LASZLO, KEEP US COVERED!

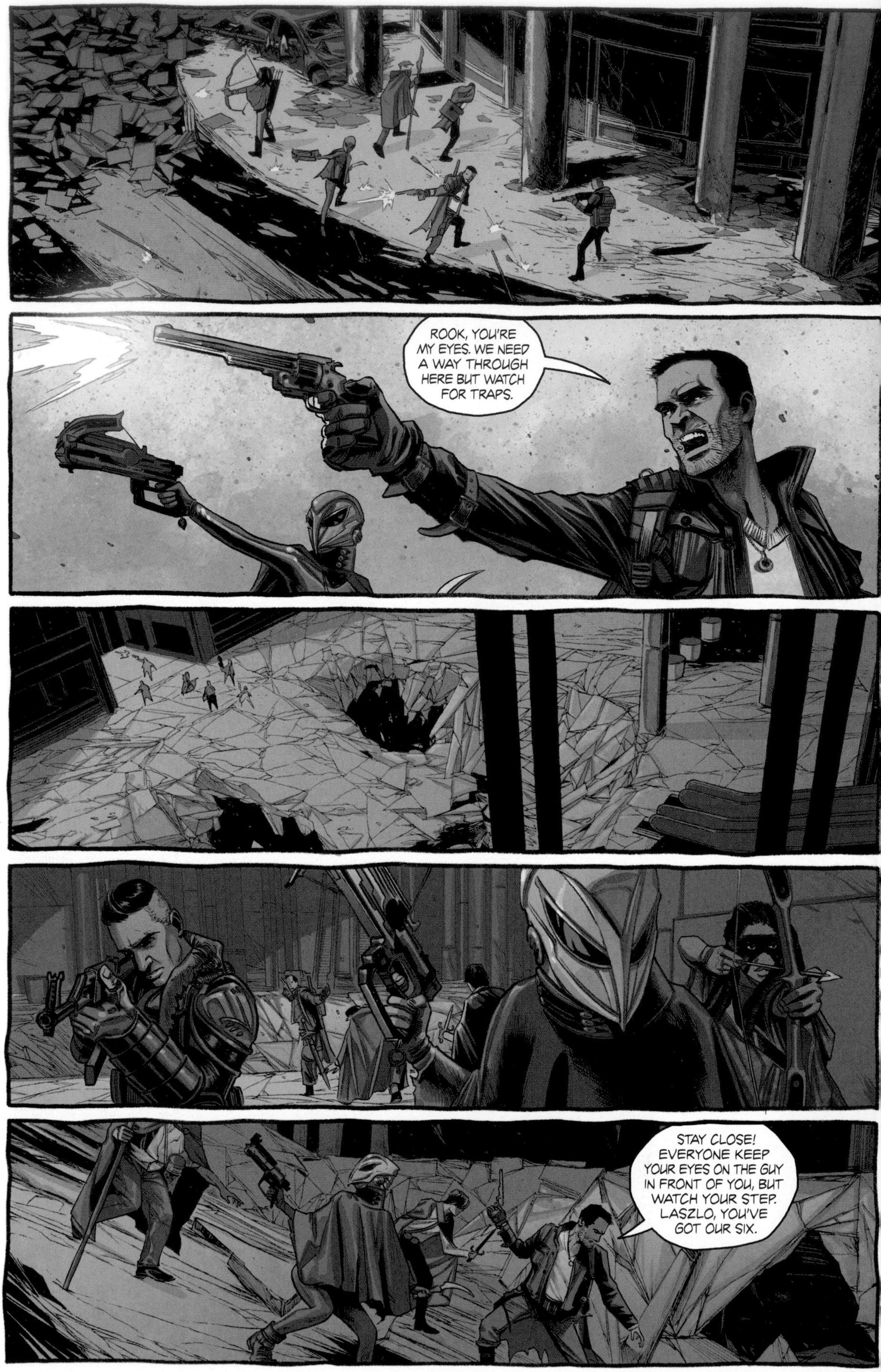
ROOK, YOU'RE MY EYES. WE NEED A WAY THROUGH HERE BUT WATCH FOR TRAPS.
STAY CLOSE! EVERYONE KEEP YOUR EYES ON THE GUY IN FRONT OF YOU, BUT WATCH YOUR STEP. LASZLO, YOU'VE GOT OUR SIX.

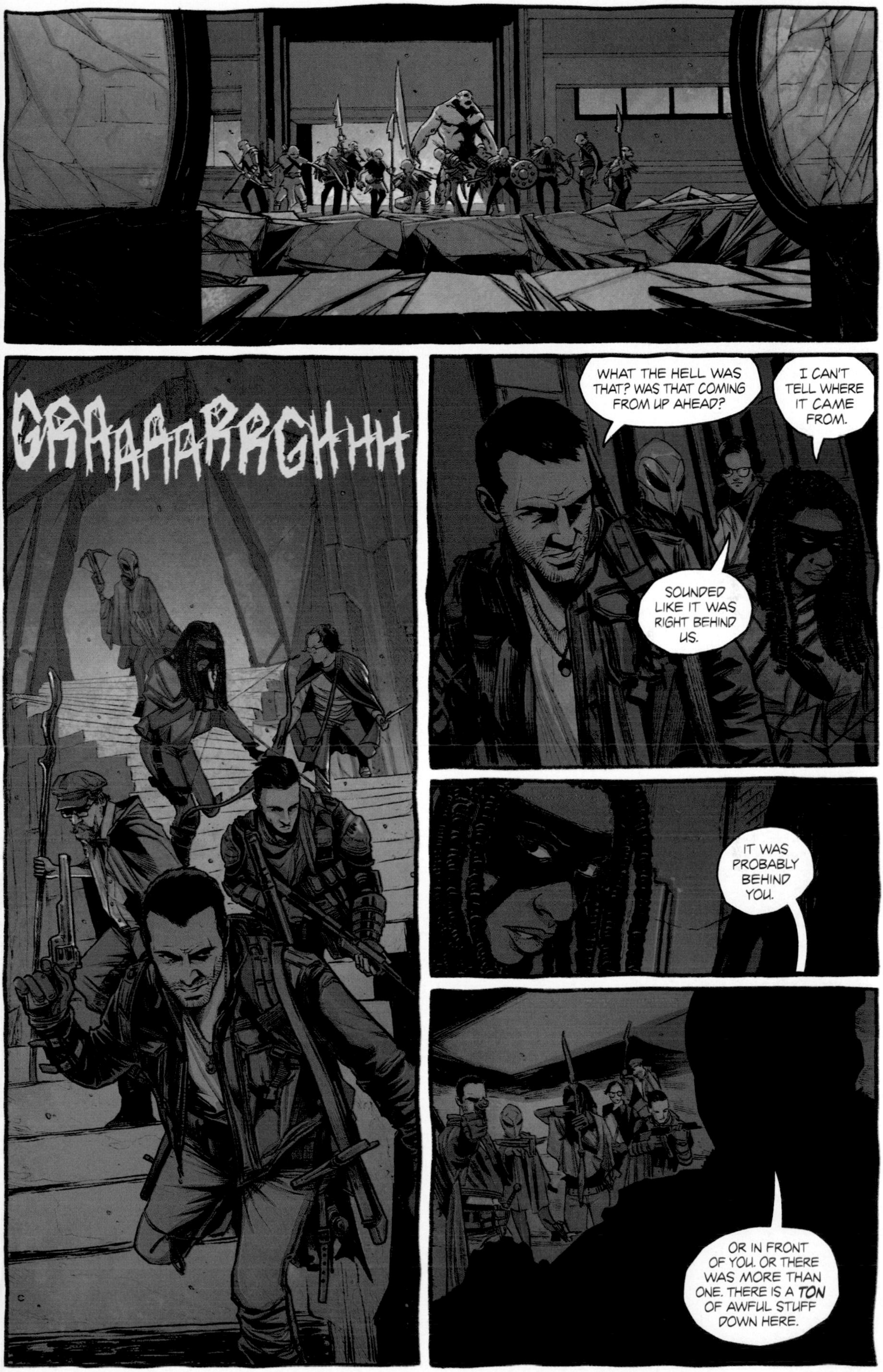
GRAAARRGHHH
WHAT THE HELL WAS THAT? WAS THAT COMING FROM UP AHEAD?
I CAN'T TELL WHERE IT CAME FROM.
SOUNDED LIKE IT WAS RIGHT BEHIND US.
IT WAS PROBABLY BEHIND YOU.
OR IN FRONT OF YOU. OR THERE WAS MORE THAN ONE. THERE IS A TON OF AWFUL STUFF DOWN HERE.

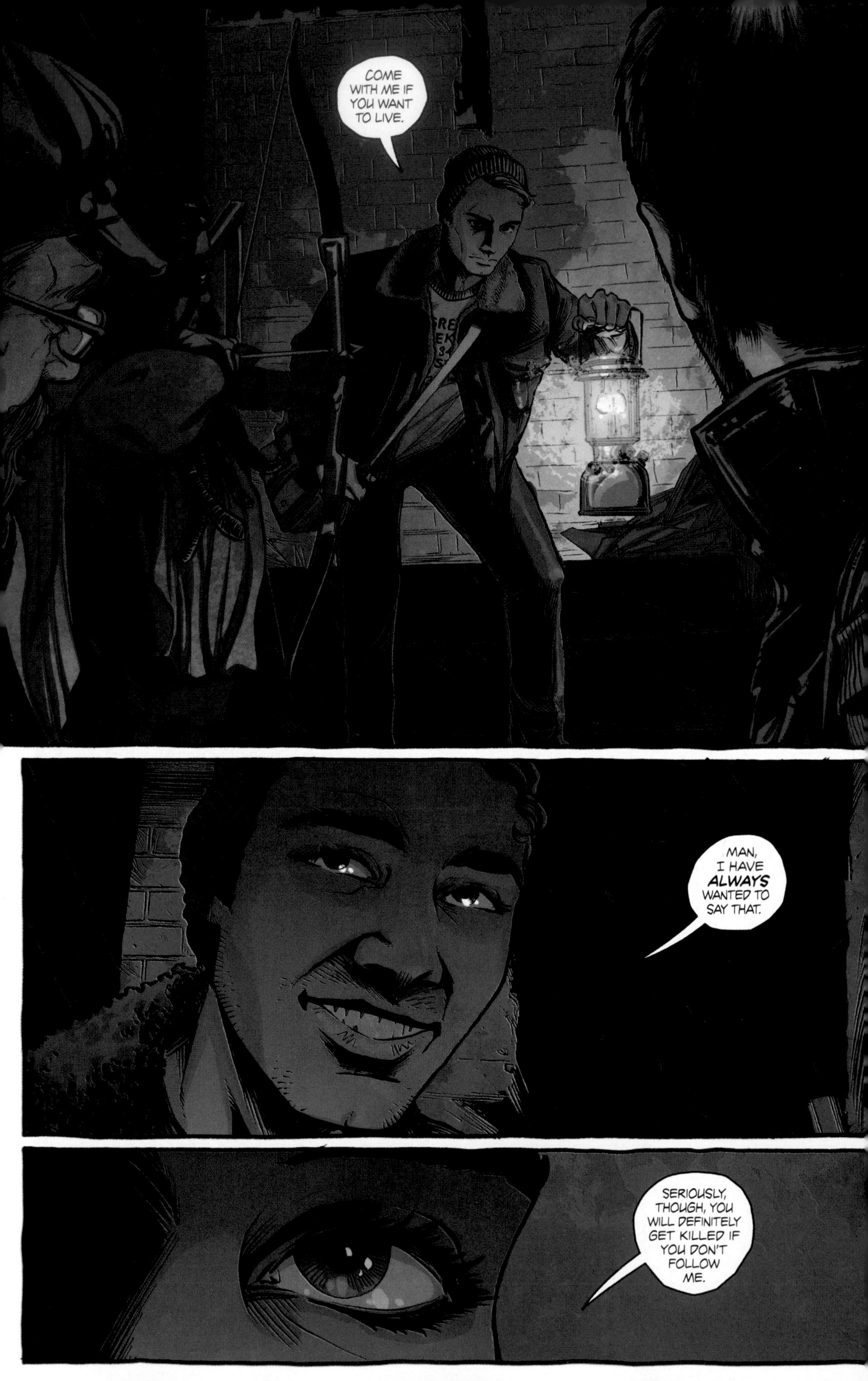
COME WITH ME IF YOU WANT TO LIVE.
MAN, I HAVE ALWAYS WANTED TO SAY THAT.
SERIOUSLY, THOUGH, YOU WILL DEFINITELY GET KILLED IF YOU DON'T FOLLOW ME.

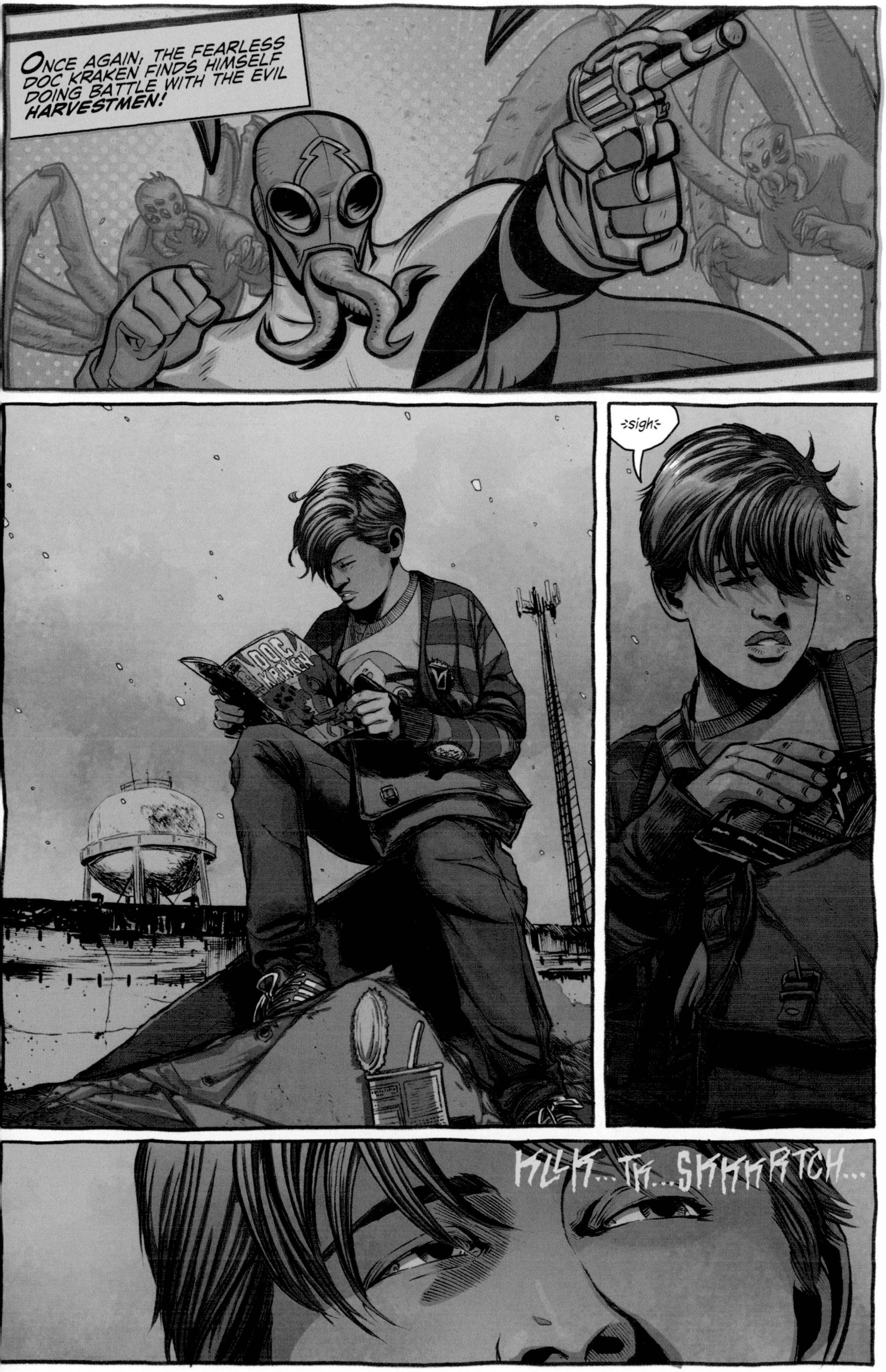
ONCE AGAIN, THE FEARLESS DOC KRAKEN FINDS HIMSELF DOING BATTLE WITH THE EVIL HARVESTMEN!
DOC KRAKEN
sigh
KLIK... TK... SKKKRTCH...

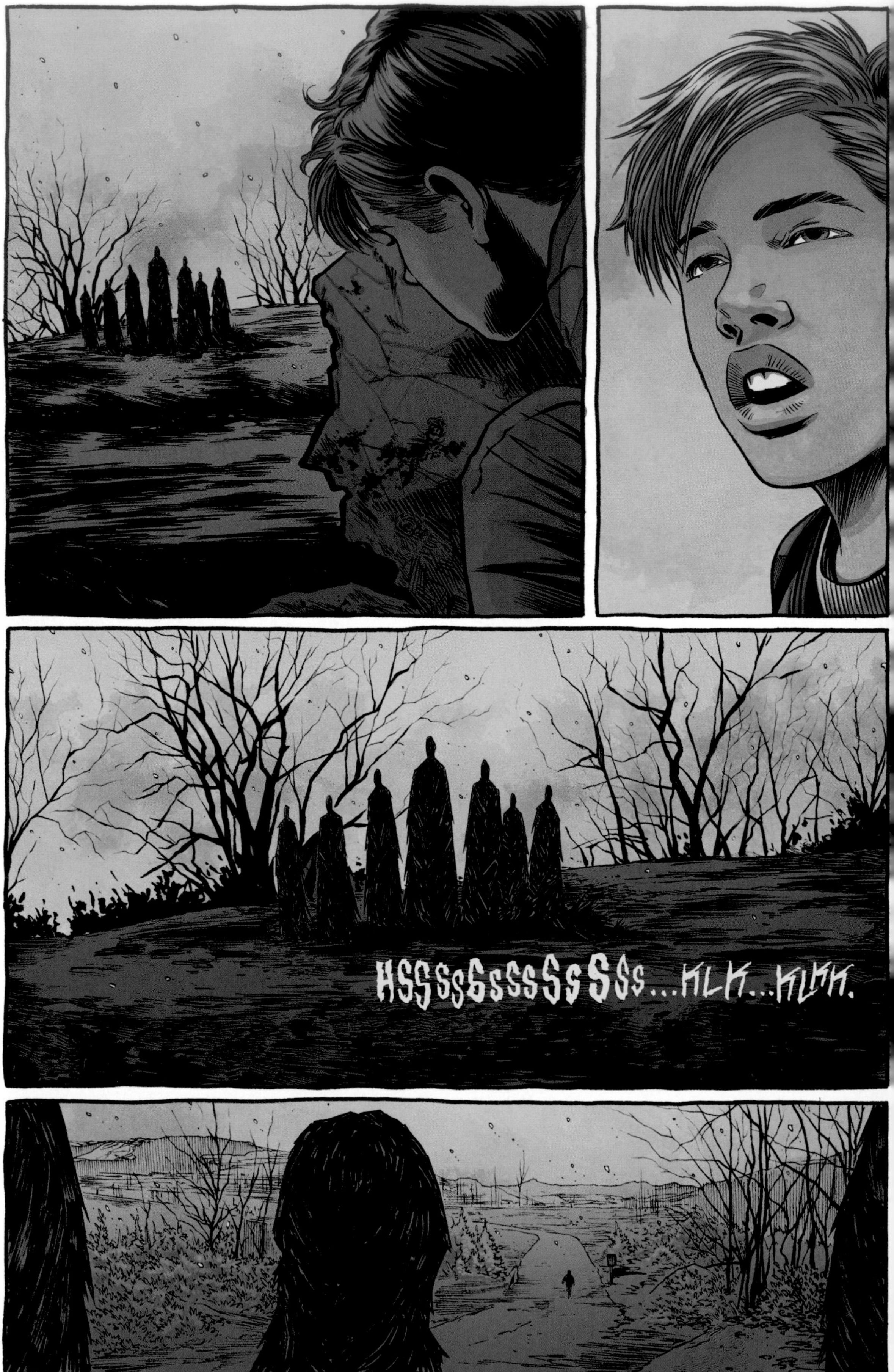
HSSSSSSSSSSSSSs...KLK...KLKK.

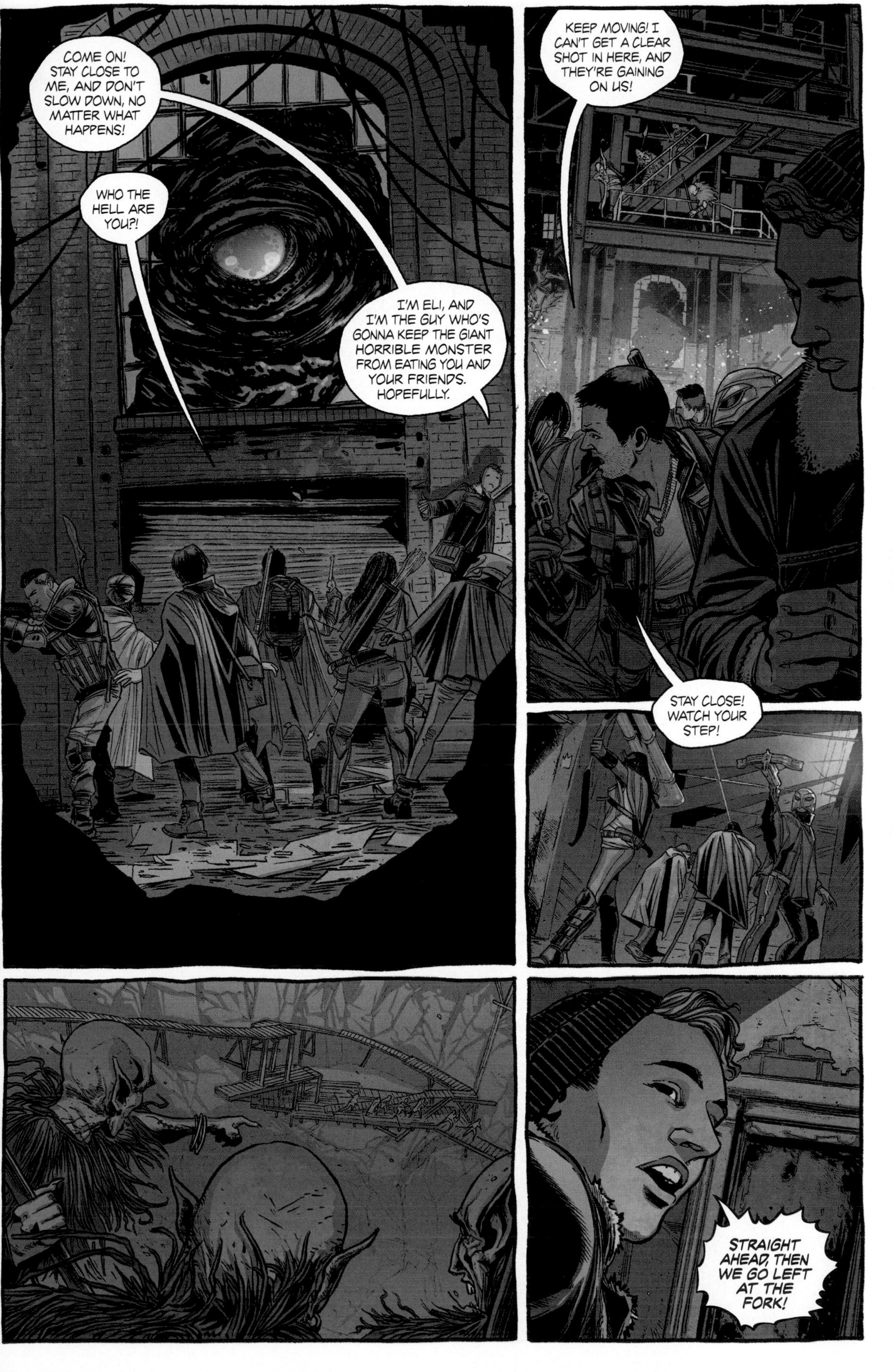
COME ON! STAY CLOSE TO ME, AND DON'T SLOW DOWN, NO MATTER WHAT HAPPENS!
WHO THE HELL ARE YOU?!
I'M ELI, AND I'M THE GUY WHO'S GONNA KEEP THE GIANT HORRIBLE MONSTER FROM EATING YOU AND YOUR FRIENDS. HOPEFULLY.
KEEP MOVING! I CAN'T GET A CLEAR SHOT IN HERE, AND THEY'RE GAINING ON US!
STAY CLOSE! WATCH YOUR STEP!
STRAIGHT AHEAD, THEN WE GO LEFT AT THE FORK!

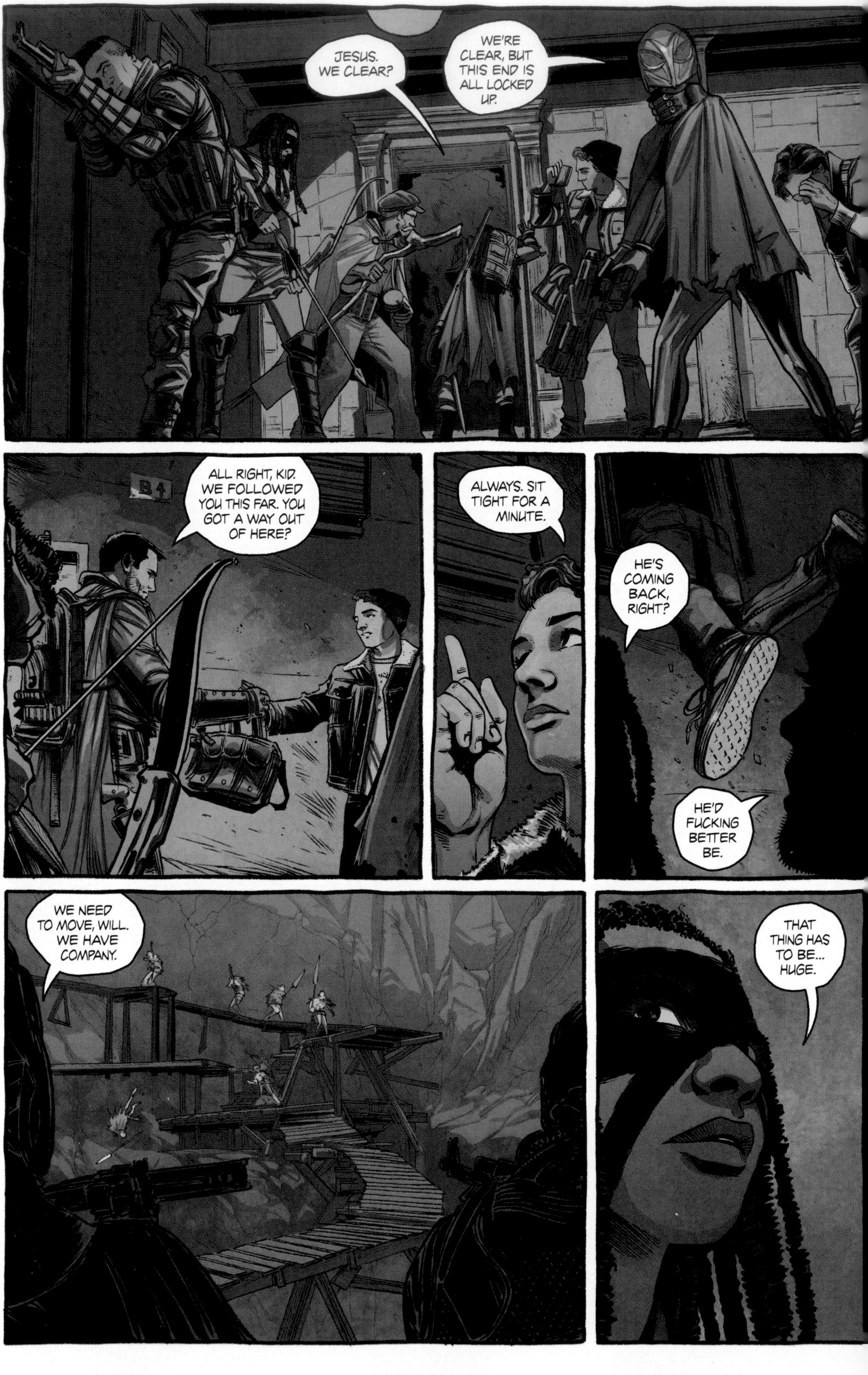
JESUS. WE CLEAR?
WE'RE CLEAR, BUT THIS END IS ALL LOCKED UP.
ALL RIGHT, KID. WE FOLLOWED YOU THIS FAR. YOU GOT A WAY OUT OF HERE?
ALWAYS. SIT TIGHT FOR A MINUTE.
HE'S COMING BACK, RIGHT?
HE'D FUCKING BETTER BE.
WE NEED TO MOVE, WILL. WE HAVE COMPANY.
THAT THING HAS TO BE... HUGE.

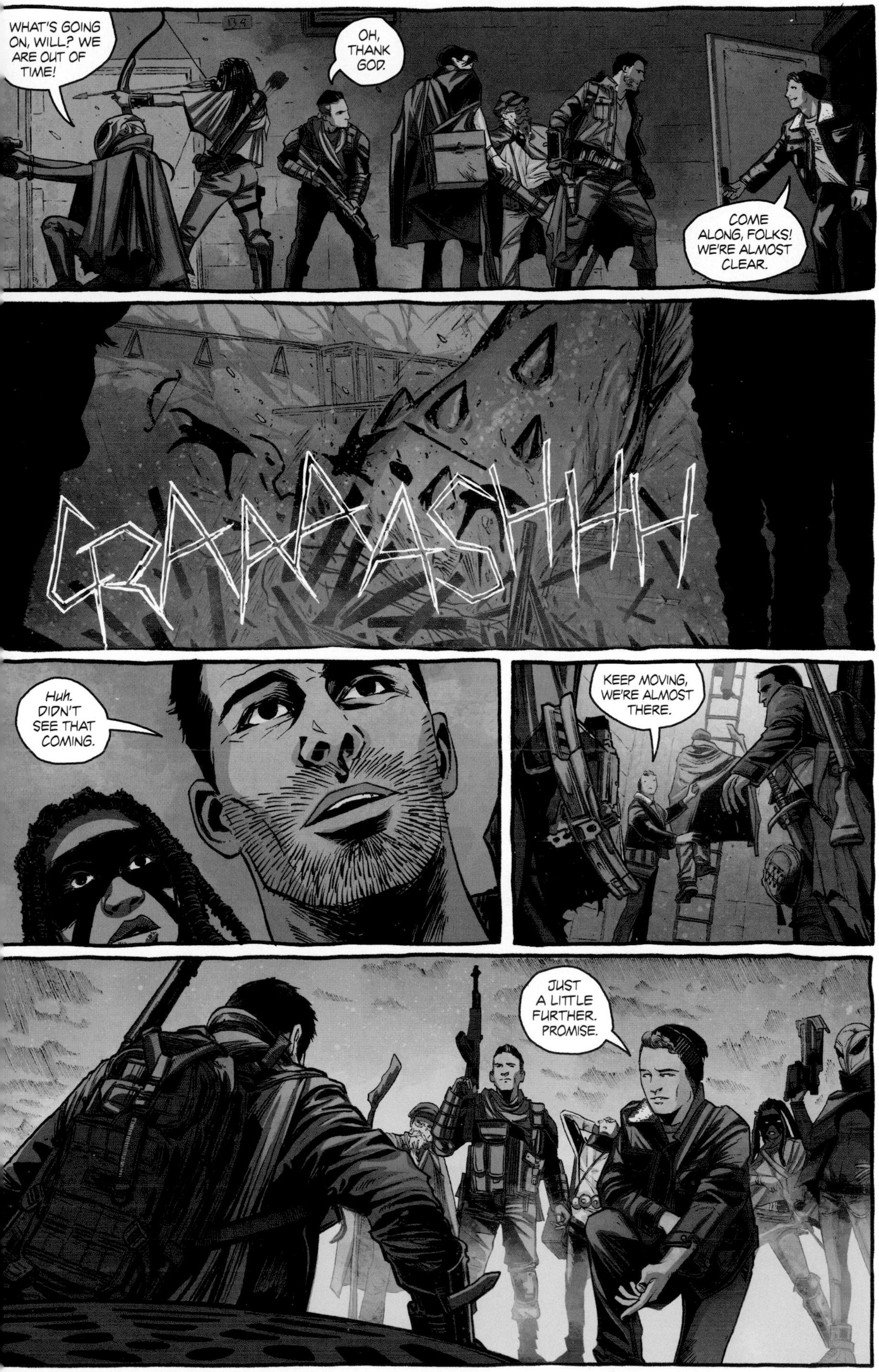
WHAT'S GOING ON, WILL? WE ARE OUT OF TIME!
OH, THANK GOD.
COME ALONG, FOLKS! WE'RE ALMOST CLEAR.
CRAAASHHH
Huh. DIDN'T SEE THAT COMING.
KEEP MOVING, WE'RE ALMOST THERE.
JUST A LITTLE FURTHER. PROMISE.

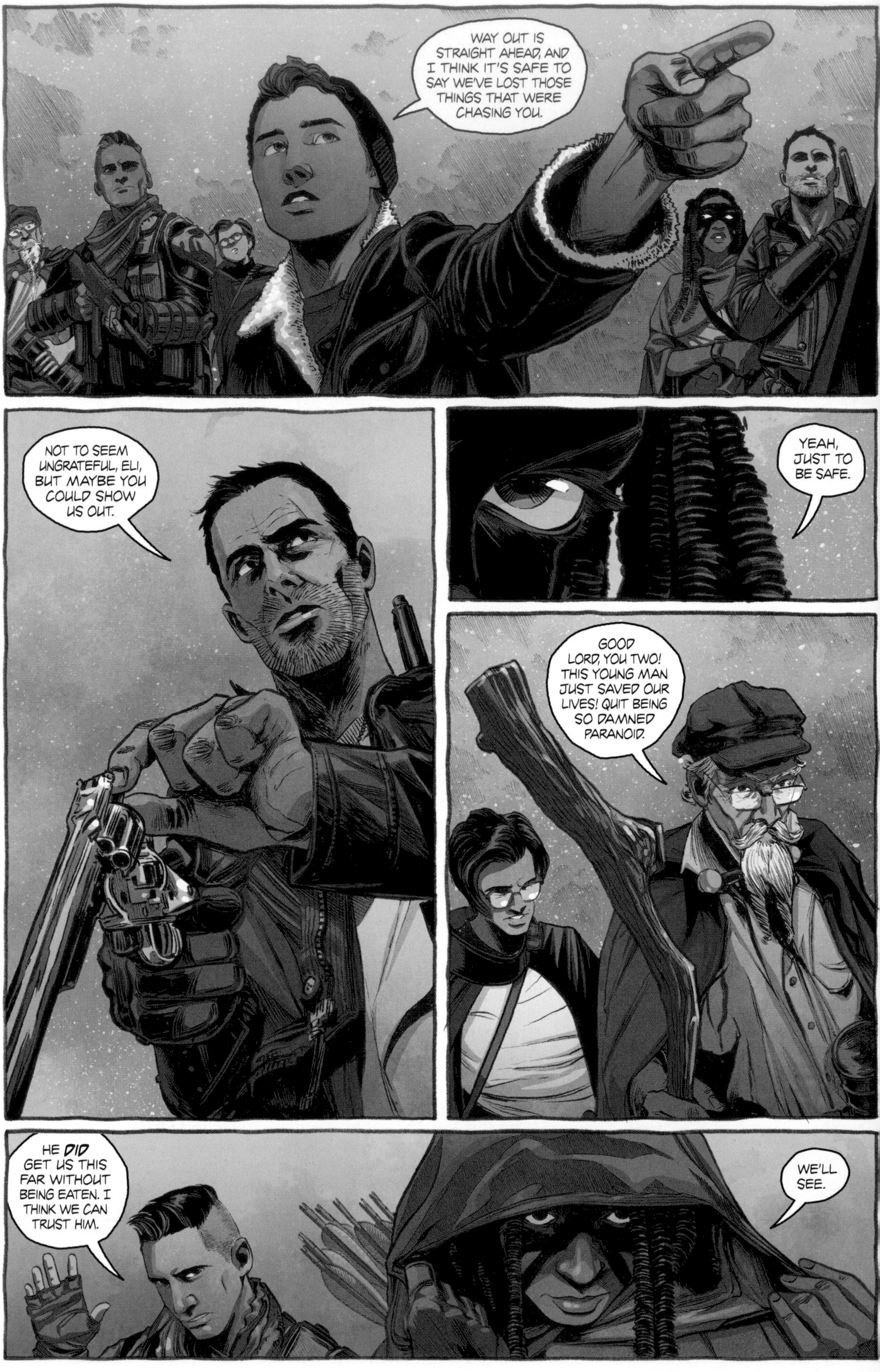
WAY OUT IS STRAIGHT AHEAD, AND I THINK IT'S SAFE TO SAY WE'VE LOST THOSE THINGS THAT WERE CHASING YOU.
NOT TO SEEM UNGRATEFUL, ELI, BUT MAYBE YOU COULD SHOW US OUT.
YEAH, JUST TO BE SAFE.
GOOD LORD, YOU TWO! THIS YOUNG MAN JUST SAVED OUR LIVES! QUIT BEING SO DAMNED PARANOID.
HE *DID* GET US THIS FAR WITHOUT BEING EATEN. I THINK WE CAN TRUST HIM.
WE'LL SEE.

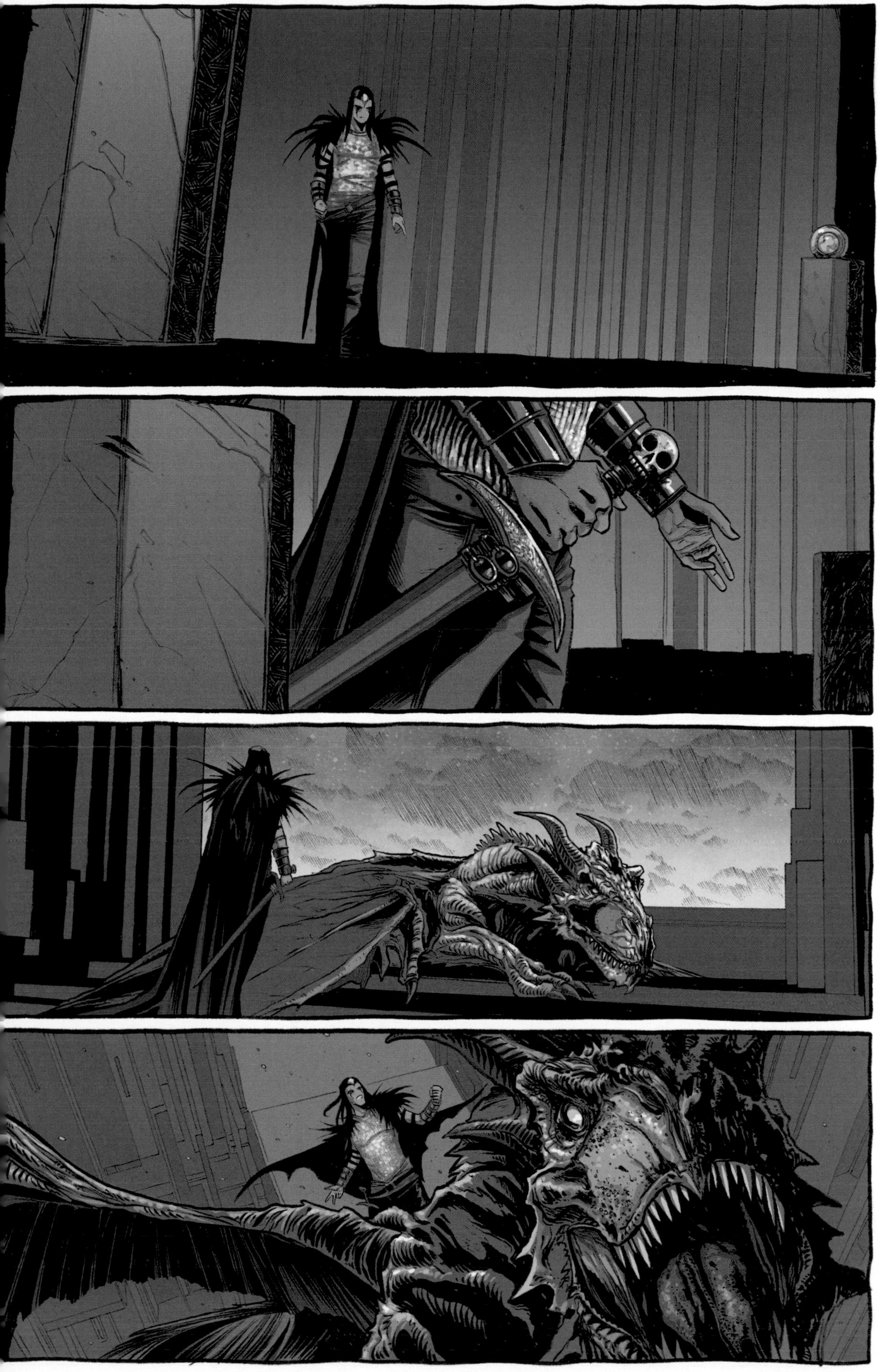

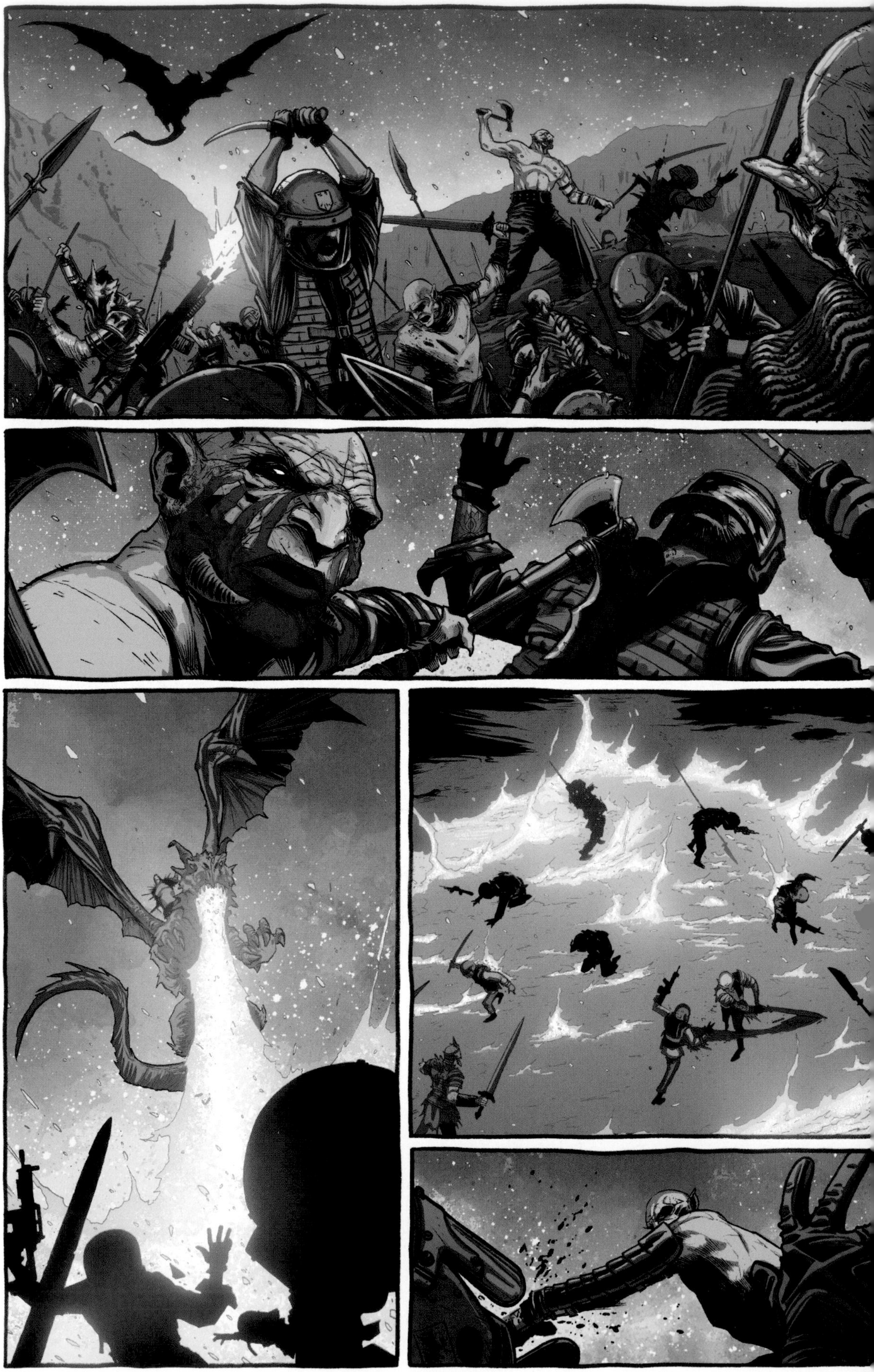

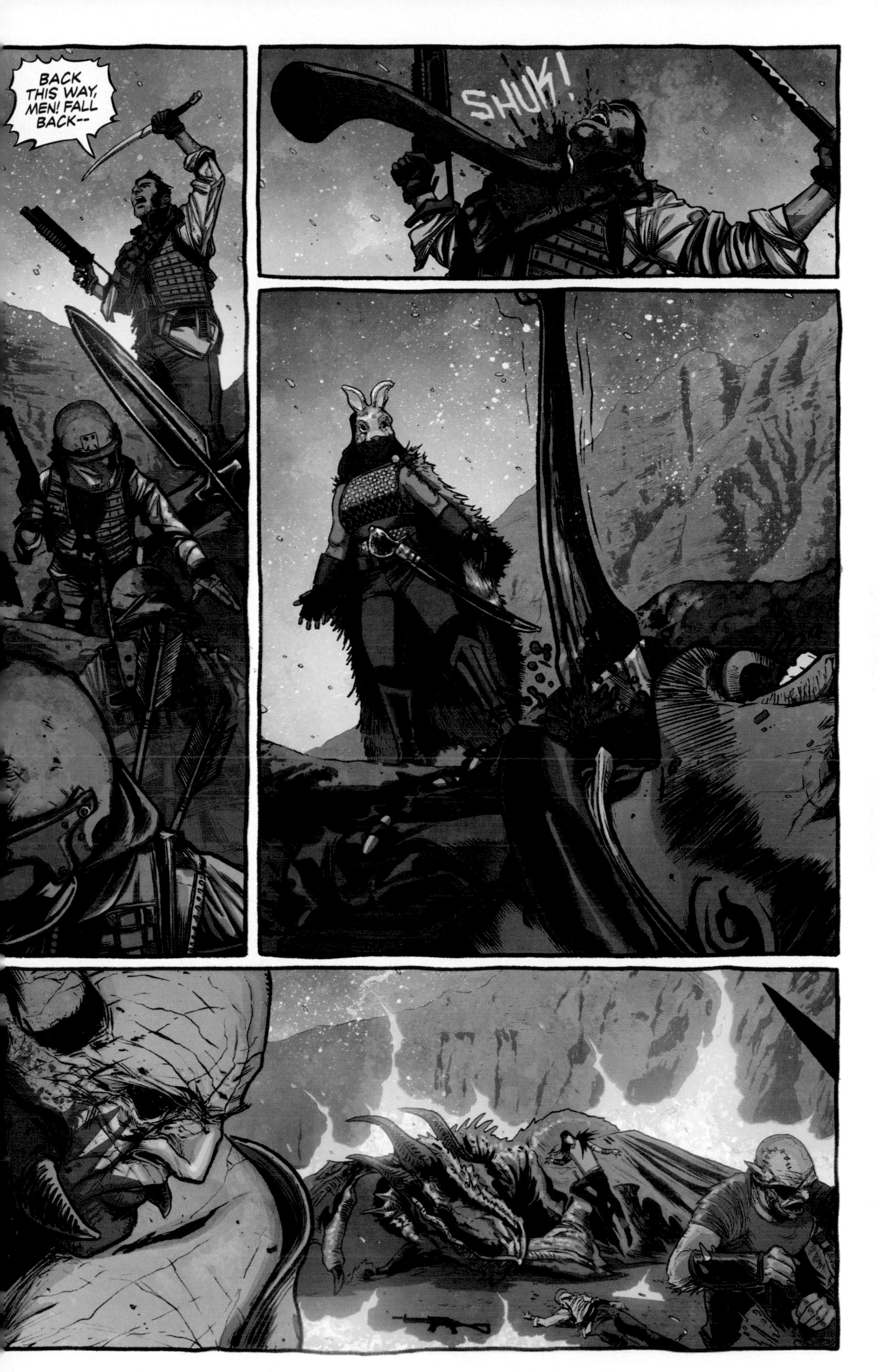
BACK THIS WAY, MEN! FALL BACK--
SHUK!

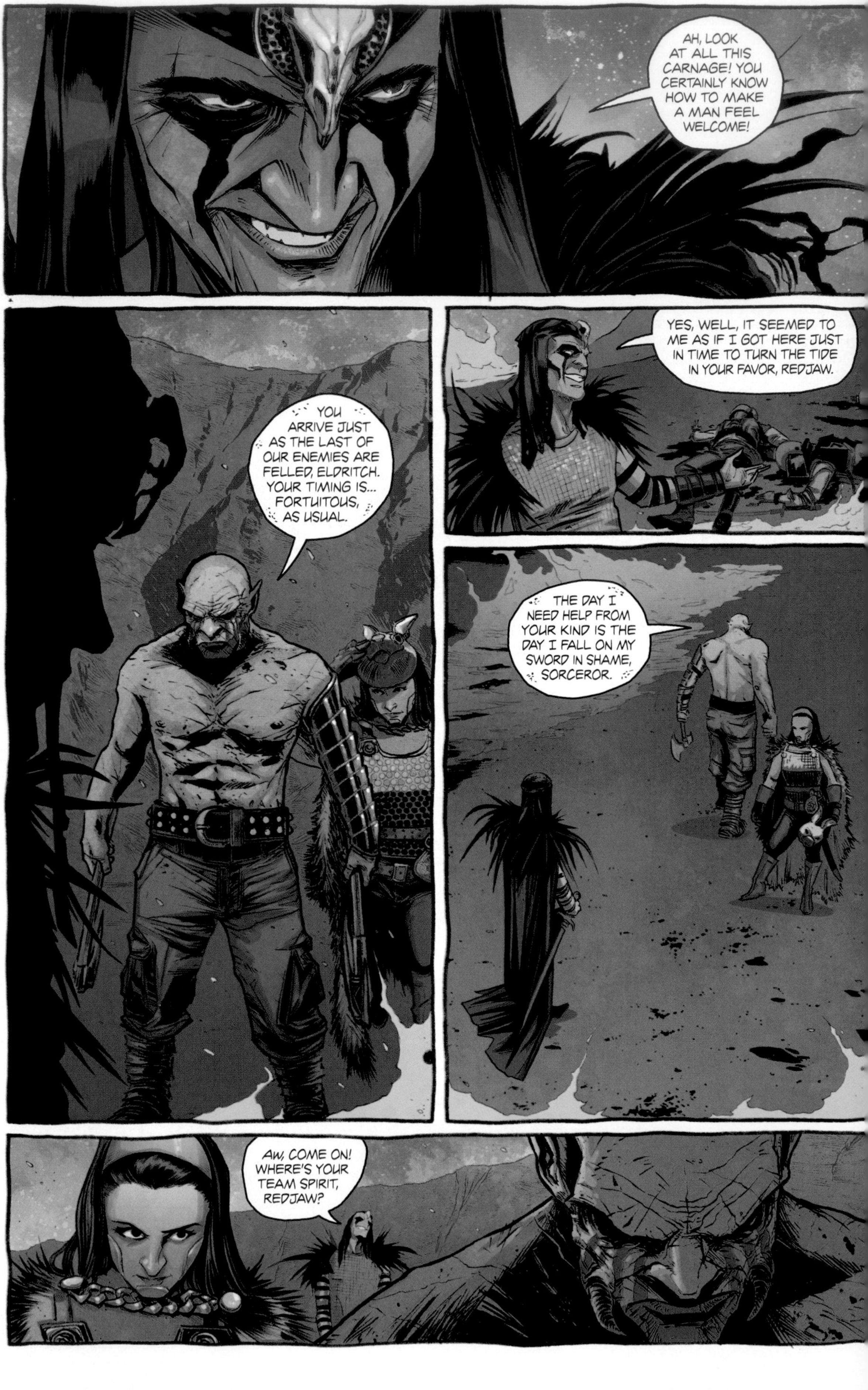
AH, LOOK AT ALL THIS CARNAGE! YOU CERTAINLY KNOW HOW TO MAKE A MAN FEEL WELCOME!
YOU ARRIVE JUST AS THE LAST OF OUR ENEMIES ARE FELLED, ELDRITCH. YOUR TIMING IS... FORTUITOUS, AS USUAL.
YES, WELL, IT SEEMED TO ME AS IF I GOT HERE JUST IN TIME TO TURN THE TIDE IN YOUR FAVOR, REDJAW.
THE DAY I NEED HELP FROM YOUR KIND IS THE DAY I FALL ON MY SWORD IN SHAME, SORCEROR.
AW, COME ON! WHERE'S YOUR TEAM SPIRIT, REDJAW?

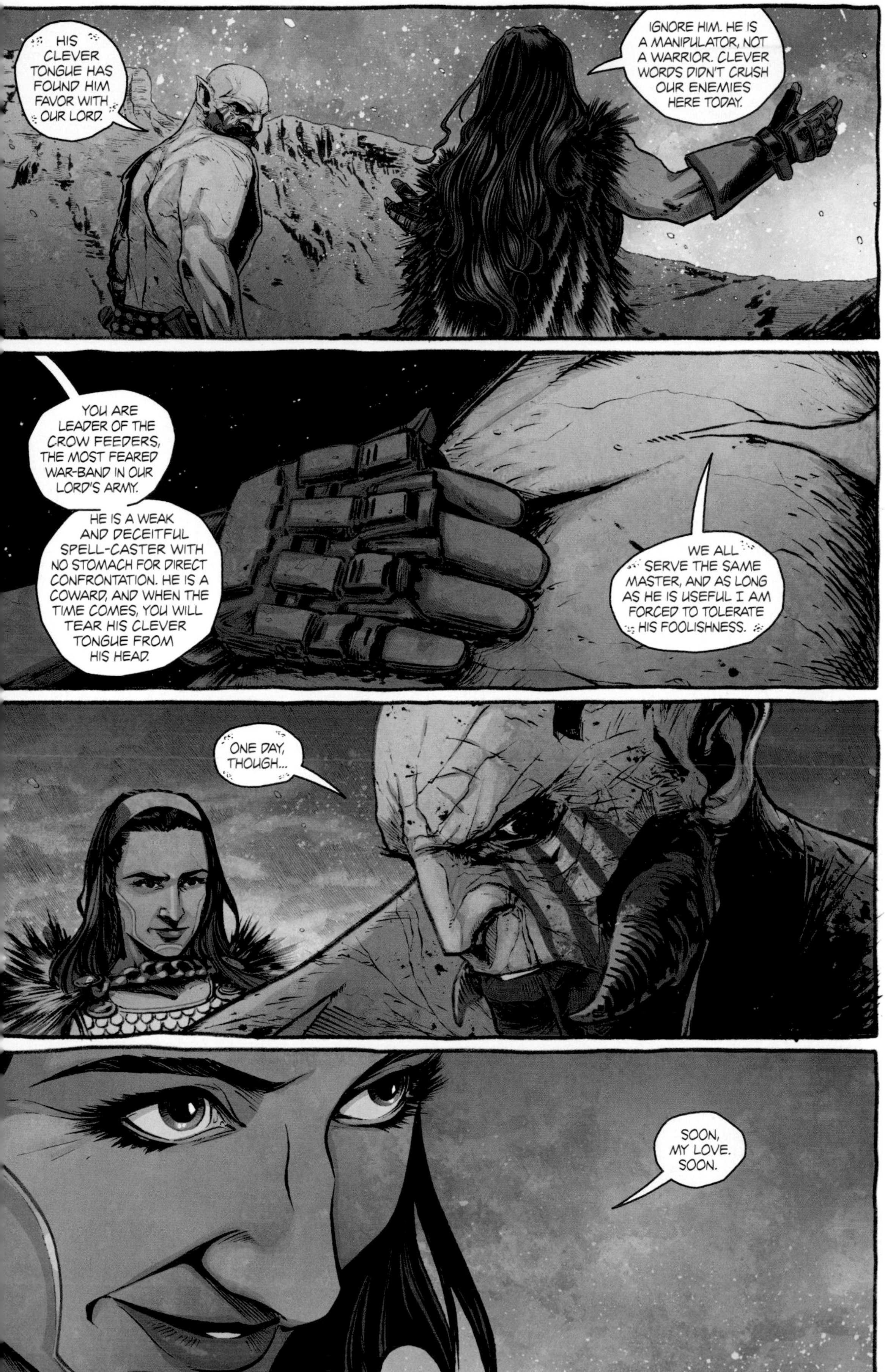
HIS CLEVER TONGUE HAS FOUND HIM FAVOR WITH OUR LORD.
IGNORE HIM. HE IS A MANIPULATOR, NOT A WARRIOR. CLEVER WORDS DIDN'T CRUSH OUR ENEMIES HERE TODAY.
YOU ARE LEADER OF THE CROW FEEDERS, THE MOST FEARED WAR-BAND IN OUR LORD'S ARMY.
HE IS A WEAK AND DECEITFUL SPELL-CASTER WITH NO STOMACH FOR DIRECT CONFRONTATION. HE IS A COWARD, AND WHEN THE TIME COMES, YOU WILL TEAR HIS CLEVER TONGUE FROM HIS HEAD.
WE ALL SERVE THE SAME MASTER, AND AS LONG AS HE IS USEFUL I AM FORCED TO TOLERATE HIS FOOLISHNESS.
ONE DAY, THOUGH...
SOON, MY LOVE. SOON.

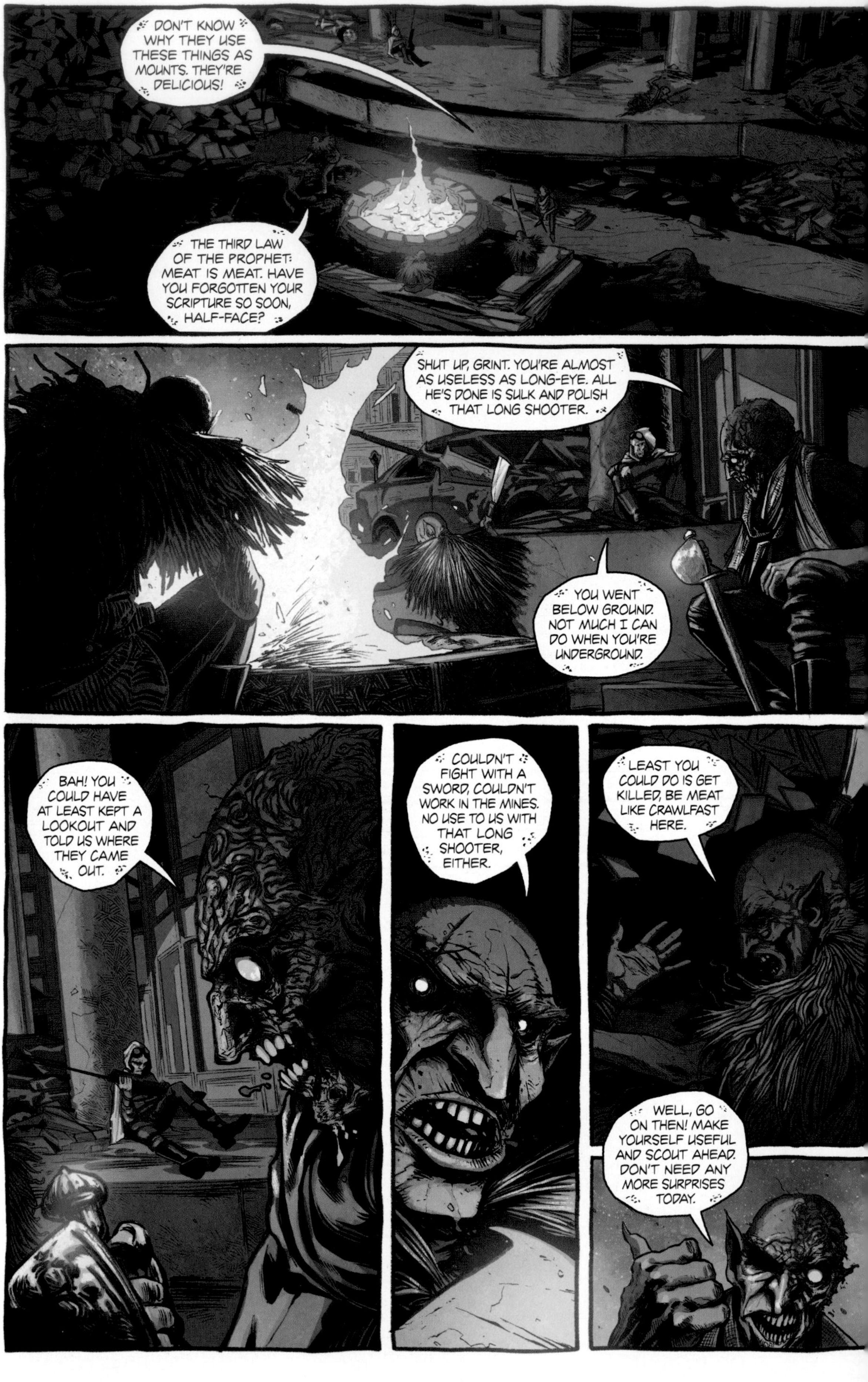
DON'T KNOW WHY THEY USE THESE THINGS AS MOUNTS. THEY'RE DELICIOUS!
THE THIRD LAW OF THE PROPHET: MEAT IS MEAT. HAVE YOU FORGOTTEN YOUR SCRIPTURE SO SOON, HALF-FACE?
SHUT UP, GRINT. YOU'RE ALMOST AS USELESS AS LONG-EYE. ALL HE'S DONE IS SULK AND POLISH THAT LONG SHOOTER.
YOU WENT BELOW GROUND. NOT MUCH I CAN DO WHEN YOU'RE UNDERGROUND.
BAH! YOU COULD HAVE AT LEAST KEPT A LOOKOUT AND TOLD US WHERE THEY CAME OUT.
COULDN'T FIGHT WITH A SWORD, COULDN'T WORK IN THE MINES. NO USE TO US WITH THAT LONG SHOOTER, EITHER.
LEAST YOU COULD DO IS GET KILLED, BE MEAT LIKE CRAWLFAST HERE.
WELL, GO ON THEN! MAKE YOURSELF USEFUL AND SCOUT AHEAD. DON'T NEED ANY MORE SURPRISES TODAY.

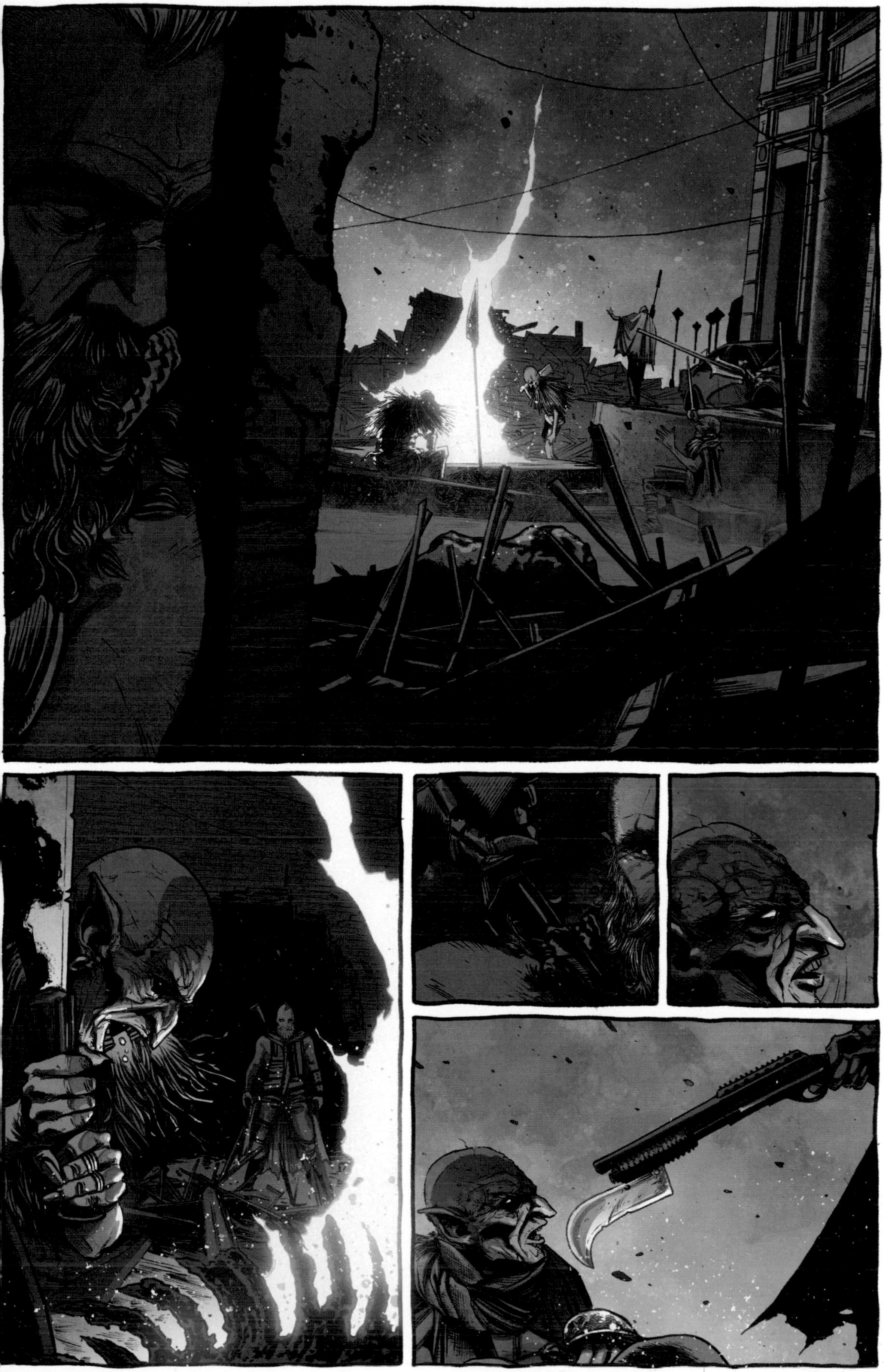

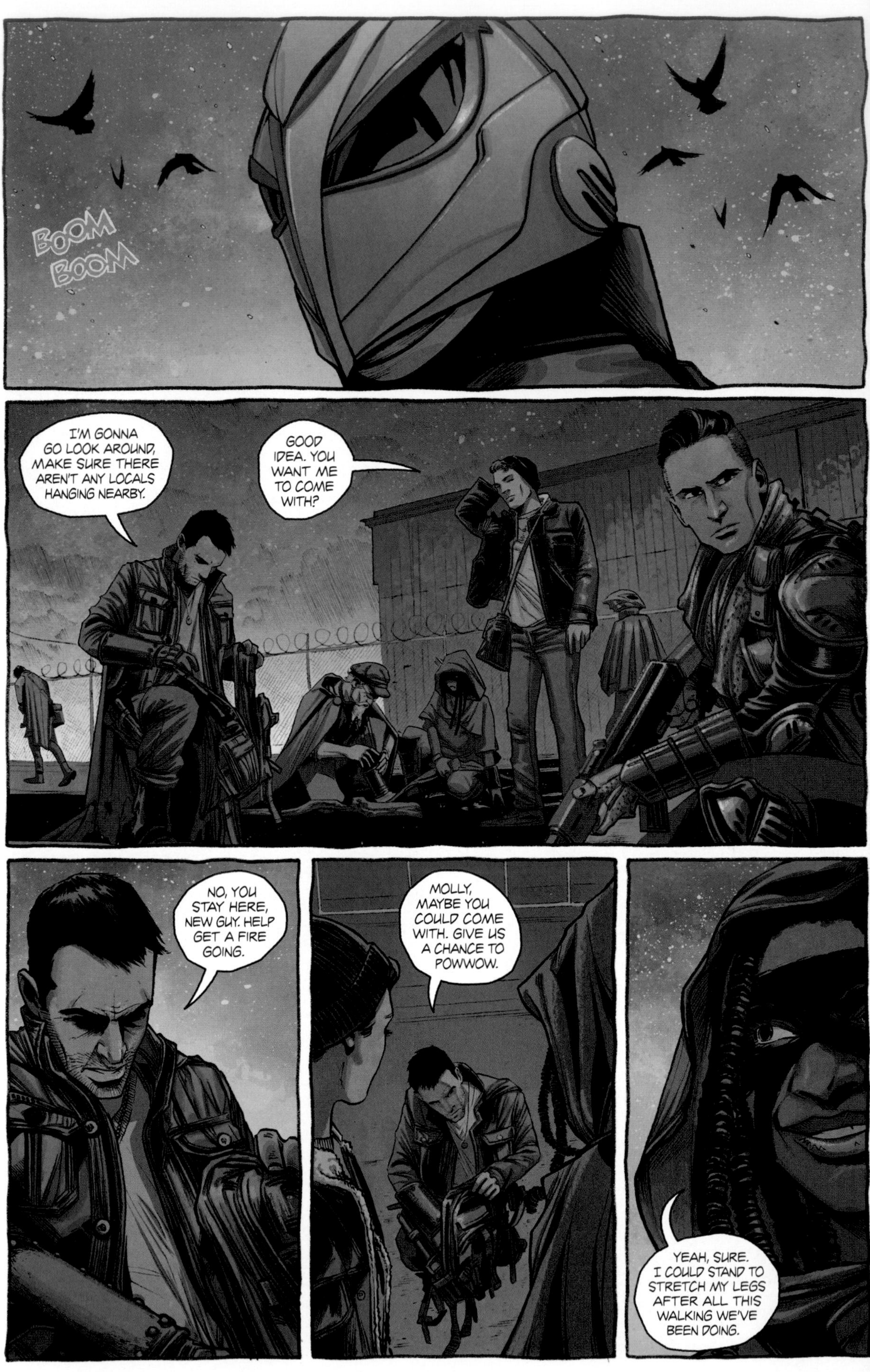
BOOM BOOM
I'M GONNA GO LOOK AROUND, MAKE SURE THERE AREN'T ANY LOCALS HANGING NEARBY.
GOOD IDEA. YOU WANT ME TO COME WITH?
NO, YOU STAY HERE, NEW GUY. HELP GET A FIRE GOING.
MOLLY, MAYBE YOU COULD COME WITH. GIVE US A CHANCE TO POWWOW.
YEAH, SURE. I COULD STAND TO STRETCH MY LEGS AFTER ALL THIS WALKING WE'VE BEEN DOING.

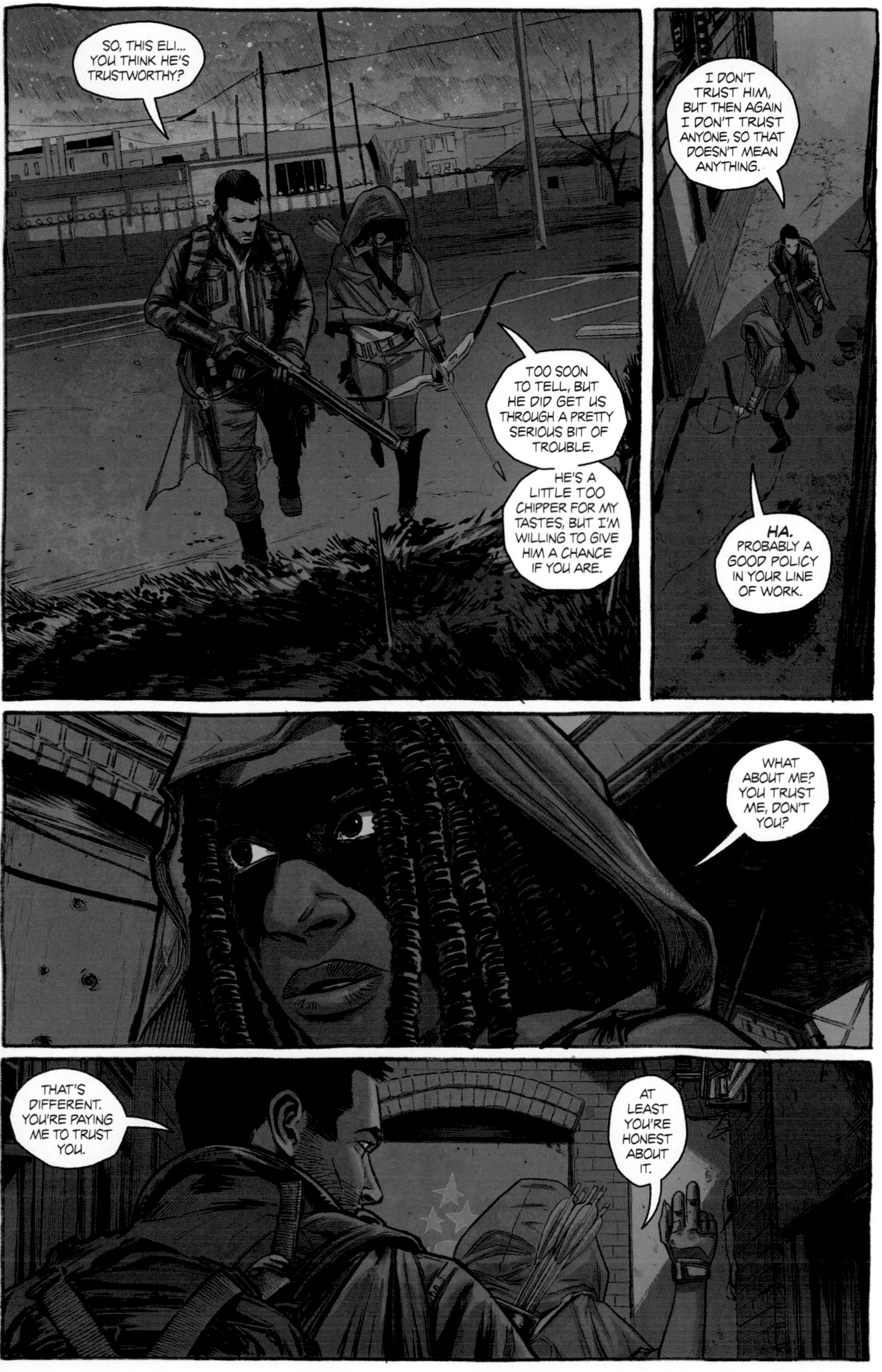
SO, THIS ELI... YOU THINK HE'S TRUSTWORTHY?
TOO SOON TO TELL, BUT HE DID GET US THROUGH A PRETTY SERIOUS BIT OF TROUBLE.
HE'S A LITTLE TOO CHIPPER FOR MY TASTES, BUT I'M WILLING TO GIVE HIM A CHANCE IF YOU ARE.
I DON'T TRUST HIM, BUT THEN AGAIN I DON'T TRUST ANYONE, SO THAT DOESN'T MEAN ANYTHING.
HA. PROBABLY A GOOD POLICY IN YOUR LINE OF WORK.
WHAT ABOUT ME? YOU TRUST ME, DON'T YOU?
THAT'S DIFFERENT. YOU'RE PAYING ME TO TRUST YOU.
AT LEAST YOU'RE HONEST ABOUT IT.

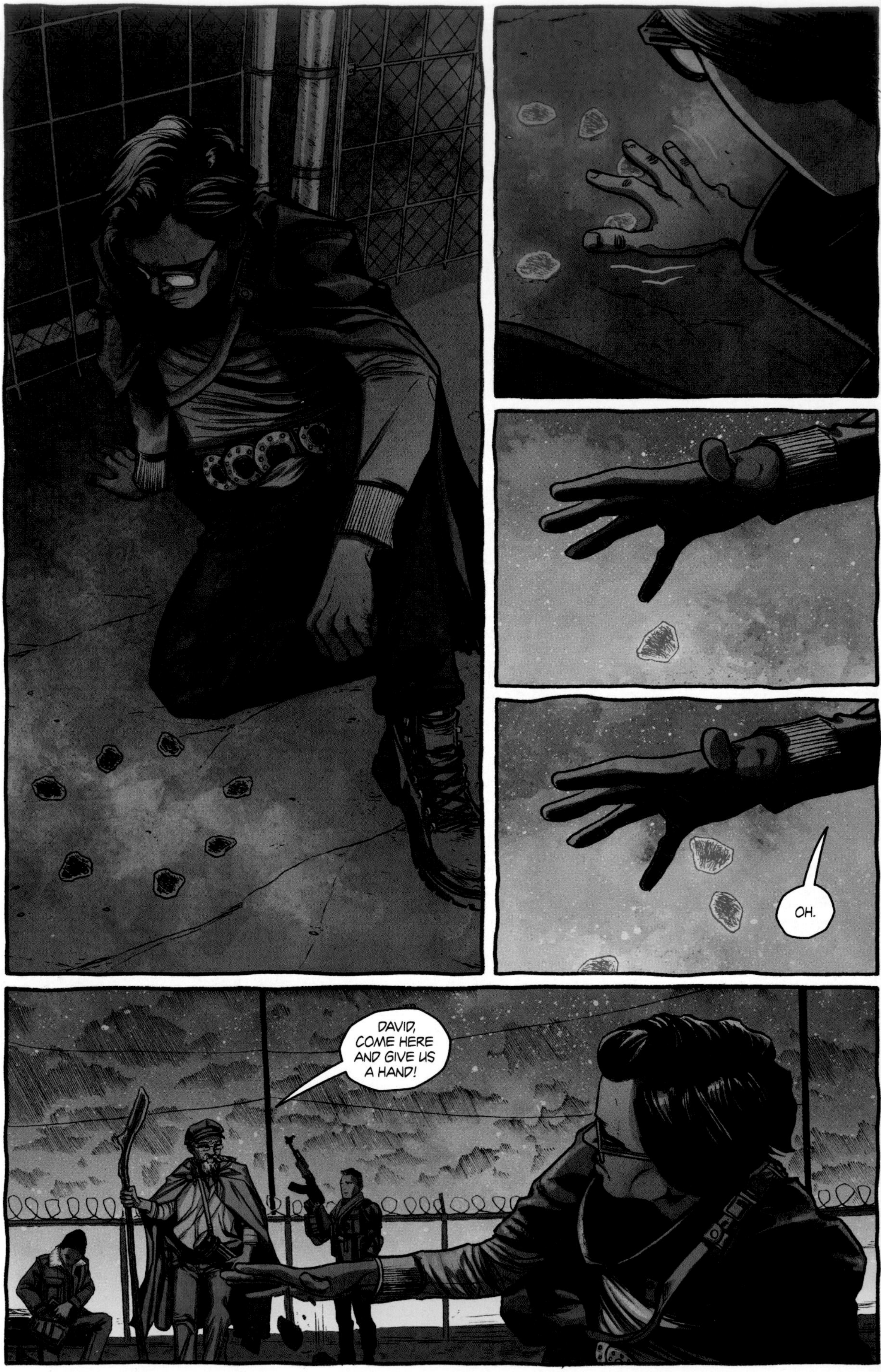
OH.
DAVID, COME HERE AND GIVE US A HAND!

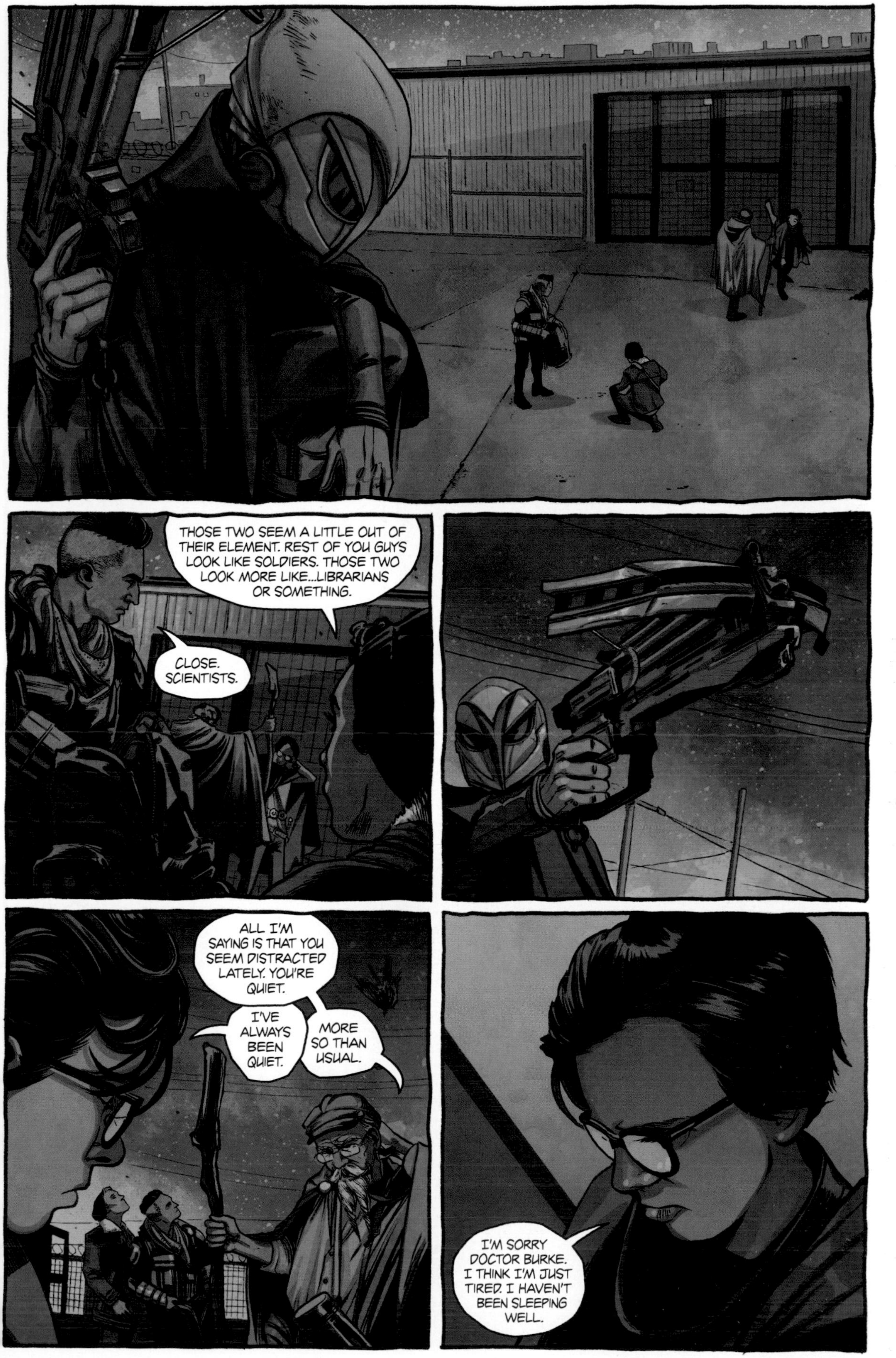
THOSE TWO SEEM A LITTLE OUT OF THEIR ELEMENT. REST OF YOU GUYS LOOK LIKE SOLDIERS. THOSE TWO LOOK MORE LIKE...LIBRARIANS OR SOMETHING.
CLOSE. SCIENTISTS.
ALL I'M SAYING IS THAT YOU SEEM DISTRACTED LATELY. YOU'RE QUIET.
I'VE ALWAYS BEEN QUIET.
MORE SO THAN USUAL.
I'M SORRY DOCTOR BURKE. I THINK I'M JUST TIRED. I HAVEN'T BEEN SLEEPING WELL.

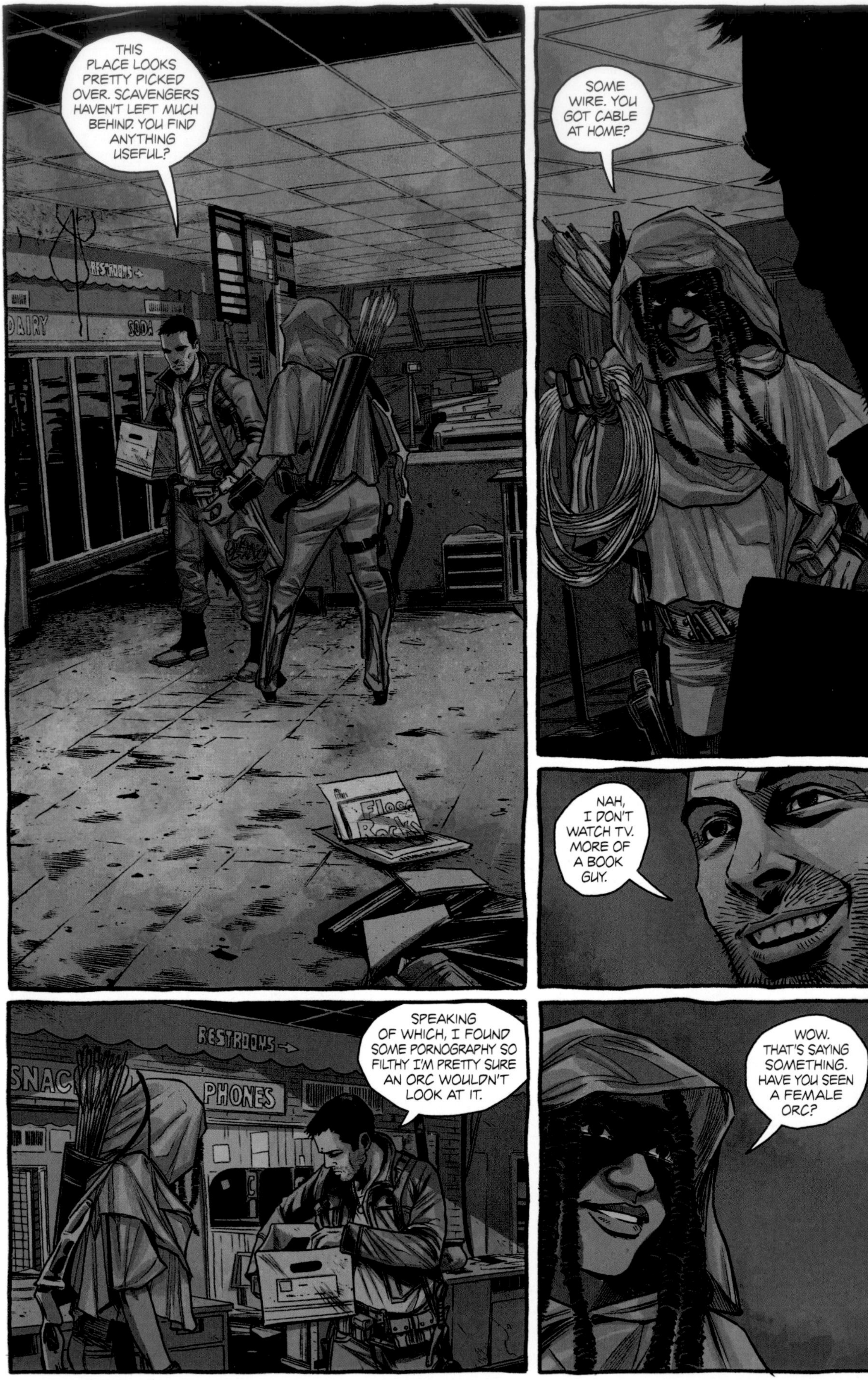
THIS PLACE LOOKS PRETTY PICKED OVER. SCAVENGERS HAVEN'T LEFT MUCH BEHIND. YOU FIND ANYTHING USEFUL?
RESTROOMS →
DAIRY
SODA
SOME WIRE. YOU GOT CABLE AT HOME?
NAH, I DON'T WATCH TV. MORE OF A BOOK GUY.
RESTROOMS →
PHONES
SPEAKING OF WHICH, I FOUND SOME PORNOGRAPHY SO FILTHY I'M PRETTY SURE AN ORC WOULDN'T LOOK AT IT.
WOW. THAT'S SAYING SOMETHING. HAVE YOU SEEN A FEMALE ORC?

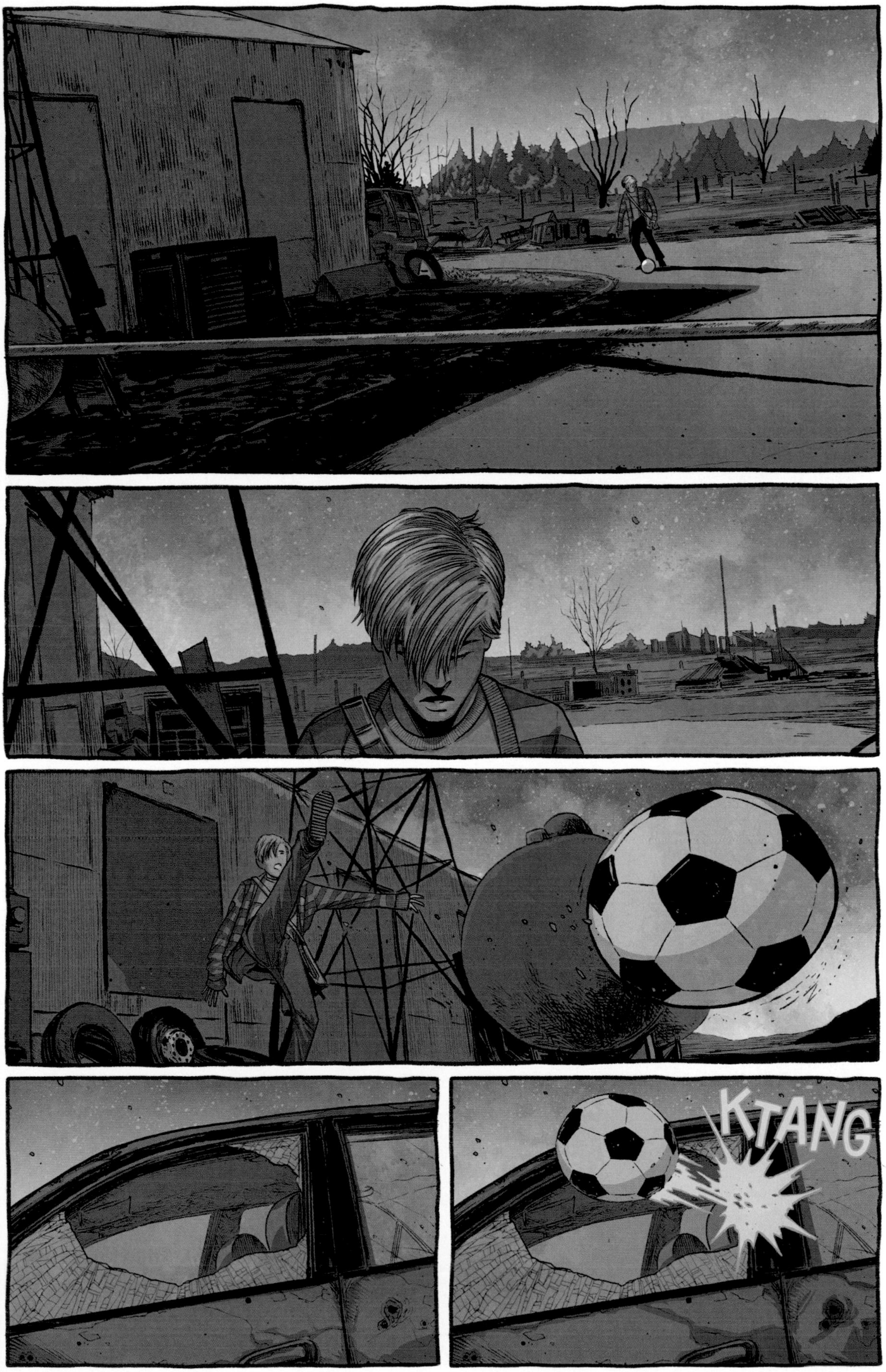
KTANG

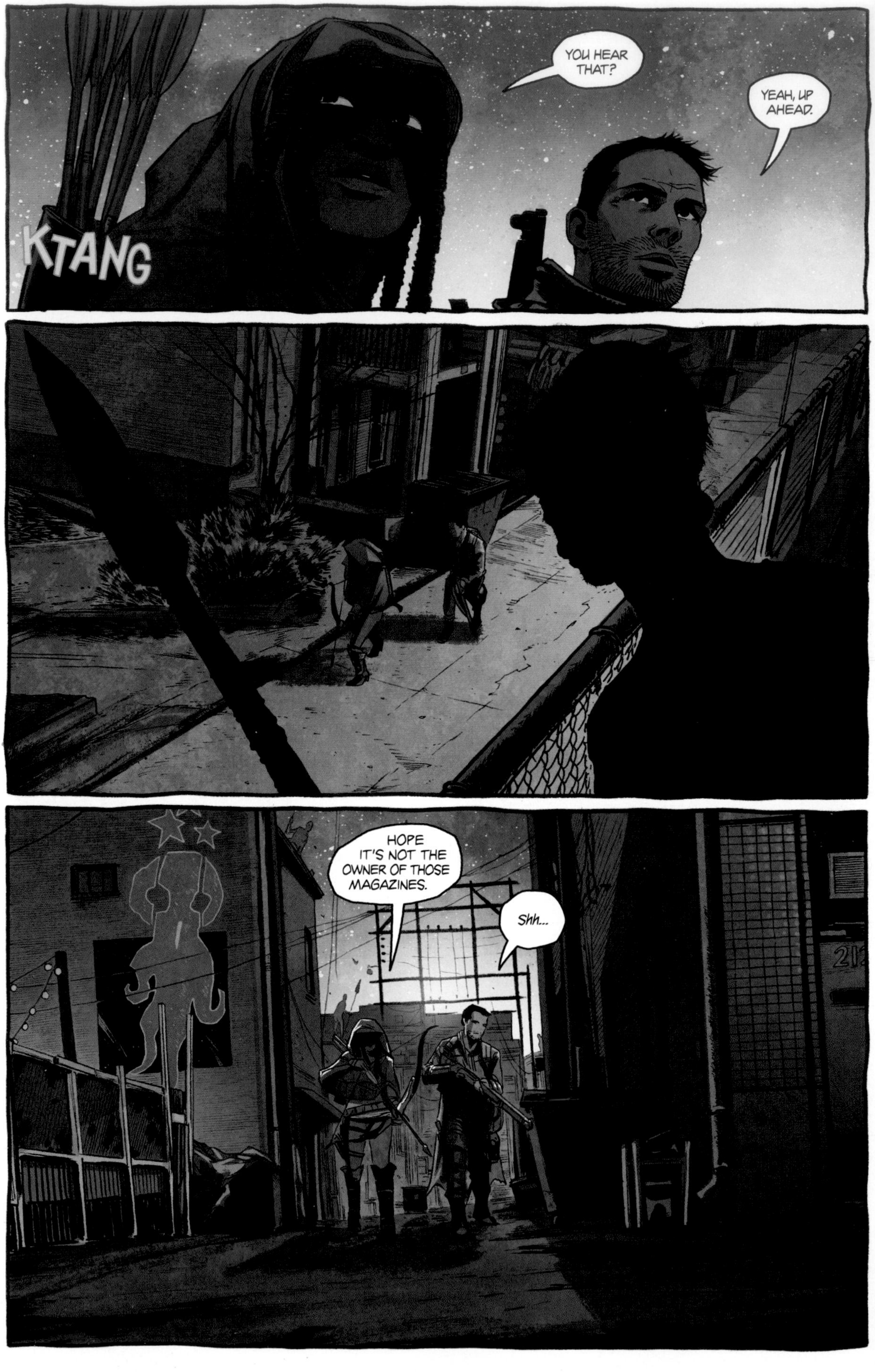
YOU HEAR THAT?
YEAH, UP AHEAD.
KTANG
HOPE IT'S NOT THE OWNER OF THOSE MAGAZINES.
Shh...

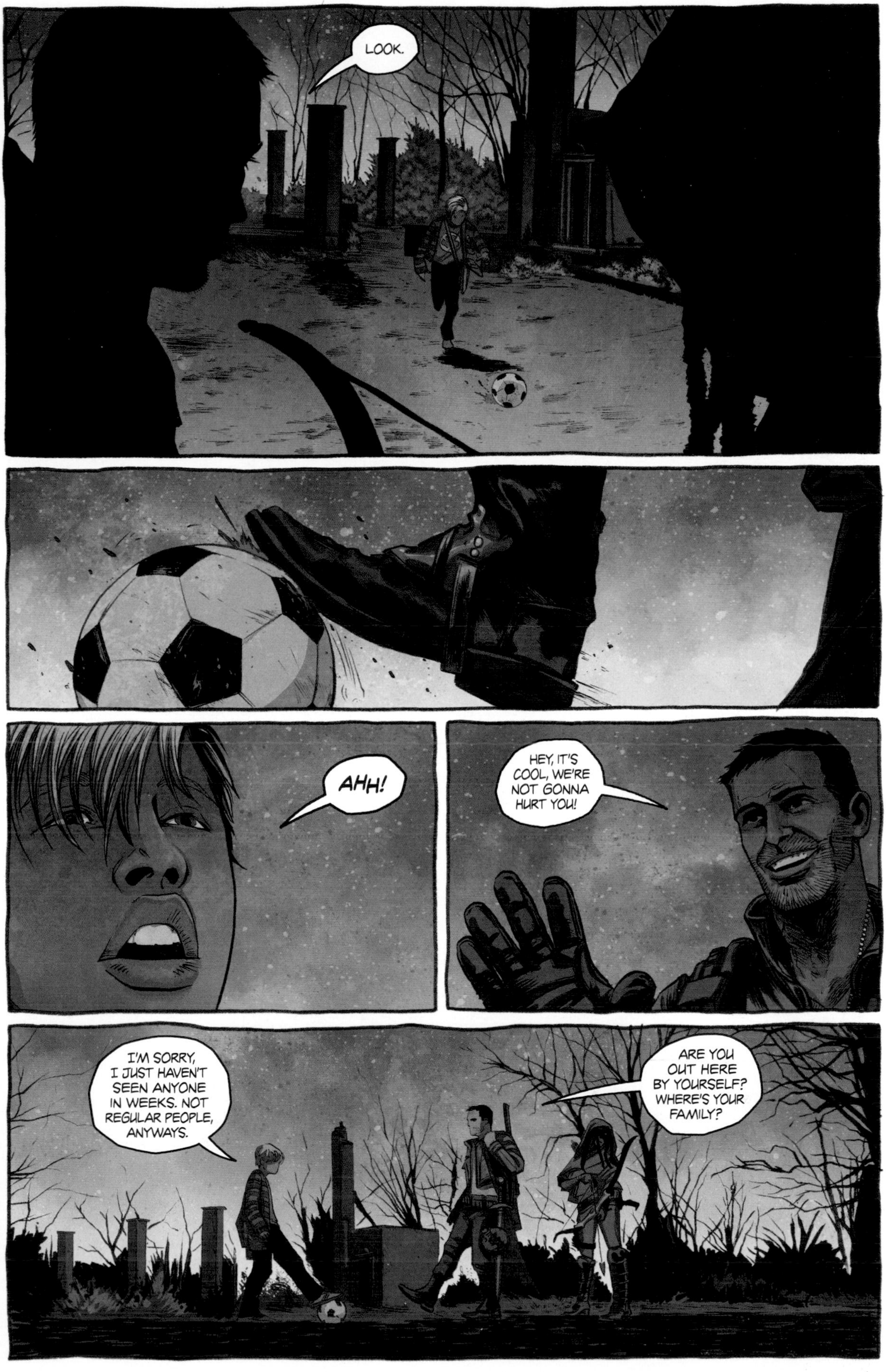
LOOK.
AHH!
HEY, IT'S COOL, WE'RE NOT GONNA HURT YOU!
I'M SORRY, I JUST HAVEN'T SEEN ANYONE IN WEEKS. NOT REGULAR PEOPLE, ANYWAYS.
ARE YOU OUT HERE BY YOURSELF? WHERE'S YOUR FAMILY?

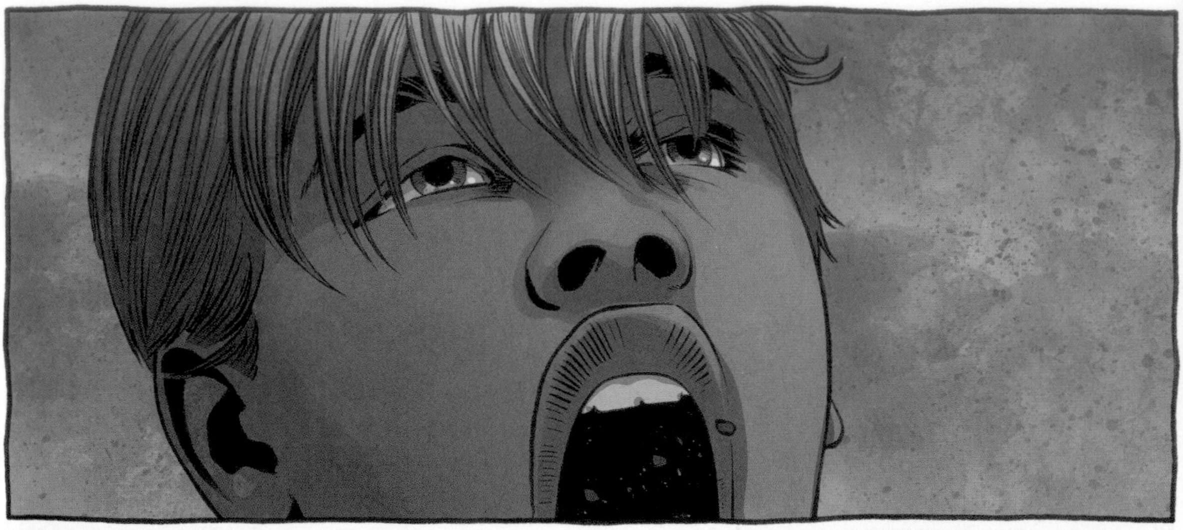

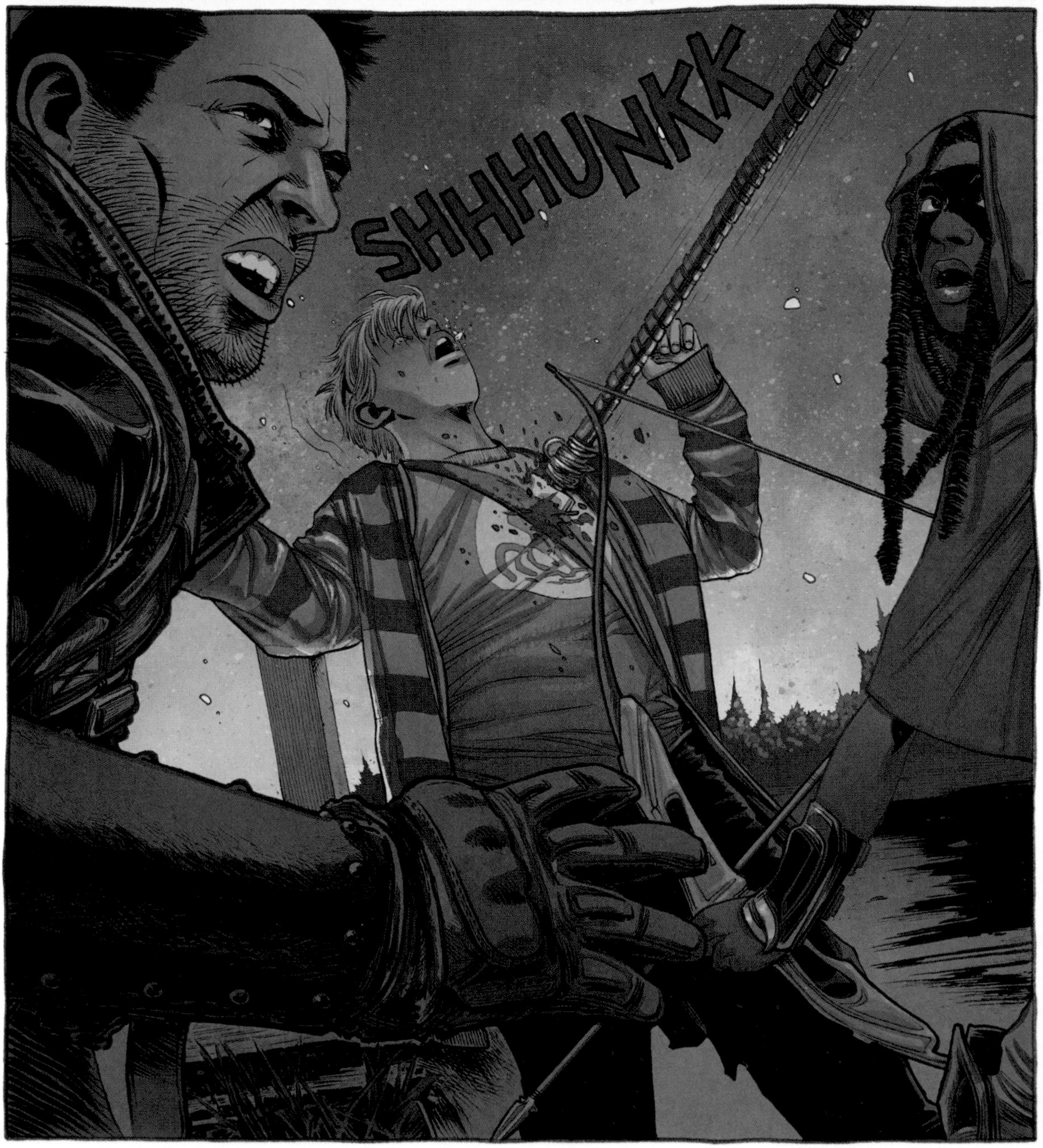
SHHHUNKK

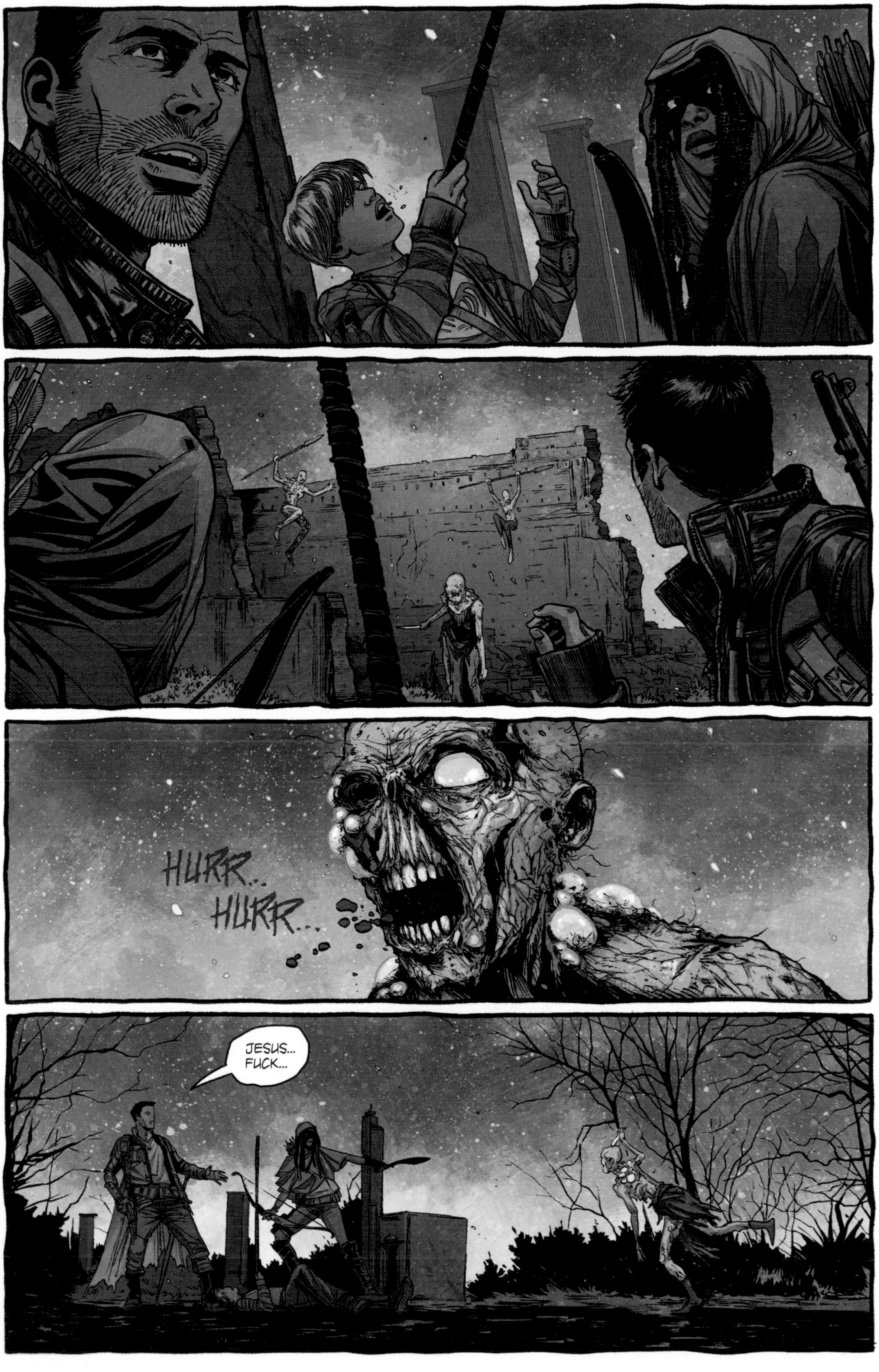
HURR...
HURR...
JESUS...
FUCK...

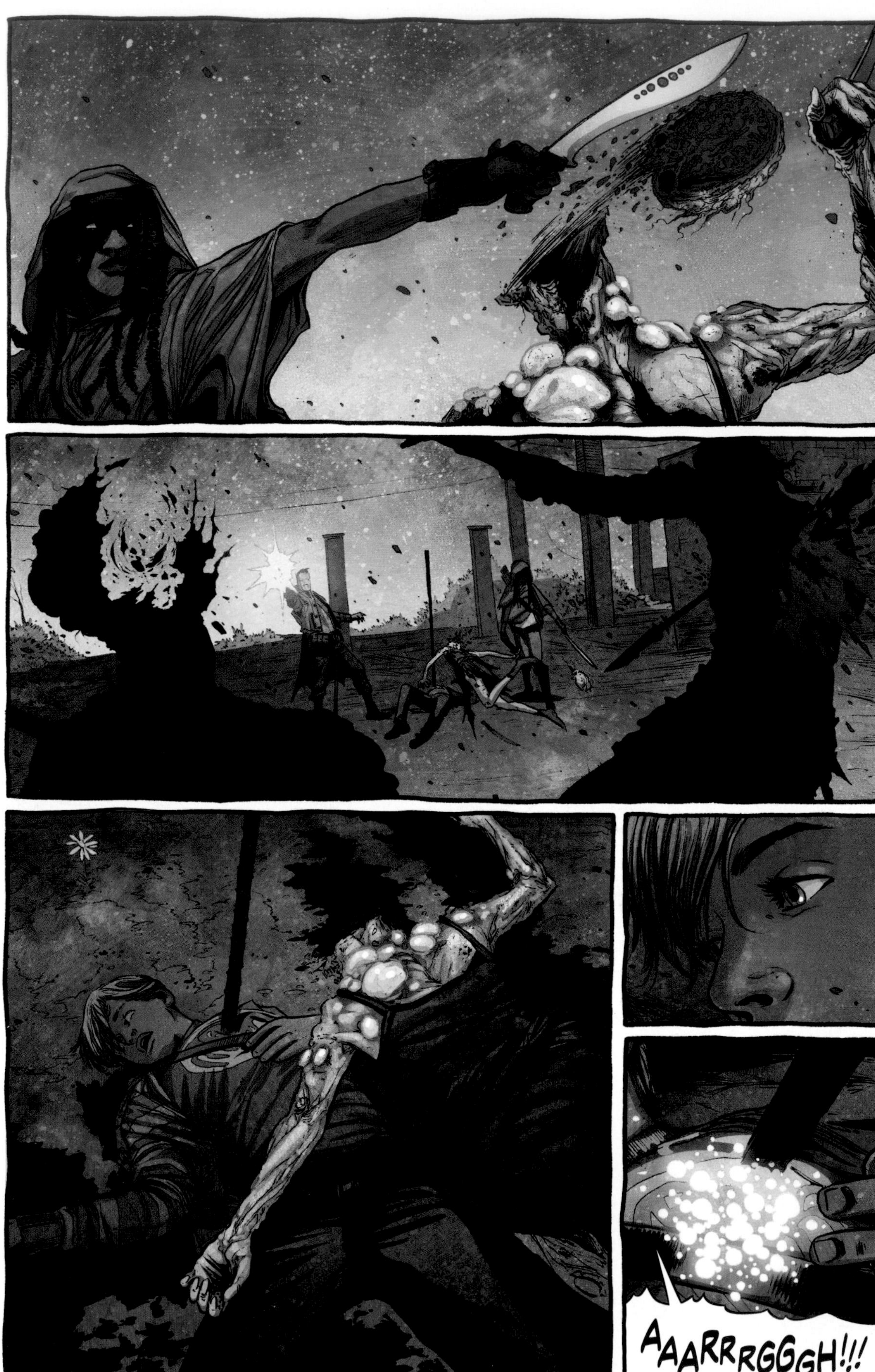
AAARRRGGGH!!!

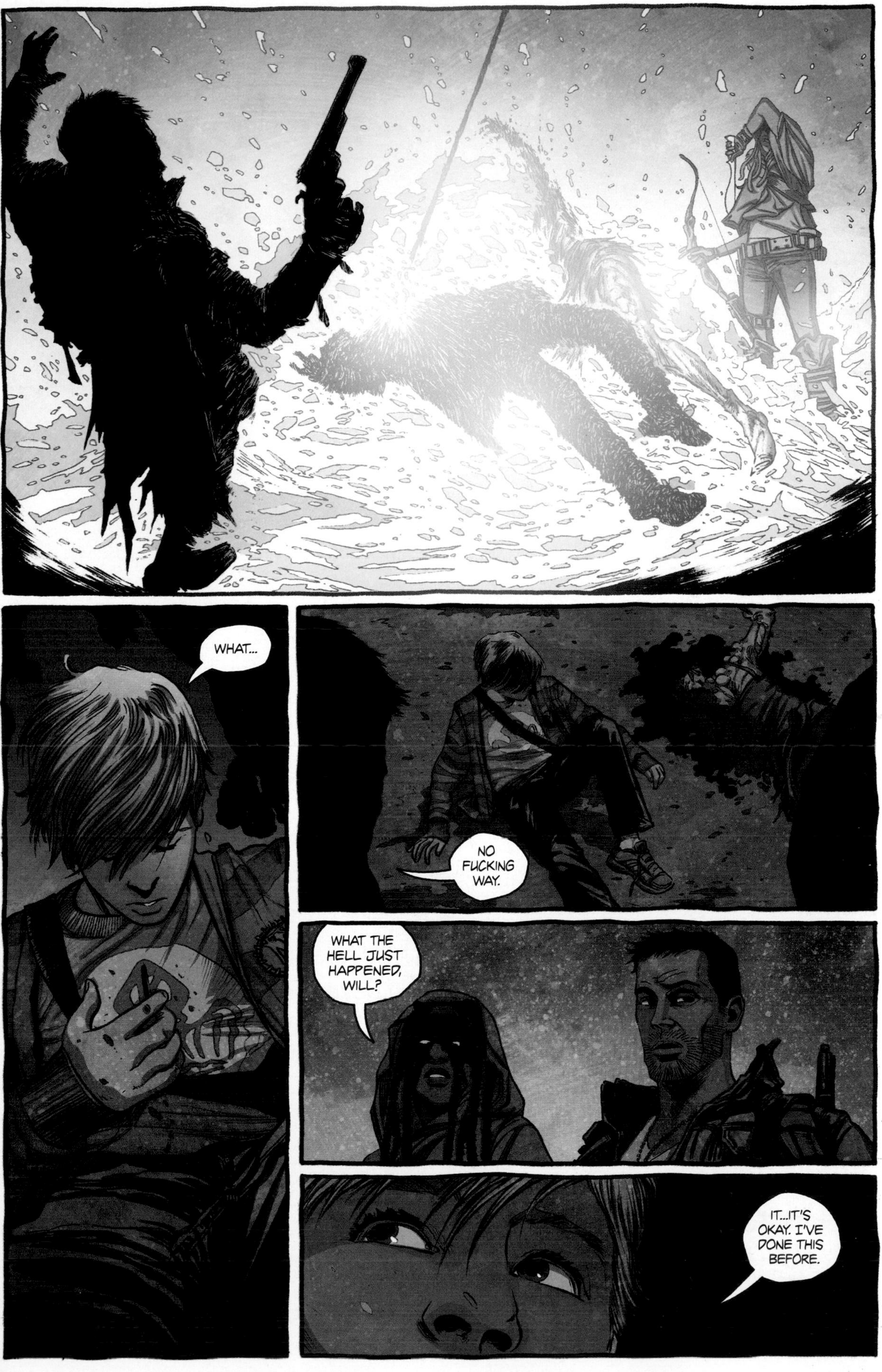
WHAT...
NO FUCKING WAY.
WHAT THE HELL JUST HAPPENED, WILL?
IT...IT'S OKAY. I'VE DONE THIS BEFORE.

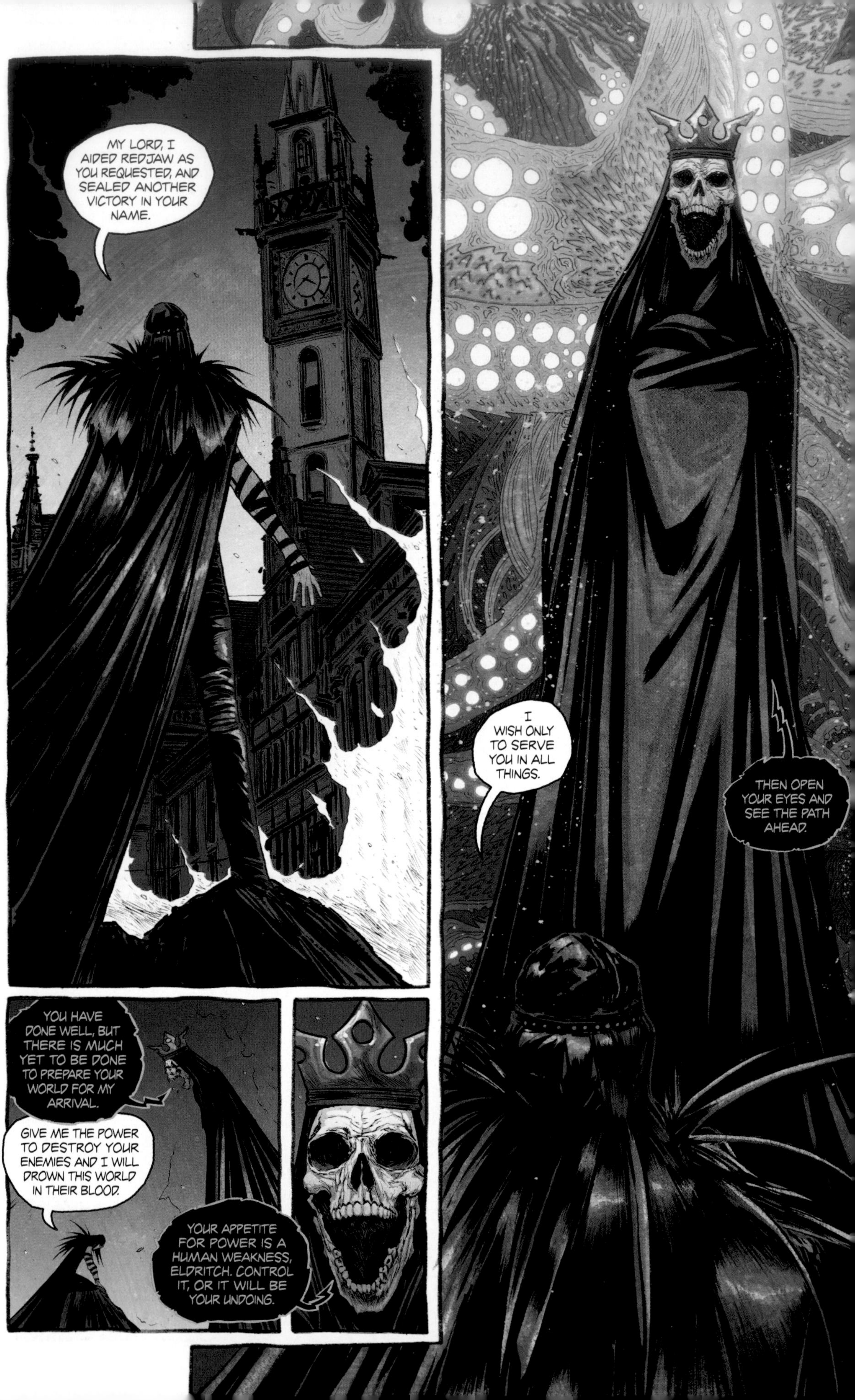
MY LORD, I AIDED REDJAW AS YOU REQUESTED, AND SEALED ANOTHER VICTORY IN YOUR NAME.
I WISH ONLY TO SERVE YOU IN ALL THINGS.
THEN OPEN YOUR EYES AND SEE THE PATH AHEAD.
YOU HAVE DONE WELL, BUT THERE IS MUCH YET TO BE DONE TO PREPARE YOUR WORLD FOR MY ARRIVAL.
GIVE ME THE POWER TO DESTROY YOUR ENEMIES AND I WILL DROWN THIS WORLD IN THEIR BLOOD.
YOUR APPETITE FOR POWER IS A HUMAN WEAKNESS, ELDRITCH. CONTROL IT, OR IT WILL BE YOUR UNDOING.

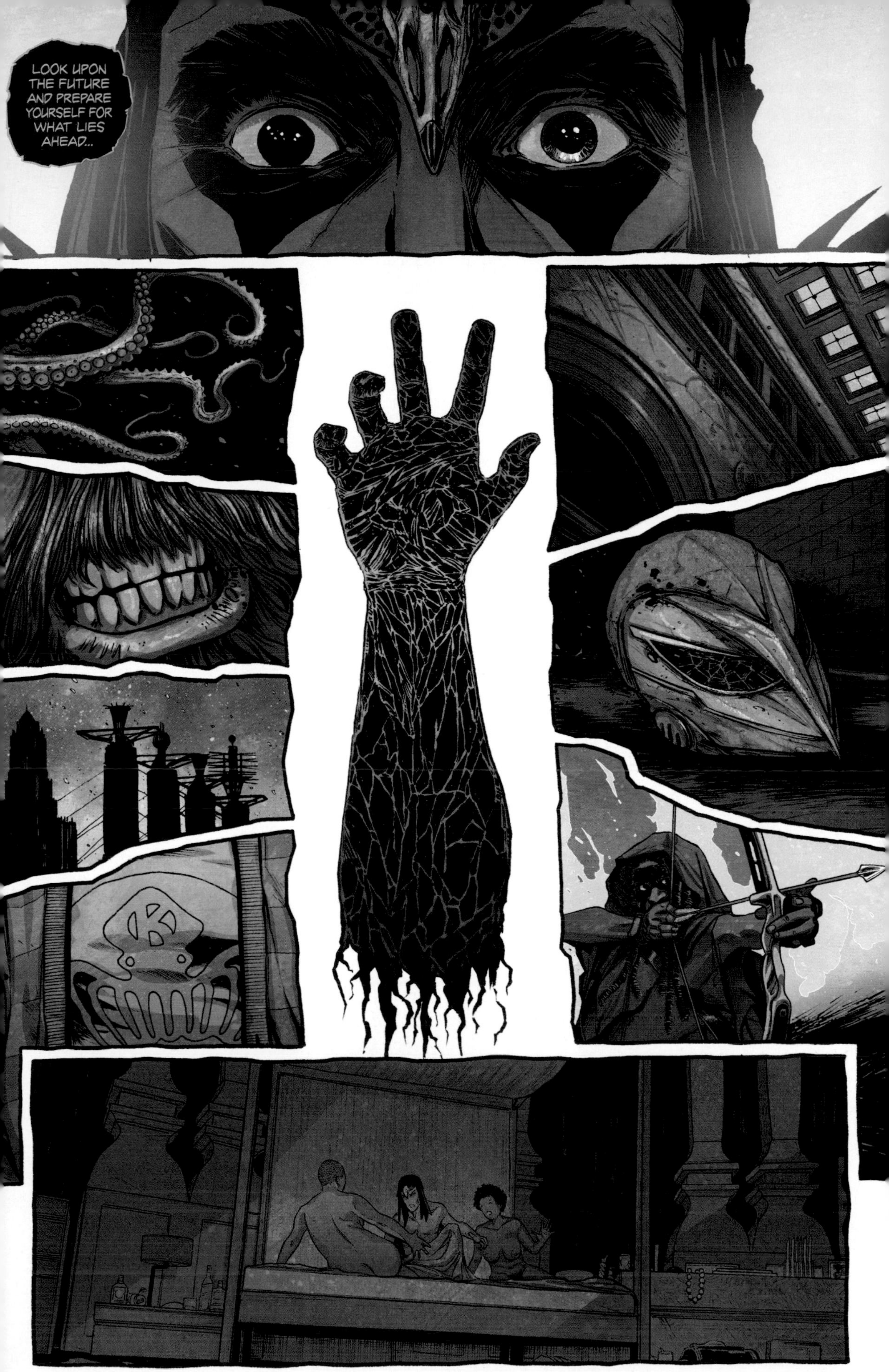
LOOK UPON THE FUTURE AND PREPARE YOURSELF FOR WHAT LIES AHEAD...

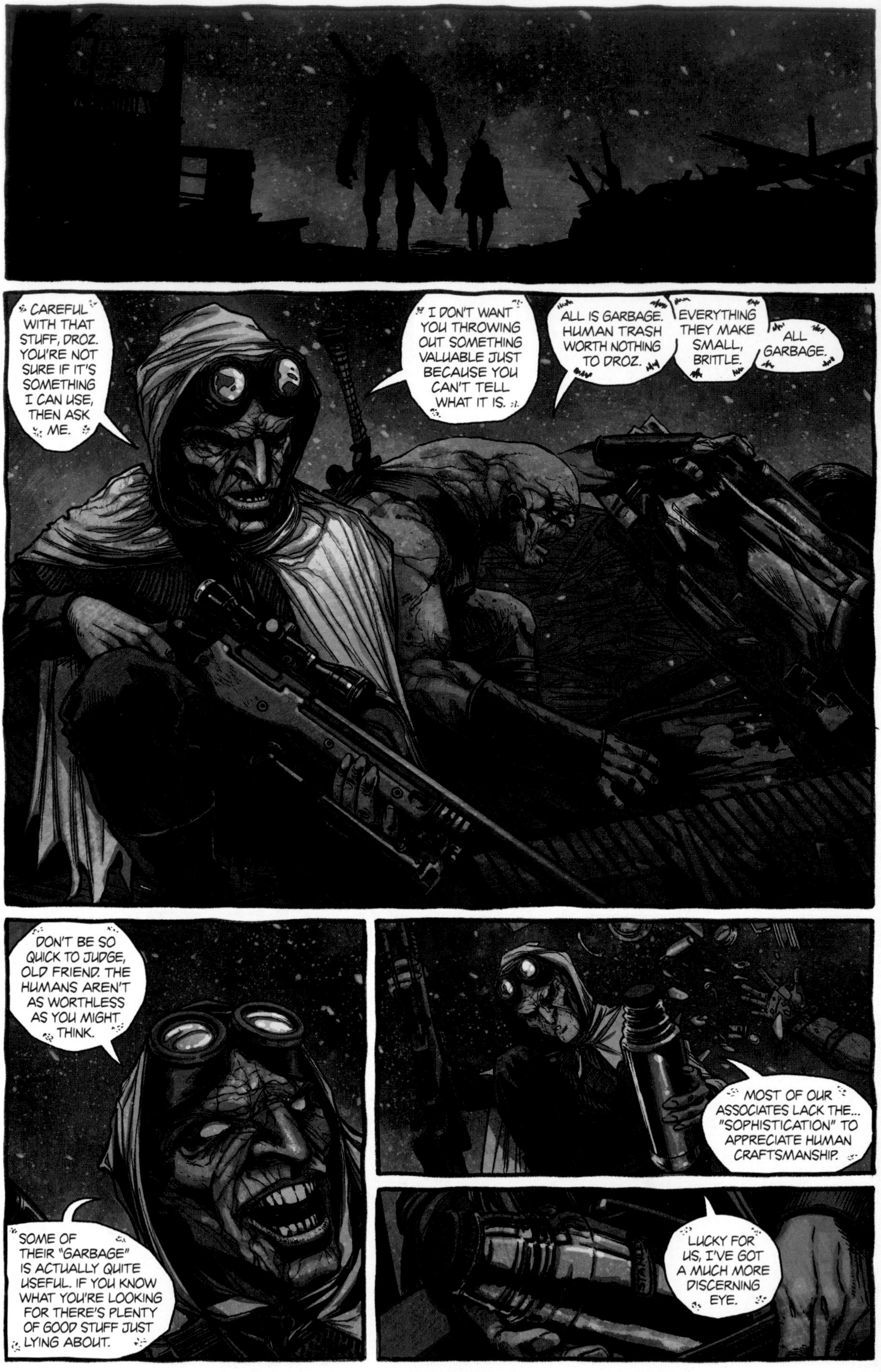
CAREFUL WITH THAT STUFF, DROZ. YOU'RE NOT SURE IF IT'S SOMETHING I CAN USE, THEN ASK ME.
I DON'T WANT YOU THROWING OUT SOMETHING VALUABLE JUST BECAUSE YOU CAN'T TELL WHAT IT IS.
ALL IS GARBAGE. HUMAN TRASH WORTH NOTHING TO DROZ.
EVERYTHING THEY MAKE SMALL, BRITTLE.
ALL GARBAGE.
DON'T BE SO QUICK TO JUDGE, OLD FRIEND. THE HUMANS AREN'T AS WORTHLESS AS YOU MIGHT THINK.
SOME OF THEIR "GARBAGE" IS ACTUALLY QUITE USEFUL. IF YOU KNOW WHAT YOU'RE LOOKING FOR THERE'S PLENTY OF GOOD STUFF JUST LYING ABOUT.
MOST OF OUR ASSOCIATES LACK THE... "SOPHISTICATION" TO APPRECIATE HUMAN CRAFTSMANSHIP.
LUCKY FOR US, I'VE GOT A MUCH MORE DISCERNING EYE.

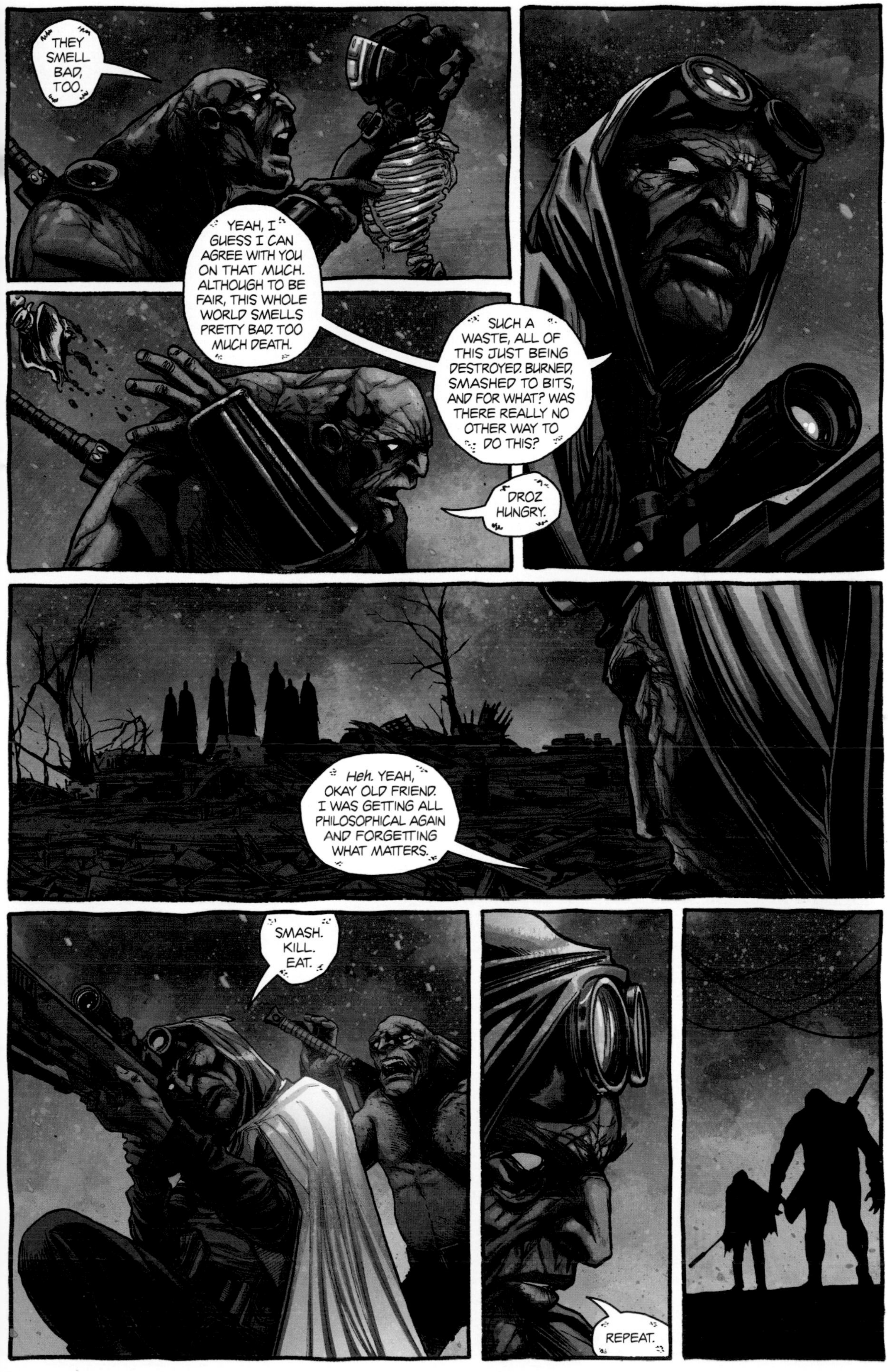
THEY SMELL BAD, TOO.
YEAH, I GUESS I CAN AGREE WITH YOU ON THAT MUCH. ALTHOUGH TO BE FAIR, THIS WHOLE WORLD SMELLS PRETTY BAD. TOO MUCH DEATH.
SUCH A WASTE, ALL OF THIS JUST BEING DESTROYED. BURNED, SMASHED TO BITS, AND FOR WHAT? WAS THERE REALLY NO OTHER WAY TO DO THIS?
DROZ HUNGRY.
Heh. YEAH, OKAY OLD FRIEND. I WAS GETTING ALL PHILOSOPHICAL AGAIN AND FORGETTING WHAT MATTERS.
SMASH. KILL. EAT.
REPEAT.

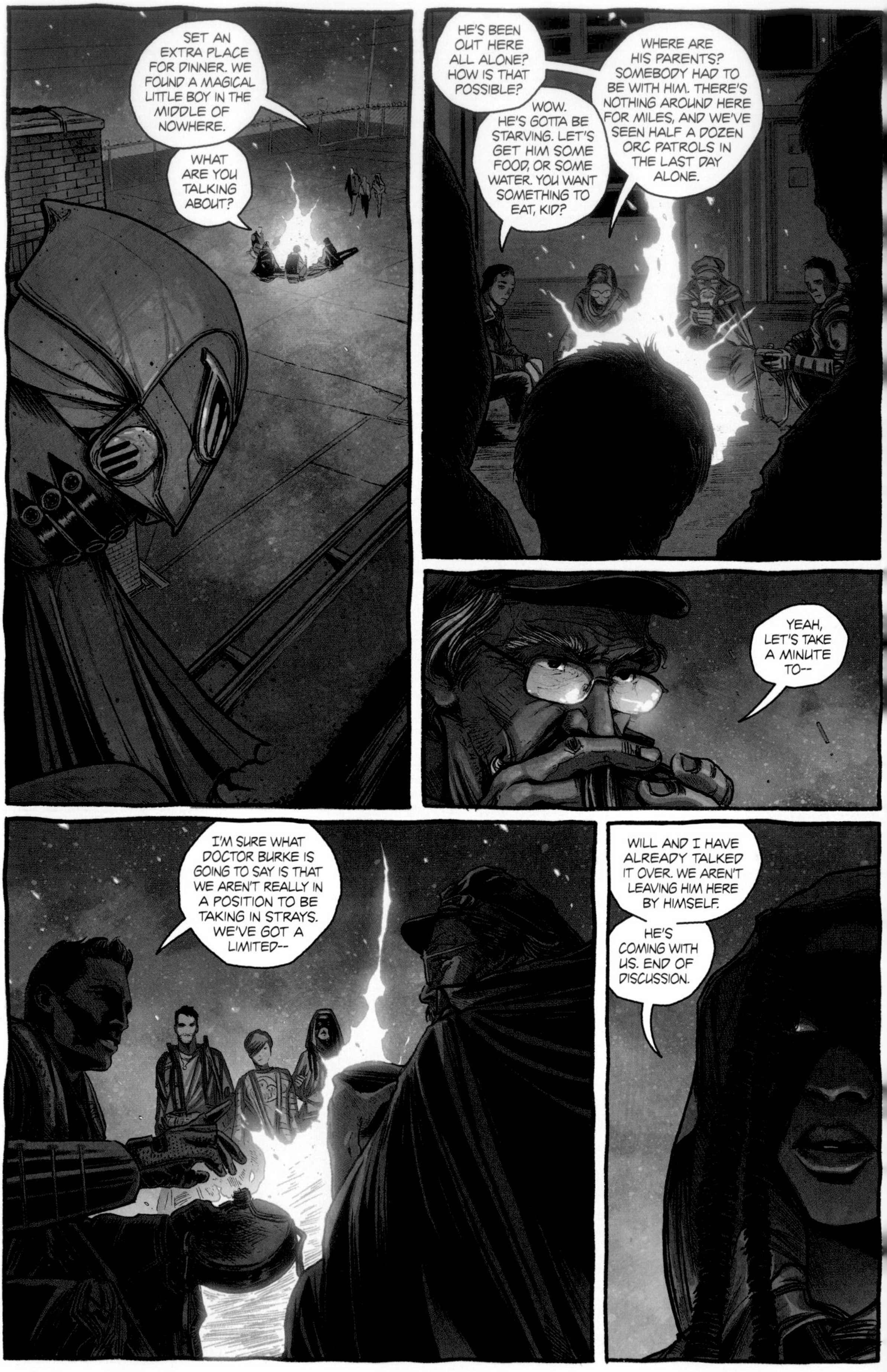
SET AN EXTRA PLACE FOR DINNER. WE FOUND A MAGICAL LITTLE BOY IN THE MIDDLE OF NOWHERE.
WHAT ARE YOU TALKING ABOUT?
HE'S BEEN OUT HERE ALL ALONE? HOW IS THAT POSSIBLE?
WHERE ARE HIS PARENTS? SOMEBODY HAD TO BE WITH HIM. THERE'S NOTHING AROUND HERE FOR MILES, AND WE'VE SEEN HALF A DOZEN ORC PATROLS IN THE LAST DAY ALONE.
WOW. HE'S GOTTA BE STARVING. LET'S GET HIM SOME FOOD, OR SOME WATER. YOU WANT SOMETHING TO EAT, KID?
YEAH, LET'S TAKE A MINUTE TO--
I'M SURE WHAT DOCTOR BURKE IS GOING TO SAY IS THAT WE AREN'T REALLY IN A POSITION TO BE TAKING IN STRAYS. WE'VE GOT A LIMITED--
WILL AND I HAVE ALREADY TALKED IT OVER. WE AREN'T LEAVING HIM HERE BY HIMSELF.
HE'S COMING WITH US. END OF DISCUSSION.

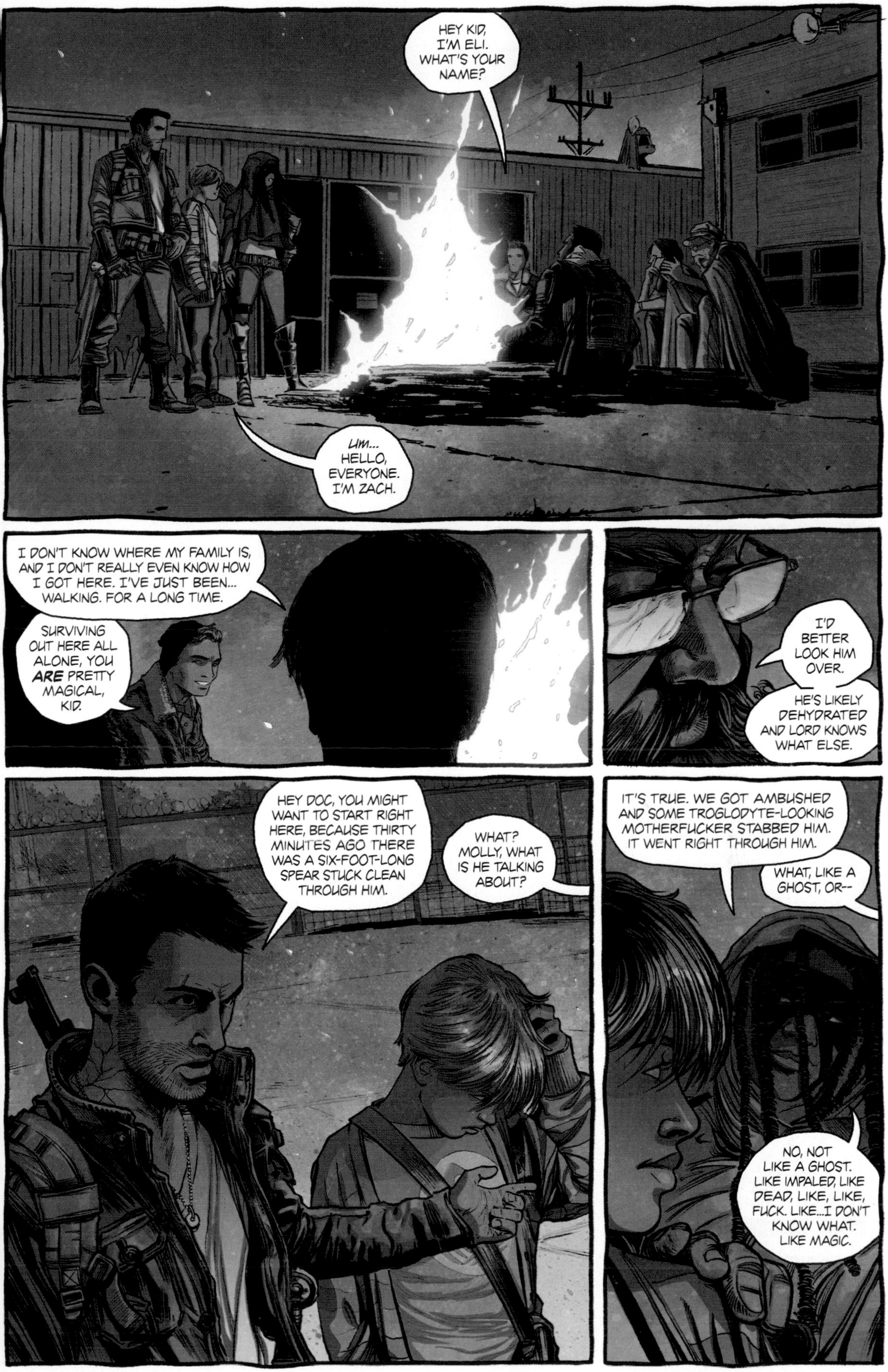
HEY KID, I'M ELI. WHAT'S YOUR NAME?
UM... HELLO, EVERYONE. I'M ZACH.
I DON'T KNOW WHERE MY FAMILY IS, AND I DON'T REALLY EVEN KNOW HOW I GOT HERE. I'VE JUST BEEN... WALKING. FOR A LONG TIME.
SURVIVING OUT HERE ALL ALONE, YOU ARE PRETTY MAGICAL, KID.
I'D BETTER LOOK HIM OVER.
HE'S LIKELY DEHYDRATED AND LORD KNOWS WHAT ELSE.
HEY DOC, YOU MIGHT WANT TO START RIGHT HERE, BECAUSE THIRTY MINUTES AGO THERE WAS A SIX-FOOT-LONG SPEAR STUCK CLEAN THROUGH HIM.
WHAT? MOLLY, WHAT IS HE TALKING ABOUT?
IT'S TRUE. WE GOT AMBUSHED AND SOME TROGLODYTE-LOOKING MOTHERFUCKER STABBED HIM. IT WENT RIGHT THROUGH HIM.
WHAT, LIKE A GHOST, OR--
NO, NOT LIKE A GHOST. LIKE IMPALED, LIKE DEAD, LIKE, LIKE, FUCK. LIKE...I DON'T KNOW WHAT. LIKE MAGIC.

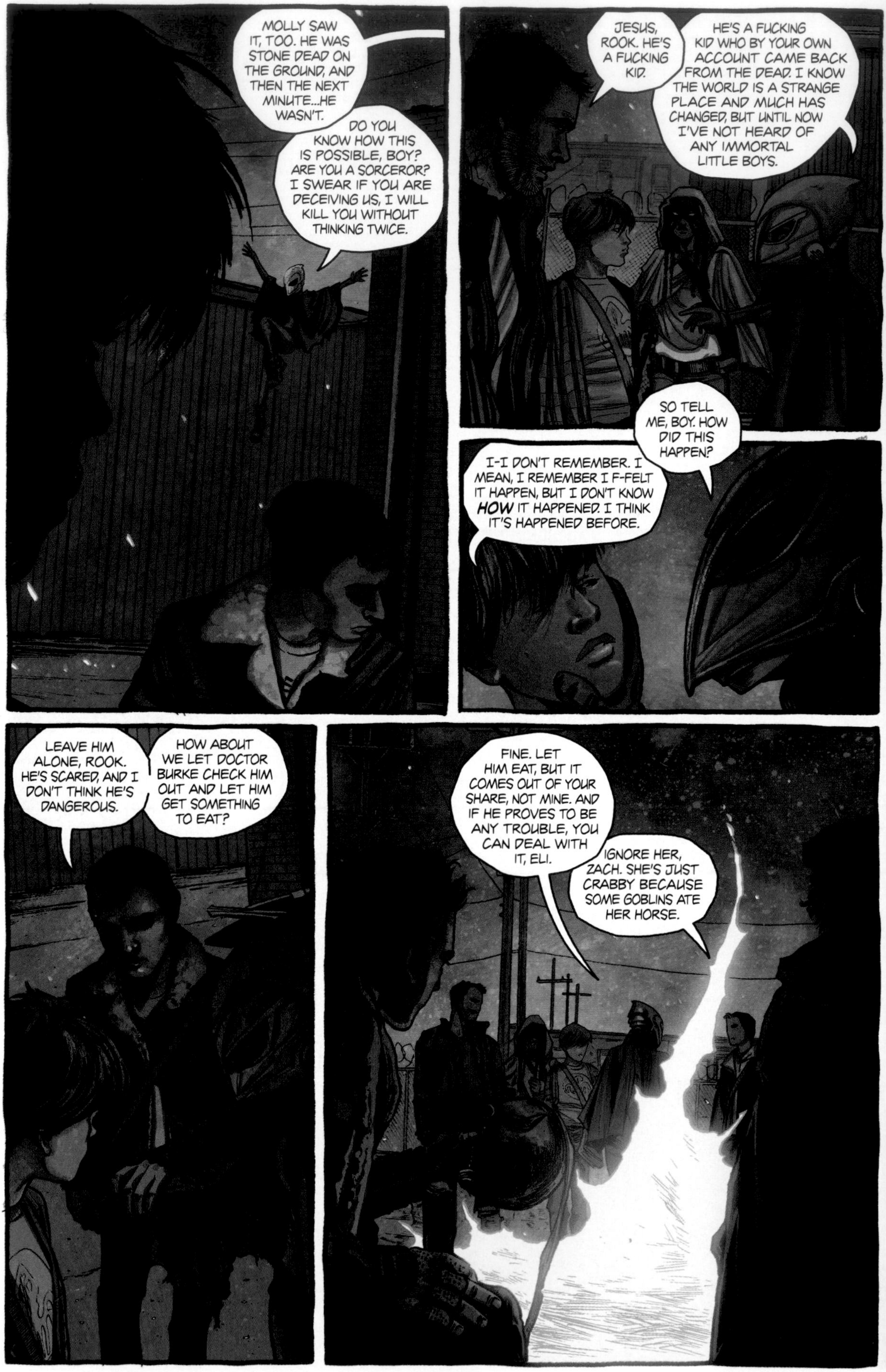
MOLLY SAW IT, TOO. HE WAS STONE DEAD ON THE GROUND, AND THEN THE NEXT MINUTE...HE WASN'T.
DO YOU KNOW HOW THIS IS POSSIBLE, BOY? ARE YOU A SORCEROR? I SWEAR IF YOU ARE DECEIVING US, I WILL KILL YOU WITHOUT THINKING TWICE.
JESUS, ROOK. HE'S A FUCKING KID.
HE'S A FUCKING KID WHO BY YOUR OWN ACCOUNT CAME BACK FROM THE DEAD. I KNOW THE WORLD IS A STRANGE PLACE AND MUCH HAS CHANGED, BUT UNTIL NOW I'VE NOT HEARD OF ANY IMMORTAL LITTLE BOYS.
SO TELL ME, BOY. HOW DID THIS HAPPEN?
I-I DON'T REMEMBER. I MEAN, I REMEMBER I F-FELT IT HAPPEN, BUT I DON'T KNOW HOW IT HAPPENED. I THINK IT'S HAPPENED BEFORE.
LEAVE HIM ALONE, ROOK. HE'S SCARED, AND I DON'T THINK HE'S DANGEROUS.
HOW ABOUT WE LET DOCTOR BURKE CHECK HIM OUT AND LET HIM GET SOMETHING TO EAT?
FINE. LET HIM EAT, BUT IT COMES OUT OF YOUR SHARE, NOT MINE. AND IF HE PROVES TO BE ANY TROUBLE, YOU CAN DEAL WITH IT, ELI.
IGNORE HER, ZACH. SHE'S JUST CRABBY BECAUSE SOME GOBLINS ATE HER HORSE.

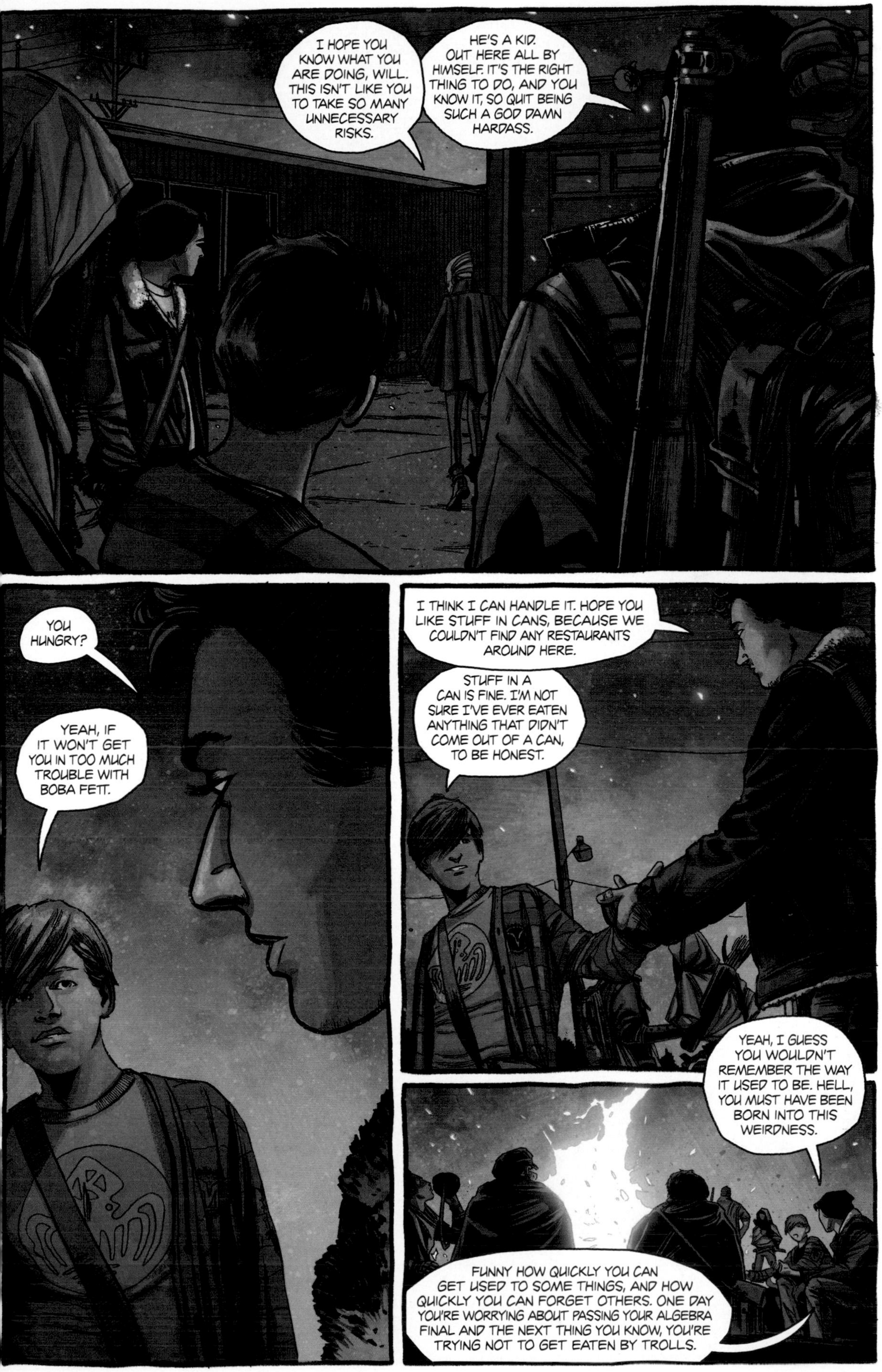
I HOPE YOU KNOW WHAT YOU ARE DOING, WILL. THIS ISN'T LIKE YOU TO TAKE SO MANY UNNECESSARY RISKS.
HE'S A KID. OUT HERE ALL BY HIMSELF. IT'S THE RIGHT THING TO DO, AND YOU KNOW IT, SO QUIT BEING SUCH A GOD DAMN HARDASS.
YOU HUNGRY?
YEAH, IF IT WON'T GET YOU IN TOO MUCH TROUBLE WITH BOBA FETT.
I THINK I CAN HANDLE IT. HOPE YOU LIKE STUFF IN CANS, BECAUSE WE COULDN'T FIND ANY RESTAURANTS AROUND HERE.
STUFF IN A CAN IS FINE. I'M NOT SURE I'VE EVER EATEN ANYTHING THAT DIDN'T COME OUT OF A CAN, TO BE HONEST.
YEAH, I GUESS YOU WOULDN'T REMEMBER THE WAY IT USED TO BE. HELL, YOU MUST HAVE BEEN BORN INTO THIS WEIRDNESS.
FUNNY HOW QUICKLY YOU CAN GET USED TO SOME THINGS, AND HOW QUICKLY YOU CAN FORGET OTHERS. ONE DAY YOU'RE WORRYING ABOUT PASSING YOUR ALGEBRA FINAL AND THE NEXT THING YOU KNOW, YOU'RE TRYING NOT TO GET EATEN BY TROLLS.

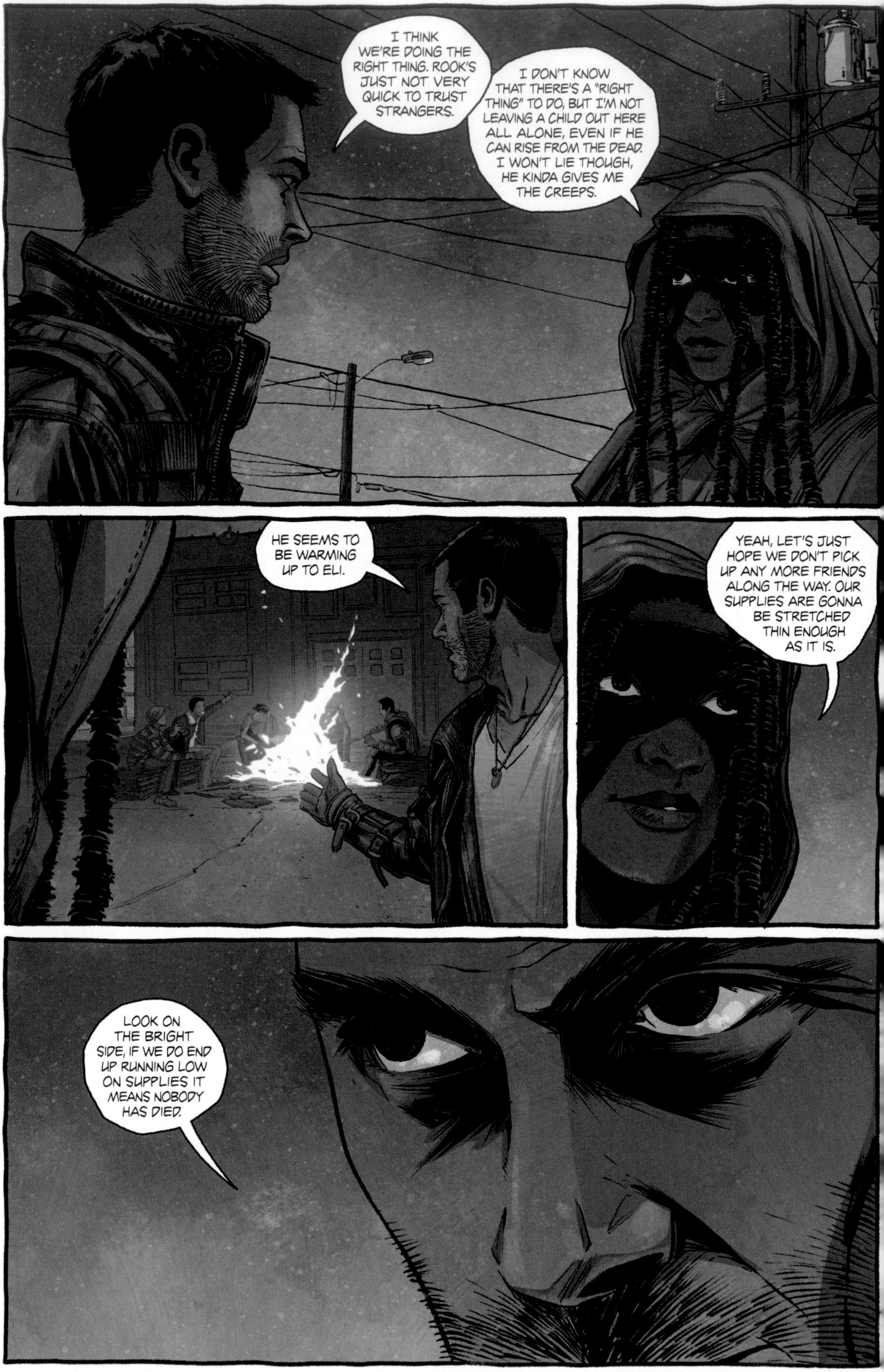
I THINK WE'RE DOING THE RIGHT THING. ROOK'S JUST NOT VERY QUICK TO TRUST STRANGERS.
I DON'T KNOW THAT THERE'S A "RIGHT THING" TO DO, BUT I'M NOT LEAVING A CHILD OUT HERE ALL ALONE, EVEN IF HE CAN RISE FROM THE DEAD. I WON'T LIE THOUGH, HE KINDA GIVES ME THE CREEPS.
HE SEEMS TO BE WARMING UP TO ELI.
YEAH, LET'S JUST HOPE WE DON'T PICK UP ANY MORE FRIENDS ALONG THE WAY. OUR SUPPLIES ARE GONNA BE STRETCHED THIN ENOUGH AS IT IS.
LOOK ON THE BRIGHT SIDE, IF WE DO END UP RUNNING LOW ON SUPPLIES IT MEANS NOBODY HAS DIED.

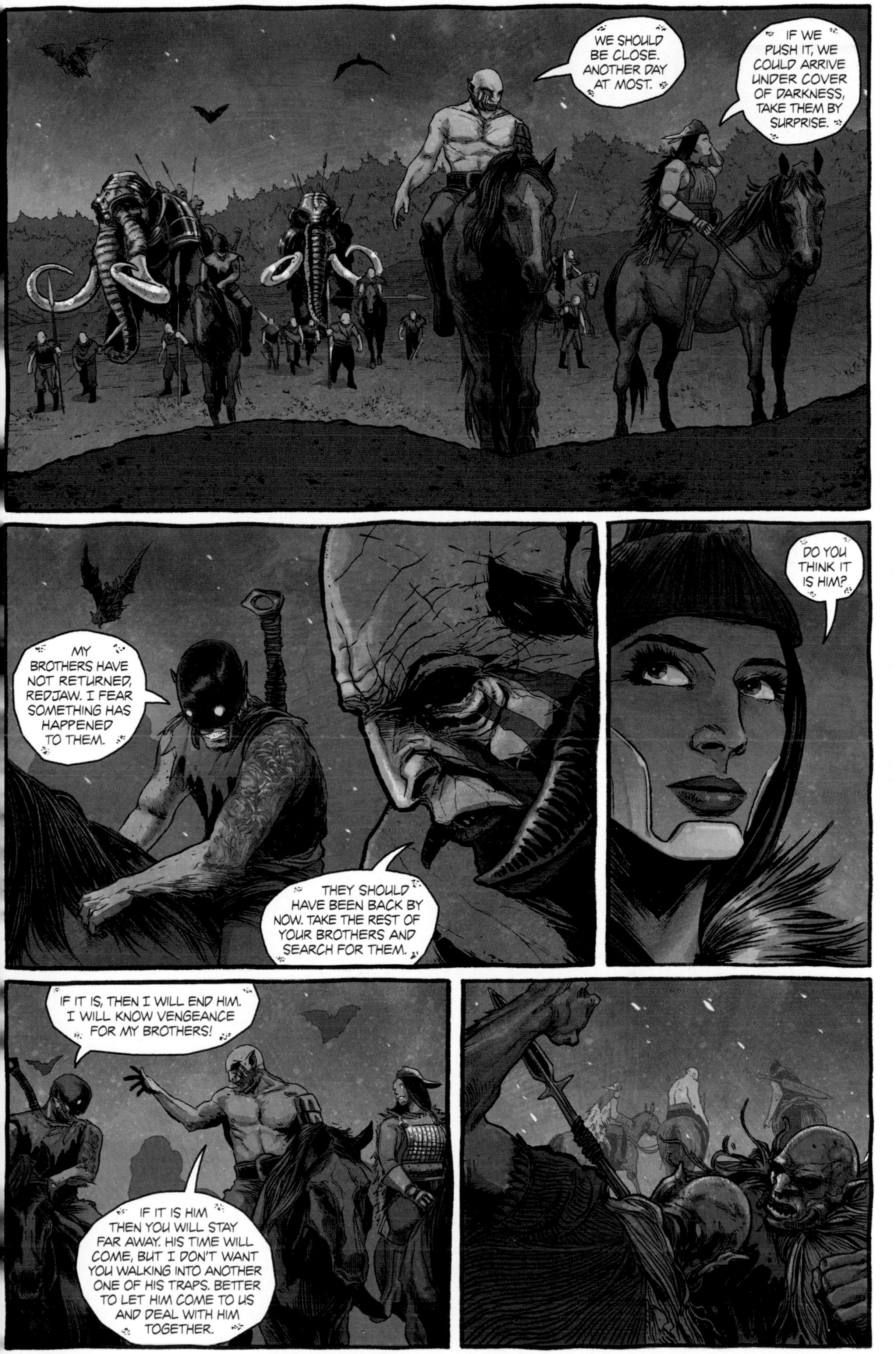
WE SHOULD BE CLOSE. ANOTHER DAY AT MOST.
IF WE PUSH IT, WE COULD ARRIVE UNDER COVER OF DARKNESS, TAKE THEM BY SURPRISE.
MY BROTHERS HAVE NOT RETURNED, REDJAW. I FEAR SOMETHING HAS HAPPENED TO THEM.
THEY SHOULD HAVE BEEN BACK BY NOW. TAKE THE REST OF YOUR BROTHERS AND SEARCH FOR THEM.
DO YOU THINK IT IS HIM?
IF IT IS, THEN I WILL END HIM. I WILL KNOW VENGEANCE FOR MY BROTHERS!
IF IT IS HIM THEN YOU WILL STAY FAR AWAY. HIS TIME WILL COME, BUT I DON'T WANT YOU WALKING INTO ANOTHER ONE OF HIS TRAPS. BETTER TO LET HIM COME TO US AND DEAL WITH HIM TOGETHER.

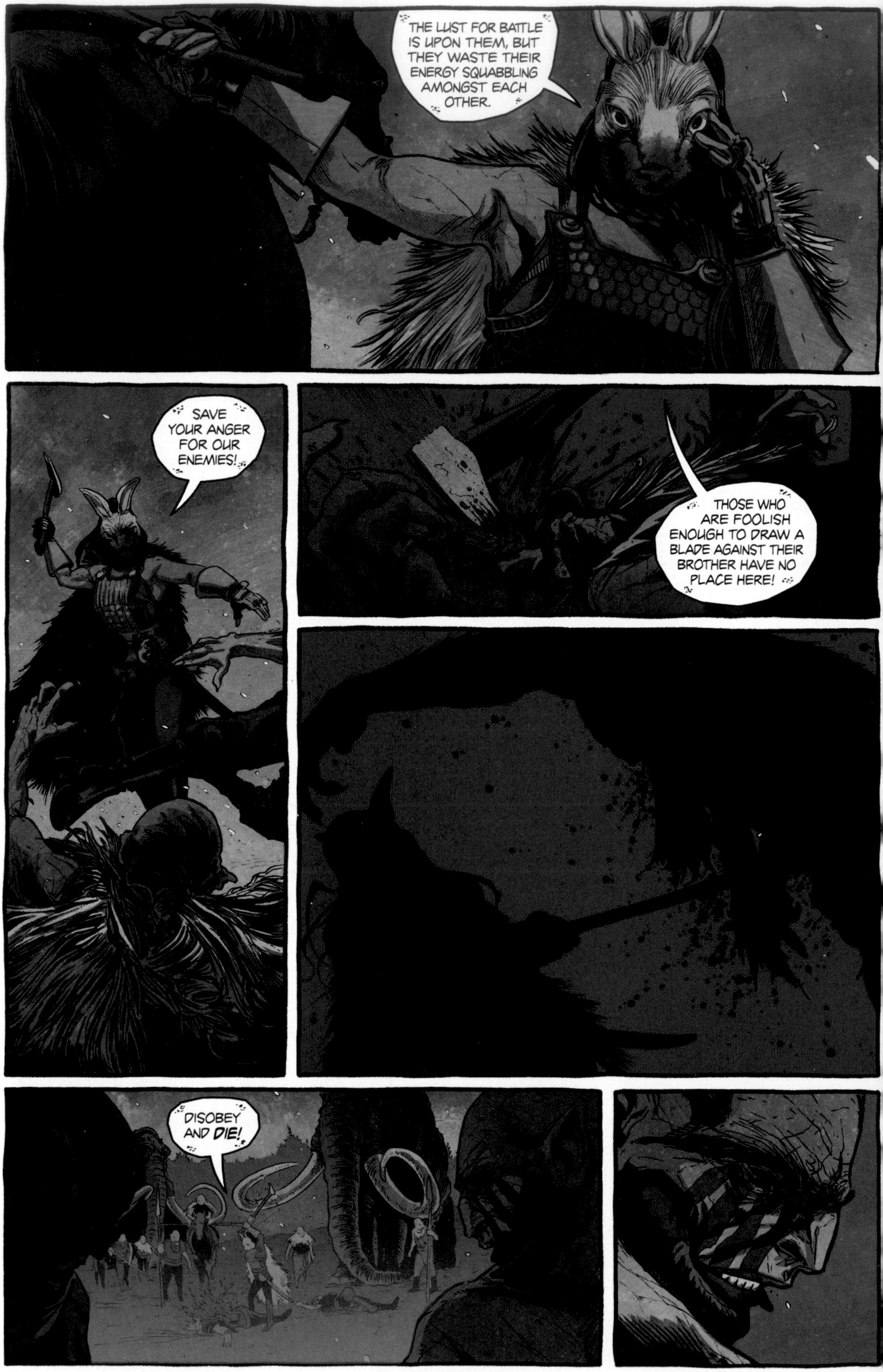
THE LUST FOR BATTLE IS UPON THEM, BUT THEY WASTE THEIR ENERGY SQUABBLING AMONGST EACH OTHER.
SAVE YOUR ANGER FOR OUR ENEMIES!
THOSE WHO ARE FOOLISH ENOUGH TO DRAW A BLADE AGAINST THEIR BROTHER HAVE NO PLACE HERE!
DISOBEY AND *DIE!*

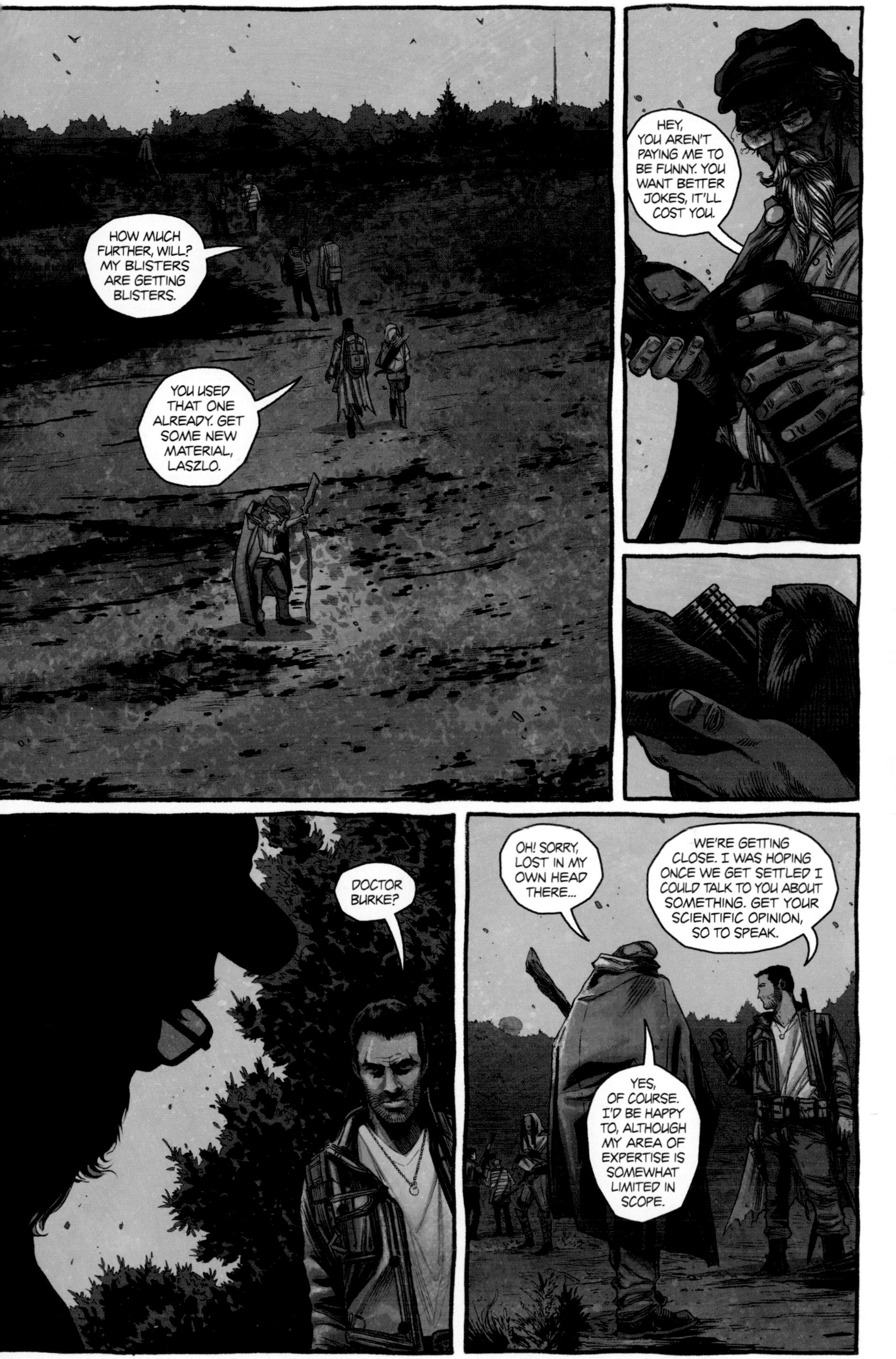
HOW MUCH FURTHER, WILL? MY BLISTERS ARE GETTING BLISTERS.
YOU USED THAT ONE ALREADY. GET SOME NEW MATERIAL, LASZLO.
HEY, YOU AREN'T PAYING ME TO BE FUNNY. YOU WANT BETTER JOKES, IT'LL COST YOU.
DOCTOR BURKE?
OH! SORRY, LOST IN MY OWN HEAD THERE...
WE'RE GETTING CLOSE. I WAS HOPING ONCE WE GET SETTLED I COULD TALK TO YOU ABOUT SOMETHING. GET YOUR SCIENTIFIC OPINION, SO TO SPEAK.
YES, OF COURSE. I'D BE HAPPY TO, ALTHOUGH MY AREA OF EXPERTISE IS SOMEWHAT LIMITED IN SCOPE.

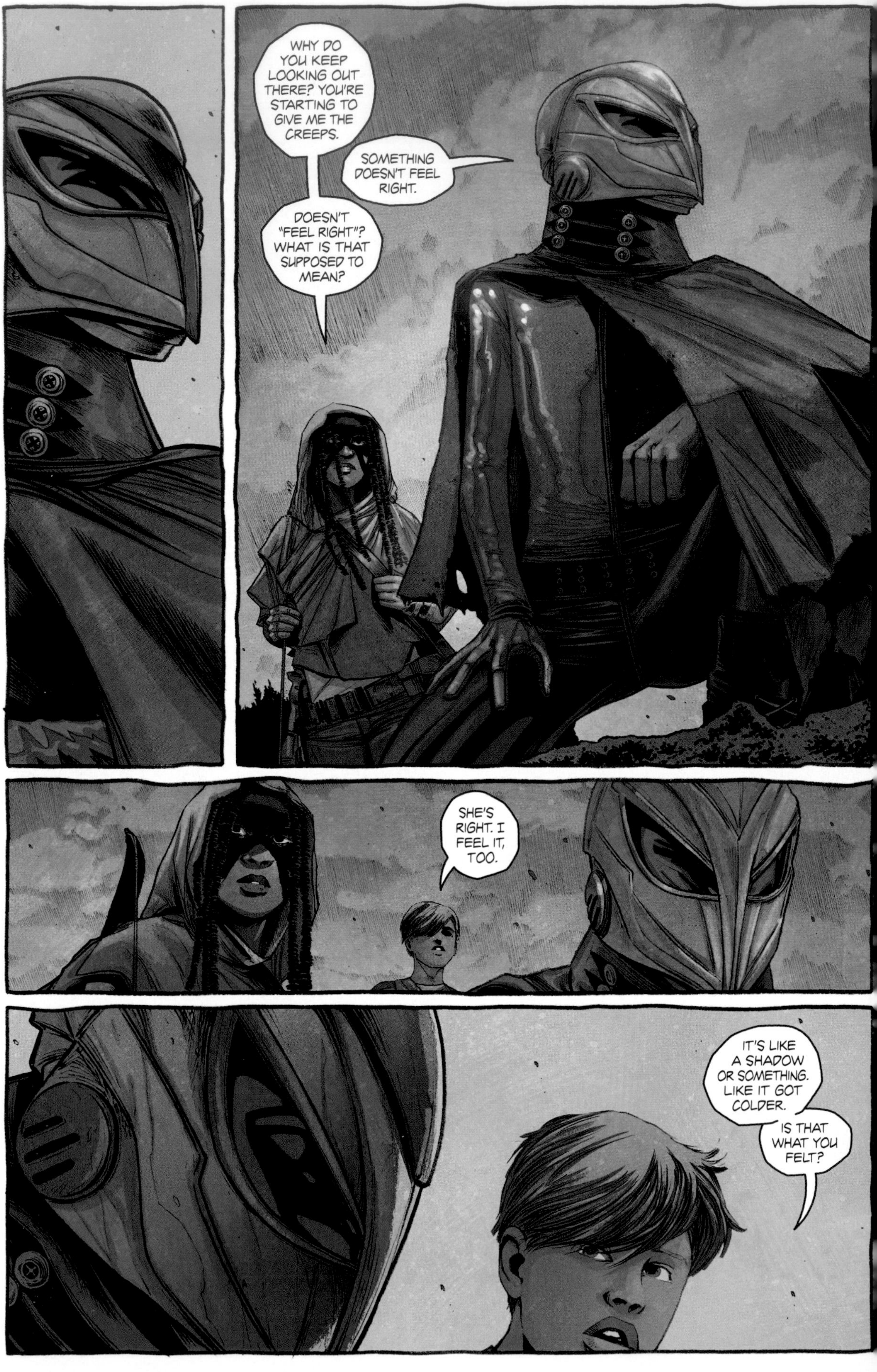
WHY DO YOU KEEP LOOKING OUT THERE? YOU'RE STARTING TO GIVE ME THE CREEPS.
SOMETHING DOESN'T FEEL RIGHT.
DOESN'T "FEEL RIGHT"? WHAT IS THAT SUPPOSED TO MEAN?
SHE'S RIGHT. I FEEL IT, TOO.
IT'S LIKE A SHADOW OR SOMETHING. LIKE IT GOT COLDER.
IS THAT WHAT YOU FELT?

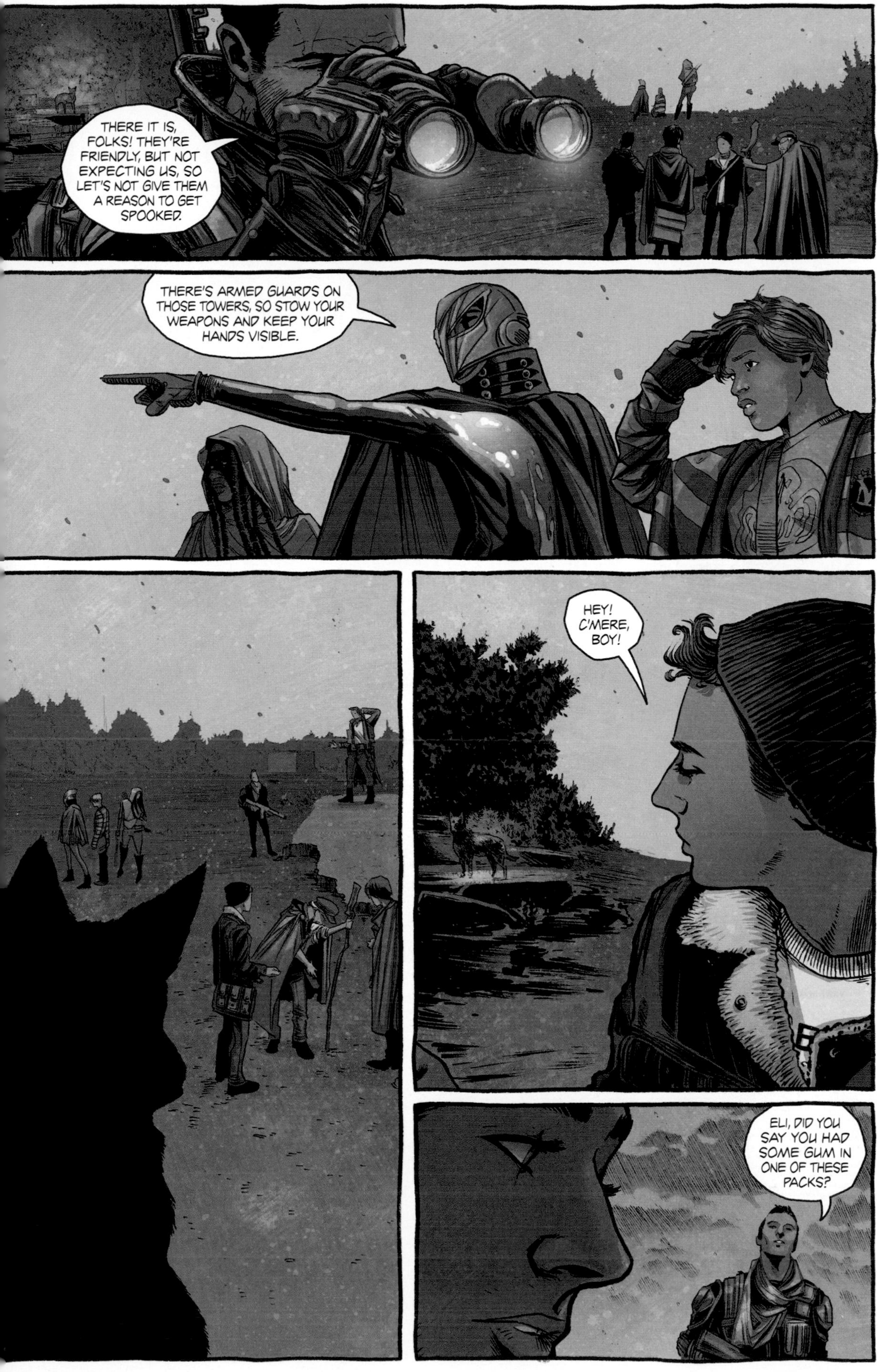
THERE IT IS, FOLKS! THEY'RE FRIENDLY, BUT NOT EXPECTING US, SO LET'S NOT GIVE THEM A REASON TO GET SPOOKED.
THERE'S ARMED GUARDS ON THOSE TOWERS, SO STOW YOUR WEAPONS AND KEEP YOUR HANDS VISIBLE.
HEY! C'MERE, BOY!
ELI, DID YOU SAY YOU HAD SOME GUM IN ONE OF THESE PACKS?

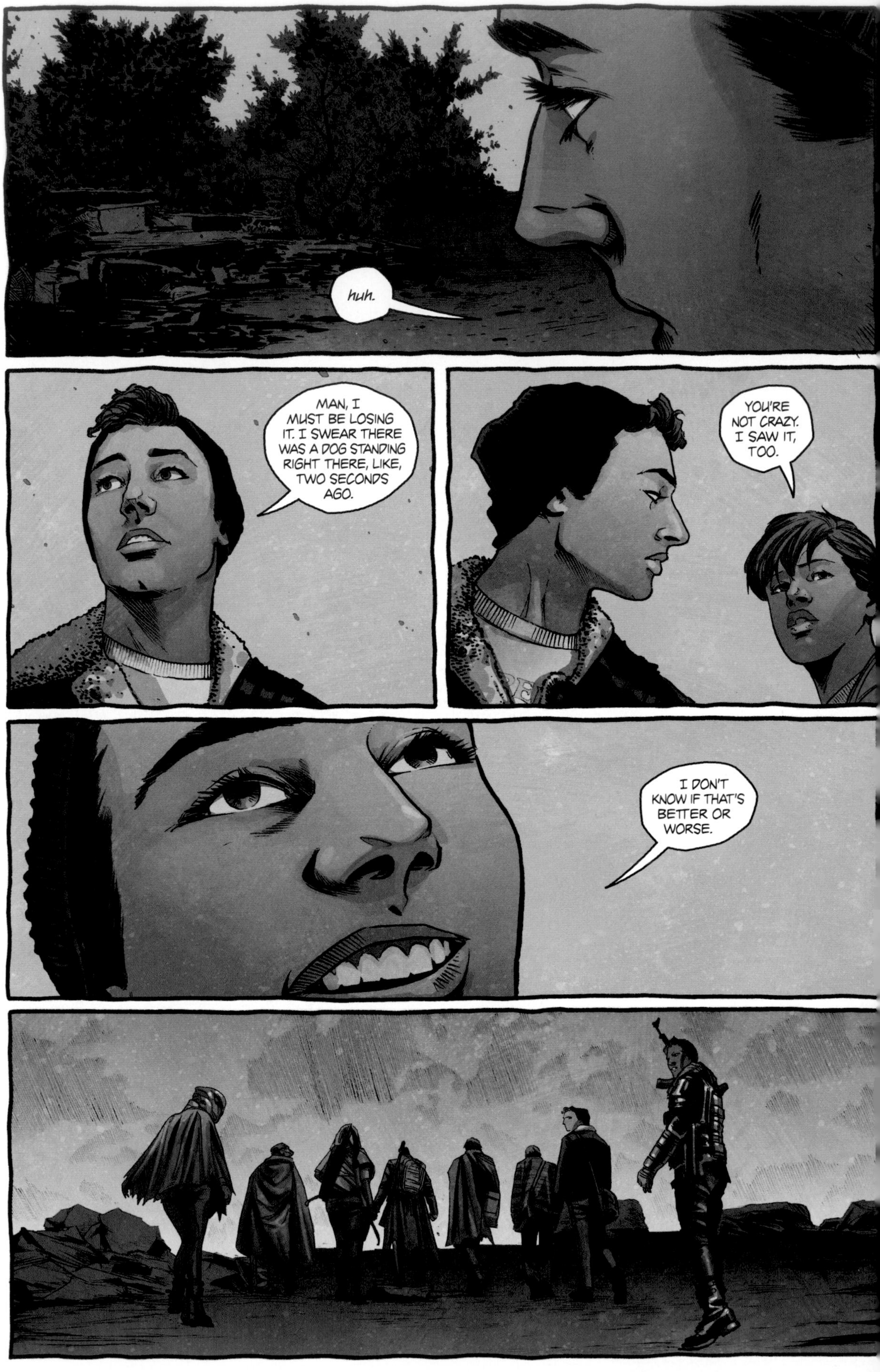
huh.
MAN, I MUST BE LOSING IT. I SWEAR THERE WAS A DOG STANDING RIGHT THERE, LIKE, TWO SECONDS AGO.
YOU'RE NOT CRAZY. I SAW IT, TOO.
I DON'T KNOW IF THAT'S BETTER OR WORSE.

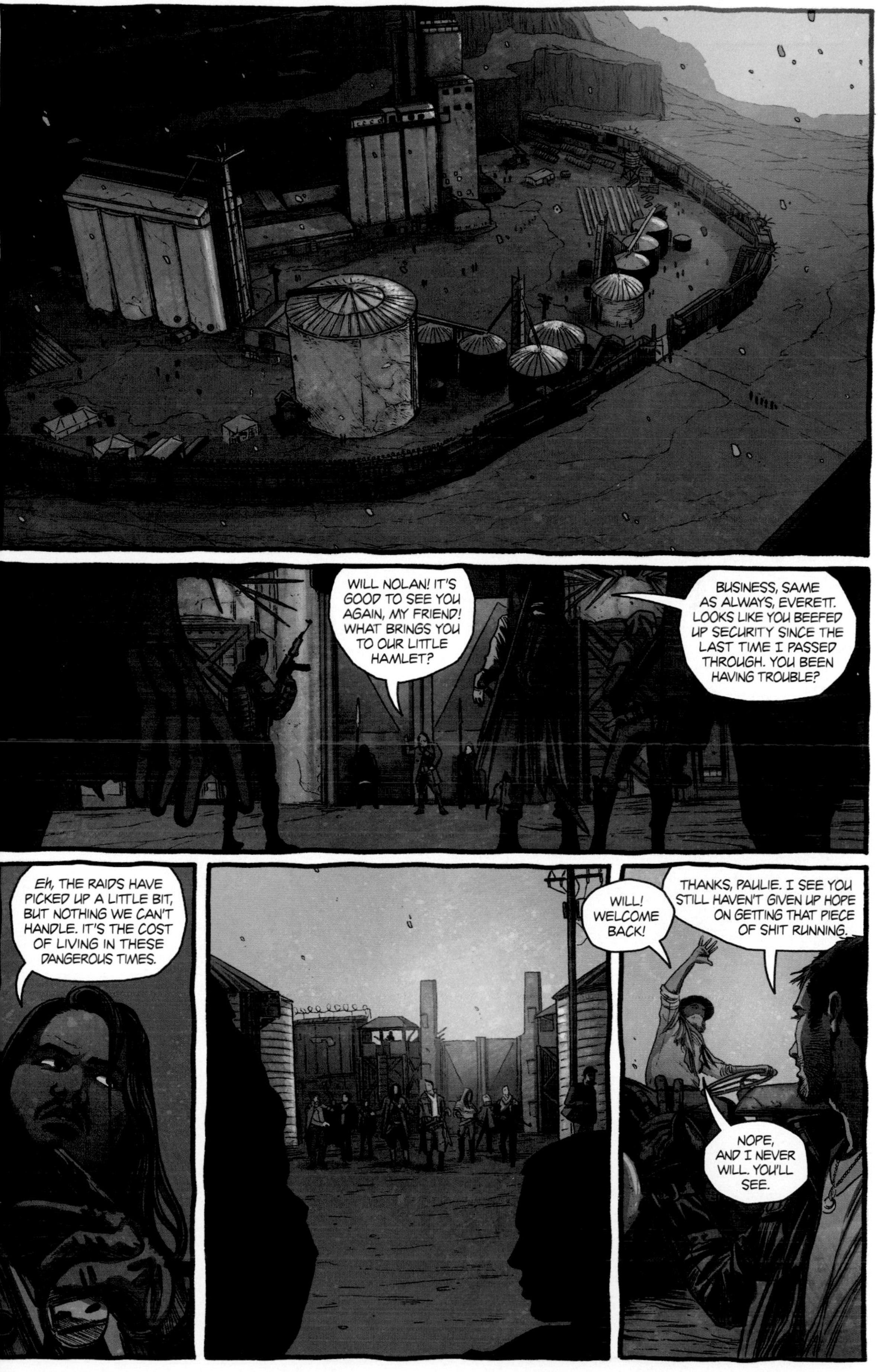
WILL NOLAN! IT'S GOOD TO SEE YOU AGAIN, MY FRIEND! WHAT BRINGS YOU TO OUR LITTLE HAMLET?
BUSINESS, SAME AS ALWAYS, EVERETT. LOOKS LIKE YOU BEEFED UP SECURITY SINCE THE LAST TIME I PASSED THROUGH. YOU BEEN HAVING TROUBLE?
Eh, THE RAIDS HAVE PICKED UP A LITTLE BIT, BUT NOTHING WE CAN'T HANDLE. IT'S THE COST OF LIVING IN THESE DANGEROUS TIMES.
WILL! WELCOME BACK!
THANKS, PAULIE. I SEE YOU STILL HAVEN'T GIVEN UP HOPE ON GETTING THAT PIECE OF SHIT RUNNING.
NOPE, AND I NEVER WILL. YOU'LL SEE.

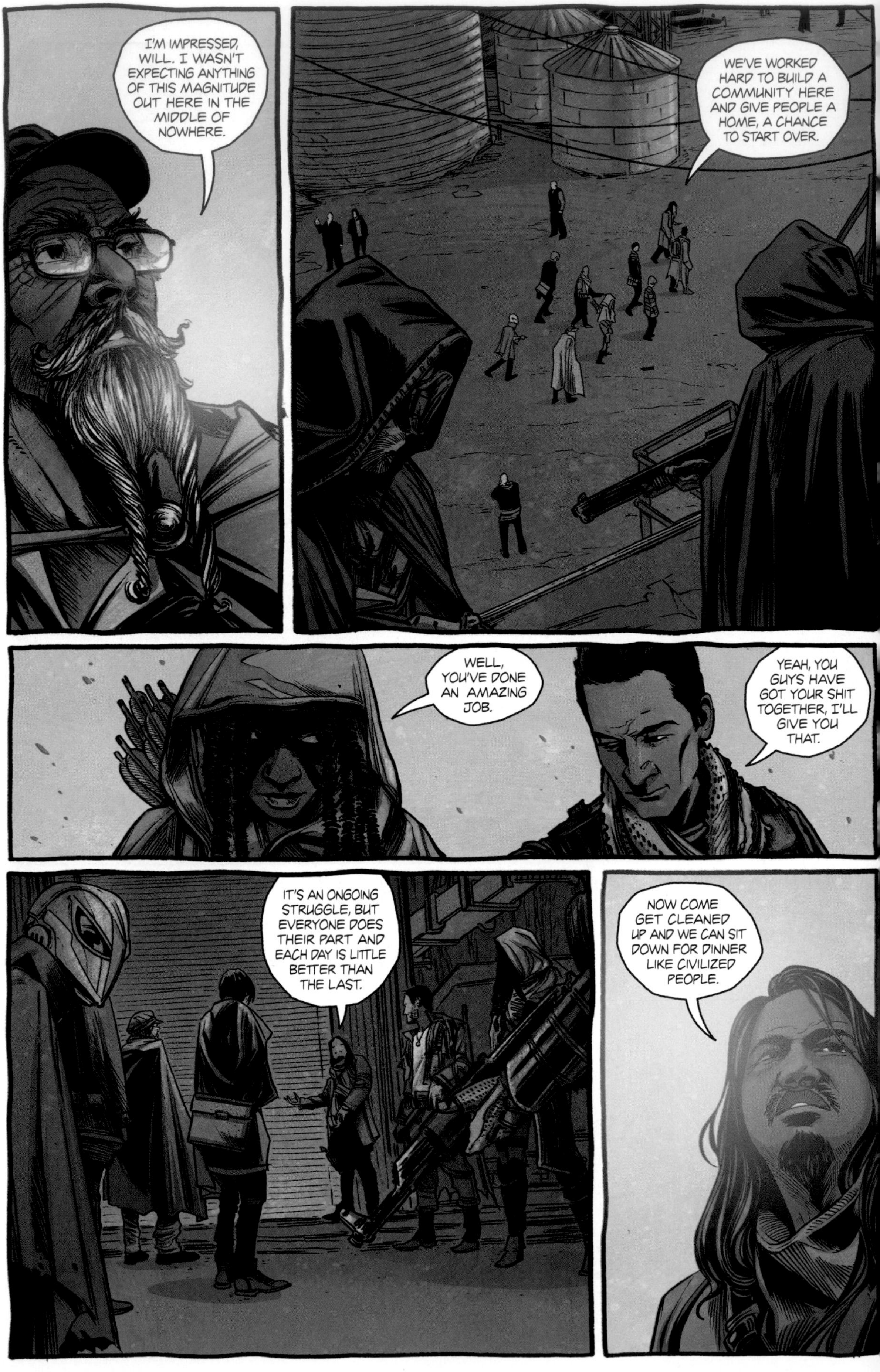
I'M IMPRESSED, WILL. I WASN'T EXPECTING ANYTHING OF THIS MAGNITUDE OUT HERE IN THE MIDDLE OF NOWHERE.
WE'VE WORKED HARD TO BUILD A COMMUNITY HERE AND GIVE PEOPLE A HOME, A CHANCE TO START OVER.
WELL, YOU'VE DONE AN AMAZING JOB.
YEAH, YOU GUYS HAVE GOT YOUR SHIT TOGETHER, I'LL GIVE YOU THAT.
IT'S AN ONGOING STRUGGLE, BUT EVERYONE DOES THEIR PART AND EACH DAY IS LITTLE BETTER THAN THE LAST.
NOW COME GET CLEANED UP AND WE CAN SIT DOWN FOR DINNER LIKE CIVILIZED PEOPLE.

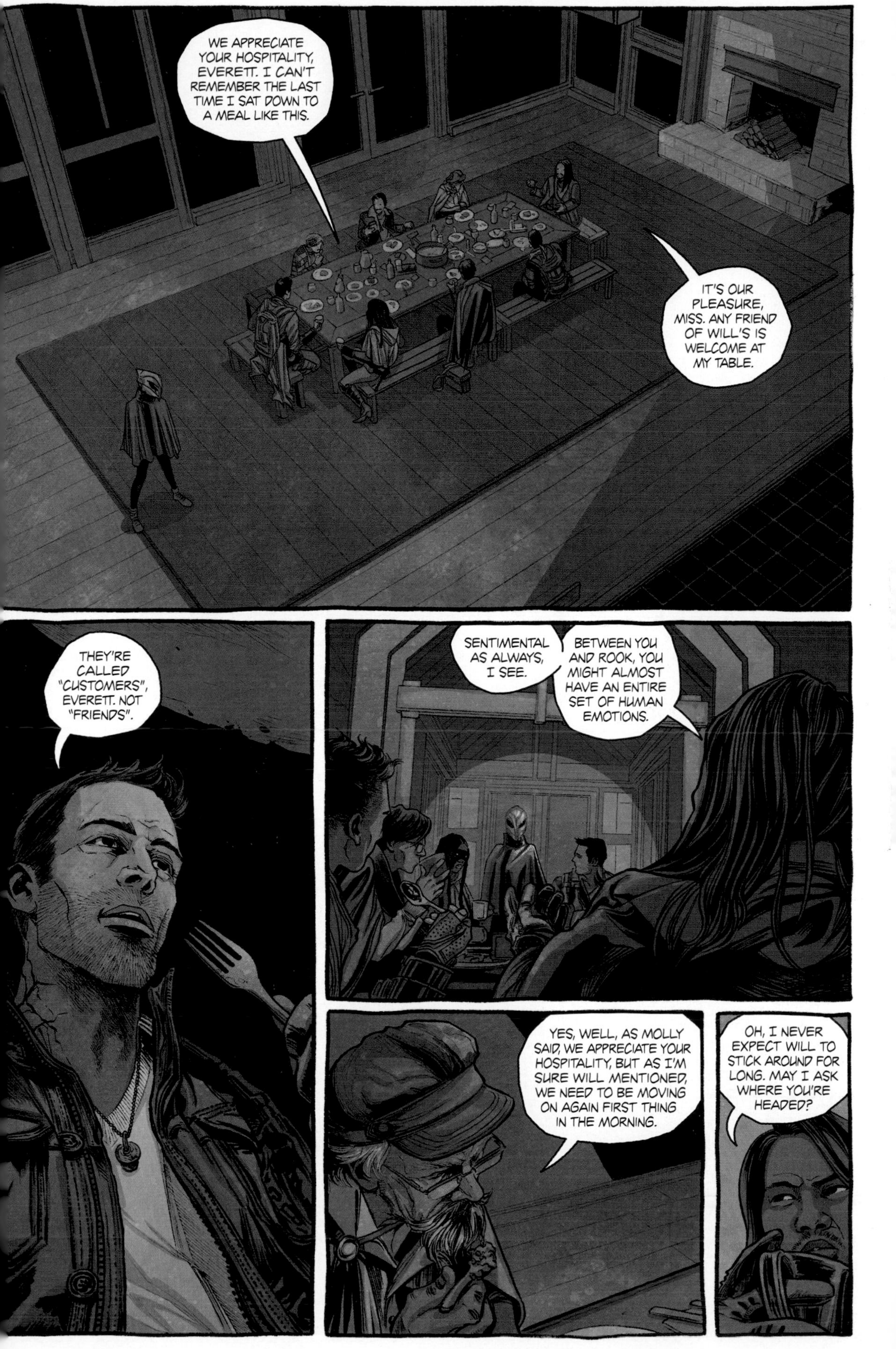
WE APPRECIATE YOUR HOSPITALITY, EVERETT. I CAN'T REMEMBER THE LAST TIME I SAT DOWN TO A MEAL LIKE THIS.
IT'S OUR PLEASURE, MISS. ANY FRIEND OF WILL'S IS WELCOME AT MY TABLE.
THEY'RE CALLED "CUSTOMERS", EVERETT. NOT "FRIENDS".
SENTIMENTAL AS ALWAYS, I SEE.
BETWEEN YOU AND ROOK, YOU MIGHT ALMOST HAVE AN ENTIRE SET OF HUMAN EMOTIONS.
YES, WELL, AS MOLLY SAID, WE APPRECIATE YOUR HOSPITALITY, BUT AS I'M SURE WILL MENTIONED, WE NEED TO BE MOVING ON AGAIN FIRST THING IN THE MORNING.
OH, I NEVER EXPECT WILL TO STICK AROUND FOR LONG. MAY I ASK WHERE YOU'RE HEADED?

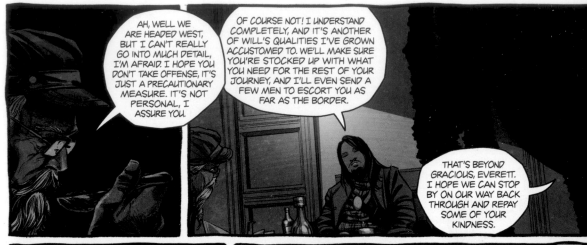

AH, WELL WE ARE HEADED WEST, BUT I CAN'T REALLY GO INTO MUCH DETAIL, I'M AFRAID. I HOPE YOU DON'T TAKE OFFENSE, IT'S JUST A PRECAUTIONARY MEASURE. IT'S NOT PERSONAL, I ASSURE YOU.

OF COURSE NOT! I UNDERSTAND COMPLETELY, AND IT'S ANOTHER OF WILL'S QUALITIES I'VE GROWN ACCUSTOMED TO. WE'LL MAKE SURE YOU'RE STOCKED UP WITH WHAT YOU NEED FOR THE REST OF YOUR JOURNEY, AND I'LL EVEN SEND A FEW MEN TO ESCORT YOU AS FAR AS THE BORDER.

THAT'S BEYOND GRACIOUS, EVERETT. I HOPE WE CAN STOP BY ON OUR WAY BACK THROUGH AND REPAY SOME OF YOUR KINDNESS.

I WOULD LIKE THAT VERY MUCH.

WILL? ARE YOU ALL RIGHT?

WHAT? YEAH...I JUST PULLED SOMETHING, I THINK. IT'S FINE.

YOU SHOULD STOP BY THE INFIRMARY AND GET IT LOOKED AT. AT LEAST GET SOMETHING FOR THE PAIN.

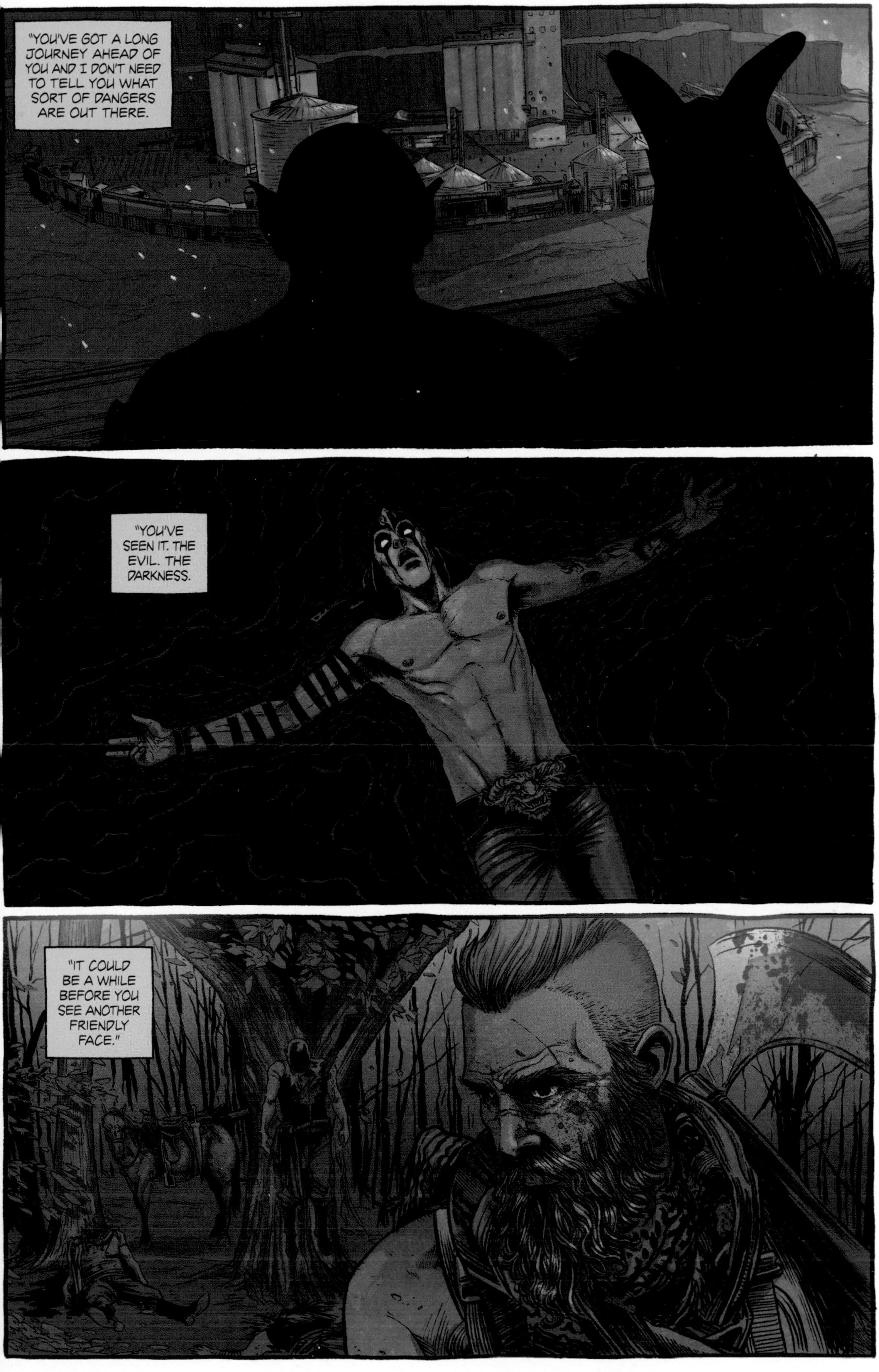
"YOU'VE GOT A LONG JOURNEY AHEAD OF YOU AND I DON'T NEED TO TELL YOU WHAT SORT OF DANGERS ARE OUT THERE.
"YOU'VE SEEN IT. THE EVIL. THE DARKNESS.
"IT COULD BE A WHILE BEFORE YOU SEE ANOTHER FRIENDLY FACE."

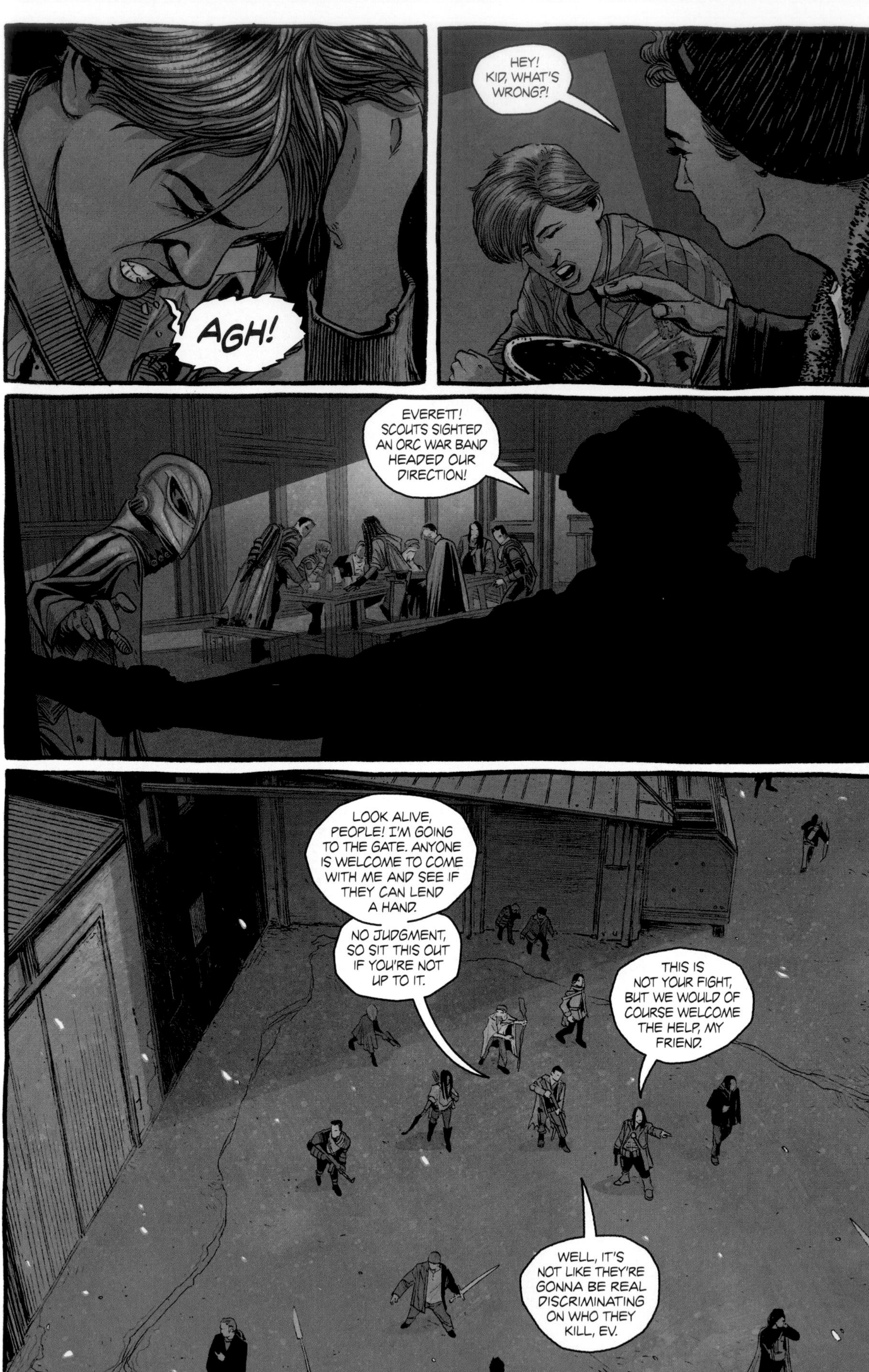
AGH!
HEY! KID, WHAT'S WRONG?!
EVERETT! SCOUTS SIGHTED AN ORC WAR BAND HEADED OUR DIRECTION!
LOOK ALIVE, PEOPLE! I'M GOING TO THE GATE. ANYONE IS WELCOME TO COME WITH ME AND SEE IF THEY CAN LEND A HAND.
NO JUDGMENT, SO SIT THIS OUT IF YOU'RE NOT UP TO IT.
THIS IS NOT YOUR FIGHT, BUT WE WOULD OF COURSE WELCOME THE HELP, MY FRIEND.
WELL, IT'S NOT LIKE THEY'RE GONNA BE REAL DISCRIMINATING ON WHO THEY KILL, EV.

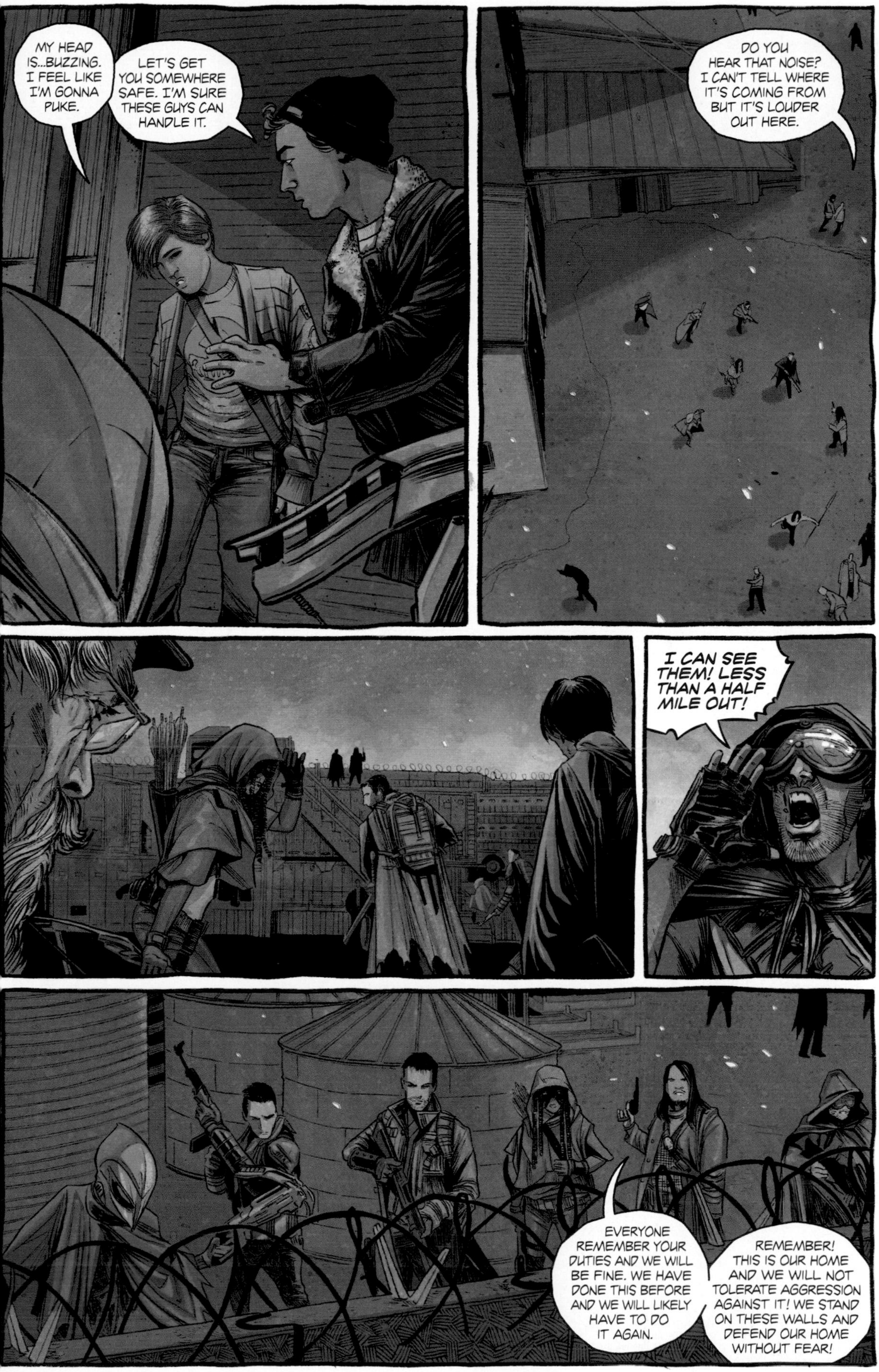
MY HEAD IS...BUZZING. I FEEL LIKE I'M GONNA PUKE.
LET'S GET YOU SOMEWHERE SAFE. I'M SURE THESE GUYS CAN HANDLE IT.
DO YOU HEAR THAT NOISE? I CAN'T TELL WHERE IT'S COMING FROM BUT IT'S LOUDER OUT HERE.
I CAN SEE THEM! LESS THAN A HALF MILE OUT!
EVERYONE REMEMBER YOUR DUTIES AND WE WILL BE FINE. WE HAVE DONE THIS BEFORE AND WE WILL LIKELY HAVE TO DO IT AGAIN.
REMEMBER! THIS IS OUR HOME AND WE WILL NOT TOLERATE AGGRESSION AGAINST IT! WE STAND ON THESE WALLS AND DEFEND OUR HOME WITHOUT FEAR!

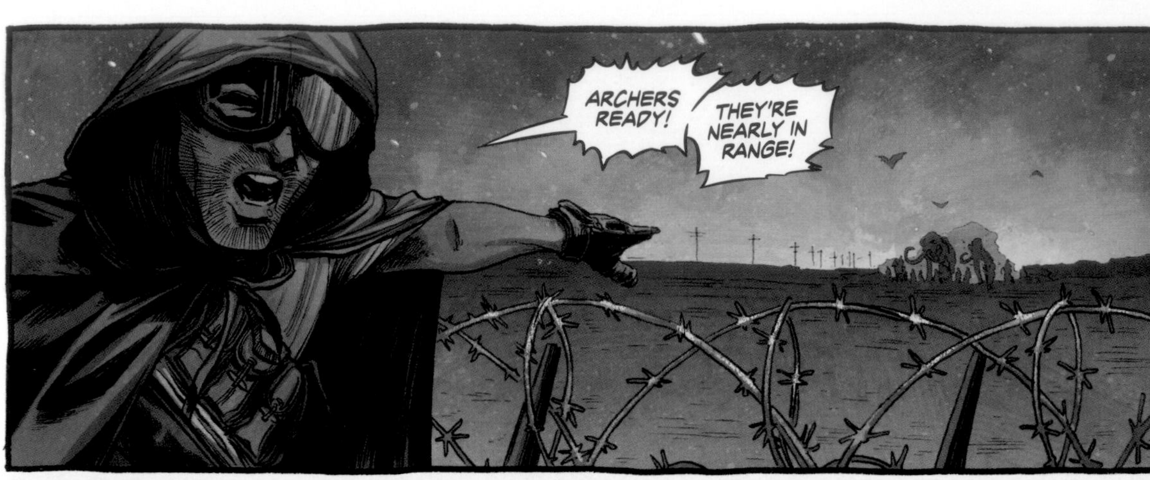
ARCHERS READY!
THEY'RE NEARLY IN RANGE!
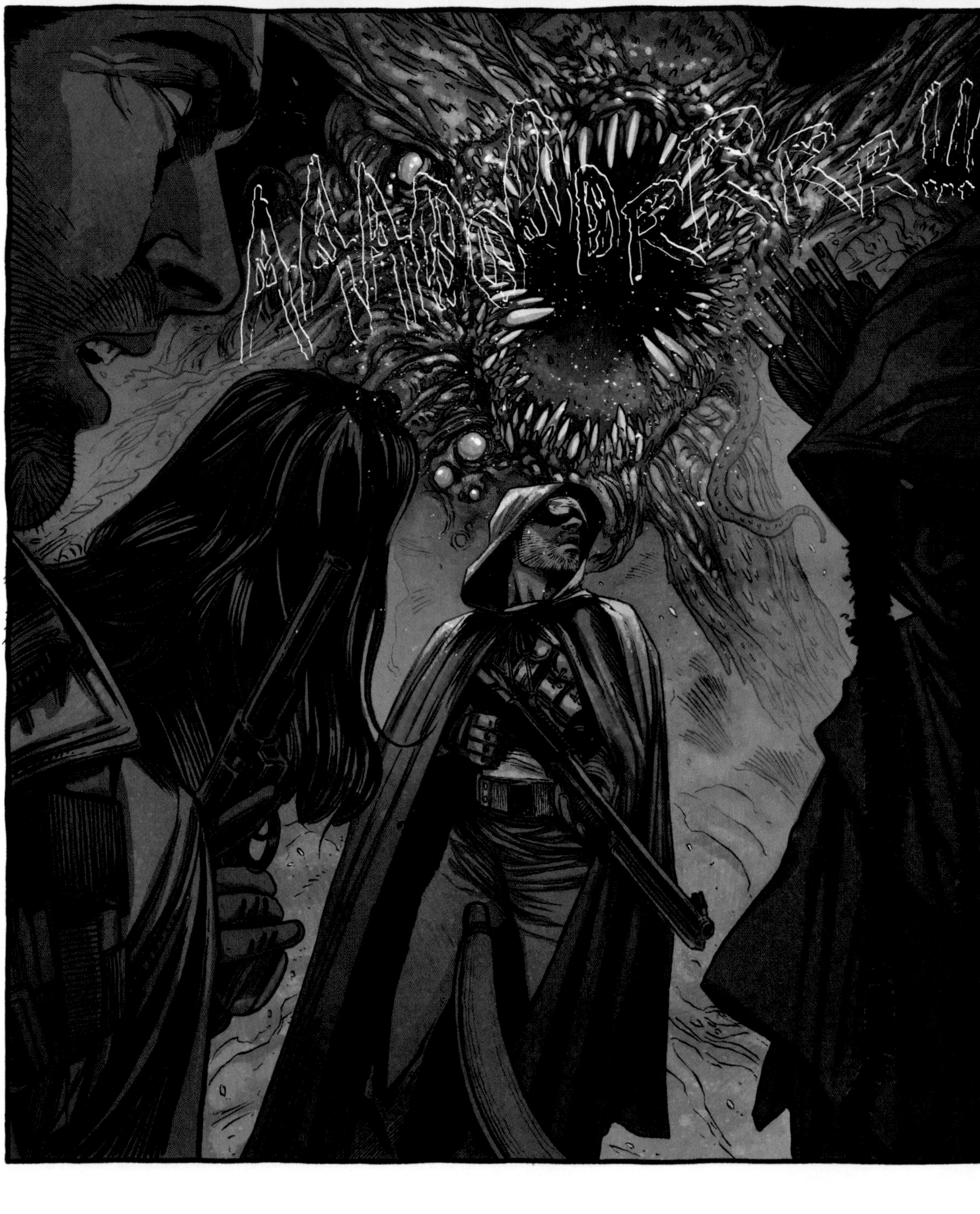

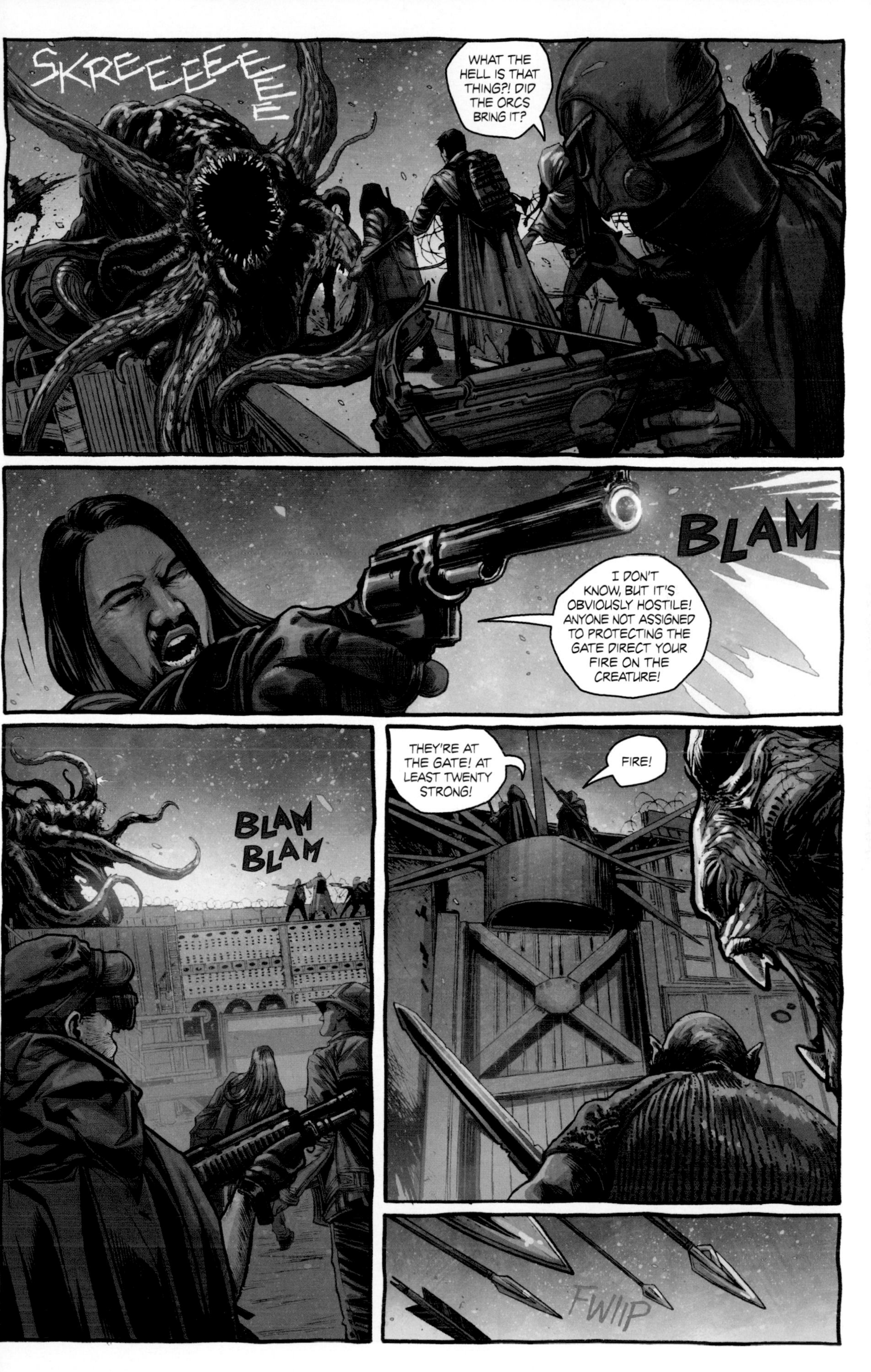
SKREEEEEEEE
WHAT THE HELL IS THAT THING?! DID THE ORCS BRING IT?
BLAM
I DON'T KNOW, BUT IT'S OBVIOUSLY HOSTILE! ANYONE NOT ASSIGNED TO PROTECTING THE GATE DIRECT YOUR FIRE ON THE CREATURE!
BLAM BLAM
THEY'RE AT THE GATE! AT LEAST TWENTY STRONG!
FIRE!
FWIIP

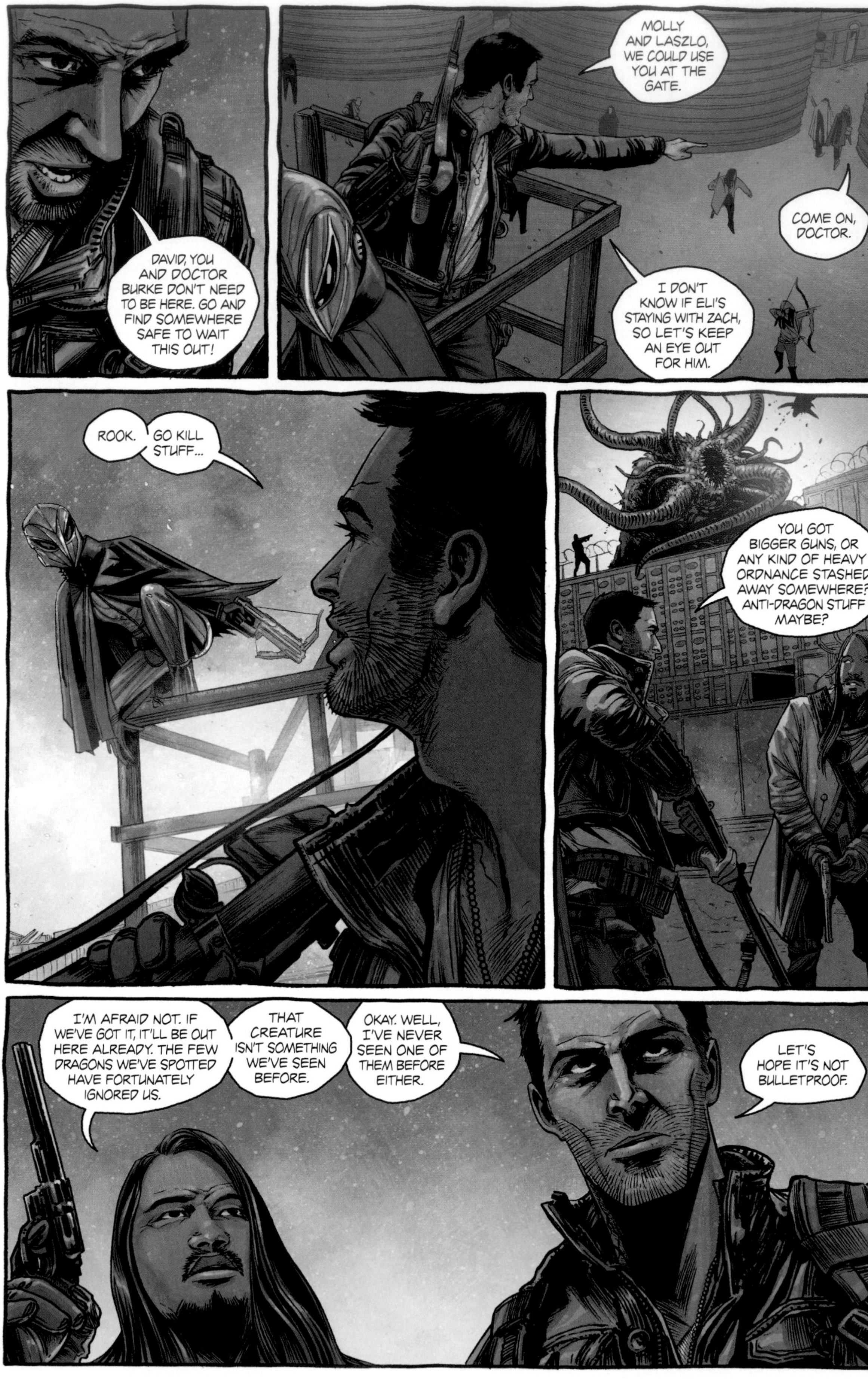
DAVID, YOU AND DOCTOR BURKE DON'T NEED TO BE HERE. GO AND FIND SOMEWHERE SAFE TO WAIT THIS OUT!
MOLLY AND LASZLO, WE COULD USE YOU AT THE GATE.
I DON'T KNOW IF ELI'S STAYING WITH ZACH, SO LET'S KEEP AN EYE OUT FOR HIM.
COME ON, DOCTOR.
ROOK.
GO KILL STUFF...
YOU GOT BIGGER GUNS, OR ANY KIND OF HEAVY ORDNANCE STASHED AWAY SOMEWHERE? ANTI-DRAGON STUFF MAYBE?
I'M AFRAID NOT. IF WE'VE GOT IT, IT'LL BE OUT HERE ALREADY. THE FEW DRAGONS WE'VE SPOTTED HAVE FORTUNATELY IGNORED US.
THAT CREATURE ISN'T SOMETHING WE'VE SEEN BEFORE.
OKAY. WELL, I'VE NEVER SEEN ONE OF THEM BEFORE EITHER.
LET'S HOPE IT'S NOT BULLETPROOF.

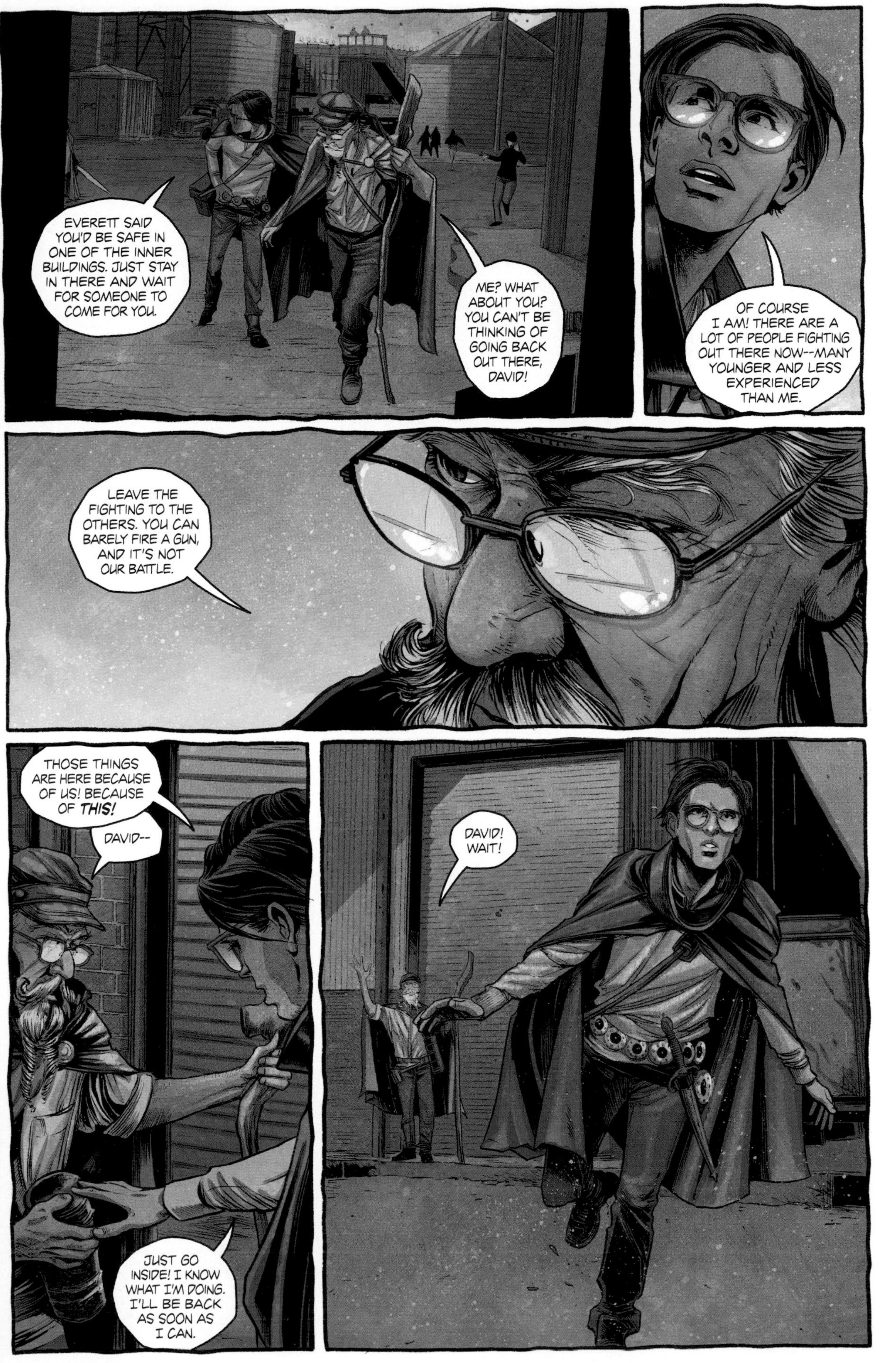
EVERETT SAID YOU'D BE SAFE IN ONE OF THE INNER BUILDINGS. JUST STAY IN THERE AND WAIT FOR SOMEONE TO COME FOR YOU.
ME? WHAT ABOUT YOU? YOU CAN'T BE THINKING OF GOING BACK OUT THERE, DAVID!
OF COURSE I AM! THERE ARE A LOT OF PEOPLE FIGHTING OUT THERE NOW--MANY YOUNGER AND LESS EXPERIENCED THAN ME.
LEAVE THE FIGHTING TO THE OTHERS. YOU CAN BARELY FIRE A GUN, AND IT'S NOT OUR BATTLE.
THOSE THINGS ARE HERE BECAUSE OF US! BECAUSE OF **THIS!**
DAVID--
JUST GO INSIDE! I KNOW WHAT I'M DOING. I'LL BE BACK AS SOON AS I CAN.
DAVID! WAIT!

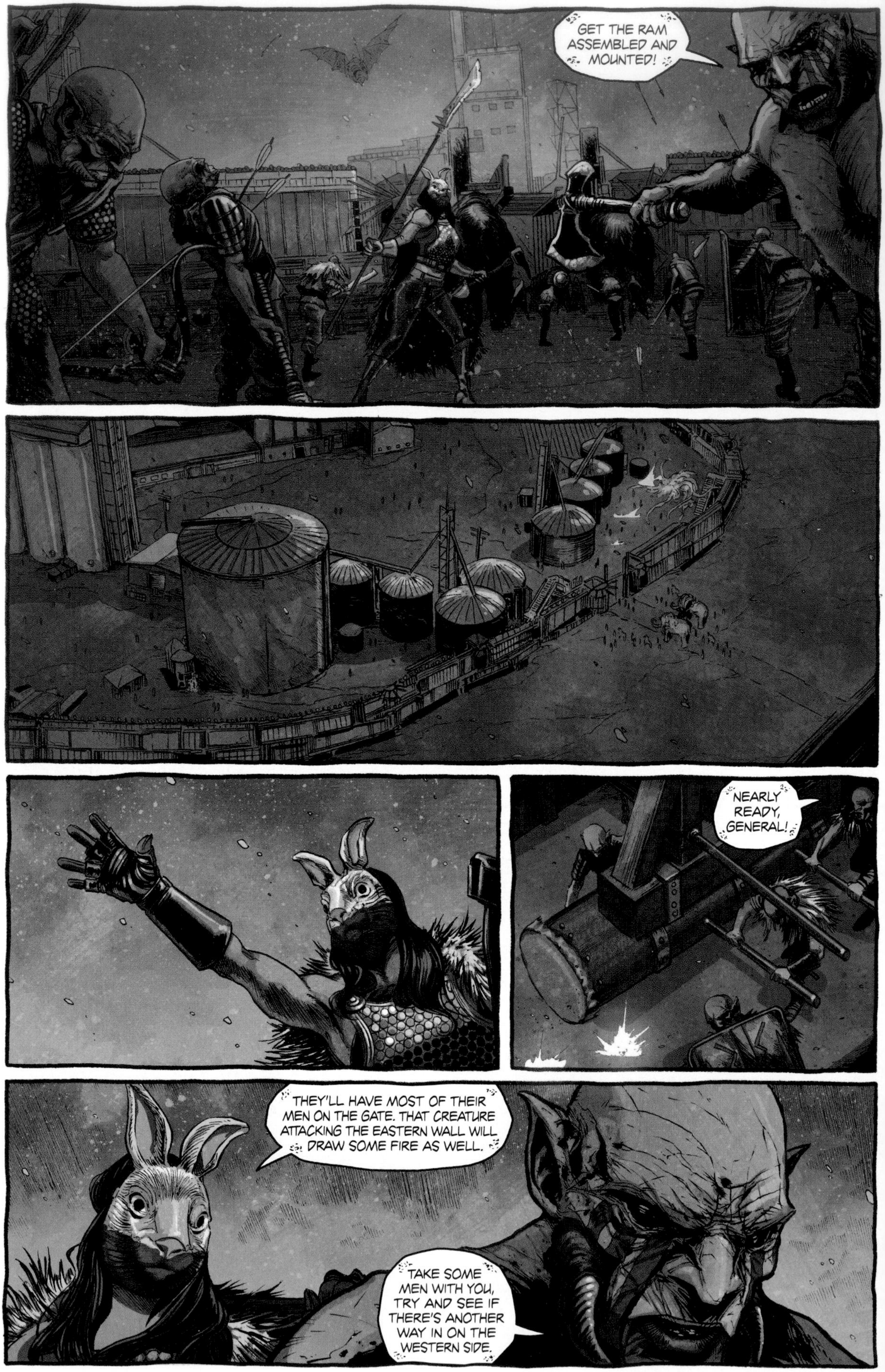
GET THE RAM ASSEMBLED AND MOUNTED!
NEARLY READY, GENERAL!
THEY'LL HAVE MOST OF THEIR MEN ON THE GATE. THAT CREATURE ATTACKING THE EASTERN WALL WILL DRAW SOME FIRE AS WELL.
TAKE SOME MEN WITH YOU, TRY AND SEE IF THERE'S ANOTHER WAY IN ON THE WESTERN SIDE.

ZACH IS SAFE INSIDE WITH SOME OF YOUR PEOPLE, BUT I DIDN'T WANT TO SIT AROUND WHEN ALL THE ACTION WAS OUT HERE. HOW SECURE IS THIS GATE?

THE GATE IS STURDY, BUT WE'VE GOT TO RUN THEM OFF. IT WON'T HOLD FOREVER.

THEY'VE GOT SOME KIND OF BATTERING RAM OUT THERE. WE NEED TO FOCUS ON THE ONES PUSHING IT. DON'T LET THEM GET A GOOD RUN AT IT.

THOSE MAMMOTHS ARE ARMORED, BUT IF WE CAN PUT ONE OF THEM DOWN THE RAM'S USELESS.

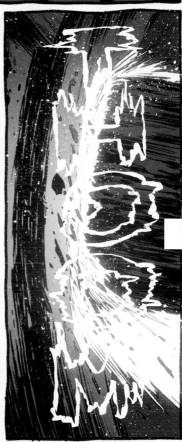

SHIT! WE'D BETTER DO IT QUICK. I DON'T KNOW HOW MANY MORE HITS LIKE THAT IT CAN TAKE!

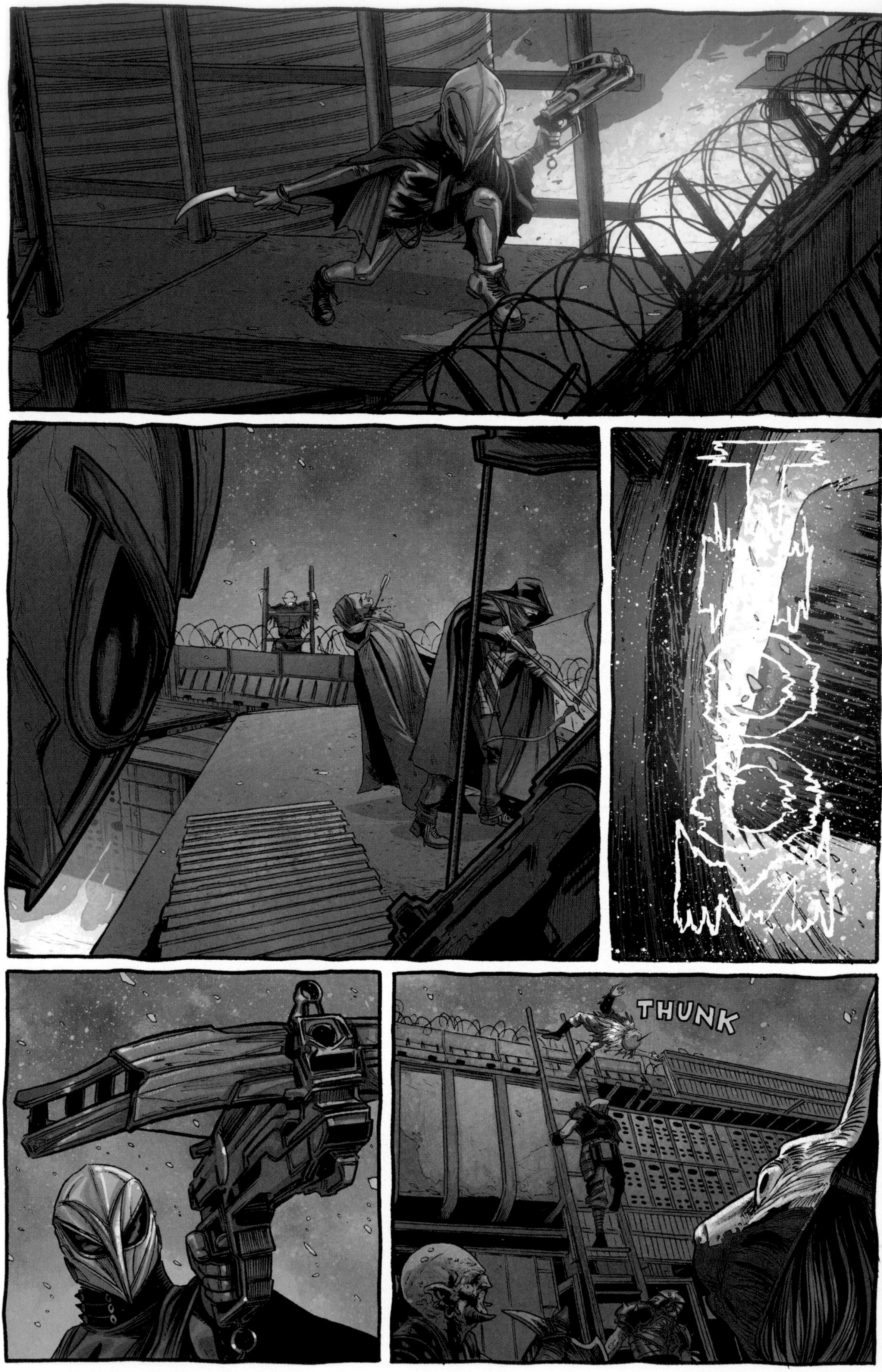
THOOM
THUNK

SKREEEE

DIE, YOU UGLY FUCKING--

SPLUCH

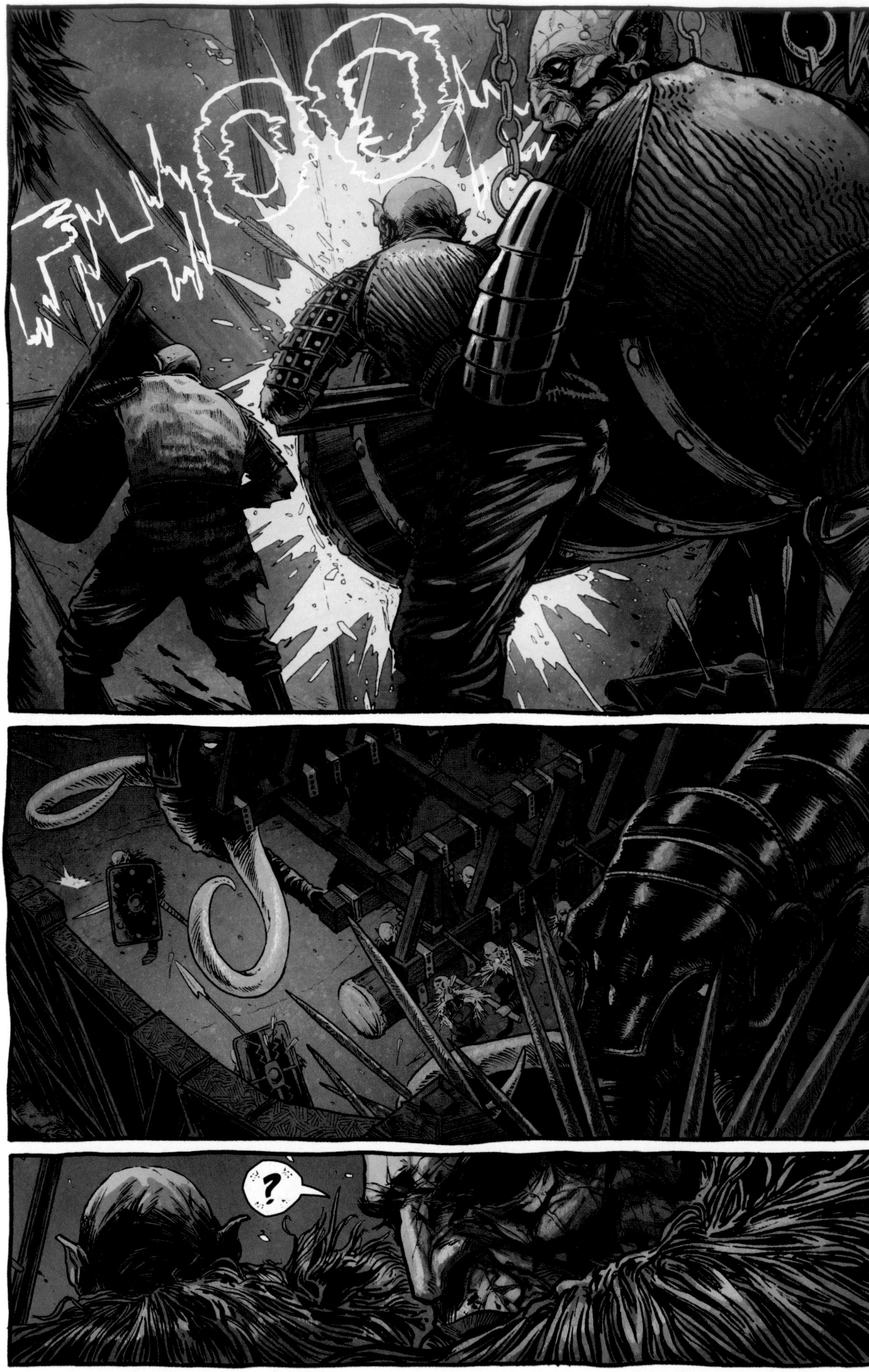
THWOOM
?

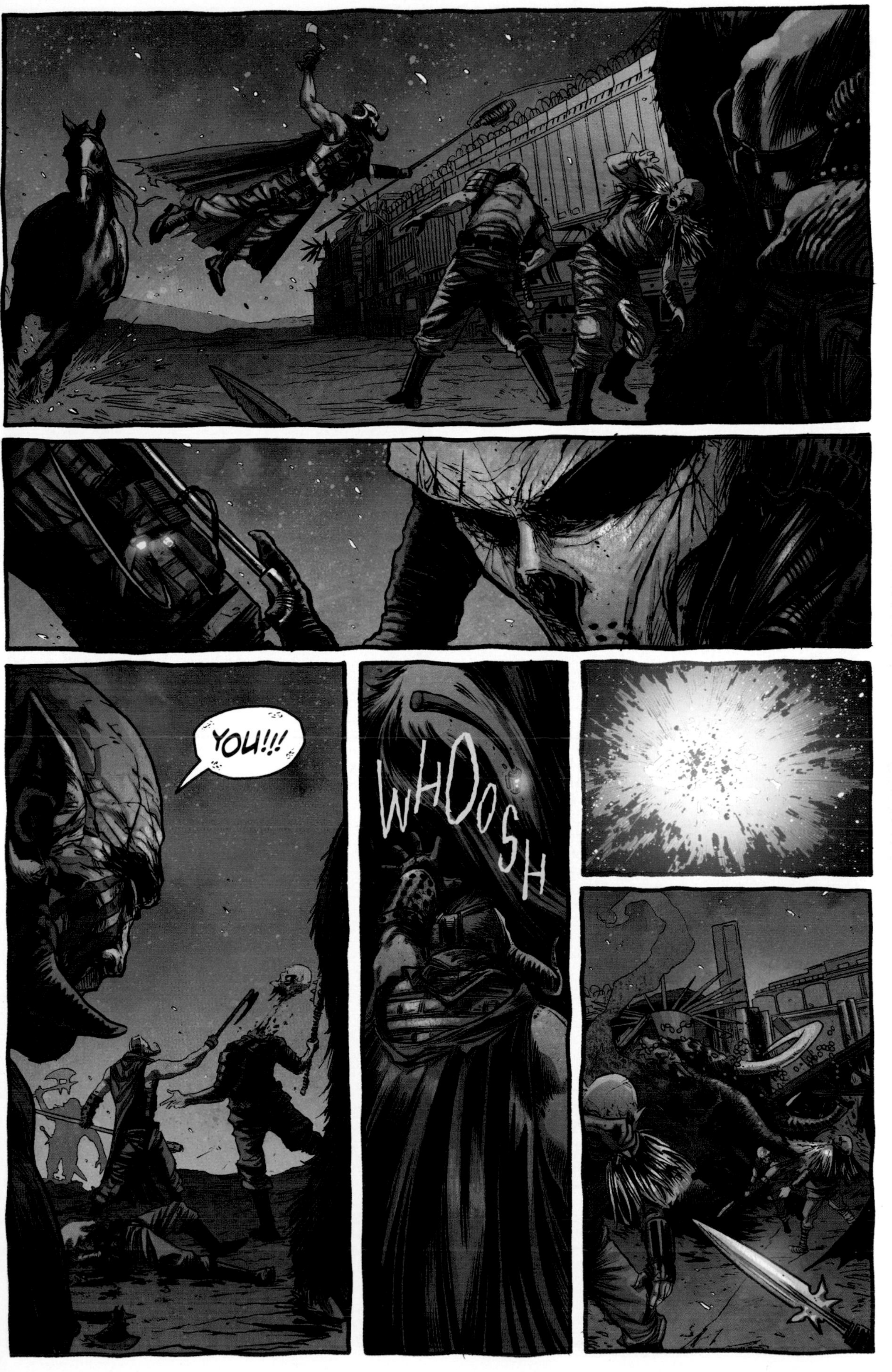
YOU!!!
WHOOSH

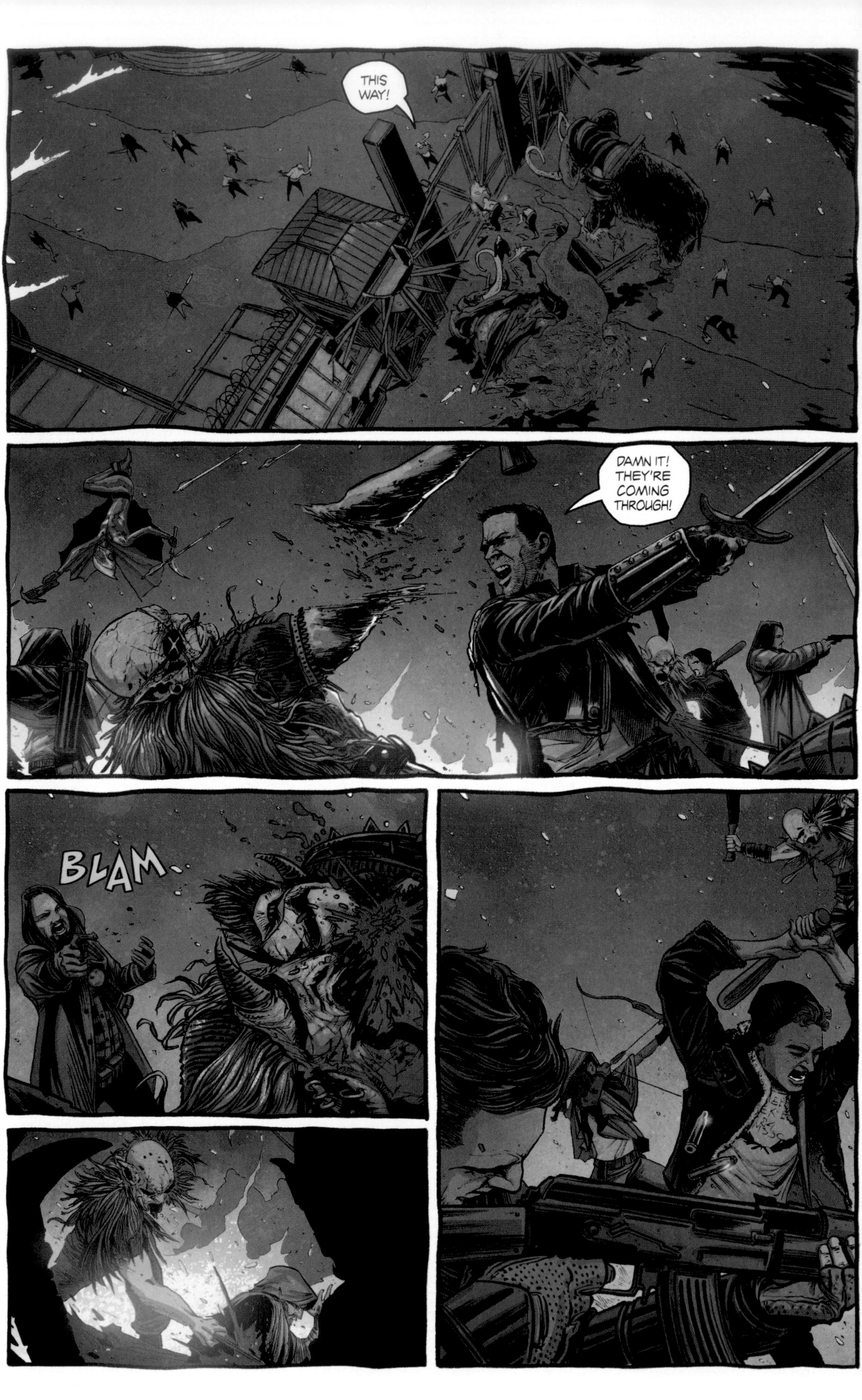
THIS WAY!
DAMN IT! THEY'RE COMING THROUGH!
BLAM

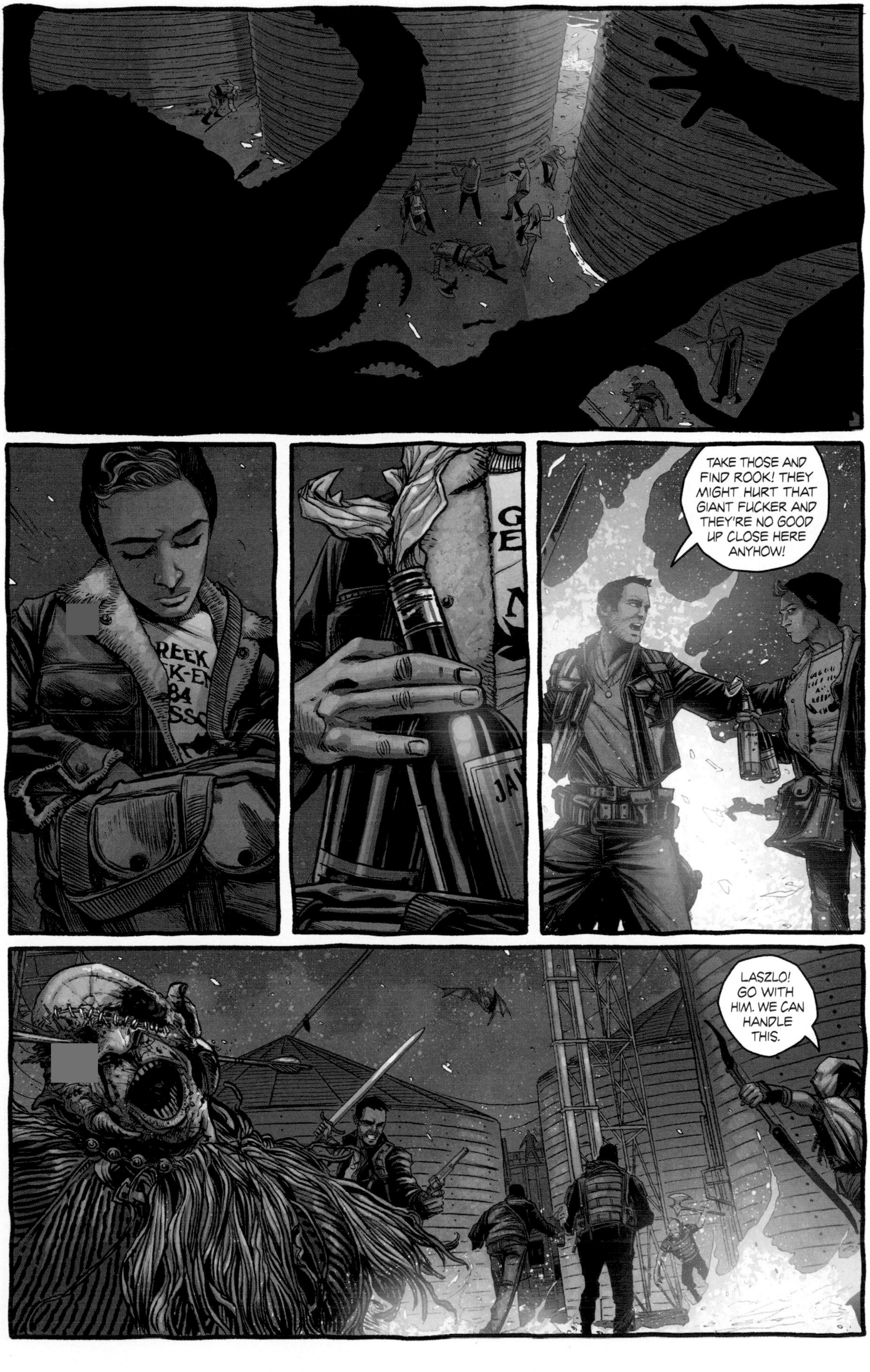
TAKE THOSE AND FIND ROOK! THEY MIGHT HURT THAT GIANT FUCKER AND THEY'RE NO GOOD UP CLOSE HERE ANYHOW!
LASZLO! GO WITH HIM. WE CAN HANDLE THIS.

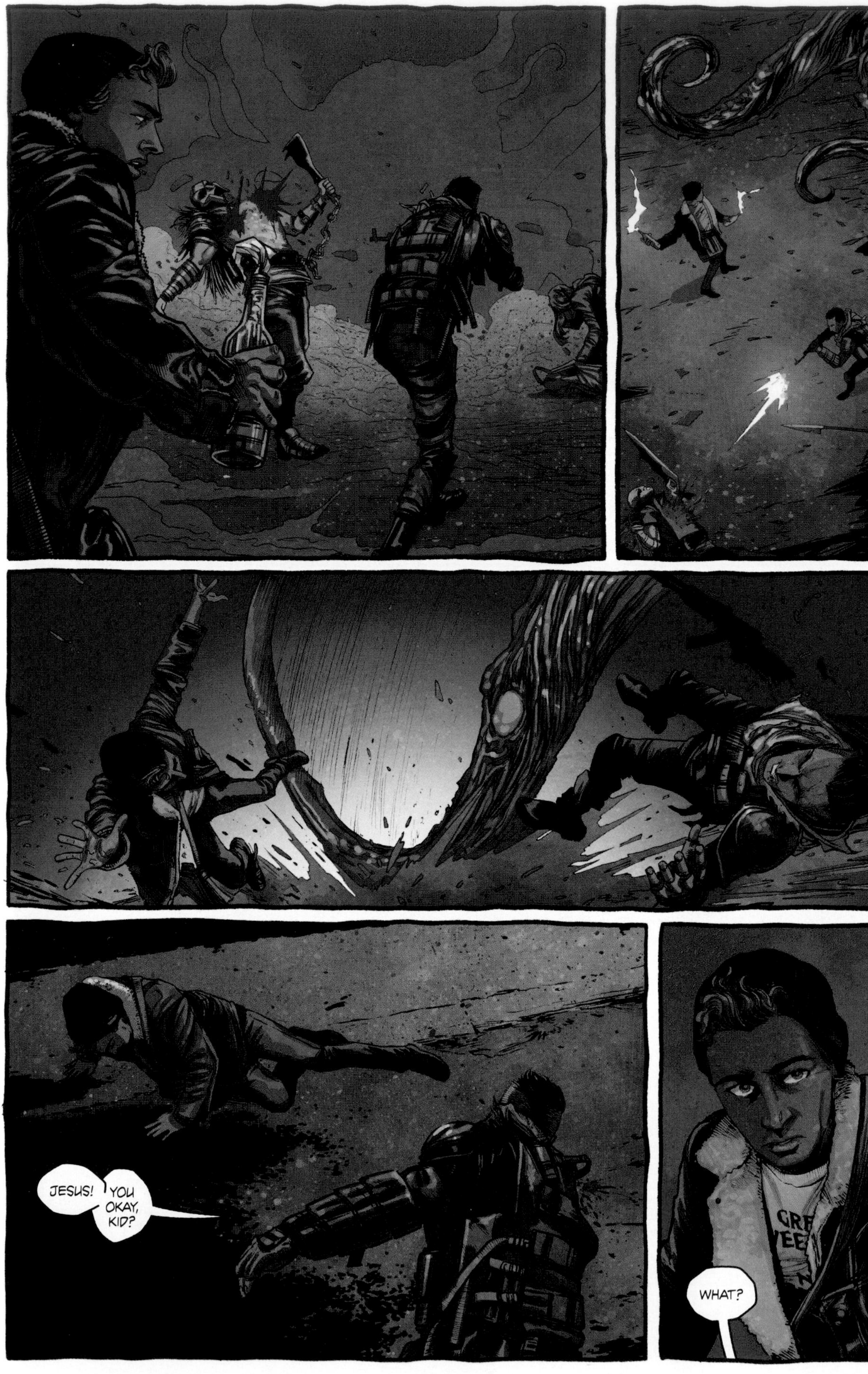
JESUS!
YOU OKAY, KID?
WHAT?

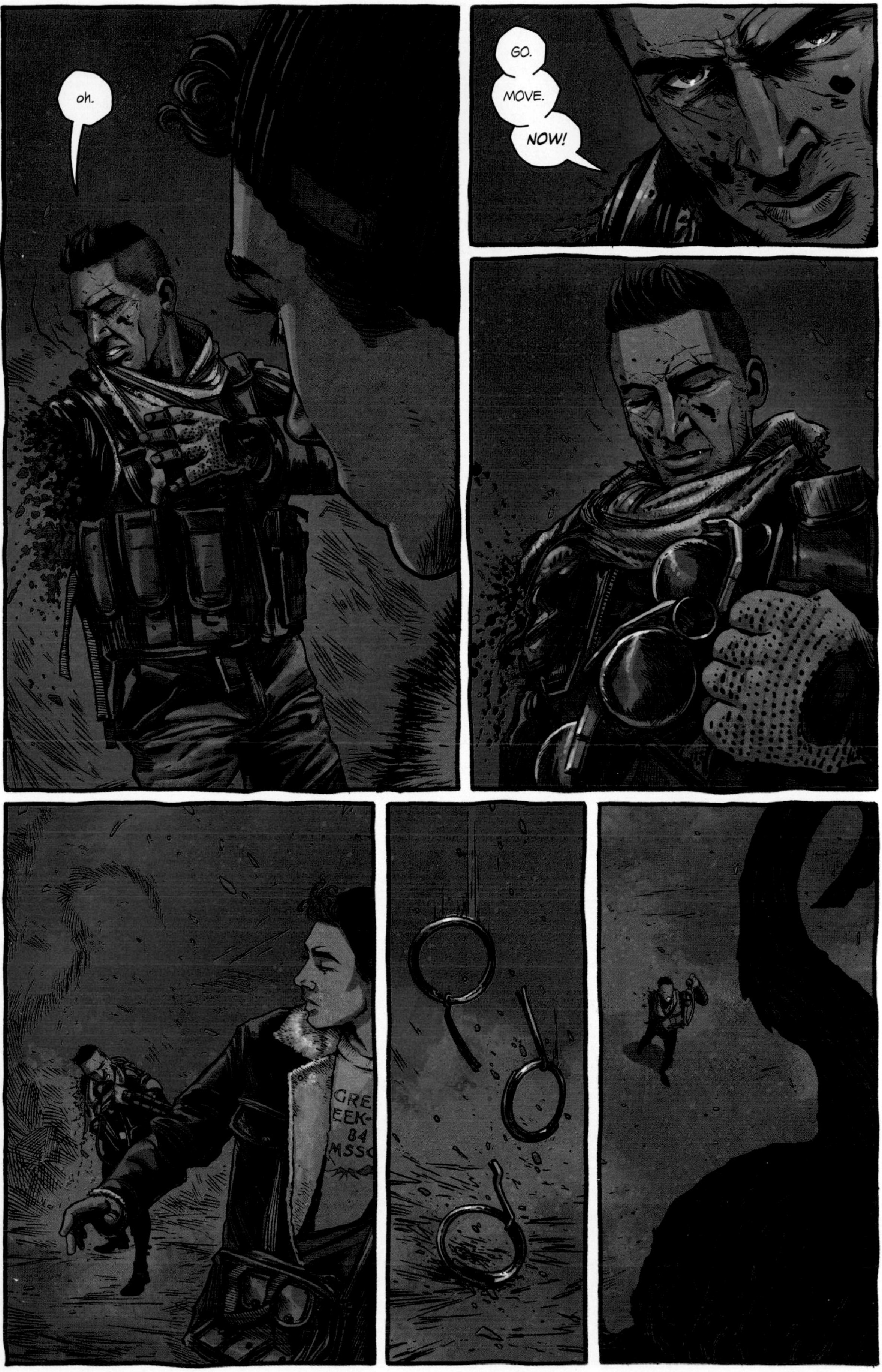
oh.
GO.
MOVE.
NOW!

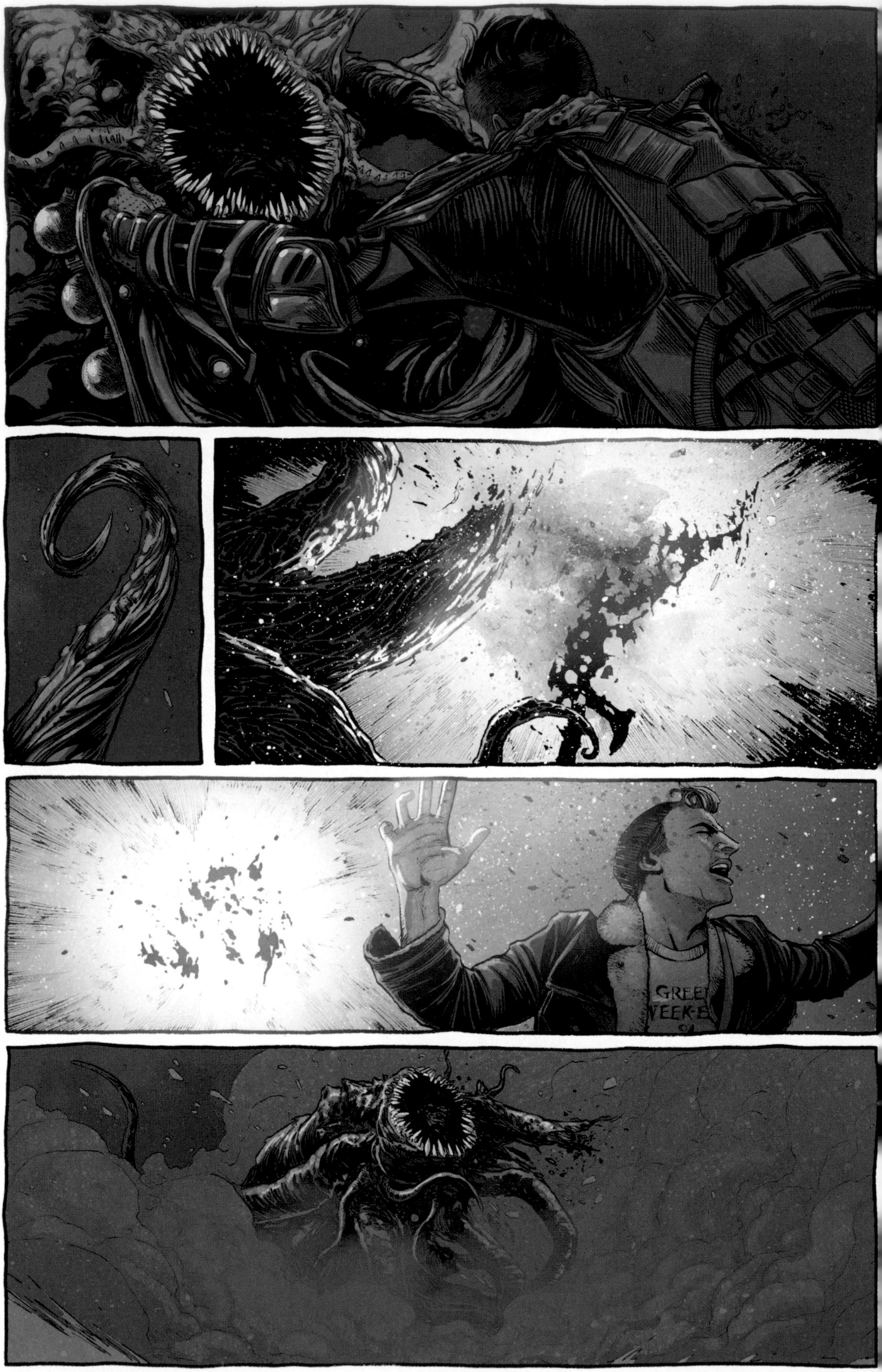

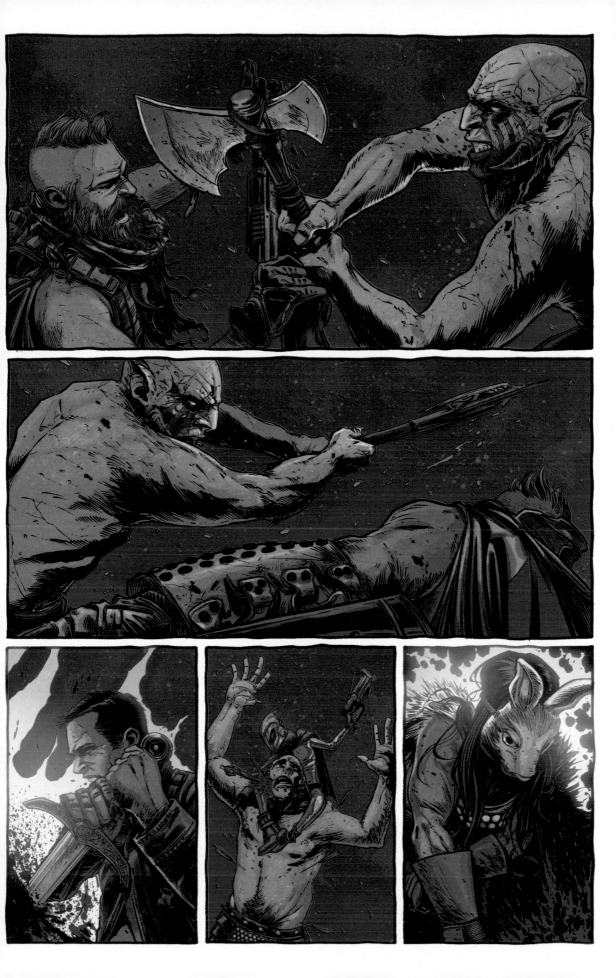

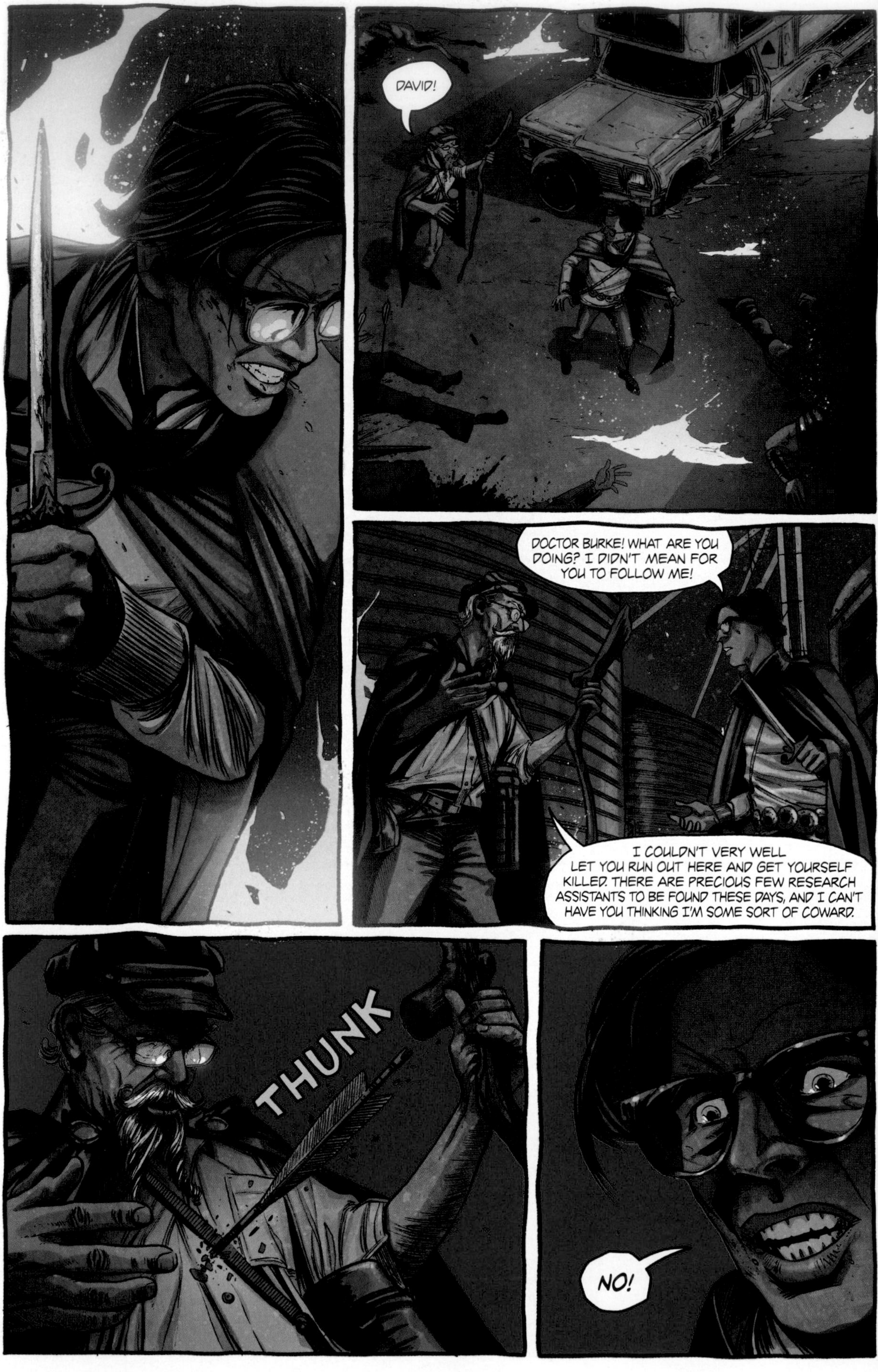
DAVID!
DOCTOR BURKE! WHAT ARE YOU DOING? I DIDN'T MEAN FOR YOU TO FOLLOW ME!
I COULDN'T VERY WELL LET YOU RUN OUT HERE AND GET YOURSELF KILLED. THERE ARE PRECIOUS FEW RESEARCH ASSISTANTS TO BE FOUND THESE DAYS, AND I CAN'T HAVE YOU THINKING I'M SOME SORT OF COWARD.
THUNK
NO!

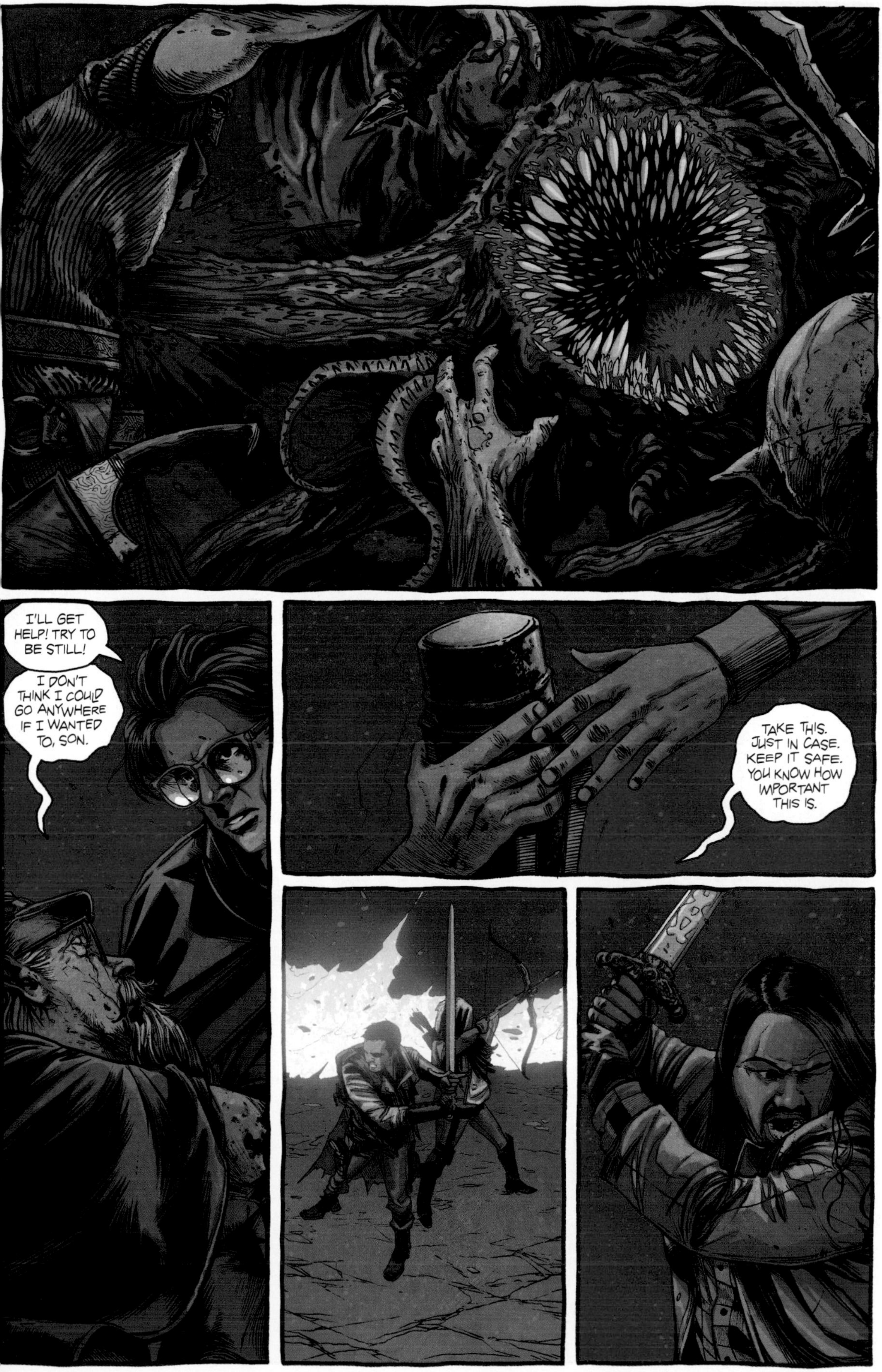
I'LL GET HELP! TRY TO BE STILL!
I DON'T THINK I COULD GO ANYWHERE IF I WANTED TO, SON.
TAKE THIS. JUST IN CASE. KEEP IT SAFE. YOU KNOW HOW IMPORTANT THIS IS.

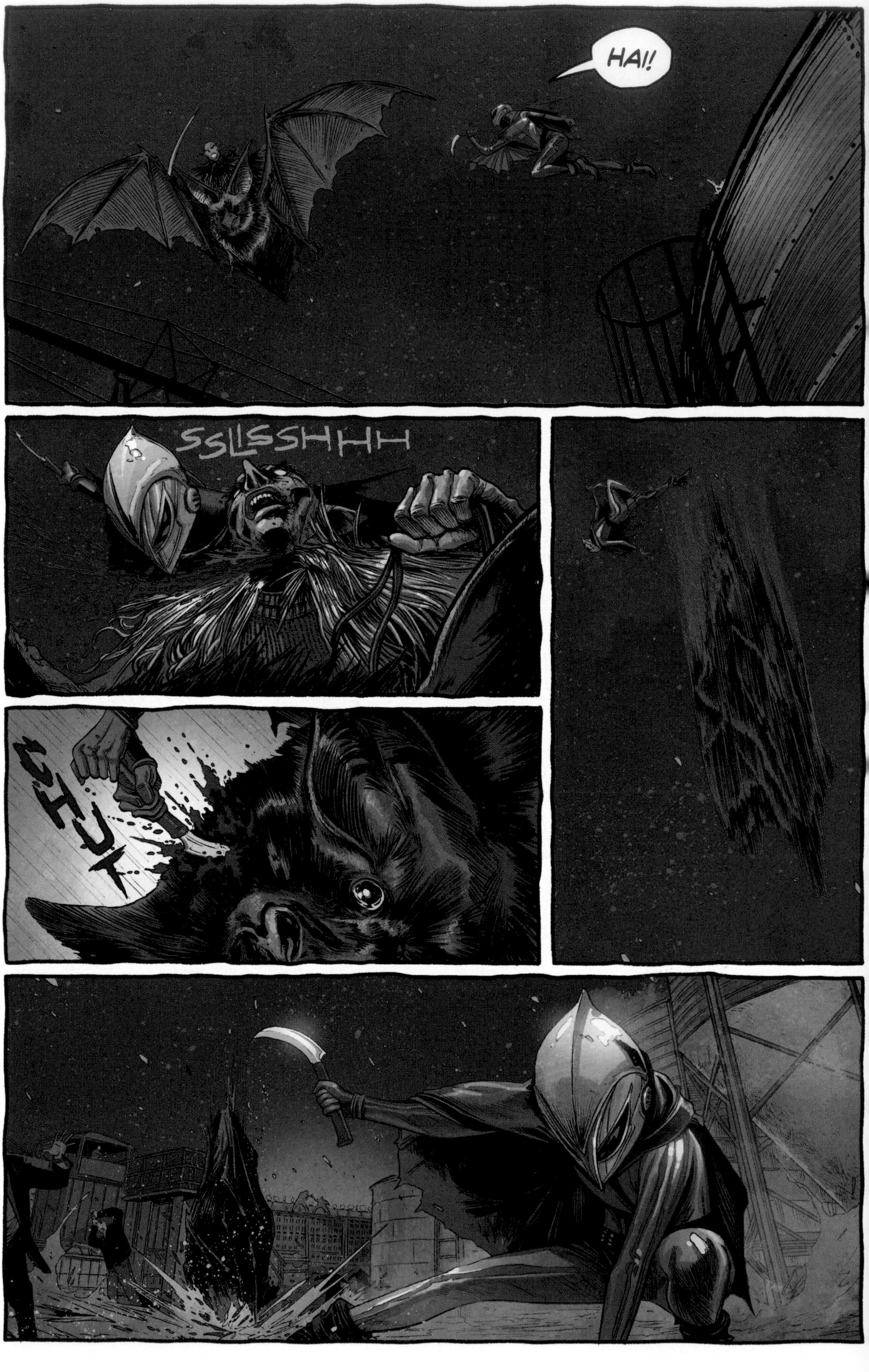
HAI!
SSLISSHHH
CHUK

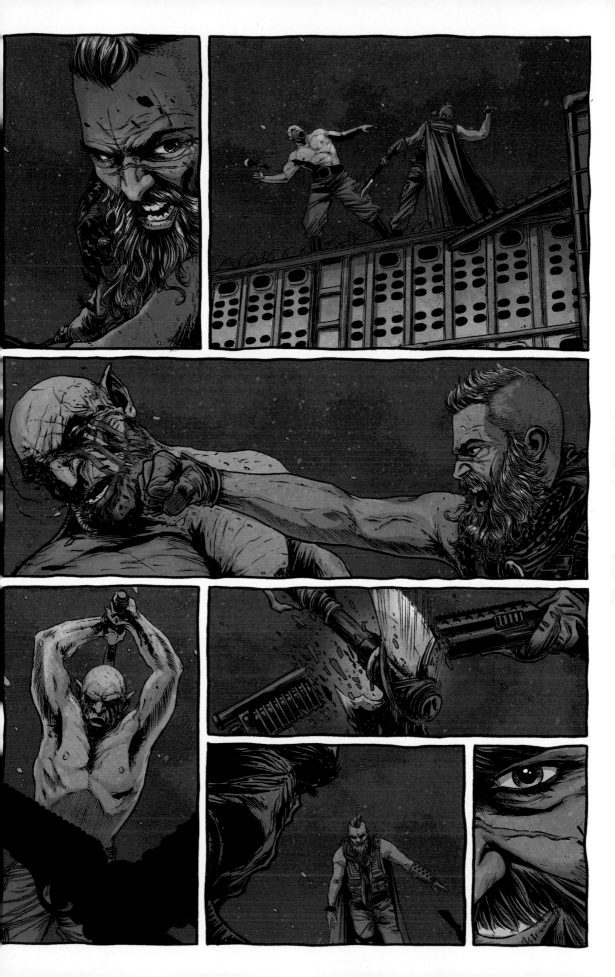

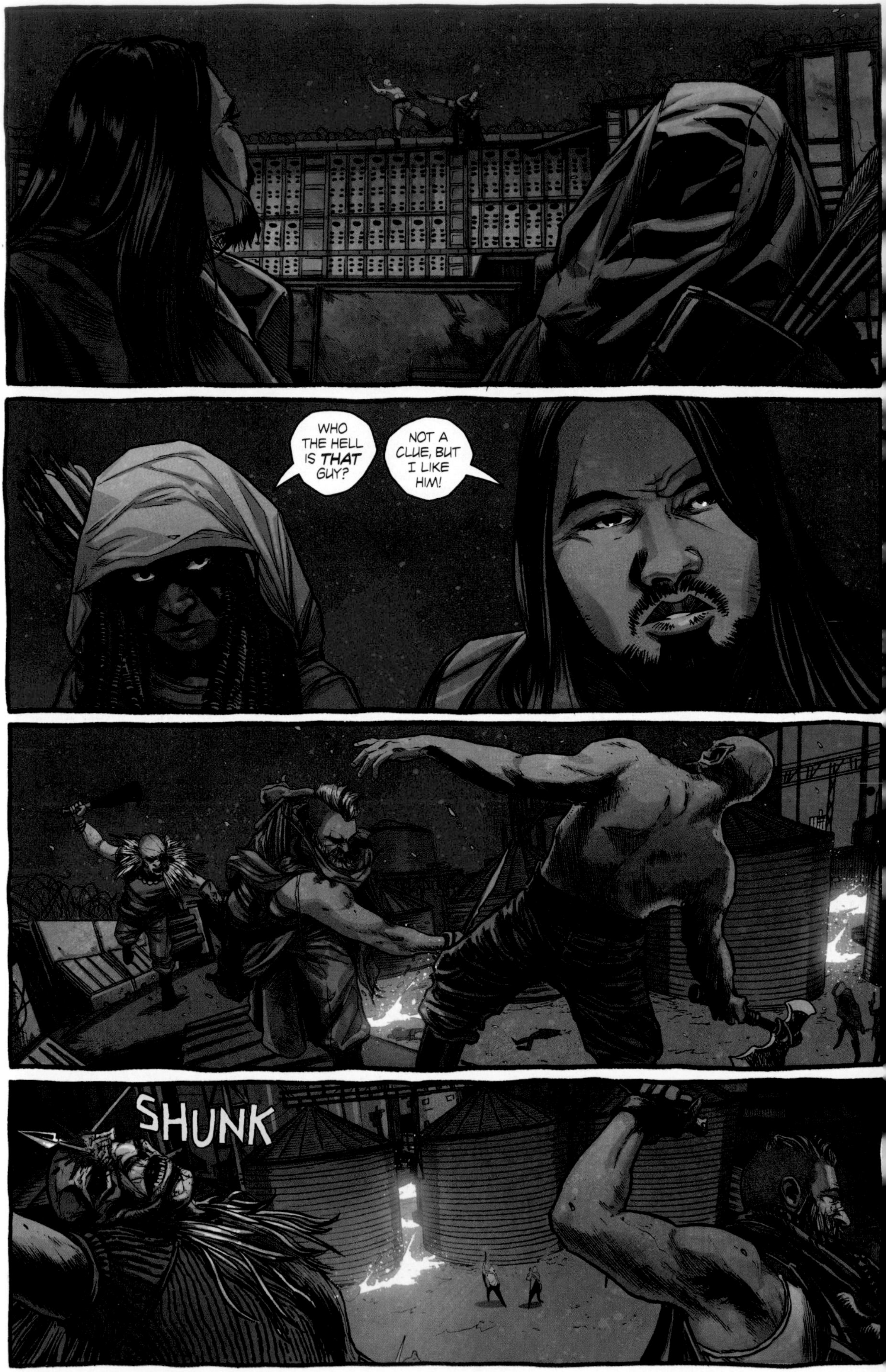
WHO THE HELL IS **THAT** GUY?
NOT A CLUE, BUT I LIKE HIM!
SHUNK

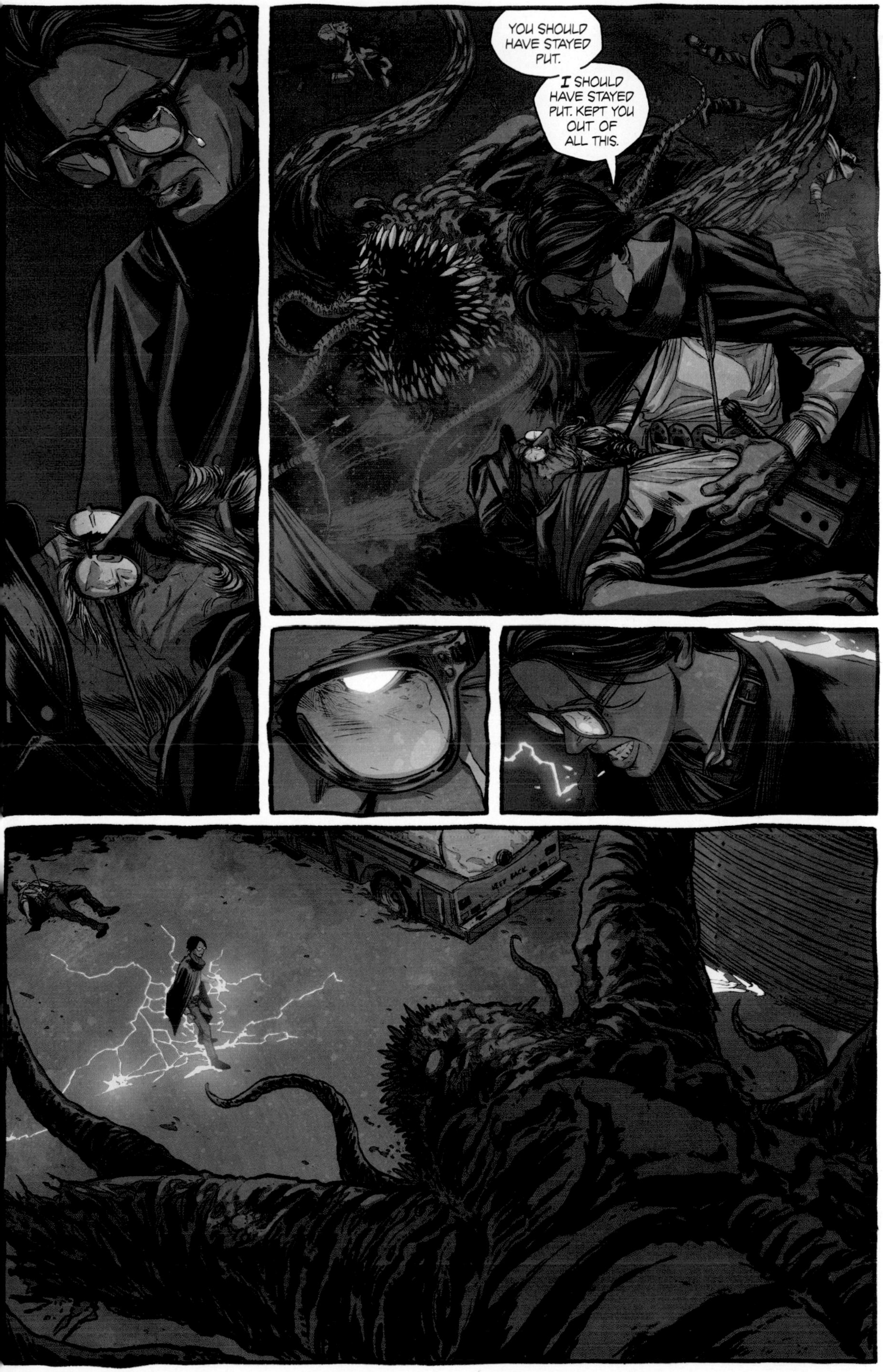
YOU SHOULD HAVE STAYED PUT.
I SHOULD HAVE STAYED PUT. KEPT YOU OUT OF ALL THIS.

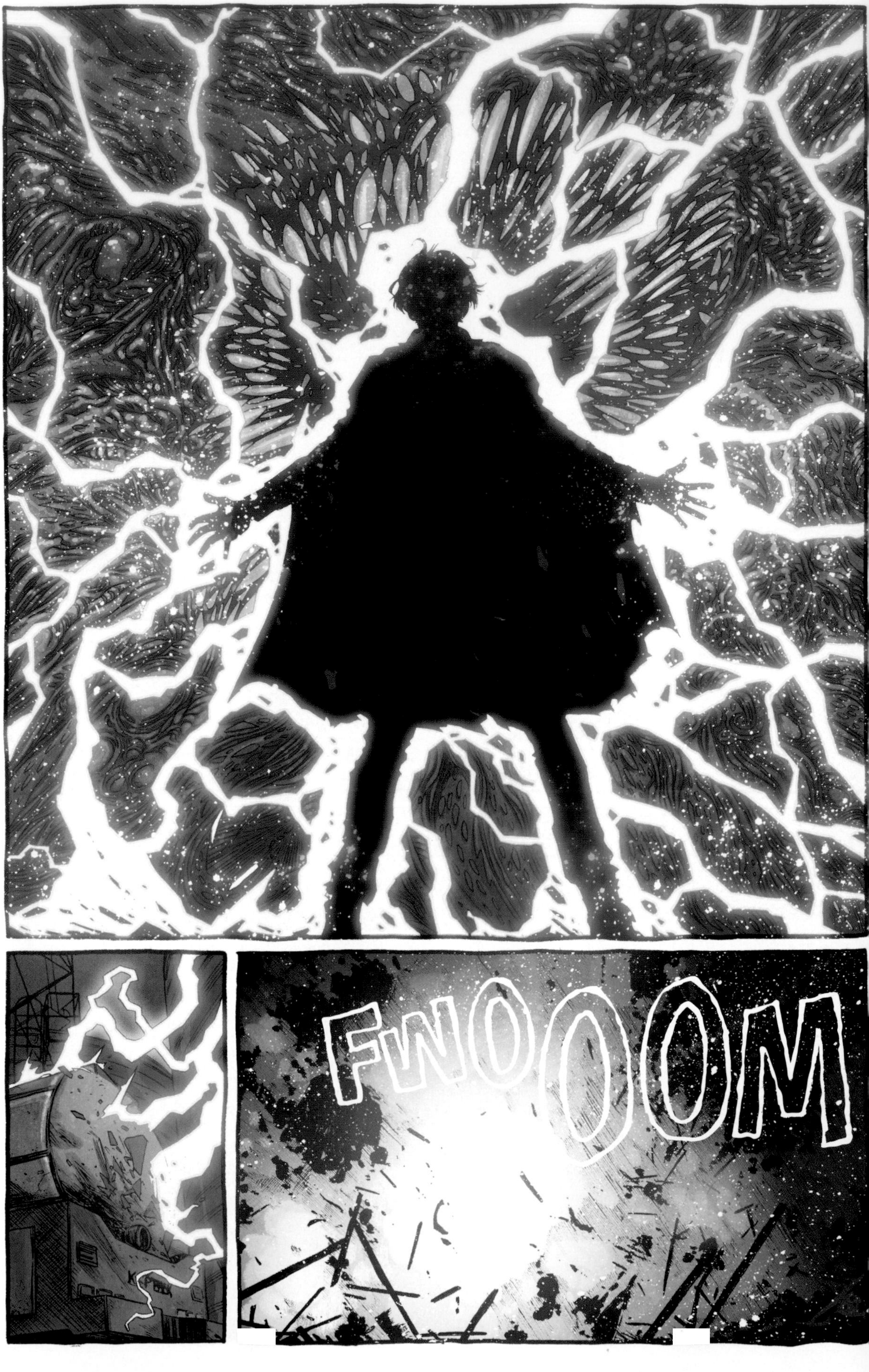
FWOOOM

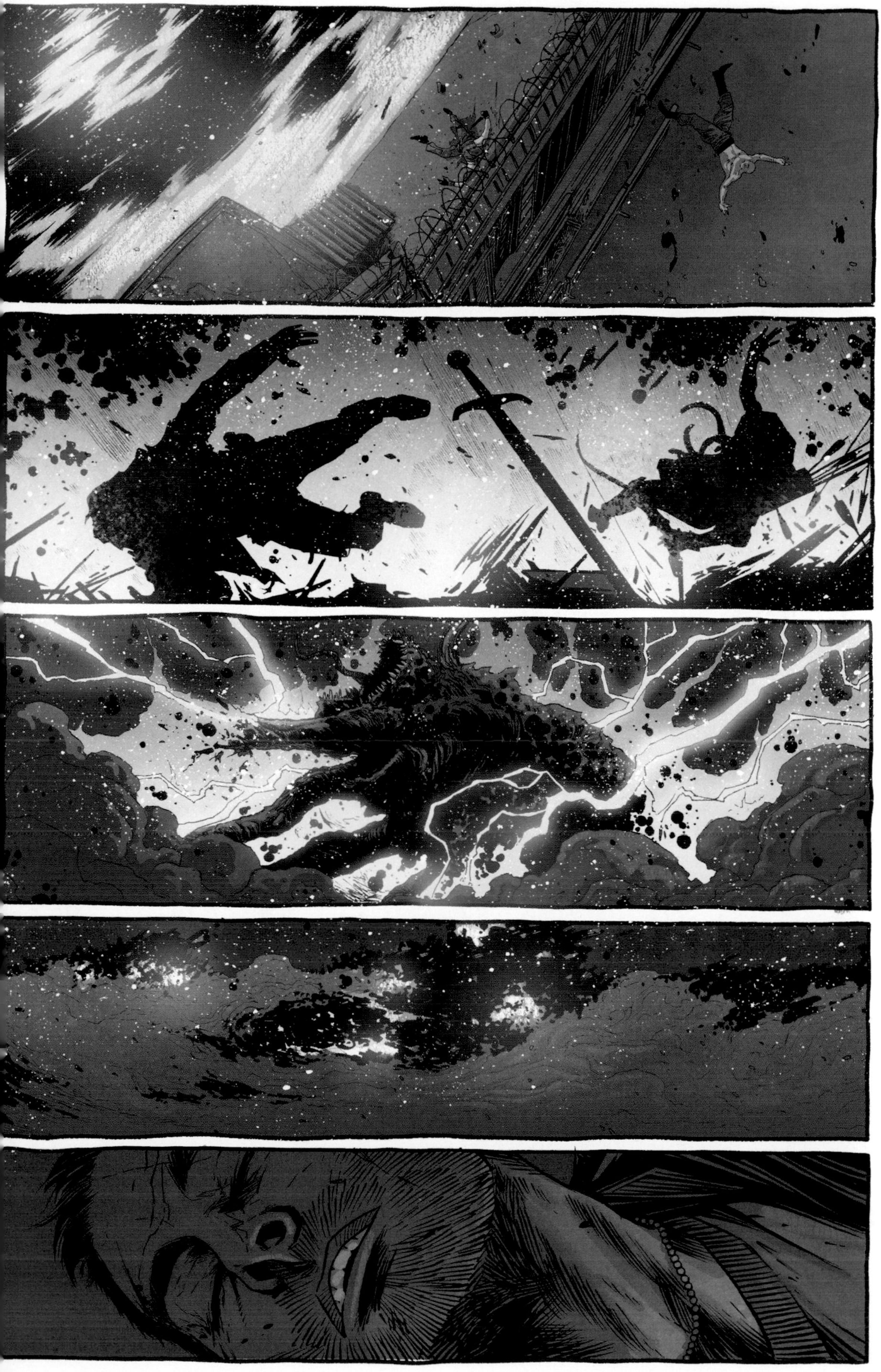

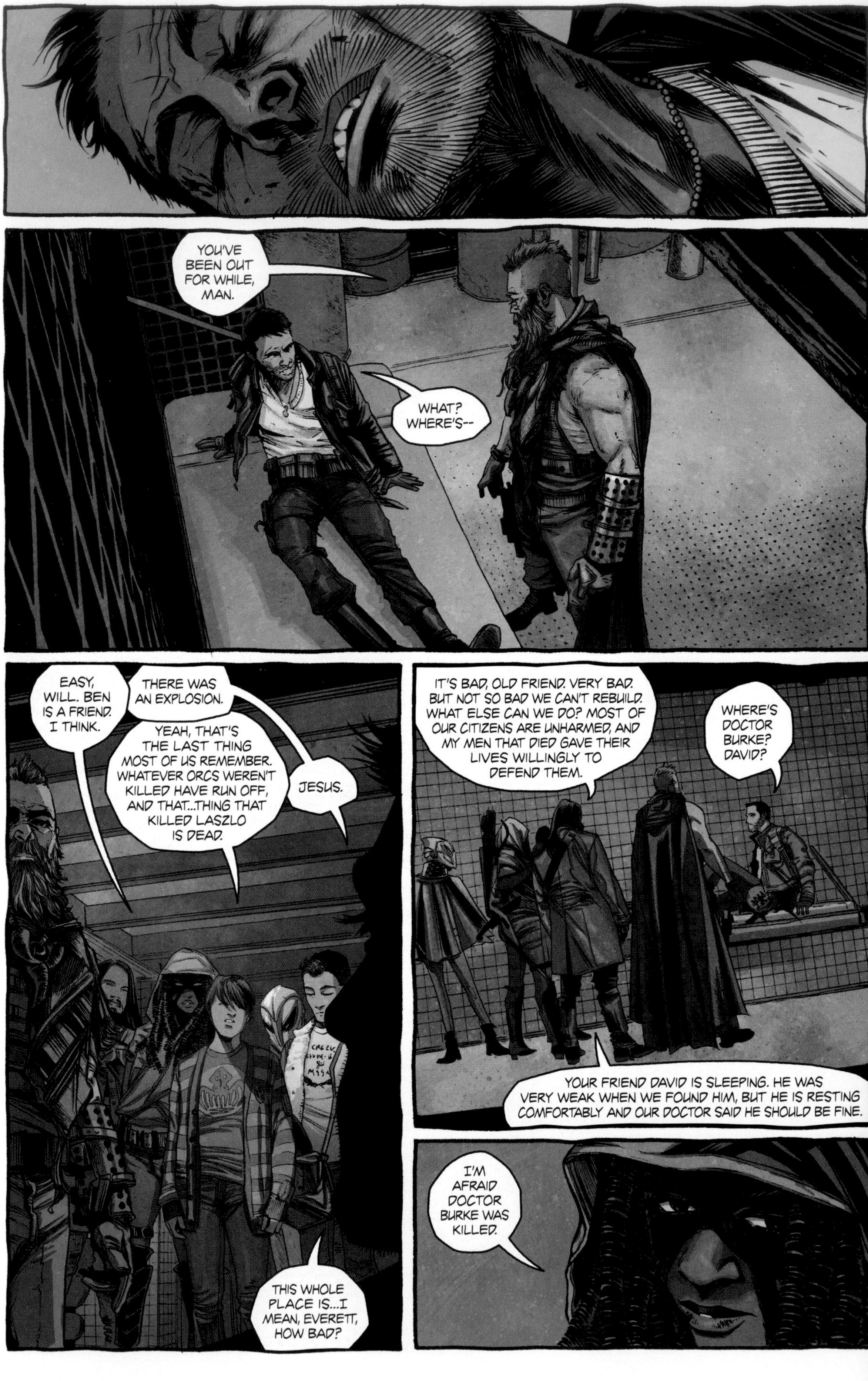
YOU'VE BEEN OUT FOR WHILE, MAN.
WHAT? WHERE'S--
EASY, WILL. BEN IS A FRIEND. I THINK.
THERE WAS AN EXPLOSION.
YEAH, THAT'S THE LAST THING MOST OF US REMEMBER. WHATEVER ORCS WEREN'T KILLED HAVE RUN OFF, AND THAT...THING THAT KILLED LASZLO IS DEAD.
JESUS.
THIS WHOLE PLACE IS...I MEAN, EVERETT, HOW BAD?
IT'S BAD, OLD FRIEND. VERY BAD. BUT NOT SO BAD WE CAN'T REBUILD. WHAT ELSE CAN WE DO? MOST OF OUR CITIZENS ARE UNHARMED, AND MY MEN THAT DIED GAVE THEIR LIVES WILLINGLY TO DEFEND THEM.
WHERE'S DOCTOR BURKE? DAVID?
YOUR FRIEND DAVID IS SLEEPING. HE WAS VERY WEAK WHEN WE FOUND HIM, BUT HE IS RESTING COMFORTABLY AND OUR DOCTOR SAID HE SHOULD BE FINE.
I'M AFRAID DOCTOR BURKE WAS KILLED.

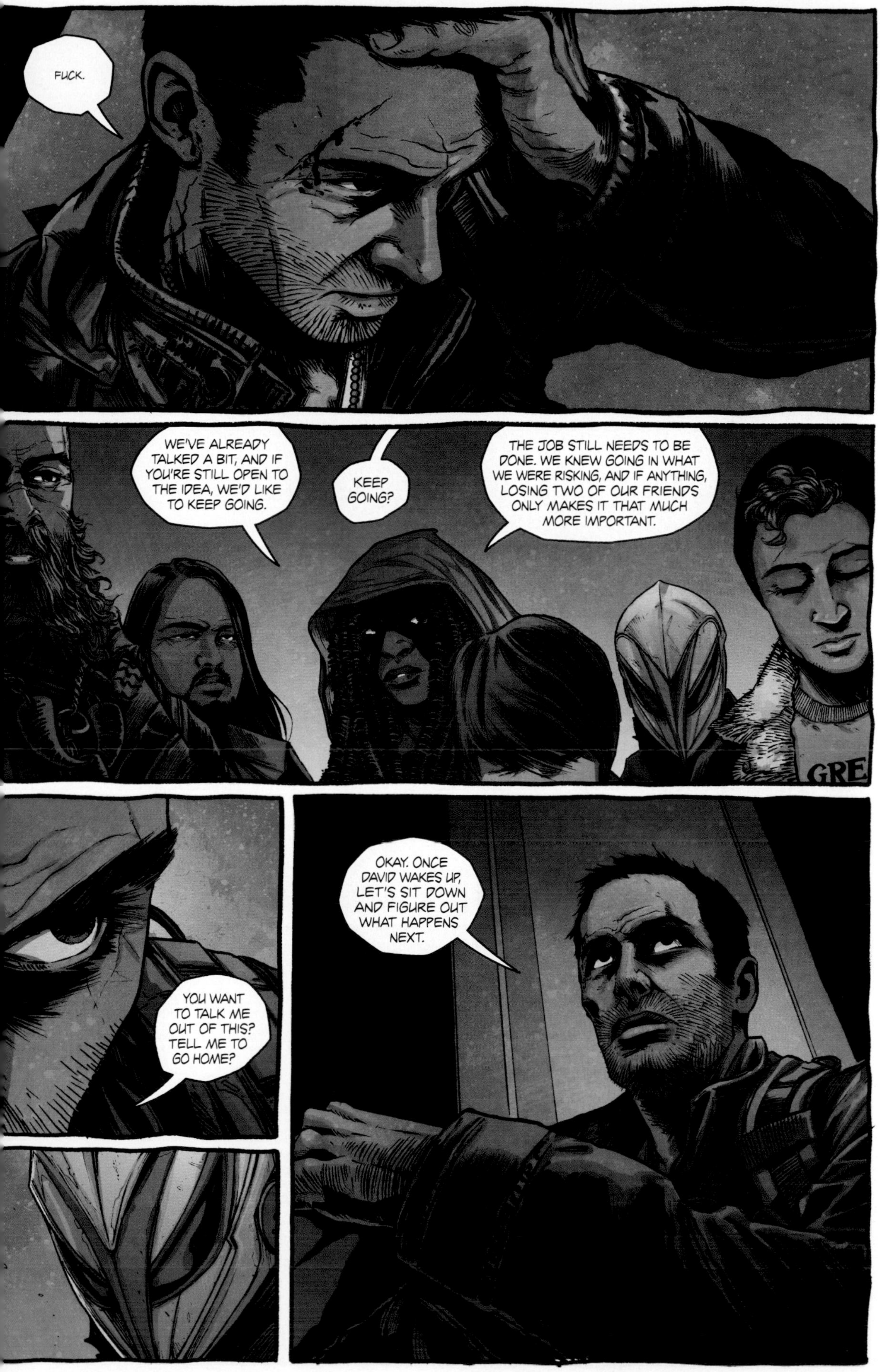
FUCK.
WE'VE ALREADY TALKED A BIT, AND IF YOU'RE STILL OPEN TO THE IDEA, WE'D LIKE TO KEEP GOING.
KEEP GOING?
THE JOB STILL NEEDS TO BE DONE. WE KNEW GOING IN WHAT WE WERE RISKING, AND IF ANYTHING, LOSING TWO OF OUR FRIENDS ONLY MAKES IT THAT MUCH MORE IMPORTANT.
GRE
YOU WANT TO TALK ME OUT OF THIS? TELL ME TO GO HOME?
OKAY. ONCE DAVID WAKES UP, LET'S SIT DOWN AND FIGURE OUT WHAT HAPPENS NEXT.

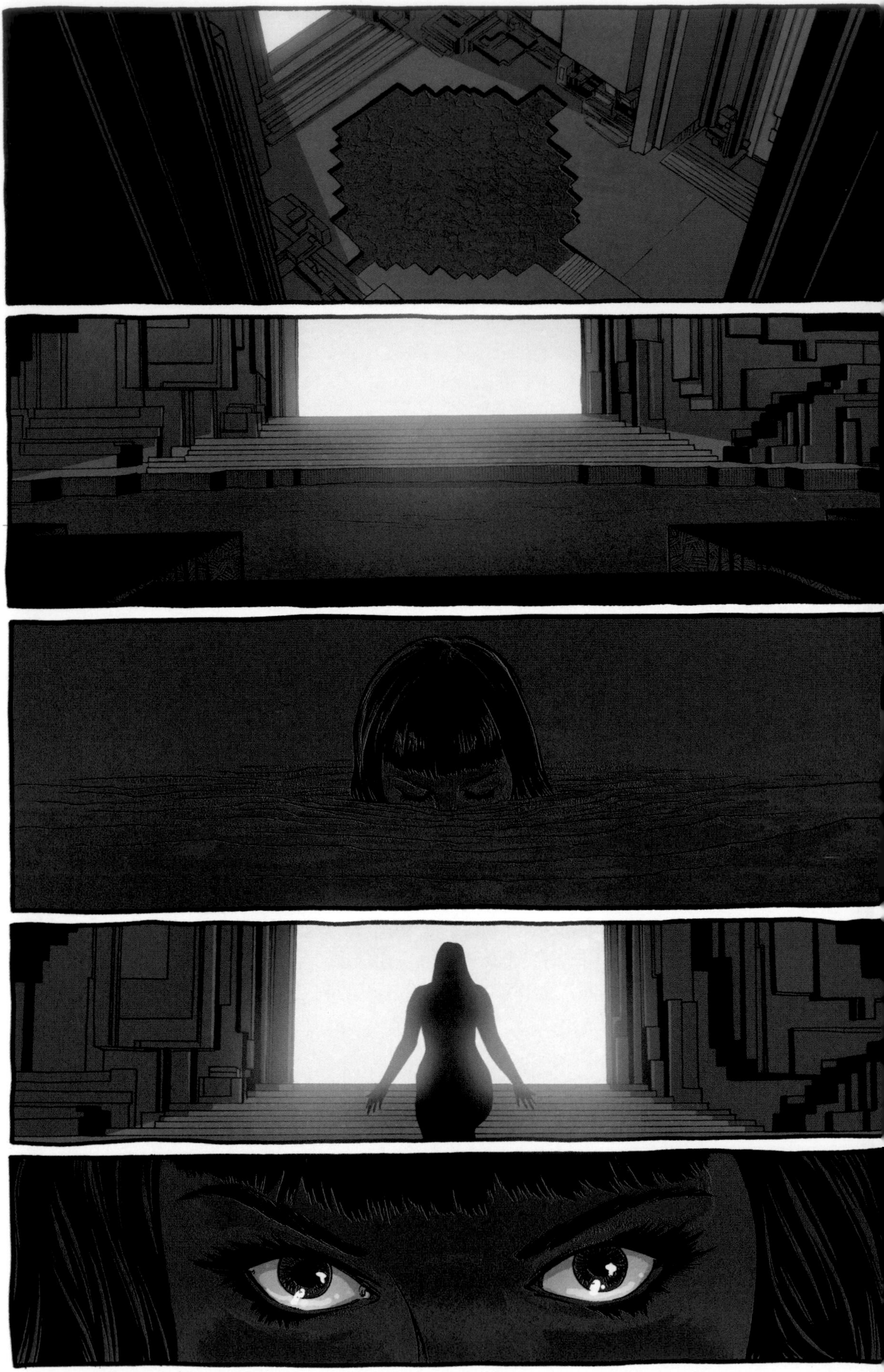

NOTES ON YOUR GUIDES

SETH PECK was born in St. Louis and raised on a steady diet of books and hockey. He likes dogs more than people and plans to die on the moon.

JEREMY HAUN, co-writer, co-creator, and artist of THE REALM, has also worked on *Constantine* and *Batwoman* from DC. Over the past decade plus, along with wearing calluses on his fingers doing work for DC, Marvel, Image, and others, he has created and written several projects. Some you might know are the graphic novel *Narcoleptic Sunday, The Leading Man, Dino Day,* and THE BEAUTY. He is a part of the Bad Karma Creative group, whose *Bad Karma Volume One* debuted at NYCC 2013, thanks to Kickstarter funding.

Jeremy resides in a crumbling mansion in Joplin, Missouri, with his wife and two superheroes-in-training.

NICK FILARDI has colored for just about every major comic book publisher including DC, Marvel, Oni Press and Dark Horse. He's currently also coloring covers for THE BEAUTY. When he isn't buried in pages, you can find his digital likeness pulling up other colorists with tips and tricks at twitch.tv/nickfil, making dad jokes at twitter.com/nickfil, and just spreading dope art at instagram.com/nick_filardi. He lives in Florida with his 3-legged dog and fiancée.

THOMAS MAUER has lent his lettering and design talent to numerous critically acclaimed and award-winning projects. Among his recent work are COPPERHEAD, CRUDE, ELSEWHERE, and THE BEAUTY, as well as *4 Kids Walk Into A Bank,* and the World Food Programme's *Living Level-3* educational comics.

JOEL ENOS is a writer and editor of comics and stories and is currently editing the series THE REALM, THE BEAUTY and REGRESSION, all three published by Image Comics.

NEW TOURS AVAILABLE SOON.